THE ANOINTING
BOOK 5

RESURRECTION DAWN SERIES
In the Continuing Saga of Victoria Martin Tempest

BY M. SUE ALEXANDER

SUZANDER PUBLISHING, LLC
BOOK 5: RESURRECTION DAWN SERIES

THE ANOINTING

FIRST EDITION 2006, USA
Copyright © 2006 by M. Sue Alexander

Cover design by Ron Watson of Clarksville, Tennessee
Photo provided by M. Sue Alexander

SUZANDER PUBLISHING, LLC
PO BOX 135
VANLEER, TN 37181
www.resdawn.net

READER OPINION

"Blessed with the gift of creative writing, Sue has written a story of intrigue interwoven with the strength of biblical truths I find useful in all life's situations," says Georgie Brooks of Dickson, TN

"From the moment I picked up the first book, I found an addiction! I love the characters, the plot, and the mystery. I wish the author could write the books as fast as I can read them!" states Jen Marceaux, a Christian talk radio host in Lakeland, FL

"The author has just the right mixture of strength, weakness and quirkiness to make her characters come alive. Each sequel holds me spellbound as I race through the pages to see what happens to the characters," exclaims Lin Taylor Branch in Lakeland, FL

"I have enjoyed every book in this Christian-based series. The mystery, romance, and dramatic succession of events makes this a truly special story," says Reba Cates of Dickson, TN.

"Your writing is unusual, characterized by a display of different personalities and continual action." Lucille Hix of Dickson, TN.

"I especially like Victoria Tempest and Texas Holmes, spirited people who always obey the Lord and act cautiously. I look forward to what the future holds for them and more about the alleged Antichrist," states Patricia Wilkins from Vanleer, TN.

"A fast-paced page-turner, I can hardly wait for the next book to come out. The characters are very believable, the story on target with current events," claims Dana Smith from Sardis, TN.

"This series captures the essence of what is taking place in American society today—scary but believable," states Nada Pitts, a West Tennessee resident. "Keep up the good writing!"

M. Sue Alexander

AUTHOR'S DEDICATION

To my three children, their spouses, and six grandchildren, who motivate me to greater achievements and keep my life interesting.

AUTHOR'S NOTES

Resurrection Dawn 2014 is a novel series set in the arena of pre-Rapture, Biblical "end times," and is not to be viewed as prophetic fact. A specific time frame has been selected that best fits this story, but only God knows when the Antichrist will rise to power.

At the conclusion of Book 4, *Veil of Lies*, Victoria Martin Tempest was only beginning to discover the depth of deception clouding the facts of her husband Jeffrey's death on April 13, 1989. Attending her daughter Karen and Mark James' wedding was daring, but turned out all right when she used a little trickery to escape arrest. Texas Holmes was Johnny-on-the-spot in the limousine waiting to carry Victoria to safety. Love bloomed.

Victoria's understanding of what occurred on the night Jeffrey was shot to death at his office enlarges her friendships as critical information regarding the unsolved murder case is shared. There is so much more to the story than meets the eye, she surmises.

The Dickson, Tennessee, cave revival proves inspirational as Victoria and Texas repair their broken relationship. However, she is not thinking about marriage, and is off to Switzerland again.

Promised her old life back in exchange for information regarding Victoria, PI Georgie Hendricks travels with Donald Wetherfield to Switzerland and confers with Alexander Luceres Ramnes. The unbelievable happens when her path crosses Victoria's.

"Do not touch my anointed ones; do my prophets no harm," I Chronicles 16:22, The NIV Study Bible.

SATURDAY, JUNE 28

1

Fernwood, Tennessee

Officer Sarah Boswell stopped by the Fernwood Police Precinct to pick up her bi-monthly check when her attention was diverted to her younger cohort, Josh Tenny. Overly excited, he was talking to Sheriff Andrew Grimes on the horn about an important matter. "Yeah," he said. "We're on it, Chief!"

"On to what, Josh?" Sarah privately approached her fellow officer with anticipation. "What's up?"

Huh? He spun around, looking confused.

"Got a robbery going down at the Union Federal Bank?" Sarah inquired, trailing Josh as he walked. The only bank in town, it had never been robbed, but there was a first time for everything.

"No, there's a ruckus going down at the country club." Josh shoved Sarah out of his way. "Can't explain now. Gotta see that the area is cordoned off before the fugitive escapes."

"Wait!" Sarah followed Josh into Sheriff Andrew Grimes' office, aware that Victoria Tempest was at her daughter's wedding ceremony to Dr. Mark James. Dog it! She wanted the facts.

"Not now, Sarah." Josh was too busy to fraternize.

"Talk to me, Josh. Put down the blasted phone and give it to me straight." Sarah grabbed his hand, hating to see an innocent person cornered. But then Victoria was clever and had not yet gotten caught—a miracle, no less. Maybe there was a way to help.

But Josh wasn't listening to Sarah, his lips already pressed against a microphone as he pushed a red button on the phone system to collectively alert all squad cars dispatched on the streets.

"Got a fugitive cornered at the country club wedding chapel. Sheriff Grimes says to block off the area," Josh excitedly blasted.

Sarah stewed, helpless to intervene.

"Yeah." Josh listened as one of the officers called on another line and threw him a few tough questions. "Use force if necessary, but bring in Victoria Martin Tempest!"

Shoot, Sarah had been right about the infamous debutante's being in trouble again. No use askin' more questions, she knew exactly what needed doing. And time was of the essence.

Before Victoria was arrested and brought in for questioning, Sarah had one idea that might pay off big. However, it required some major risks. *Should she do it?* That was a huge question.

A couple of weeks back, Sarah had visited the police archives in an attempt to locate Jeffrey Tempest's unsolved murder file. It wasn't there. About to board the elevator going up, she hadn't counted on bumping into Henry T. Carter. But there he was, big as life, hobbling down the long hallway toward her, maintaining his balance through the use of a sturdy but crooked wooden cane.

Heavens to Betsy! She had barely recognized the old cop in his blue-jean overalls, skin-bald head, and bushy gray sideburns. The bright glimmer in Henry's blue eyes said he still had some life left inside his sick body. Man, was he a sight for sore eyes.

Sarah had waited patiently for him to draw closer . . .

"Henry? Is that you?" She crooked her head and asked, realizing he was scrutinizing her just as diligently. "I thought you was dead by now," the insensitive person inside Sarah croaked before thinking. "I meant—" she didn't get out her apology.

"Sarah, my child!" Recognition emanated from Henry's poignant gaze. "Quit teasin' an ol' man like me, ya hear? Death 'll come soon enough, trus' me." His laugh was so vigorous it shook his belly and swelled his broad chest. Sarah laughed, too.

"It's me, all right, Henry—not that I'm a spring chick anymore by any man's ruler." She prepared to receive his usual robust greeting—a hug and sloppy kiss—like the one he usually delivered when she visited him alongside her daddy years before.

"Come here, honey. You know I gotta have a hug." Henry extended his burly arms and received Sarah into his muscular grasp with surprising strength, staring into her dark eyes like he could actually see deep into her soul. "Now there, don't that make you feel better? Everybody needs a hug now and then."

"It does," Sarah agreed. "I heard you were out in New Mexico for a while. When did you get back?"

"Coupl'a months ago," Henry replied. "Lausy, child, am I glad to see the likes of you!" His wide-stretched smile revealed one large, gold-filled front tooth, a couple missing at the side.

Henry smelled like Brut Cologne, always Sarah's daddy's choice. Next came his sloppy kiss, still all right in Sarah's book.

Back in the good ol' days—before life hammered down a series of blows that had left a lot of good folks in Fernwood staggering with disbelief—Sarah's daddy and Henry used to take a day off work and go fishing for bream in the Hatchie River.

When they came rolling down the dusty road in Henry's old Ford truck toward the house, she would be sittin' on the front porch steps waiting, almost tasting the fish before her mama basted them in cornmeal and slapped 'em in a sizzling frying pan.

So much had changed since then, her mama and daddy long dead, and all. Sarah usually got sappy when fond old memories crept in. But here was ol' Henry Carter—proof that life was stronger than death. Somehow just seeing him again brought life back into her tired bones. She could do the right thing, she could.

After Hearty Meats arrived in town, many of the regulars at the police precinct were offered early retirement to make way for new blood to be brought in—not necessarily for the best.

Andrew Grimes was a little "big shot" back then, his mouth a whole lot bigger than he was—not that he was small. A good six feet in height, the rookie was muscle-bound from working out at the gym. Not too bad looking as a young man, either, his muddy-brown eyes revealing his true reprobate character. Meaner than a snake on any good day, Andy could stare down any contender.

Sarah recalled how Andy had flirted with the young female recruits. Some claimed he made their toes curl he was such a good kisser. Back then, being black, Sarah had plenty of opportunity to observe Andy's moves and chuckle at his failures.

Who would guess they had attended the Police Academy together? Andy's career had taken off fast, rising up the ladder of success, while Sarah was left answering the phones year after year.

A fate thing, she guessed. *Anyhow* . . .

"I can't believe it's you." Sarah recalled another segment of her conversation with Henry, how she'd reached out and felt the stubble prickling his trembling chin. "How's the wife?"

Mary Ann Carter, a fine cook, had owned a small diner off Second Street for years. Henry cooked for her sometimes and did great with hamburgers and fries. Those were good ol' days.

"Mary Ann's dead. Three sons gone now, too," Henry declared with a sigh. "Life sucks." His expression went as blank as a blackboard as he leaned on his cane, old and feeble now.

Sarah was taken back by Henry's callous comment. He usually hid his hurt well and seldom complained that she could recall. He'd been around long enough to see Fernwood change from a friendly little community run by a town council to a bustling city with leaders preying on the innocent and defenseless.

Henry had turned in his cop badge a few months after the highly publicized Jeffrey Tempest case was abandoned by the police and declared unsolved. Sarah never knew why and hadn't dared ask. *Some things were best left unsaid*—a phrase coined by the vivacious Beverly James, Mark's ex-wife.

"I'm so sorry, Henry," Sarah said about the loss of his family. "I know you miss 'em." Being a stubborn old man, he had outlived the ones he most loved, including many of his friends.

"All of us is sorry, Sarah." Henry's sad gaze incited empathy. "So whut ar'ya doin' down here in this dark hole?" he asked, withered face quizzically tilted to one side in speculation.

She chuckled. "I might ask you the same thing, Henry."

"Wull, I'm here to see my niece. She still works in the police archives, you know . . ." he leaned close and whispered in Sarah's ear, "whur all those secret files are kept." Mischievousness gleamed in his round blue eyes as he chuckled. "Did'ja ever meet Bessie? She wus the pretty one who looks a whole lot like me."

"It's been a spell." Sarah noted how Henry's expression brightened at the mention of Bessie's name.

"'Course that was when I was younger and much cuter," he professed, being a big tease. But that was okay, Sarah decided. Fantasizing about the past to endure the future was acceptable.

Humph. "Elizabeth Carter," Sarah recollected. The woman was nigh on to sixty by now—no budding sunflower—which would put Henry way up in his eighties.

"Yep, tha's my Bessie," Henry replied with a chuckle. "So, Sarah, whut brings you down to the cellars?" he asked again.

"You remember Jeffrey Tempest, don't you?" Sarah thought it was worth her time to pry. The folks who worked in records sometimes read old reports out of shear boredom.

"That attorney fellow who bit the dust one stormy night in 1989." Henry grimaced, glancing down the hall to see who might be listening in on their conversation. "Ain't nobody likely to forgit that case if they had a mind to try. Why do you ask, child?"

Henry supported the bulk of his weight on his wooden cane, looking perplexed as he waited for Sarah's answer.

"I'd sure like to get my hands on that ol' police file if it was possible," Sarah declared, hoping Henry had a bright idea about how to accomplish the feat. "It's really important to me."

"Wull . . ." Henry scratched his stubbly chin with the hand not holding the cane. "Do you think it's wise to ask questions about *that* case, considering all that's been a'goin' on?"

All that's going on? Sarah had pondered Henry's reply. About that time, the elevator doors had yawned open and closed again.

"Reading that file might clear up a few things in my mind," Sarah informed Henry. "Do you have any idea how I might go about askin' to see that file?" Injustice had reigned far too long.

"Wull, I guess I could ask Bessie about the file. If it ain't in the archives, maybe she'd have some idée where it went." Henry's bulbous lips were pursed. "But if I was you, Sarah, I wouldn't go around announcing to just anyone whut you're up to."

"Oh, I won't, Henry," Sarah assured him. "Would you mind talkin' to Bessie for me? I could wait right here while you go inside the library and inquire. As far as I'm concerned, we never had this conversation." Shivers had gone down Sarah's backbone.

"No, problem, child. Only thing is . . ." Henry's bushy eyebrows arched a notch, "I might want you to buy me a cup of coffee so we kin catch up on ol' times." His sunny smile was cracked with wrinkles. "Sometimes I gits lonesome."

"Sure. But not today, I'm in a hurry," she responded.

Bumping into Henry Carter had been more than coincidence, Sarah thought. For her to check out the Tempest file would require an affidavit. With no official reason to review the unsolved case, she was sure to be denied access.

Although, Sarah thought, *I could steal a form from Andy's desk and forge his signature. No, that was a bad idea.*

Borrowing the file for a few hours seemed a better option, Sarah decided. She would only need to see it once to judge the value of its contents. But if Andy Grimes found out she had been at the archives asking about the case, it would mean losing her job.

Worse, Dick Branson and his motley crew would croak if they got wind of her prying. *No, I have to be discreet*, Sarah vowed.

Thinking Victoria would approve, Sarah had even said a little prayer to help Henry along while he ventured inside the archives to talk to his niece, Elizabeth. Surely, God was on their side.

Sarah had waited in the hall by the elevators a good fifteen minutes for Henry to return. When he did, he was grinning from ear to ear. "Bessie said the Tempest file was checked out a couple nights ago—by Sheriff Andy Grimes, his self. Is that a help to you?" The old man victoriously thumped his cane on the floor.

"You bet it is!" Sarah planted a kiss on Henry's cheek.

It was no secret that Andy and Dick fraternized on occasions. Now that Sarah thought about it, maybe Andy had some help in rising to political fame. So what did the town's sheriff have to do to get on Dick Branson's good side? What was in that file?

"Henry, you're a winner!" Sarah hugged her daddy's fishing buddy. "I'll call you about coffee." She would and soon.

"Don't forgit, I'm in the *Yellow Book*." Again, Henry thumped his cane on the floor. "Now you jes' be careful about takin' unnecessary chances, you hear? I want my date, darlin'."

"I hear," Sarah answered. "You can't imagine how much you have helped me, Henry!" She pressed the button to call the elevator. "You're a mighty angel under all that limping!"

Henry chuckled. "Leastwise, I got some good left in me. More 'n some folks I know who claim to be upstanding citizens!" He huffed and hobbled on the elevator with Sarah.

"Don't worry about me, Henry." She pressed the button for the first floor and bid him a fond goodbye as they left the building. The groundwork for a sting had been laid.

Today, all Sarah needed to do was muster the courage to act on her plan. She jolted to the present as Josh Tenny closed down the phone system and rushed from Andy Grimes' office. Shoving aside memories of Henry Carter, Officer Boswell had a job to do.

Now where would Sheriff Grimes have taken the Tempest file?

Seeing that a red alert was on to arrest Victoria at the country club, and Andy Grimes had his hands full, it seemed the opportune time to check out his private residence. Just to make it official, Sarah would borrow a slip of paper from the sheriff's personalized notepad and scribble a meaningful note to his wife.

13

The rest would require a little ingenuity.

Sarah smiled, thinking she had to make the diabolical scheme work to Victoria's advantage. Talk about not getting involved.

Baloney!

2

The Rose Garden Wedding Chapel

Victoria Tempest realized she was not categorized as a woman of few words. Too many times she had offered a judgmental opinion when she should have shut up and listened. Having just witnessed her daughter Karen's marriage to Dr. Mark James, her former lover, she was barely able to utter a polite "thank you" as the new husband escorted her to the stretch-white limousine set to carry away his blushing bride—which Karen definitely was not.

Life had certainly gone askew—not always a good thing.

Mark smiled at Victoria, signifying that he understood what she was experiencing in saying goodbye again. No one could be certain when it would be safe for her to return to Fernwood.

In response, she squeezed his arm.

When Mark had stepped away from the vehicle, and the door was shut, Victoria called out to the driver: "Make my day, honey!"

And the guy behind the wheel certainly knew how to do that.

"Hello, Victoria," a husky male voice said through the overhead microphone. "Are you comfortable back there?"

"What?" She started, pulse leaping to attention at the utterly familiar voice. As if in slow motion, her gaze wandered to the front of the limousine. There sat Texas Holmes in the driver's seat, staring at her through the rearview mirror with a pair of eccentric seaweed colored eyes, looking as suave as a prince.

Huh? Victoria blinked as the Texan's gaze burned a hole straight through her skittering heart. Tongue-tied and starry-eyed, brandished with love, her hero had once again come to her rescue.

In the driver's seat, as always, he was just too much.

Of course, Mark had helped, too. Without his assistance, Victoria never would have made it out of the Rosewood Wedding Chapel without getting grabbed, handcuffed, and arrested by the testy Andy Grimes. But Karen's clever ruse had worked, and God was in the deal, for sure. So how did Texas Holmes get in the act?

Jon Branson, Victoria smiled, loving the guy even more.

"So you just happened to be in Fernwood?" Victoria raised an arched eyebrow. "How come you're so smart?" the words stumbled off her tongue like rocks off a crumbling cliff.

Texas grinned and shrugged his shoulders.

"Even I didn't know I was coming to Fernwood."

It was the truth. The chain of events that had occurred during the afternoon had unfolded like a movie script written by the unseen hand of some mastermind storyteller. Minutes before, Victoria had been trapped with Karen in the Bride's Room, surrounded by police personnel itching to arrest her for murder.

"A little birdie told me?" he teased.

"Really!" Victoria wondered what would have happened if she hadn't traded places with Karen. "A *Jon* bird."

"Yeah," Texas confessed, lowering the glass window separating the cab from the sleek interior of the limousine. "Can we kiss and make up now? You're not still mad, are you?"

Victoria gave the questions some consideration.

"Come on, honey, I got Lucas up here with me and he's dying to give you a hug." The lad unbuckled his seat belt and perched on his knees to peek over the backseat.

"Lucas! He's here?" Victoria crawled to the front of the limousine and extended her arms to embrace the lad. "Oh, baby! I'm so glad to see you! You taking good care of your papa, here?"

The mirror reflected Texas' extreme pleasure.

"Your papa's quite a risk-taker." Victoria's adoring eyes drew Texas like a magnet. She couldn't possibly stay mad at her hero.

"Hi, Ms. Victoria. We was so . . . worried about you."

"Were," Texas corrected Lucas's English.

The unpretentious lad offered Victoria a second ferocious hug through the snug opening. "I knew you'd come home."

"Well, this isn't quite *home*, but it's nice," she said, brown eyes skittering to Texas again, skyrocketing her emotions.

"You ready to go somewhere?" Texas asked Victoria as his gaze wafted on her. "I would say that time is of the essence."

"Yeah!" She laughed. "You're the driver. Any ideas?"

"I have a few, but it doesn't include driving."

Collapsing in the back seat of the sleek white limousine like a found Cinderella, Victoria gathered her thoughts and emotions so her words would later make more sense. *What does he have in mind?*

Texas stepped on the accelerator and the limousine eased forward. "You do have a plan," Victoria uttered, glancing back at all the distraught people exiting the chapel.

"Trust me," he said.

"I do," she peeped, sensuously mellow as she inhaled Stetson cologne and recalled his warm embrace with lingering kisses.

"Good!" He winked at her through the rearview mirror. "Just sit back and enjoy the ride, honey. You're safe now."

Honey? Victoria felt completely safe for the first time in a while with the vehicle doors locked and Texas in the driver's seat.

Poor Mark. She glanced back at the chapel and couldn't help but wonder what lay ahead of him. More than likely he would be blamed for her escape and catch havoc from Dick Branson, nobody's true friend. And Andy Grimes would be positively livid.

Then what would happen to Karen?

No! Victoria refused to let worry diminish her feelings of success. *She was free, wasn't she?* Karen could take care of herself.

Texas drove down the street. Peering through the dark-tinted windows of the limousine, Victoria spied unsuspecting officers of the law tipping their hats at her, the alleged bride, as she eased past them. With JUST MARRIED inscribed in black paint on the vehicle's exterior windshield, roadblocks in front parted like the Red Sea when the Israelites escaped the diabolical Egyptians.

God was still very much in the delivery business. Only the Almighty could have inspired so clever an escape plan. When Victoria had shown up at the wedding chapel, she had absolutely no idea how to escape arrest should someone alert the authorities.

Obviously, someone had. Dick Branson, no doubt, since he had the most to gain from her conviction. *The cad!*

The second Sheriff Andrew Grimes learned Victoria was hiding out at the wedding chapel he was on the job with an arrest warrant. Although it appeared there was no possible way of escape, Andy's plans had been foiled, thanks to her ingenious, adorable daughter. Other than dispatching mighty angels, didn't God sometimes use ordinary people to carry out His plans?

All Victoria had envisioned moments before showing up for the wedding was hearing Karen say "I do" to Mark James without her being there. It had been worth the risk of getting caught just to share in those precious moments with her beloved daughter.

When it came time to leave, when the drama ended, Victoria had walked away untouched. Indeed, how would everyone feel when Karen traipsed out of the Bride's Room in her place?

Stunned, no less. Victoria smiled to herself. *Good!*

About now, Mark would be explaining his rash actions to the authorities for not leaving in the limousine with his new wife. At his side, Dick Branson would be giving him the devil of a time for it. His answer would be a bunch of clever baloney, but believable.

Dr. James would come out a winner, no doubt. Hadn't he avoided prosecution for years despite his part in Jeffrey's death?

Although the capable surgeon hadn't held the gun that fired the two deadly shots, wounding and killing Jeffrey, he had definitely been privy to the incident. Beverly James had early on confirmed it was so. An expert liar, Mark would wiggle out of this unsavory predicament just like he did every other time.

In Victoria's way of thinking, the money Mark used to pay off his gambling debts and the IRS had come from Dick Branson's deep pockets—funds which may have been stolen from Jeffrey's life-insurance policy, the one she supposedly initiated.

One day the truth was bound to surface and justice would have its day in court. When Victoria learned what happened the terrible night Jeffrey died, Mark would own up to his mistakes.

All things were forgivable under grace.

The clever surgeon had some virtues, Victoria realized. Hadn't he watched over her children following her debilitating accident? According to Beverly, Mark had received her into their home and paid for her medical care. Despite his shortcomings, hadn't she previously trusted him enough to agree to marry him?

Which would certainly have happened had she not had a memory switch. Now Mark, her former lover, was her son-in-law.

Try that switched relationship on for size.

Had life turned out differently, Victoria might have been Mrs. Mark James, rightfully riding in the limousine beside her new husband. Karen would have been left standing on the sidewalk, throwing rice at the limousine, a heartbroken bridesmaid.

And Texas would not even be a passing thought.

Over the years, Victoria's poor choices had weirdly scrambled her relationships. With a confused set of memories, she had not always acted responsibly. Karen was right about that.

But one thing now was for certain: Victoria's loyalty in seeing that Jeffrey's killers brought to justice was unshakable!

She glanced back down the street again and caught sight of Mark standing outside the wedding chapel, hands stuffed in his pockets like a little boy as he conversed with Dick Branson.

What lies is he telling?

3

Mark James was in no big hurry to explain his actions to Dick Branson or Andy Grimes. It was turning into a more beautiful evening than anticipated, cool winds stirring, the sunset promising a spectacular escape over the horizon—like Victoria.

Standing loosely in the yard in front of the chapel, hands coyly placed in his pockets, Mark waited for Karen to come out of the Bride's Room and the axe to fall when everyone realized what had occurred. It was fun he didn't want to miss. *Glory be!*

The angel of mercy tottered over to Mark. "What?" Dick whispered. "You ain't goin' with the bride? This ain't no way to start a marriage," he fussed. "Why not?"

Mark glared at Dick's fat face etched in displeasure. "Why do you care?" he remarked, then thought better of antagonizing Dick.

"Actually . . ." Mark continued, "I told Karen to go ahead to the airport and I would catch up with her in thirty minutes or so."

"What's got to be done here so important someone else won't do?" Suspicion grew in Dick's gaze. "Are you two okay?"

Mark winced. "I thought Vicki would need someone here when Sheriff Grimes arrested her. Where is he, by the way?" He glanced around the yard for the pompous police official. So far, so good! Life for Andy Grimes was about to get uncomfortable.

In arresting Victoria Martin Tempest, a high-profile fugitive, Andy was counting on bolstering his political career to stardom. With one eye on a state senate seat, he would easily settle for the mayor's job. It was sickening to think so shallow a man could actually win a political election. However, Dick was behind him.

"Thinkin' of Victoria first!" Dick quipped.

"Speak up, man. What's stuck in your craw?" Mark slapped Dick on his back, harder than he should have.

"Mighty nice of you, I'd say," Dick huffed. "And Karen is fine with that, I suppose. I'm not so sure you can be trusted around Victoria, if you ask me." Dick puffed hard on a cigar.

"Who asked you?" Mark grew weary of talk.

"Why don't we go back inside the chapel and get your *Little Vicki*, convince her to turn herself in to the police and avoid a big skirmish?" Dick scrubbed out his fiery cigar butt with his heel.

"One woman against a dozen policeman?" Mark played Dick to the hilt. "Really, buddy, do you believe Victoria has one chance in a million of escaping?" He lingered on the porch steps to explore the topic. That Dick looked rattled pleased him.

"She can't get out the back, right?" Dick rocked on his feet, appearing more than a little concerned. "How come you're so calm? Shoot, I knew it! You got somethin' up your sleeve." Worry tore at his face. "Aiding and abettin's a crime, you know."

"Look, Dick!" Mark held up his hands. "I'm not wearing a piece. I don't know anymore about what's going on with Victoria than you do. Let Andy do his job." He suppressed a smug grin.

"It's not what you *know* that concerns me, it's what you're not sayin'!" Dick snapped. "I'm goin' over and have a talk with Andy. It's time to end this mess." He trotted off with plenty of attitude.

Mess is right. Mark parked his expensive black tuxedo against the white porch banister. Crossing arms over his chest, he contemplated how much fun he'd have watching Andy Grimes swallow his political pride. Muck would soon smear the cop's smug face as townsfolk swore obscenities at his failing to apprehend one defenseless woman—who in Mark's opinion had more gumption and foresight than all Andy's men put together.

Let Dick and Andy play out the little game. He'd watch, Mark thought to himself. *Yep.* It was really turning out to be a nice day.

***

Andy and Cheryl Grimes lived in a gated neighborhood in a two-story brick house—certainly nothing to brag about, but far more expensive than Sarah Boswell's own house.

Standing on the front door, Sarah glanced at her watch. *2:45 p.m.* The wedding nuptials between Karen Tempest and Mark James were probably over by now. If she knew Andy, he would go back to the station to check on things before coming home.

Sarah rang the doorbell and waited.

Cheryl Grimes answered the door, wearing a chenille robe like she'd just stepped out of the shower. "Can I help you?"

Sarah erected her body and prepared for the performance of her life. In fact, it was Victoria's life that was at stake. "I hope I haven't come at a bad time," she said, less than confident.

"Is this about what happened at Dr. Mark's wedding?"

Huh? For a second, Sarah didn't know how to respond.

"You did know that Tempest woman—the one who killed her attorney husband—is holed up at the country club wedding chapel as we speak?" Cheryl's eyes grew large with speculation.

"That's why I've come." Sarah swallowed hard.

"The foolish woman showed up at the last minute to see her daughter get married. Imagine the gall! Victoria Tempest really takes the cake." Cheryl stared at Sarah like she had some answers.

"I see." So much for innocent until proven guilty. "As I said, that's why I've come." It was time to improvise and move forward. "Boss sent me over for the Tempest file."

"Of course." Cheryl's blond eyelashes fluttered. She was a tall woman with glassy blue eyes, and slender, with enough muscle to signify she ate properly and worked out regularly at the gym.

"Do you know where the file is?" Sarah asked.

"Yes. Step inside and I'll get it."

"Thank you, Mrs. Grimes." Sarah's heart slapped a high-five, pleased that her instincts had proven correct. Without a doubt,

Victoria would have labeled her stroke of good luck as an act of God's grace. Sarah stepped into the foyer and closed the door.

"The file is on Andy's desk. He brought it home a couple of nights ago to review the contents," Cheryl said. "Does this mean Victoria Tempest is already in custody?"

"The Sheriff's working on it." Sarah handed Cheryl the note from Andy that stated, GIVE OFFICER SARAH BOSWELL THE TEMPEST FILE. I NEED IT ASAP.

"I'll only be a moment." Cheryl hurried up the stairs and disappeared around a corner, leaving Sarah anxiously waiting for her prize. *Yes!* She had no idea the deed would prove so painless.

However, explaining to the sheriff why she had the file and what she was about to do with it for the next hour would require sheer ingenuity. A big fat lie was a necessary evil, to put it simply.

Sarah glanced at her watch, growing anxious to copy the contents of the file and get it back to Mrs. Grimes before her feisty husband finished his official business and returned home.

What happened next wouldn't be pretty if she got caught. Sarah liked her skin—shiny black with no bullet holes.

"Here it is, Officer Boswell." Cheryl handed over the thick manila folder containing critical information that could free or convict Victoria Tempest of a murder charge.

"Thank you," said Sarah, tentatively clasping the file bound with two thick rubber bands like it was hot and going to explode in her shaky hands. "Have a nice day."

"Oh," said Cheryl, detaining Sarah a couple of seconds.

"Yes?" Sarah slowly turned around and faced Cheryl.

"If you don't mind, tell Andy his supper is in the oven. I have an errand to run." She waited for a response.

"Of course," Sarah replied with a smile. "No problem."

4

Texas Holmes took his time driving through Fernwood in the white limousine designed to carry the deliriously happy bride and lucky groom. Police were out in numbers on the lawn of the three-story historic courthouse but nobody made an attempt to stop the marked vehicle. Wearing a smile and an official cabby cap, Texas casually waved to pedestrians and moved on.

"So where are we going?" Victoria scooted to the front of the limousines to be nearer Texas.

"Where do you want to go?" He kept his eyes forward, left hand on the steering wheel while he grasped Victoria's cold hand with the right. "I'm open to suggestions and Lucas doesn't care."

"Somewhere safe," was all Victoria could think to murmur.

"How 'bout Jackson, Tennessee?" Texas asked. "What do you say to ditching the limousine and getting up with Jon Branson? From there, we'll head east toward Nashville."

"To Dickson County," Victoria clarified, holding on to Texas' hand for dear life. If she let go he might evaporate like a dream.

No, this had to be real. It felt too good, too compelling—like God had designed their reunion. "Jon has agreed to meet us?"

"One call and it's done," Texas replied.

"Good, I have friends who are going to attend the cave revival," Victoria said, thinking of Jacob Cooley from Nashville and his remarkable granddaughter, Angela. "You'll love them."

"*Them?* What friends?"

Texas approached a red light, stopped, and swung his head around to meet Victoria's fond gaze. She was beautiful, more

24

radiant than he remembered. "I hope you didn't divulge the revival meeting to strangers." He didn't mean to scold.

Victoria slowly withdrew her hand, a pout on her lips. "I wouldn't do that, Texas!" Her stormy gaze reflected hurt. "Just because I didn't meet with your buddy, Luceres, doesn't mean I don't know how to conduct myself when it comes to keeping others safe." She immediately regretted her harsh response.

Women! Texas sighed, not commenting, off on the wrong foot again. Victoria was touchy and he understood why. Her life was in constant jeopardy. Like Jesus, she had no safe place to lay her head on this green Earth. And he had to go and fuss at her.

Lucas stuck his head into the cab opening. "Now, don't you two go gettin' into a fuss just when we're back together again," the boy wisely advised. "Papa?" He turned to Texas.

"What, son?" Bewildered eyes displayed his feelings.

"Is Mr. Jon coming by his self to get us?"

"No, Lucas. Jon's mother is with him."

"Marilyn Branson?" Victoria leaped into the conversation, forgetting her anger at Texas for his accusations of incompetence.

"Yes," Texas replied.

"She has terminal cancer, doesn't she?" The idea of Marilyn Branson's facing a horrible death brought tears to Victoria's eyes.

"Is she going to die?" Lucas innocently asked.

"Everyone dies," Texas remarked. "Apparently Marilyn's most recent trip to the hospital had some positive affects. After receiving multiple blood transfusions, she was sent home."

Victoria blinked, not knowing what to say.

Emotion gripped Texas. "I'm afraid the leukemia is still eating away at her." Compassion ruled his heart. On a more personal note, he wanted to apologize to Victoria for criticizing her but pride closed his lips. What man sabotaged his happiness?

Only someone very foolish! Texas concluded. The silence in the limousine was threatening. He could hear his own heart tick.

"I'm so sorry, Texas. For *everything*." Victoria's lips trembled. "I never should have left you in Rome without first explaining." Regret weighed heavily. "My son kidnapped me in the hallway as I came out of the Marriott's Grand Ballroom. He wouldn't let me tell you I was leaving. It was never my choice to leave."

Telling the truth didn't make Victoria's actions any less damaging to their relationship, but she hoped the benevolent man in her life would understand and forgive her many transgressions.

"I know," Texas said, releasing a sigh like a deflating balloon.

"You *know*?" Victoria's pupils vibrated with confusion. "Did you *also* know that the authorities were planning to arrest me after the banquet?" Her dander was up and stirring all over again.

"Of course not!" he reacted, cranking his head around.

The idea that Texas didn't chase after her was even more unsettling to Victoria. "Then how?" She needed to understand.

"Karen told me later."

Lucas was soaking in the conversation like a sponge.

"Later? How late?" Revelation shot up to disbelief.

"Evidently your son, Daniel, asked his sister to intervene on your behalf. What she did was quite interesting."

"Intervene how?" Victoria was on the edge of her seat.

"Your daughter is rather clever." Texas glanced back at Victoria. "Dressed as a banquet server, at first I didn't recognize her. But neither did Dick Branson." He recalled the scene.

"Wait! Dick was there when Karen talked to you?" Victoria reacted. "How is it she got past Dick without his knowing?"

"Well, Karen didn't actually talk to me. She served me a cup of gourmet coffee with a very challenging note attached: GET OUT! YOUR COVER HAS BEEN BLOWN."

Victoria smiled. "And she did it right under Dick's nose?"

"Yes ma'am. Apparently Dick assumed Jackson Lloyd Hammerstein was someone important or he would not have made it a point to venture over for a friendly chat."

"Sounds like the creep." Victoria grimaced.

"When I blew the meatpacker off, he huffed off speechless, tripping over Karen on his way out the door." Texas couldn't help but smile, reliving the scenario. "Mission accomplished."

"Wow! Talk about clandestine meetings."

"I'm tired of clandestine, Victoria," Texas soberly declared. "I'm ready for a little peace and quiet." He missed having a wife to go home to at the end of a tiring workday. "Aren't you?"

Victoria privately pondered the question as the limousine departed Fernwood's city limits heading north toward Jackson, passing Branson Meatpacking Company on the right.

"What's going on at Branson?" Victoria couldn't help but notice people wearing metallic-looking suits and gas facemasks.

"It's the Environmental Protection Agency folks. It was in the local newspaper," Texas revealed.

"What was in the newspaper?" Victoria asked. "Sorry, I guess I'm a little out of touch. What's happened?"

"The details are sketchy," Texas answered.

Victoria wasn't at all surprised. She'd been adding two and two for years and coming up with five. Apparently Attorney Devin Baldwin had turned in Georgie's evidence proving that Dick Branson was operating his business on environmentally unsafe soil. Couple that with illegal drug trafficking and he could get life. If all went well, she'd be back in Fernwood in no time.

"I hope they lock up Dick and throw away the key!" The bitterness in Victoria erupted. Her anger ran much deeper than she realized, teetering on hate. "He's absolutely ruthless."

"That's not what the papers are reporting," Texas remarked.

"*What?* Dick hides toxic materials on his property, and they let him get away with it? I don't think so." Victoria straightened her suit skirt and leaned back in the seat. "Give me a break, partner." Her anger stepped up a notch. "Justice is overdue."

"So it is." Texas took a moment to collect his thoughts before continuing. Victoria had no idea how clever her adversary was—just short of brilliant. She could forget about obtaining justice in this instance. But how to break the news was troubling.

"Okay, explain. I know you will anyhow," Victoria insisted.

"According to this morning's editorial in the *Fernwood Gazette*, when Dick learned that a puddle of toxic sludge was on his property, he immediately phoned the governor to report the incident. The Environmental Protection Agency was notified and sent out a crew of chemists to investigate. Dick is being applauded for a good-citizenship deed. I'm so sorry, Victoria."

"I swear . . ." Victoria knew it was wrong to do so, "Dick could puke all over the citizens of Fernwood, and they would thank him." She was up to her chin in outrage.

Victoria's comment brought Lucas to life with a rage of chuckles. "Sorry, Papa," he covered his face with his ball cap.

"You didn't hear that, Lucas," Texas warned. "Miss Victoria is just upset. Tell him, Victoria."

"Right. Sorry, Lucas."

Victoria stewed over the matter, a chill invading her spine as she considered how close she'd come to getting caught at the wedding chapel. Forget that anyone would be so compassionate to her as they had been with Dick. Whatever happened, she was not going to make it easy for the crooks to win. Dick Branson was guilty of murdering Jeffrey, and he would pay in full!

Silence filled the limousine as Texas eased past another roadblock erected north of town. "Are you okay?"

"No. Did the paper mention what happened to Georgie Hendricks, my private eye?" Victoria dared to ask. "If Dick did anything to harm her . . ." she left her threats undefined.

"According to one news article I read, Georgie is deceased," Texas informed Victoria. "But she left behind quite a legacy."

"Huh? What are you talkin' about?"

"A reporter for the *Memphis Commercial Appeal* discovered Georgie's damaging evidence buried in Attorney Devin Baldwin's backyard. A dog dug it up," Texas revealed.

"Oh wonderful! Now we've got a canine sticking its nose in my business," Victoria remarked. "I suppose Devin proclaimed that he had no idea how the evidence got there."

"Exactly," answered Texas.

"Papa? Did you say a puppy dog dug up the evidence?" Lucas asked, finding a topic that truly interested him.

"That's right, Lucas. A neighbor noticed the attorney's dog running around acting strange. A white powder was caked on the fur around his mouth, so the reporter investigated the incident."

"Cocaine," said Victoria, deflating over the news. "Georgie went undercover to help clear my name. She must have taken photos of Dick's crew packing drugs between layers of meat."

"Too bad Georgie isn't alive to tell her side of the story," said Texas. "Her incriminating photos were printed in the Memphis paper," he expounded. "A lot of good that did."

Victoria stiffened. "And, of course, Dick said it was all a pack of lies aimed at destroying his business." Her face was contorted with anger. "And since Georgie died in an apartment fire, how could she have possibly snapped the incriminating photos of Branson employees packing cocaine between meats?"

"It appears so," Texas said. "It's what most folks believe."

"Dick's clever, I'll give him that!" Victoria would prefer giving the lying, meatpacker a swift kick for his rare contribution to society. Her feelings for him bordered on hate.

"Unfortunately," Texas pointed out, "you are beginning to sound like a raving maniac bent on destroying Dick's company. At least, that's what Dick would like folks to think."

Seeing the anger displayed in Victoria's face, Texas immediately regretted his words. "Sorry, dear, I know this is a bitter pill to swallow. I know your heart is in the right place."

"I'm not so sure," Victoria admitted. "If I never saw Dick Branson again, it would be too soon!" she exploded. "I hate—" she clammed up and sulked. She could wring his neck herself.

"Victoria?" The chastisement in Texas' voice concerned her. "You know that Dick won't give up until he finds you. Somebody has to take the fall for Jeffrey's death, and people like him avoid prosecution at all costs." Texas was brutally honest.

Victoria visibly wilted. "Why me? I loved my husband. I'm a good person. I tried to be a good mother. I went to church and I had friends over to eat." She would not cry. "This isn't fair."

"Of course, it isn't. But you are a straight shooter, Victoria, and I love you for it," said Texas. "Don't give up yet."

Love? Victoria was too confused to deal with her feelings for Texas. This was a nightmare, and she would soon awaken.

"Georgie isn't dead!" Victoria passionately declared. "I feel it in my bones. My friend didn't die in the fire because she wouldn't let anyone kill her. I'd bet my boots on it."

"You don't have any boots." Texas grinned. "Forget about getting even with Dick Branson. Settle down in Texas with me, and I'll have a pair of red boots custom made to fit your lovely feet. We'll spend the rest of our lives wrapped up in each other."

"That sounds almost like a proposal." A light flickered in Victoria's eyes as she relaxed a bit. "Maybe."

"Something to think about, isn't it?" Texas pointed out.

Victoria didn't comment, but he knew by the expression on her face that she was touched by his attentiveness.

Texas picked up speed as they left the city of Fernwood behind. Jackson, Tennessee was forty minutes north, and if Mark James managed to stall the police a little longer, they just might make it to safety. Home free, again. What a blessing.

Victoria relaxed and tried to let the anger go. It had already been a long day, and who could say what would happen next.

5

Miami, Florida

Private Eye Georgie Hendricks heard the breaking news on the radio while riding over to the Miami International Airport with Donald Wetherfield. The Fernwood police had Victoria Martin Tempest cornered at the country club wedding chapel.

Too bad, she thought to herself. But it was too late for her to help. She had committed her life to self-preservation.

A few days before, Georgie was withering away in a Colombian camp with no thought of how to remedy her insidious predicament. No thanks to Anthony Vorices, the attorney-thug who abducted her in Memphis outside Attorney Devin Baldwin's house and hauled her off to South America. No doubt, it was Dick Branson's idea of a bad joke. *Ha, ha*. She wasn't laughing.

For weeks she had labored in the coffee fields, part of that time too sick with a high fever to think straight. Certain that she would never again fully appreciate the dark beverage made from beans, she had but one prayer: Get me out of this God-forsaken country! Chalk up her predicament to meeting Victoria Tempest.

But every good detective was blessed with at least one client who managed to turn life upside down. Georgie grimaced. Unfortunately, that was what made life intriguing, she recalled that dark, stormy evening in April when she first hooked up with the troubled debutante at an O'Charley's Restaurant in Memphis.

After hearing Victoria's unbelievable story and her earnest plea for help in solving her husband's murder, Georgie had thrown caution to the wind and taken on the difficult assignment.

Ugh! What an error in judgment!

So much had happened from that point forward, it was mind-boggling. Mildly put, life had been running steadily downhill since. Georgie had actually believed she could outwit Victoria's big bad wolf. She would never forget her first trip to Fernwood in pursuit of proving that Richard Branson the Third had a motive for canceling Jeffrey Tempest's life twenty-five years before.

Posing as Allison Black, she had worn her deceased half-sister's Tennessee Gas Authority suit and illegally obtained permission from Branson Meatpacking Company to check out their gas lines. In reality, she was there to collect soil samples. By a stroke of luck, she'd stumbled upon a toxic lake of sludge.

The samples were overnighted to Clint, a friend of Georgie's who worked for the Environmental Protection Agency. Forty-eight hours later, Clint had verified the soil contained toxic substances. PCBs—the kind that gives people cancer and costs millions to clean up. Just as Victoria suspected, Branson was illegally operating his meatpacking business on contaminated soil.

Georgie had gone over to Victoria's condo to present the incriminating evidence, but the meeting never happened since her client was flat on a stretcher being hauled away in the back of an EMS ambulance. The timing was awfully suspicious.

Oh yeah, Dick Branson had a motive for wanting Victoria's mouth permanently shut. She'd asked far too many questions about her husband's unsolved murder for Dick's comfort. Hadn't they both learned the hard way that nobody pushed the pompous man around without facing enormous consequences? *Duh.*

Georgie had trailed the ambulance carrying Victoria to Hardeman County General Hospital, bent on reporting her findings. To accomplish this, she had cleverly created a diversion.

A 1-800 Hotline call to Channel 5 News had done the trick. Kelly Nobel had jumped on the tip and headed off to Hardeman County General Hospital to obtain the newsworthy story—how a Fernwood celebrity recovering from amnesia, and about to reopen her husband's unsolved murder case, had ended up in ER.

Every player was present at the hospital, including Dick.

In spite of the ruckus at the hospital, Georgie was unable to get into Victoria's hospital room because of the big dude stationed at the door. Frustrated, she had questioned the sanity of risking her life for a woman she barely knew. Instead, she had returned to Memphis with seeds of doubt planted in her mind regarding the worth of pursuing so volatile a case. *Was Victoria's problem hers?*

Then Georgie's Memphis apartment was bombed. That was when Victoria Martin Tempest's business became personal.

Barely escaping death, she had driven around Memphis in a daze, finally going over to Devin Baldwin's house. With his help, she became officially deceased and assumed the identity of a burnt-to-a-crisp corpse and got Dick Branson off her back.

A talk with Colburn Gordon in Southaven, Mississippi, provided the lead Georgie needed to find his missing sister, Gloria. Afterwards, she'd spoken with Officer Sarah Boswell in Fernwood. Turned out Sarah's friend Tanya Mason knew where Gloria was hiding out, in a Florida trailer court south of Orlando.

So off on Devin Baldwin's motorcycle Georgie had gone in search of the former soda jerk. Gloria was shocked when she showed up at her front door, finally admitting she had tried to warn Victoria about Mark James' association with Dick Branson before freaking out at seeing Jon Branson walk into the drugstore.

Georgie soon learned that Gloria had received a substantial wad of cash and a note telling her to leave town after speaking with Victoria on Saturday. Under the circumstances, quitting her job and starting a new life somewhere new was a no-brainer.

Other stuff went down in Orlando before Georgie returned to Memphis and met with Victoria to share information.

With Gloria's input, a chunk of the Tempest murder puzzle had fallen into place. Learning how three plaintiffs had hired Attorney Jeffrey Tempest to represent them in an environmental complaint against Hearty Meats for improper disposal of toxic substances was proof enough for Georgie that Dick Branson had hired thugs to break into Jeffrey's office and steal the pertinent files. That Jeffrey died was an error. That Victoria wrecked her car and was left in a coma gave Dick the edge. With no proof of existing files and no witnesses, the murder case was mute.

The unsolved case had many layers like an onion. With each shiny layer peeled away, the stink got worse. At the core, it was pure rotten. And now she was in the middle of it.

Following the bombing of her apartment, she had gone undercover to spy on Dick Branson's business practices. Needing a new identity, she had posed as Jaycee Moore, a homeless person, and landed a job at Branson Meatpacking Company.

After only one week, she had obtained proof that Branson employees were illegally packing cocaine inside packages of fresh meat. She'd even taken photos of the Branson employees in the act and stolen a package of the lethal white substance as proof.

Hindsight, it would have been the opportune time for her to contact the FEDS, but thinking it would endanger her life even more, she had mailed the evidence to Attorney Devin Baldwin.

Who knew he would bury the package in his backyard and try to forget she existed? Georgie scowled. *If that's what friends are for . . .*

All hell broke out when she went to see Devin at his home. Enter Anthony Vorices and his thugs from Miami, who beat, drugged, and hauled her off to somewhere south of the border.

So now, here she was, weatherworn PI Georgie Hendricks in the clutches of yet another thug: Donald Wetherfield.

"They won't get her," Georgie mumbled as her captor drove the rental car, en route for the Miami International Airport.

"What?" Donald momentarily took his eyes off the interstate and set them on Georgie. A muscle-bound jujitsu expert, he didn't let much get past him. "Speak up, detective!"

"Not that you care—I said the Fernwood police won't get their hands on Victoria." Might as well express an opinion, thought Georgie. Playing it cool hadn't yet loosened her chains.

Donald chuckled. "What is it about you girls that makes you think you can outsmart trained law-enforcement personnel? Is there something I'm missing?" He was privately considering switching their two international tickets for the next flight to Tennessee. Victoria Martin Tempest had been spotted at the country club, and the police were on site to arrest her.

Georgie glared at Donald and said, "You don't know Victoria Tempest like I do. She's got God on her side."

"God? Like, as in the *Almighty* Creator?" There was a smirk as big as Kansas on the thug's tanned face. "I think not. Victoria is cornered in a wedding chapel with no way to get out." He would not let this two-bit pathetic private eye get his goat.

"Like I said . . ." Georgie stuck to her opinion, "Andy Grimes' team of officers are wastin' their time at the country club. I'm willing to bet you my freedom that Victoria escapes."

Not so bad a bet if Donald agrees, thought Georgie. There was nothing more she wanted to do than to go home to Memphis.

However, to accomplish the feat, it would require protection from Dick Branson. And, as much as Georgie detested the idea of hobnobbing with Alexander Luceres Ramnes on his European turf, he was probably the only one with enough clout to help her.

"Okay, Georgie, so say I'm curious. Why are you convinced Victoria will escape?" Her reasoning seemed ludicrous.

She glared at the bulldozer. "I don't think I can explain how life works for my client." She stared out the car window, yawning from fatigue. "What do I know about anything?"

"Try, Georgie." Donald's jaw was set with determination.

"If you insist . . ." Georgie cleared her throat. "It seems that my client has the uncanny ability to waltz into any sticky situation that definitely doesn't favor her and somehow walk out untouched—like at the hospital when she nearly died and escaped harm's way." There was the dude at her door, big as Godzilla.

"When was that?" Donald inquired as the cab stopped in front of the Miami International Airport. "Get out, Georgie. We'll talk on our way over to the Delta ticket counter."

"Why are you wasting your time on me?" Georgie kept up with Donald as he pushed through the revolving doors.

"I like you," Donald quipped.

"No, you don't. I'm a nobody, a PI without clout." *True, as of late,* Georgie thought. "Why don't you go after Victoria and skip the middleman?" *And leave me alone!*

"Interesting question," Donald commented. "Why don't you answer my question first and then I'll answer yours?" The half-breed was full of intriguing insight. "A deal?"

"For instance," said Georgie, "take the episode at the hospital." She wondered how much information to dole out to the creep who had nabbed her in Columbia—not that her life hadn't already been in jeopardy. "It's a long story, pal. Are you sure you want to hear this?" She had no idea how to explain supernatural intervention. "It's spiritually complex."

"I've got the time," Donald replied, feeling like slapping the broad around until she came clean. "At the beginning, please."

"Whatever," Georgie said as they approached the Delta counter. "Get out your credentials and show the gal," he ordered.

Georgie obeyed. Donald proved his intent to ruin her day by purchasing two tickets to Zurich, Switzerland. Walking away from the ticket counter, she picked up the conversation where they had left off. "What about the bet? The one about Victoria escaping the police and me going free?" She might was well go for broke.

"What's in it for me, then?" Donald wisecracked. "I don't get the fugitive or you. Now is that fair? Besides, I work for

Alexander Luceres Ramnes, and he is the only one who can really help your client—unless you've got a better idea."

Georgie sighed. She didn't.

"Anyhow, didn't I promise you a new life if you cooperate?"

Georgie nodded as they made their way down the corridor leading to the Delta concourse. "I'd still like an update on what's happening at the country club," she said and threw out a suggestion, "Why not call the Fernwood police station and ask?"

"You think we should cancel our trip to Switzerland and fly into Memphis?" It was still a tempting idea.

"That would be nice," Georgie replied, thinking how Brer Rabbit had absolutely loved his briar patch, such as it was.

"But wouldn't it be a wasted trip if Victoria isn't there?" Donald said. "I fear we'd be too late to help."

Help? Georgie halted in her tracks. "Funny man. Well, one phone call will put our minds at ease, won't it?"

"Perhaps." Donald toyed with Georgie's proposal.

"Do it!" Georgie's turquoise eyes flashed with emotion. "If Victoria's still there, I want to go to Fernwood as bad as you do. If not. . ." The alternative route was Zurich.

With their international tickets in hand, Donald stepped into the long line at the checkpoint and pulled his cellphone from his belt to dial information. Georgie trailed him, crossing her fingers.

"The Fernwood, Tennessee Police Precinct," Donald conversed in Spanish with the party at the other end of the line.

Hooray! Georgie impatiently waited for the outcome, a smile tucked underneath her lips as her leverage increased.

"Got it." Donald pushed the *End* button and dialed the number. Thirty seconds later, he was talking with Officer Josh Tenny. "Yeah?" he said. "Uh huh."

"What's happening?" Georgie impatiently inquired.

Donald cupped the phone with his hand. "All he can tell me is what the news media is reporting."

"Which is?" Georgie was on pins and needles.

"That the Christian fugitive has been cornered in the wedding chapel at the Branson-Fernwood Country Club."

"Com' on!" Georgie cursed at the turn of events.

Donald shook his head at Georgie. She could only imagine the fiasco that was taking place at the country club—Dick Branson's team of thugs jumping up and down to get their dirty hands on Victoria. Karen and Mark fighting for her.

"Well, that's that." Donald snapped shut his cellphone. "Officer Josh Tenny is certain the fugitive will soon be apprehended. That's all the information I could glean."

Donald stood motionless in the throws of decision-making. Should they journey to Fernwood? What good would it do?

"She won't be," Georgie declared with certainty.

"How can you be so positive?" Donald's eyes narrowed to gray slits. "If she's cornered and there's no way out."

"There's always an exit route. I know my client, and she wouldn't show up in Fernwood without an escape plan. No way. Victoria's going to nail her husband's murderers or die trying."

Donald was paralyzed a few seconds in retrospection. "Move on down with the line." He nudged Georgie with a hand.

"So do I get to go free? I won the bet, didn't I?" She pushed her luck. "I said she wouldn't get caught, and she hasn't."

"No." Donald grasped Georgie by the elbow and pushed her into the throws of the checkpoint. "I'll let you explain your client's mental state to my boss." He removed his laptop from his briefcase and laid it in the plastic bucket, along with a set of keys.

"Your boss? The Antichrist?" Georgie emptied her pockets of some loose change and sent the plastic box sailing along the conveyor belt. Seeing the anger displayed on Donald's face, she considered apologizing. "Hey, don't get all bent out of shape." She eyed him. "I was only stating the opinion of my client."

They passed through the metal detector and retrieved their belongings. Donald's distorted expression relaxed as they continued down the concourse. "So Victoria thinks my boss is

God's greatest enemy?" Donald's lips evolved into a subtle grin as he shook his head in total disbelief. "Do you honestly believe Luceres is evil because he opposes the dogma of Christianity?"

Georgie shrugged, knowing when to shut up.

"Never mind giving an opinion. I know my mentor, and he's a good person. Keep going, girl!" He gave a nudge.

"Obviously, you trust your boss explicitly and truly believe that Victoria is wrong in her assessment of him." No use getting on Donald's bad side this early in the game, Georgie thought.

"So what's your take on Luceres?"

Huh? "Why does it matter?"

"What do you think motivates Alexander Luceres Ramnes, the 2014 recipient of the *International Man of the Year Award?* A savvy politician who has convinced millions of peoples of all religions and cults to quit their bickering over moral differences?"

"Don't forget about the author of PEACE FIRST," Georgie sarcastically quipped, then bit her tongue thinking that she should just keep her opinions to herself and go on breathing the earth's air. "Look, I'm an atheist. You can have religion, give me peace."

It wasn't worth arguing the point. Georgie respected Victoria for her faith, but begged to differ, seeing God had never done her any favors. For now, she had appeased Donald Wetherfield.

Georgie's toughest problem was deciding exactly what to say to the famous Italian politician when she faced him in Switzerland. "Good to meet you, Mr. Ramnes. Pay me my hundred thousand dollars and I'll go get your victim." *I don't think so.*

Regardless how the conversation went, Georgie would agree to the leader's terms. Didn't she need to get home? And that took money and a lot of protection. It'd only be a little white lie.

6

Fernwood, Tennessee

Sarah Boswell couldn't believe what her heart had convinced her to do: commit a crime. Removing the Tempest folder from Sheriff Grimes' house without authorization was definitely breaking the law. However, in lieu of the trumped-up charges against Victoria, she saw no other way to ascertain the truth.

Just the facts, Ma'am!

And if the written evidence in the file showed that Victoria Tempest hadn't committed a crime, hadn't planned her husband's murder, what would she then do? Sarah questioned if she had the guts to stand up against Dick Branson and his cronies.

Was she any different from any other criminal on the streets?

After all, she'd stolen the Jeffrey Tempest file and was about to read it. Indeed, she hoped Victoria was right in saying the blood of Jesus Christ covered every conceivable sin.

Sarah walked into the Speedy Print Copy Shop and obtained a page counter. Throwing caution to the wind, she fed the first page of the Jeffrey Tempest file folder into the copy machine.

"So what are you copying?" Eleanor Mayo came over and asked. "Don't you people have copiers down at the station?"

"This is personal," said Sarah, standing between the copy machine and nosy Elli. No way was she letting the woman see what she was copying. The sounds of flipping pages continued.

"Well . . ." Elli mewed, wrinkling her pug nose, "just let me know how many copies you make and we'll settle the bill at the front desk." She turned and walked away.

"Fine by me," Sarah agreed, grateful to put some distance between them. If anyone found out, her goose was cooked.

Sarah gathered the first of the materials and entered another batch into the copier. So what was she going to do with this information when she finished? *Privileged* information?

Naturally, she would return the originals to Cheryl Grimes for safekeeping. *But then what?* Sarah began to invent a scenario.

"So why did you bring back the files so soon?" Cheryl would likely inquire. "Sheriff says he don't need 'em," Sarah would answer. "Says he's too busy right now, to bring the file back."

Would Cheryl believe her?

"Why?" she'd ask.

"I have no idea, Mrs. Grimes. Just doin' my job."

"Is there anything else you need, Officer Boswell?" Cheryl was sure to add with a polite smile, aiming to please.

"No," Sarah would say. "Sorry about the bother."

The copier spit out the sheets of paper like it was angry.

You see . . . Sarah pointed out to herself, *one crime leads to another,* all the while watching eight-by-eleven-inch pages flip off the end of the machine into a neat little illegal pile.

By chance, if Cheryl Grimes happened to mention lending Sarah the files, she could forget about growing old and collecting a government pension. Her career would be over, possibly her life.

***

Jackson, Tennessee

"What's this place?" Lucas queried in Spanish.

Victoria silently read the sign through the limousine window glass: THOMAS CREMATING SERVICES, in no hurry to enlist their services. Let Texas do the explaining, she gulped in air.

"C R E M A T I N G," Lucas spelled out the middle word. "What's it mean, Papa? Does it have to do with ice cream?"

Texas chuckled, glancing down at his inquisitive adopted son. "No, it's a funeral home," he explained. "Some folks don't want to be buried in the ground." He wasn't going into any details, how the bodies were burned and their ashes placed in urns.

"Why not? If they're dead, I mean." Lucas climbed out of the plush stretch-white limousine, getting the willies as he saw a corpse hauled out of the end of a black limousine. "Who is *that*?"

Texas made eye contact with Victoria and smiled.

"Someone who is heaven-bound," he said to Lucas, praying it was true. "If not, it's too late for them to make the right choice."

"Oh," Lucas replied, kicking at a loose stone on the concrete pad. "If they don't know Jesus, guess they'll go the other way."

Lucas' response brought chuckles to the grownups.

Texas walked around the back of the vehicle, opened the limousine door, and let Victoria out. Without any forethought, she fell into his strong arms and planted a wet kiss on his lips.

"What was that for?" he asked, dazzled, clinging to Victoria as he yearned for a bit more of her sweet affection.

"Rescuing me." She flashed a winsome smile "So where is Jon and his mother?" She distanced herself from Texas and glanced around at the parking lot rapidly filling up with cars for the next scheduled funeral. Attendees gathered at the entrance.

Texas looked around for their ride. "Jon ought to be here soon. We need to get going. I don't want to be late for the revival." He didn't comment how dangerous it was to delay.

"What happens to the ashes of the dead people when Jesus comes back?" Lucas was still puzzling over the act of cremation. "Does Jesus put their dead bodies back together again?"

"Lucas . . ." Texas knelt beside the disturbed lad, "I really don't have time to go into the details of all the Bible has to say about the subject of death. All you need to know is that Christians will be bodily resurrected from the grave when Christ summons His church to Heaven. Those of us who are alive will be changed in the twinkling of an eye and instantly receive new heavenly bodies. It will be a gloriously supernatural event."

"The rapture," Lucas clarified, walking alongside his papa.

"That's correct, son." Texas grasped Victoria's hand, eyeing her for approval. "We have much to look forward to."

Victoria shook her head in agreement, feeling like a schoolgirl on a field trip with Texas, a smile dancing across her face as their eyes met. Don't pinch her if this was a dream.

Texas was about to go back for a second kiss when Lucas tugged on his arm. "There they are!" the lad exclaimed. "Let's go, Papa!" He ran across the parking lot to greet Jon Branson.

"Hi." Jon rounded the corner of the building. "Mother's waiting in the van across the street. Ready to roll?" His gaze shot from Texas to Victoria. "Did you two just make up?" he teased. "I detect a giddiness in your faces that spells love."

"Yes—no!" Victoria said, embarrassed, grabbing Jon and hugging him with all her might. "Where would I be if my friends didn't stand up for me?" Her respect grew with each encounter.

"That's what friends are for." Jon recalled the title to an old song written on the subject. "We'd better hurry. The police are bound to be looking for you guys by now."

"We made up," said Texas, taking the time to embrace Victoria and give her a lingering kiss. It was a minute before she came up for air. "Ain't that right, honey?"

"Right," said Victoria. "Very right."

7

Back at the wedding chapel

Sheriff Grimes complained to Mark James, "I've given Victoria Tempest forty-five minutes of my valuable time. Now I'm going in there to get her." He pointed a stumpy finger at the Bride's Room, believing that Victoria was trapped inside.

"No, let me do it," the groom offered. "I'll see there is no resistance." He trekked down the hallowed path of the wedding chapel where brides had gone for two decades, noticing the pretty white bows attached to the ends of the reserved benches. His foot was heavy as it hit the stage with a thud. Father Crosby was seated in a chair at the corner of the stage, appearing traumatized.

"The wedding's over, Father, you can go home," Mark said to the stunned minister. "I'll call you the first of the week and drop by with a nice-sized check for the church." He planned on paying the man for his patience as well as the quick ceremony.

"I'm worried about that woman—in there." The rector pointed to the Bride's Room. "What will they do with her? Is she going to be arrested and put in jail?" Sweat poured off his face.

"No need to worry, I've taken care of everything," Mark replied. "We're done here. You should go on home now before the police detain everyone for questioning."

"I don't understand, is there a problem?" Crosby's layered chin was quivering, never having seen a wedding like this one.

"There will be shortly." Mark's lips were set hard in his lower jaw. "Thank you for a beautiful ceremony. We'll call you to have our children christened. Go home." It was not a request.

The tired minister gathered up his white robe in his pudgy arms and tromped down the center aisle, talking to himself like a babbling lunatic. Mark didn't care as long as he left, and quickly.

Now, to do the inevitable! Mark stood at the door marked THE BRIDE'S ROOM, about to tap on the locked door.

"Well, ain't you gonna go in to get her?" Dick demanded.

In response, the groom spun around and faced his stalker. "I swear, Dick, you look like a starving piranha about to dine on human flesh," he accurately assessed the situation.

"Quit the chatter, Mark. The jig's up! Just go on in there and get Victoria and let's get this show over with," Dick barked. "Marjorie's tired and wants to go home. And I've had it."

"Then, let her go home. Call a taxi." Mark opened the door to the Bride's Room and stepped inside.

Dick huffed as the door slammed in his face.

"Hi, sweetie," Mark said to Karen. "I hope you didn't get too lonely." He kissed her lightly on the lips. "How's my baby doin'?" He felt her paunch. "We'll go have a nice dinner somewhere, as soon as this fiasco passes. It might take a while, considering Dick's state of mind and Andy's posse."

"Don't worry about me, I'm fine." Karen wore her mother's pretty size-eight beige suit. Lowering the veil attached to a pillbox hat over her face, she said: "You really think I can walk out of here posing as my mother?" She giggled. "I love you, Dr. James."

"Me, too. Now let's get this ruse over with." Mark took Karen's arm and exited the room. "Back up, Dick. I'm taking Vicki to Sheriff Grimes. Go home, I'll call you later."

"Sure." He glared at the bride's veiled face.

Karen acknowledged Dick's presence with a nod then slowly walked down the aisle toward the front entrance, holding to Mark's arm for dear life, fully expecting to be grabbed by Andy, handcuffed, and dragged off to jail. But they made it safely outside the chapel into the waning daylight.

In light of their success, Karen wished the wedding reception had not been cancelled. At least the honeymoon was still on.

"Victoria Martin Tempest," Sheriff Grimes met the bride at the bottom of the chapel steps. "You have the right to an attorney . . ." he read her Miranda Rights with an air of authority.

Mark stood beside Karen, a smug expression tearing at his face. He'd given Victoria and that handsome Texan friend of hers plenty of time to escape. Soon, everyone would know what had happened, including the media. Karen planned on taking the blame, being the dutiful daughter. But he was guilty, too, unwilling to see Vicki behind bars for a crime she didn't commit.

Balancing the truth was tricky and that continually required practice. And believe it or not, Mark was getting good at it.

"Remove that veil and look at me!" Andy tired of the fugitive's nonchalance. "Now!"

Slowly, Karen unveiled her face. "Sorry, Sheriff, but I didn't have a choice." Her fierce gaze targeted Andy's blazing eyes.

Mark thought Sheriff Grimes was going to explode and burn, his face turned so red. Andy shot a glance at Dick that scalded everyone standing close enough to see it. Then he slowly turned around and faced Dr. Mark James. "Where is she?"

"Vicki? I have no idea," Mark responded. "This was Karen's idea." He had his palms up, signifying innocence.

"But you went along with it, didn't you?" Andy's fat lips twisted into a knot. "That's aiding and abbettin', and I'm taking in the both of you. Forgit about the honeymoon!"

"No, don't." Dick put his hand on Andy's arm. "Use your energy to get the fugitive. She can't have gone far in a limousine. Put out an APB on the vehicle. Do your job, buddy."

"So that's all you have to say?"

"Yep." Dick was unyielding.

"Okay." Andy got in his squad car and called the precinct.

"Well, you've sure gone and done it now, bud," Dick addressed Mark. "If Victoria gets away again, it's all your fault."

"Prove it's my fault," said Mark. "Did you see me do anything wrong?" His chilly blue gaze shot to Karen.

"Admit it, Mark. You know you knew it was Vicki when you walked her to the limousine," Dick attempted to get a confession.

"No, I didn't. I thought it was Karen," Mark lied. "She told me to stay with her mother while she went by the condo to pick up an item she'd forgotten. I'm an obedient husband now."

"What item?" Dick defied Mark's story. "You know you're lying." His bulbous brown eyes chased after Karen.

"A lot of people lie about a lot of things." Mark wasn't talking about Victoria anymore. Dick had effectively fabricated his way through life. One day the string of lies was going to amass and hang him. Mark knew he would probably go down, too.

Such was life.

8

Sarah Boswell pulled her Buick into the single garage of her house and manually let down the door. Sweat poured from beneath her arms, and it wasn't from the oppressive Tennessee heat settling like thick fog over the mid-South. It was fear.

Why had she committed the crime?

For twenty-five years Sarah had been a law-abiding citizen, an officer of the law paid to keep criminals off the streets. Never had she once taken a nickel lying around at the precinct, always placing any loose change she found in a glass jar designated for purchasing goodies. How could she possibly justify her actions?

Sarah's conscience was hurting, but not enough to stop her. Only a first-class, fool-hearty person would risk losing a twenty-five-year-long career. But that was exactly what she was doing.

Marching into the house, Sarah tossed her purse on the sofa. "Victoria, I swear, girl. If this information doesn't get you off the hook, I am washing my hands of the matter. You hear?"

Sarah knew the fugitive couldn't hear her, but saying so made her feel a heap better. Picking up the phone, she dialed Tanya Mason's number to confess. "Thank God, Tan. This is Sarah."

"I know who it is, girlfriend. You don't sound good at all."

"I'm not good." *Good* was a word used to describe honest folk, and Sarah had failed to pass that test. "I have a hot item in my hand." She could not spell out her sin in plain English.

"I take it you don't need a potholder to relieve the heat."

"No. I'm making you my partner." She was talking about sharing the information illegally taken from Sheriff Grimes' house.

"What?" Tanya reacted.

"Don't even think about saying 'no.'"

"Is this gonna cost me?" Tanya asked.

"Probably," Sarah replied.

"What's the deal?"

"I'm off tomorrow. Thought we could meet somewhere."

"This sounds *really* serious." Tanya noted the soberness in her friend's voice, Sarah's heavy breathing over the phone.

"Life-and-death serious," Sarah breathlessly replied. "If you haven't been watching the news, I suggest that you turn it on for an update on Fernwood's latest crisis."

"Not again," Tanya said, sighing. "When will the nightmare ever end?" She flipped on the TV, dreading what was coming.

A photo of Victoria flashed on the screen.

"I'm working on that," said Sarah. "Meet me later tonight at the place where our daddies used to take us fishing when we were kids." Tanya would know which spot she meant. "And come alone. Make up some excuse to get out of the house."

"You're scarin' me." It was short notice to batten down the helm without telling her family where the boat was setting sail.

"Be scared, but show up," Sarah insisted. "We need to put on our thinking caps, and fast. I can't do this alone."

"Okay, if you think there is no other way."

"There isn't." Sarah racked the phone. As soon as she had packed a bag, she was leaving town. No way was she getting caught with the loot. By now, Andy Grimes might know.

9

Somewhere over the Atlantic Ocean

Georgie Hendricks, airborne and belted in a seat with a fantastic window view, put on the black mask the gal wearing the Delta uniform had handed her to shut out the light for the eight-hour flight to Zurich. Seated next to her was Donald Wetherfield, needing no assistance to sleep, already snoring gourds and spitting like a camel with every breath. Why was it that men could fall asleep at the drop of a hat? No conscience?

It certainly wasn't because they were innocent, Georgie decided. It was probably because males believed themselves clever enough to never get caught at wrongdoing. While women, on the other hand, had built-in guilt complexes that convinced them they needed to confess every little misdemeanor.

That was why God had given women the children to mentor and sent the men off to work. Maybe God believed there was hope for future generations with strong feminine guidance.

Georgie cursed to herself. If she kept up this vein of thought, she would never sleep. So this was the deal, she was going to meet the newest International Man of the Year and play polite. She'd agree to do everything the world leader asked.

When the money Donald promised her was in her greedy little hand, she would hightail it back to Memphis and have a serious little talk with Attorney Devin Baldwin, her so-called friend, and find out if he knew how to find Victoria Tempest.

No monkeying around, or else!

Afterwards, Georgie would punch out Devin for his failure to report Dick Branson's crimes to the FBI and rescue her from the hands of the Columbian thugs. If Donald Wetherfield hadn't tracked her down, she'd likely be dead by now.

Georgie squirmed in her seat. Nobody would need to write her a new death certificate. There was already one on file at the Shelby County Courthouse. Dead or alive, she wasn't feeling so good. She shut her eyes beneath the black mask and counted sheep. All black. Whites ones didn't exist in her dreams.

Georgie had lied when she told Donald she was an atheist. Only God could have invented so vast a drama involving Earthlings. Besides, the universe was far too complicated to have just accidentally exploded in all directions and life happened. Even an infidel could see God's handiwork in the beauty of nature. It was people who troubled Georgie, people who troubled God. It was people who troubled people.

***

Fernwood, Tennessee

"So what's going to happen to Mark and Karen?" Marjorie Branson asked her husband on their way home from the country club. "Did they commit a crime by helping Victoria escape?"

"Of course, they committed a crime!" Dick barked, in no mood to discuss the fiasco. He should have grabbed Victoria by the neck and hauled her off to the precinct when he had the chance. Nobody was competent anymore. Nobody.

"It was nice of you to tell Andy to quit hassling the newlyweds. Mark and Karen deserve a honeymoon. How could they possibly have known that Victoria would show up for the ceremony unannounced?" Marjorie peered at her husband.

"I know they didn't," Dick admitted, calming down a tad. "But Andy needs to blame somebody besides himself. All Mark did was talk. There's no proof he knew what Karen was up to."

Dick privately considered if it was worth Andy's time to arrest Karen. No. Better to keep the channels open and wait for Victoria to reappear in Karen's life. She would, given time.

"Is she going to sell her condo and move in with Mark?" Marjorie asked, operating on a different wavelength.

"Who?" Dick turned his head toward Marjorie.

"Karen Tempest," she replied. "Does Victoria have any ownership in Karen's condo that would hinder a sale?"

"I don't know," Dick answered. "Victoria sold her house in January and moved in with Karen to plan her June wedding—which I might add didn't turn out like anyone expected. It's all water under the bridge now." He cast his eyes on the scenery.

"Such is life." Marjorie sighed.

"I'm hungry," Dick remarked. "What'd ya say we stop at Burger King and pick up two sandwiches?" The growling in his stomach was ferocious. "Maybe a couple of shakes."

"Not a chance," said Marjorie. "You're starting on a diet. Remember?" Her pale violet eyes chastised Dick.

"No, sweet pea! You know I don't handle diets well. It makes me cranky." Dick could not deal with sacrifice today.

"Life makes you cranky, Dick. You are not going to go out and buy another set of larger clothes like you did last month. Weight Watchers will help you." Marjorie's jaw was set hard.

"Oh, no! I knew it!" Dick had read his Zodiac sign in the morning paper: *Beware! A change is coming, not necessarily for good.* "Can't I wait another week?" He was dying for a burger with all the fat calories and extra cheese. "Please, Pun'kin."

"No, Dick. We're going to both have a nice spinach salad with sliced tomatoes and boiled eggs when we get home. You can have tomato juice before going to bed. Don't argue, please."

"And I have to weigh in at Weight Watchers every week?"

"That's the program," said Marjorie. "I'll go with you. I have the little calorie book that tells us how much we can eat each day. You get to pick and choose. It won't be so bad."

"Between broccoli and carrots—that's no choice." Dick was already dreaming of a hot fudge sundae. "Can't we wait until tomorrow? I've had such a ratty day."

"We've all had a ratty day, Dick. Diets aren't easy for anybody. Losing weight requires a great deal of discipline. You'll thank me when you're fifty pound lighter."

"Fifty pounds! I'll never survive long enough—won't I have to buy another set of clothes if I get too skinny?" Dick wanted to wiggle out of the D word. "Please, Pun'kin."

"No. I have the next three sizes down packed away in boxes in the attic. All I have to do is pull them out by sizes as the pounds dissolve away." She had a workable diet in mind.

Clutching the steering wheel, Dick wished for a juicy hamburger on a toasted bun. Loaded with cheese, sour pickles, Mayo, sprinkled with sautéed onions and ripe tomatoes.

Was this diet his punishment for hating Victoria's guts? Maybe there was a real devil and it had invaded his pretty wife?

Dick wanted to scream bloody murder!

10

Washington D.C., The White House

Lazarus Bacon lived with his parents in the White House: *The* White House. His daddy was the president: *The* President of the United States of America.

To those outside the presidential circle, Lazarus appeared to be an ordinary ten-year-old kid, privately tutored because of the heightened security in a risky world. To those closest to President John Anthony Bacon, the lad was trouble spelled with a capital T.

Diana Bacon was entirely too busy with political projects to monitor her son's daily activities, so she had hired a professional nanny to see that Lazarus was properly nurtured and behaved in public. On Monday of each week, Lazarus received his school assignments via e-mail from a private school system serving high-profile families in the Western Hemisphere.

Although Lazarus had everything a kid could possibly want, he still wasn't satisfied. Something inside of him whispered unrest. "Lazarus doesn't fit the usual mold," he had heard the adults comment. "He's weird," the kids at the gym said.

The problem was, Lazarus actually knew a great deal more about most things than his twenty-three-year-old nanny, whom he simply called Natalie. Possessing a razor-sharp mind, he constantly read everything in print—newspapers, novels and religious tracks. He also listened to the news: CNN, FOX, NBC, and the weather channel. He never forgot what he read, heard or observed.

Bottom line, Lazarus was a genius and knew it. Usually in control of social situations, he had the restraint to step back and give other players the first move on the great Chessboard of Life before taking a turn. To Lazarus, life was a game, a challenge of intellect. When he prevailed, he would sit back and gloat at the loser. No two games were ever alike, he had observed.

Natalie Brooster, the socially apt nanny with a college degree in child psychology was stupid in Lazarus' estimation, primarily because she cared more about earning her salary than mentoring children. Lazarus could care less whether Natalie taught him one thing as long as she gave him some space to daydream and play.

Lazarus laughed when Natalie accused him of being a precocious genius. His teasing usually made her so mad she often stormed out of the study and left him alone to complete his educational assignments. Because Lazarus liked learning, he usually completed his work on time and read a few books to boot.

Being a loner was just fine. It gave Lazarus time to think.

So the precocious lad's mother and much-in-demand father trusted that Natalie was doing a beautiful job with educating their only son and often praised her with raises. That kept her happy.

Lazarus didn't care about Natalie's quirks—which included habitually shopping for stuff at the malls. It was control that most interested him. He praised the way his daddy stood up to the United Nations when America was not getting a fair shake.

Why? Politics intrigued him.

Lazarus knew the names of all the political contenders of both Republican and Democratic Parties. Having a divine dream, he yearned to rule the world. Those grandiose ideas of fame were muses, whimsical daydreams, often playing on the fertile mounds of Lazarus' keen but mysterious mind. One day he would grow up. Then people would honor him and care what he thought.

One day . . .

Lazarus didn't remember much before he was two years old, only that he liked chocolate a lot. His daddy sometimes read fables to him when he was younger. Diana, his prim mother, kept him at bay, likely afraid he would mess up her pretty dress if they touched.   That was okay, though. Lazarus didn't need to be handled. Touchy-feely stuff was for wimps, not real boys.

Lazarus was daddy's "big" boy, all right.

By the time he had turned five, he was reading on the fifth-grade level.   Twelve months later, he comprehended general arithmetic and was able to solve simple algebraic problems.

At age eight, enrolled in a private academy, he had taken the comprehensive exam required of students to graduate high school and passed it. Learning was a contest and Lazarus loved it.

Around that time, his daddy decided to hire a nanny and remove Lazarus from the private school. "Too smart for your britches," British-born Natalie often scolded her bright student.

But if you knew a lot more than your teachers, Lazarus considered, and you were doubly smart, it didn't really matter what others said or thought of you. What those closest to him didn't know about him was his secret interest in witchcraft.

White, of course, like the house he lived in. He wasn't a bad kid compared to most, but he enjoyed playing pranks. A person could log on the Internet and order books about Wicca and learn how to cast spells. And Lazarus had.

Sometimes the spell worked, sometimes it didn't. But it was whopping fun to try, Lazarus thought. One time Natalie caught him whipping up a spell in the kitchen using raw frog legs and toadstools and threatened to expose him to his parents. He told her to go ahead and tell, that he would blame her for helping.

As usual, Natalie gave in.

And if threats didn't work, Lazarus pointed out the fact that Natalie never helped him finish his homework, her negligence likely to get her fired. Politicians called it a "bargaining chip."

Natalie liked the good pay, her comfy bedroom, and the freedom to do as she pleased and go where she wanted twenty-four seven. As long as Lazarus was not in immediate danger, his parents didn't seem to care where Natalie took him.

She was the perfect nanny.

However, Natalie had a weak spot, a boyfriend who secretly came calling a couple of times a week. They made out in the next room while Lazarus finished his schoolwork. He knew because he peeped through the keyhole and saw them necking—doing more than that, sometimes. *Sex,* they called it. *Disgusting,* he had decided. Love was stupid. He never wanted any part of *it!*

Lazarus wasn't the least bit interested in sharing his life with another person, male or female. He wanted to grow mentally and control anything he could. Why, he used to have a dog, a cute little black poodle his mother let him keep in his room in a cage.

One night Lazarus cooked up a spell and made the puppy quit breathing. It was fun watching the animal twist and holler, dying at a young age, smothering. He had no regrets. None.

But the next morning, the dog began to stink and his mother came into the bedroom and screamed for his daddy. They hugged and kissed him and said they were so sorry that the puppy had died. Pepper must have had a virus. He pretended to be sorry, but he wasn't. He could always get another puppy.

But Lazarus didn't, because if he did he knew he would kill it, too. He liked watching things die. He liked to control things—animate and inanimate objects. But it was always his secret.

So Lazarus practiced his magic arts when Natalie took him to the park to play. He would sit on the swing, gently rocking, while concentrating on the child swinging next to him.

"Fall!" he would think to himself, and the little boy or girl would get dumped out of the swing. Then, he'd laugh, jump off the swing, and help them get up. "Did that hurt?" he'd ask.

Touching another person gave Lazarus more power, he soon discovered. "Cough," he would say and they did. He was beginning to wonder if he said, "Die!" if they really would.

Death was an intriguing concept. Where did the human spirit go when it left the body? Was there a planet eons away in another universe that housed earthly disembodied spirits?

Lazarus knew the Bible said that dead people went to live with Jesus. But if the Savior could bodily raise himself from the dead after three days, why didn't he raise everybody?

His daddy, a practicing Christian, said there were a lot of unanswered questions about life that everyone would find out by and by. Lazarus never understood "by and by," but it must be someplace important. "Stay focused, Lazarus! Make something important out of yourself, so you won't waste your time living."

That was what his parents always told him.

As far as death, if people started to die while he was around, they might suspect that he had caused the trouble. Then, his parents wouldn't let him go to the park with Natalie anymore.

No, it was better to keep his psychic gifts to himself.

Today, Lazarus was playing video games at a local mall. Natalie was standing a few feet away, watching him like a hawk. Beyond her, at the door were plain-clothes CIA men. Because Lazarus' father was the President of the United States, he was constantly watched and protected twenty-four hours a day.

And being protected from life was no fun at all! Lazarus couldn't help but wonder what would happen if he told all the guards and Natalie to go to sleep. He might tell everybody in the mall to take a nap. That way he could go anywhere he pleased, take anything he wanted, and later wake them up with the snap of a finger. And absolutely nobody would know what he had done.

But first Lazarus would have to practice on someone to make sure he could really do it. Putting a little puppy to sleep was one thing. Making a thousand people sleep—well, he wasn't sure if his daddy would approve of that. He suddenly felt hungry.

Lazarus glanced around his world. The mall was bright and noisy with people rushing about. There were wonderful odors of salty peanuts, perfumes, food, and opportunities for fun.

"Natalie? Can I have a chocolate shake at Sally's Ice Cream Shop?" Lazarus pointed across the massive hallway.

"Sure. I'll walk you there." Natalie peered at Lazarus with her beautiful blue eyes, huge like windows with lights.

"No," said Lazarus. "I want to go alone. I don't want you going with me. It's just across the hall. You can watch me from here." He looked up at her, very determined to have his way.

"I don't know, sweetie." Natalie looked at the distance between her and the door of the ice cream shop.

"Please, Natalie. I'll be safe," he gently prodded.

"Well, I suppose you can," she reluctantly agreed, hugging to the railing overlooking the lower level of the mall while Lazarus walked around the open area and approached the ice cream shop.

"Don't stay in there too long, okay?" Natalie hollered.

"I won't." Lazarus peeked inside the ice cream parlor, then glanced back at Natalie. She was speaking to two of the guards. Guns bulged under their jackets, real guns that fired bullets. He'd sure like to borrow one of those weapons and shoot something. His daddy had promised to take him deer hunting sometimes.

Lazarus walked up to the lady behind the counter and laid his five-dollar bill on the counter. "I want a *big* chocolate shake."

"Me, too." A man sat down on a stool beside Lazarus. "I'll buy us both a shake. Is that all right with you, kid?"

Lazarus nodded at the stranger and pocketed his five. The man had big muscles and a nice smile. "Thanks."

"Hi, kid. I'm Gordo. What's your name?"

"I'm not supposed to talk to strangers." Lazarus glanced out the doorway to see if the guards were watching. "But I will, because I can do anything I want to." He liked breaking the rules.

Gordon chuckled. "I like you, kid. You're all right."

"You're all right, too," Lazarus said, relaxing a bit.

"Tell me, kid. What can you do that's so different from other children? You can't be more that eight, can you?"

"Ten!" Lazarus declared with certainty. "And my name isn't *Kid*, it's Lazarus. Lazarus Roger Bacon."

"Are you related to the famous poet?" Gordon asked, good with kids because he had once been a professional clown and done circus gigs. Kids liked him because he was a natural.

"No, but Roger Bacon was pretty important. And so is my daddy. He's the President of the United States," Lazarus bragged.

"Well, well now, that's pretty impressive. So tell me, Lazarus Roger Bacon, what can you do that other children can't?"

"I made my puppy go to sleep," Lazarus said, hands cupped as he whispered in Gordon's ear. "Bet you never did that. I bet you don't know one person who has done that!"

"Nope." Gordon winked an eye, chuckling as the young waitress behind the soda bar stared at them. "Hey, gorgeous, how 'bout those two sodas?" He pulled a ten from his pants pocket.

"Do you like chocolate a lot?" Lazarus asked, his eyes on the green money. "Chocolate is my favorite flavor."

"You bet, Lazarus." Gordon twisted around on the bar stool to face the lad. "I love chocolate so much I got a candy bar the size of a horse at my house." He kept a straight poker face.

"Really? Is it sculptured like an Easter bunny?"

"Yep. Carved it out myself. Melted down a ton of bunnies to make it. You wanna come see it sometimes? When you're not busy with your friends." Gordon knew that Lazarus had watchdogs at his heels. The idea was to get the kid alone.

"I'm not busy now," said Lazarus, interested. "Those men aren't my friends. They follow me because my daddy pays them. I hate them. We could slip off, just the two of us."

"What about your nanny out there? Won't she be upset if you leave with me?" Gordon asked, hoping the kid had an idea.

"Naw," said Lazarus. "She won't even have to know. I could just put her to sleep like I did my puppy. I won't make her stop breathing—that might make her die."

Gordon tilted his head to one side. "You're kidding, aren't you?" There was a lump the size of Kansas lodged in his throat.

"No sir, I'm not. I have psychic powers. My parents tell me I'm a genius," Lazarus bragged. "Do you really have a giant chocolate bunny at your house, or are you just teasing? Are you trying to trick me so you can take me away from Natalie?"

"I guess you'll never find out if you don't come and see," said Gordon. "The bunny is real, but if you don't trust me enough to go look, I guess you'll never know." A smile tugged at his lips.

Lazarus thought about what Gordo had said. How would he ever know the bunny existed if he didn't go and take a look?

"I guess," Lazarus remarked with a sigh.

"You guess what?" Gordon observed the waitress as she placed two tall icy glasses filled with liquid chocolate ice cream across the counter. "You guys want water?" she asked.

"I do," said Gordon. "What about you, kid?"

Lazarus grabbed his soda and nodded.

"Bring a water for my friend," Gordon said to the waitress.

Neither Gordon nor Lazarus said much as they polished off their sodas. Lazarus wiped his sticky lips with a paper napkin.

"I'm finished with my soda, Mr. Gordo, and I want to go see your big chocolate bunny," Lazarus declared.

"What about your nanny and the other guys?" Gordon swiped his mouth with a napkin. "Won't you get in trouble?" Gordon knew he would if he tried to leave with the kid.

"I'll take care of them. You promise to bring me back here?"

"Sure, kid. Else you might put me to sleep permanently."

Lazarus smiled. "You're my friend, right?"

"Right," said Gordon.

Lazarus perched on the barstool for another few minutes and contemplated the best way of escape. Why not put out the lights? Then he and Gordo could easily slip past the guards in the dark.

No. That wouldn't work because it would be too dark to see. He suddenly knew what to do as he spied a fat woman walking past the soda shop. "Go to sleep, lady," he mumbled.

A nanosecond later, the woman fainted.

Lazarus watched a crowd of mall walkers gathering around the victim like a flock of buzzards. Not understanding what had taken place, people abandoned their booths and rushed from the restaurant. "We're home free," Lazarus said to Gordo. "Run!"

11

Dickson County, Tennessee

Victoria Tempest yawned. "How much farther is it to Dickson?" Cuddled up against Texas, she was enjoying the feel of his strong arm draped about her shoulder.

"You should take a nap," Jon hollered from the driver's seat. "Mother's already asleep. I'll wake you up when we get there."

"Good idea," Texas pointed out to Victoria. "I expect the revival will go on until quite late. And we have the drive back to Safehouse # 36. I might just doze off, too."

Victoria didn't need much encouragement to close her eyes. She was talked out now that Texas knew everything that had happened to her since they'd last been together in Rome.

The only thing Victoria had purposely left out concerned the little gold key in her billfold—the one Karen said fit a bank safe deposit box in Zurich, Switzerland. What if Texas disapproved of her returning to Europe to collect five million dollars?

To quote the infamous Beverly James: *Some things are best left unsaid.* Victoria attempted to shut off her thoughts and relax.

"You said Joseph Glower is preaching tonight," Texas addressed Jon. "What do you know about him?

"Only what I've been told. Brother Joseph is from California. He used to be a bouncer at a nightclub—got saved at a street meeting and was baptized in the Holy Spirit. Life for him radically changed after that. Notice I didn't say for the better."

"You mean he got saved," Lucas perked up and asked.

"Yeah, that and more," Jon replied. "At the time of his salvation, Brother Joseph received a special anointing in the gifts of healing. When he lays hands on people and prays for them, Jesus honors his prayers. People are often healed in the process."

"But not always," Texas qualified.

"Correct." The van rolled over the Tennessee River Bridge. "But if what folks report is correct, Brother Joseph is a fine evangelist and knows his Bible. A friend of mine heard him speak once in Los Angeles. The man's authentic, solid as they come."

"And you're sure he's not a glory seeker?" Texas wanted no involvement with occult practices. "Seems to me as of late there is an uprising of false prophets seeking to appease the itching ears of dissatisfied church members. Satan has his followers, too."

"Bible predicted it, why should we be surprised?" Jon said. "Matthew 24, verse 11: 'False prophets will rise up and deceive many.' None of us can comprehend the horror of the end times."

"Exactly," said Texas. "I'm just waiting for Jesus to come back." He noticed that Victoria was breathing evenly, sleeping.

"The *Rapture*. What an event!" Jon exclaimed. "But first, all the prophecies of the Word must be fulfilled. Verses 22 and 23 in Matthew 24 say that God will have to shorten the days on Earth or everyone would die. False prophets are gonna rise and show great signs and wonders to deceive, if possible, even the elect."

"I guess that's what worries me," Texas shared. "I once saw a woman healed. She had a withered hand and it grew back, but the preacher didn't do anything special. It just happened."

"Likely an isolated move of the Holy Spirit."

"Correct," said Texas. "The woman prayed a lot."

"Prayer is a key factor in every miraculous healing," Jon said. "Brother Joe doesn't lay hands on anyone unless he is prompted by the Holy Spirit. As you will see, when he preaches the all-powerful Word of God, the Spirit moves mightily. Lost folks get saved, the backslidden repent, and the sick are healed. People are encouraged to persevere in times of persecution."

"I can live with that," said Texas. "I don't think Victoria has ever been in a meeting like this one. I guess I wonder if her natural gifts will be enhanced."

"Oh," said Jon. "Her ability to understand languages."

"Yes," Texas said. "Victoria doesn't make a big deal out of her ability to speak Spanish or Italian, but I can tell you it is a big deal to the Christian lay movement. What if she has the ability to interpret and speak any language? Think of the all the aborigine tribes that still need to hear God's Word."

"Truly," Jon softly whistled, "a gift of that magnitude would prove phenomenal. You think Victoria could communicate with these lost people tribes?" He made eye contact with Texas through the rearview mirror. Victoria was sleeping peacefully.

"Maybe," Texas replied. "But I wonder if she's ready."

"You mean, with all that's she's recently gone through."

"Yes. Her inability to cope with lost memories bothers me. And she's so determined to chase down her husband's killers regardless the consequences. Plus she's highly unpredictable."

"Have you mentioned your theory to Victoria?" Jon asked. "The possibility of her being able to speak multiple languages?"

"Not yet." Texas questioned where he would fit in her schedule if she became an evangelist. He selfishly wanted to marry the unique woman and reside with her on his Texas farm.

"Because you want her for yourself?" Jon was perceptive. "Isn't it awful? Getting priorities straight to please Jesus?"

Texas shrugged his shoulders as Victoria shifted her position on his shoulder. "If Jesus needs her more, I'll have to live with it." He knew Jesus wouldn't tarry too long. God's will for the lives of His people took precedence over personal gratification.

"Are you going to help Victoria solve Jeffrey's murder?"

"I don't know," said Texas. "I do know that Victoria will never abandon that goal." He sighed. "I just don't know any way to help speed up the process. The evidence is sketchy, at best. Without Jeffrey's stolen files, she's very much in the dark."

"Yeah," Jon said, "it's her word against my father's." He hated believing that his own flesh and blood was involved with the young attorney's premature death. "Time will tell, I guess."

"Yeah," said Texas, "the truth will come out given time."

"I'm afraid Victoria is right about my father."

"In what ways?" Texas inquired, now that Jon had raised the issue. "What is it you think Dick did?"

"It's a question I've pondered often. Richard Branson the Third is selfish and devious, out to get all he can financially in this life, but I can't see him as a premeditated murderer."

"You should know, growing up under the man's roof. But you know Victoria's opinion is clouded by ignorance and anger."

"Yeah. And the whole fiasco has the mark of the devil—not that my father didn't have a choice in participating."

Texas studied Jon, feeling sorry for the lad.

"I keep hoping Dad will convert to Christianity and give up his devious ways," Jon said. "Will you pray for him? And me?"

"And if he doesn't change?" Texas speculated the outcome.

"I'll confront him about the matter. If I suspect he's guilty of murder, I'll turn him in myself. It's the only ethical thing to do."

"Saying and doing are two different things." Texas knew, because he had made many promises to his wife while she was in good health and never followed through. Then it was too late.

"I refuse to let Victoria take the blame for a crime she didn't commit," Jon declared. "She has suffered enough."

"I agree. Exactly how do you think your father was involved with the crime?" Texas wanted to understand Jon's reasoning.

"I think Dad hired the thugs who broke into Jeffrey's office, and it had something to do with the company he was managing."

"Hearty Meats. What was the motive?"

"To grab hold of some incriminating files."

"Why do you think that?"

"Paul Tempest told me he'd overheard my daddy and Dr. Mark James talking about Jeffrey's death on the telephone. Dr.

Mark said he was sorry for his part. After Paul died, I went to his apartment and found a notebook hidden under Paul's pillow."

"What did it say?" Texas' eyes drew taut.

"Paul only wrote one sentence and underlined it: <u>My daddy wasn't supposed to be there</u>. I can't ignore the conclusions."

"Did Paul mention anything else about Dr. Mark James?"

"Not in that note."

"Why hasn't Mark told Victoria about the conversation?" Texas asked. "Is he trying to protect her, or himself?"

"Who knows? That Mark loves her deeply is evident."

Texas knew it was so in his heart. "Now that Branson Meatpacking Company's environmental problem has been exposed, maybe some other particulars about Jeffrey's death will come to light," he went on to say. "Victoria needs to end this."

"I hope so," said Jon. "We all want the mystery solved."

"Actually," Texas said, "I'd like to see Victoria give herself up, hire an attorney, and let her friends go to bat for her."

"And you think she would get a fair trial?"

"I didn't say that," Texas replied. "However, God is on Victoria's side and He never yet has let one of his prophets die before fulfilling their mission." Faith counted for much.

Humph. Jon mulled over the idea.

"Take John the Apostle for instance, the last of the twelve disciples, the one who eventually penned the Book of Revelation. One historian reported that John was boiled in oil before being imprisoned by the Romans on the barren island of Patmos."

"So you believe that Victoria won't die until God is finished with her," Jon concluded. "It's a spiritual application that should encourage every believer to remain true to their calling."

"I pray it's the case with Victoria."

"But you realize eventually she will be caught."

Texas sighed. "This is changing the subject, Jon, but how will your mother react if she isn't healed during the revival?"

"I suppose she'll accept that Jesus is finished with her."

Texas slapped Jon on the arm. "It is well with her soul."

"*But* . . . I don't think my mother wants to die. She very badly wants to see the Rapture." The persecution had heightened the expectation of Jesus' return to earth. Heaven sounded like a wonderful place in comparison to earth. "Her will is strong."

"Not any stronger than her faith," Texas pointed out, rubbing Victoria's cool head with his warm hand. "Rest, sweetheart. Tonight we will see what challenges God has for you."

"You sound tired, buddy," Jon noted.

"I am." Texas laid his head back on the seat and closed his eyes. *Dear God,* he prayed, *help me to accept what I cannot change.*

12

Back in Fernwood

"So darling, what shall we do now?" Karen asked as Mark opened the car door for her. "I mean, now that Mother is safely away from Fernwood." The wedding was over and it was time to begin the project of living together, hopefully in harmony.

"What do you want to do?" Mark was unsure of where the conversation was headed. Was this a philosophical question or a simple "what's next?" Back at the wedding chapel, Andy Grimes' police force had departed to parts unknown, and a cleaning committee had arrived to restore the property to its original pristine condition in readiness for the next scheduled wedding procession. Except for the twitter of a bird perched on the hood of his antiquated sports car, all appeared calm in Mark's world.

"I suppose we go on with our plans," Karen decided, totally worn out from the trying past few hours. At least, she and her mother had triumphed, winning the battle of wits against the authorities. "Soaking in some rays on a warm island in the Pacific is beginning to sound appealing." Her thoughts dared to grasp at happiness. "What do you think, Mark?"

"I think seeing you in that cute little bikini you wore last summer will be a treat." Mark closed the passenger door and walked around the back of his sunflower-yellow BMW.

"Except I can't fit into it right now," Karen remarked as Mark slid behind the wheel. "Junior is taking up a little too much space in my body." She fondly patted her stomach.

"Have you felt it kick?" Mark reached over to feel.

"Mark! The baby isn't an *it!*" Karen laughed. "I've felt some movement, yes. Likely it's gas, due to my overly spicy appetite." The fetus wasn't large enough yet for her to feel true movement. "The second I do feel a kick, I'll be sure to let you know."

"You can't imagine how happy you've made me, Karen— giving me a child in my old age. I never thought I'd be a papa, and the more I think about it, the more excited I become. Just remind me not to dote on our child too much and spoil him."

"*Him?*" Karen lent Mark her warm gaze. "We've moved from an *it* to a him. That's progress," she teased.

"Of course, a daughter is fine with me."

"As I recall, you spoiled me when I was a teeny bopper with not a shred of common sense," Karen said. "We had a great time at the mall, you waiting on me while I rummaged through every fad shop. I spent a ton of money and you never scolded me once. I can't imagine you not spoiling this baby absolutely rotten."

"You're right." Mark ignited the powerful BMW engine. "How do you think your mother feels about being a prospective grandmother? You did tell her, didn't you?"

"No, Daniel told her. Though Mother said she was happy for us, I'm sure she doesn't approve. But she's pretty adaptable."

"I see." Hurt cracked Mark's heart as he recalled how quickly Victoria had dropped him without a second's pause.

"I'm just glad Little Vicki didn't try to break us up."

"Would it have changed anything?" Mark felt a bit insecure in his new role of husband, tacked on to mentor and friend.

Karen smiled. "Not for me." She wondered about him.

"Do you need to stop by the condo for anything?" Mark grasped his new wife's hand, eyes gleaming with appreciation.

Well, that's said and done, Karen thought.

"No," she replied, "I can check my home messages from here." Removing a cellphone from her purse, she began dialing.

Mark drove away from the wedding chapel, having passed a major milestone in his life. In front of him lay many new ones.

Karen had one message: "Hi. This is Sarah Boswell from down at the police station. When you return from your honeymoon, could we possibly meet? I have information that will work in your mother's favor. I'll call back in a week. Don't' call the precinct. This is highly confidential. Just us, okay?"

Karen blinked and shut down the phone.

"You had a message from Vicki?"

"No. I had a message from mother's friend, Sarah Boswell."

"The black gal with the badge?" Mark queried. "Why did she call?" Victoria's world was expanding in new directions.

"Sarah has some information that might help Mother."

"Really?" Mark reacted. "How is that possible? What new information could she possess that Andy Grimes hasn't already reported to Dick? I think the woman's yanking your chain."

"Dick again!" Karen exclaimed. "I swear the bully pokes his nose in everybody's business. I don't think we should trust him or Andy Grimes. What is your take on their strange relationship?"

"They're friends. It's no big secret they go way back." Mark had heard rumors, but Dick had never filled him in on all the details of how he and Andy hooked up decades ago.

"Way back to *what?*" Karen leaned as the car took a curve.

"I don't want to discuss Dick. Let's just concentrate on us, okay?" What Mark knew about the past wasn't worth ruining his future. He wasn't ratting on anyone, including himself.

Karen didn't want to forget about it. "Why not?"

"Because we just got married, because you look so beautiful in your mother's new outfit. Because I want to make love."

"Quit changing the subject, dear!" Karen scolded. "Now that we're married, why don't you come clean and tell me what you know about the night my father died? Did you have anything to do with the office heist? Just tell me and I'll forgive you."

What? The hairs on Mark's back defensively stiffened like a porcupine's as Karen's insinuation of guilt sank in.

"Karen!" he burst out. "How could you think that? I loved your parents. I'd never do anything purposely to hurt them!"

He'd made one phone call on April 13, 1989, to inform Dick that Jeffrey had left the office for the day so that the hired thugs could break inside and steal some files. No one, including Dick, had expected Jeffrey to return to his office to get his umbrella.

It wasn't like *they* planned a murder.

Of course, the perpetrators had messed up Jeffrey's office and taken his new computer with them to make the theft appear like a simple robbery. No one knew about the files, so they wouldn't be missed. It could have all turned out so differently.

"What are you thinking?" Karen asked Mark.

"Nothing in particular," he lied, learning from experience that there were no *simple* fixes, no quick answers. Every act evoked a consequence and the biblical principle was still in effect.

"So you are saying you are innocent?" Karen needed to know if she could trust Mark. Truth was absolutely necessary to sustain a meaningful relationship. She would never survive sharing a bed with another conniving Teddy. Her first husband had abused and beaten her—until she saw him dead.

Mark wanted to be truthful, but he couldn't.

"Never mind, I believe you," she said.

"Thank you." Mark had squeezed through the window of lies. "I *do* promise to honor and cherish you 'til death do us part." He raised Karen's upturned palm to his lips and kissed her hand.

"Oh, Mark!" Karen was overcome with endearment.

"All I want to do for the rest of my life is make a good home for you and our child," Mark passionately declared. Victoria's daughter deserved all the happiness he could lavish on her.

Karen squeezed Mark's hand, tears materializing in her eyes on the best day of her life. "Let's not miss our flight."

***

The District of Columbia

"How far is it to your place?" Lazarus Bacon asked.

"Not far." Gordon had lied about having an apartment in Washington. However, he was making one stop before they boarded a private jet at LaGuardia in New York. But first, to assure a successful abduction, he must sedate the high-profile lad.

Oh yeah, Gordon had read Lazarus' profile compiled by the detective from Chicago, Illinois. This slick kid could do serious damage when crossed. But there was a lot of money riding on the job if he delivered Lazarus unharmed to the designated location.

Gordon didn't have to understand all that was involved in the abduction, or the motives of the player paying the bill. All he knew was, somebody badly wanted to get hold of this kid.

No problem, the sting was going without a hitch. Gordon was almost home free. *Just keep the kid happy.*

"How are you doin', Lazarus?"

"Okay, but my parents will worry if I'm gone too long." Lazarus glanced around at the buildings passing by and saw nothing familiar. "Maybe I should call Natalie and tell her where I am. She'll get in big trouble if anyone finds out I'm missing."

"But she won't tell, right?"

"Right. She likes her job."

"All right then. What's the number?" Gordon asked to placate the boy. He'd play along, too soon to sedate the kid.

"Natalie's cell number is . . ." Lazarus gave the number.

Acting as if everything was cool, Gordon pressed the buttons into his dead phone and pretended to call the nanny.

"Hi, Natalie." He paused a couple seconds. "I'm fine," he said, pretending to be answering her questions. "Lazarus is with me. My name is Gordon Smyth. We're taking a little drive over to my apartment so Lazarus can see my giant chocolate bunny."

Lazarus listened attentively and relaxed slightly.

"No problem, Natalie. I'll drop Lazarus off when we're finished here." Gordon almost chuckled. "Don't worry, he's fine." He flipped the cell shut. "Does that ease your conscience, son?" It sure did his, Gordon privately rejoiced at the ruse.

But Lazarus had a frown on his face, slightly uncomfortable with the situation. Should he be riding in a car with a stranger? "Strangers can be dangerous," Natalie had said. *"Never* trust strangers!" his daddy often warned. "You'll get hurt, Lazarus."

Gordon winced. "We can always turn around and go back."

"Are you kidnapping me, sir?"

Gordon forced a smile. "No, son. I wouldn't do that. We're friends, aren't we?" The ex-marine blinked his eyelids.

"Yeah, I guess," said Lazarus, reining in his worry. Running away from Natalie was slightly exciting. Daring. "One hour and you have to take me home. Promise, or I won't go with you!"

"Sure, son. Right to the door of the White House."

Gordon picked up speed, having arranged to meet a friend at a Texaco Station on the outskirts of D.C. There he would trade the red Mustang for another car, drug Lazarus with a sedative, and proceed on his merry way to New York in Larry's beige Pontiac.

No problem was anticipated, since Gordon's friend was returning the Mustang to the Airport Budget. Having used cash and stolen credentials to rent the car, Gordon was certain that no one would connect him to the kid's abduction even if they were spotted leaving the mall. Once Lazarus was in Baghdad, fifty grand was as good as in his pocket. It was a win-win situation.

13

"Wake up, honey, we're in Dickson." Texas nudged Victoria. The fugitive opened her eyes and wrapped them around Texas. "We're here already? I thought I was dreaming. It's hard to believe I've been sleeping in your arms."

Texas leaned over and whispered in Victoria's ear.

"But we don't have a marriage license," she protested.

Shuu! His invitation was a secret, only for her ears. He had more to say, and she listened carefully before responding.

"But I can't go home with you until I see my mother," Victoria proclaimed in a loud whisper. "What?" The whispering continued until Jon Branson could no longer hold his tongue.

"Okay, you two lovebirds! It's time to get serious about revival. You can get married Monday at the safehouse, as soon as you have a license. I'll marry the two of you myself." He was an ordained minister. "So you don't have to whisper anymore."

Marilyn Branson giggled, now fully awake, hands covering her mouth as she fondly recalled a time when she was madly in love with Jon's father, Richard, believing life was paved with roses.

"We're not getting married, folks," Victoria declared, a bit embarrassed as she erected herself in the back seat. "How much farther to the cave?" She glanced over at Texas. From the expression on his face, she wondered if she had hurt his feelings.

"About twenty-five miles," Jon replied. "So far so good, no flashing red lights signaling us to stop." His eyes fondly captured Marilyn's. "You all right, Mama?" Her complexion was sallow.

"I'm fine, son. Just enjoying the ride. It's so nice to be among Christian friends and to know that Jesus is meeting us tonight at the cave." She huddled under a warm knitted shawl.

Victoria peered at Texas, disturbed. What if God failed to heal Marilyn Branson? Would it tarnish the woman's sweet relationship with Jesus Christ? Or strengthen her in His will?

"The silence in this van tells me all of you believe I'm an old fool," Marilyn said. "Well, I am." She chuckled. "Whether I live or die, it will be for Christ. But, c'mon! Give the Holy Sprit some credit here for doin' miracles. Where's your faith, young folks?"

"Marilyn's right," Victoria agreed. "We should all be praying for many people to receive healings instead of being so skeptical. Jesus is the same yesterday, today, and tomorrow. Right? And I hear the preacher is anointed. You can't beat that qualification."

"Well said, Victoria." Jon lifted up a spontaneous prayer: "Dear God: here we are, your servants. Look down on us tonight and abundantly bless us. Bring your children together, those who are anticipating a renewal of spirit and body. We thank you for our salvation. Let us always be a light in the darkness. Amen."

Jon reached over and patted his mother's frail hand.

"That was beautiful, son," said Marilyn. "I'm so proud of you. I wish your daddy could appreciate your fervor for Christ." She hugged her body, wracked in pain. "I fear for his soul."

"Mama? I told daddy I was a born-again Christian," Jon admitted. "I hope I didn't do wrong."

"You did what?" Texas reacted. "What if he reports you?"

"He won't," said Victoria. "Dick Branson thinks he's superman, capable of convincing Jon into thinking the way he does. My guess is he will encourage his only son to give up his futile attempt at religion and return to work at Branson."

"Victoria's right. Who else will Dick leave his billions to, if not Jon?" Texas added. "The man has no spiritual scruples."

"Dad has already said as much," Jon admitted. "Please pray for his soul. God needs to break his stubborn will and bring him

76

to his knees, show Richard Branson the consequences of rejecting the Holy Spirit. Money can't buy eternal salvation. I hate the way Dad lives, but let's face it, no man deserves hell."

"Jesus Christ never gives up on saving sinners," Victoria reported. "But He has a lot of work to do if he expects Dick Branson to respond to gentle nudging. Better to use a boulder."

Texas chuckled. Victoria was correct. A sinful man like Dick was blinded by pride and would have difficulty submitting to any kind of authority, even the kingship of Jesus Christ granted by God Almighty. But one day every knee would bow down to Jesus, the One for whom and by whom all things were created.

"I wish I could feel more compassion toward your father," Victoria admitted to Jon. "It's just that the two of you are so very different, I sometimes forget you are related. But I promise to pray for Dick to do the right thing." *Could she do that?*

"Which is?" Jon opened the door for more revelation.

· "You know, the *right* thing! If your father is guilty of hiring the thugs who murdered my husband—whether planned or not— he should confess to the police and take his medicine," Victoria declared, silently praying that she could live up to her brave promise to pray for Dick's soul, the man who wanted her dead. Truly, forgiving an enemy was the greatest challenge of love.

"Don't hold your breath for that to happen," Marilyn huffed. "Remember I was married to the man for three years. Dick thinks only of himself and those who can benefit him. 'Love thy neighbor as thyself' never crosses his selfish mind."

"But salvation is for sinners," Texas reminded the three of them. "If Judas Iscariot had repented for his deed of betraying Jesus and asked God forgiveness instead of suffering remorse and hanging himself, he'd likely be in heaven today."

"You think?" Victoria blinked.

"I *know*. We don't need to become cynical about salvation," Texas remarked. "Grace is an undeserved gift, available to all who seek forgiveness by calling upon the name of Jesus." He knew because he had walked the sinner's path most of his life.

"Look, I'm chief among sinners," Victoria announced. "I shacked up with Mark James and lived like other worldly-minded people, not caring about morality or what God thought as long as I pleased myself. Unfortunately, it's difficult to truly repent with half a memory." She made a face Texas thought was priceless. "Sorry to burst your bubble, but I'm far from perfect."

"But you are going to have brain surgery?" Texas turned to Victoria. "And get that memory of yours fixed."

What would that mean to their relationship?

"I'm seriously considering it," Victoria confessed.

"You now have Christian friends who will see you through it," Jon interjected. "You are not alone in this."

"I know, and I love all of you for supporting me." Victoria sighed. "That's why I'm going to check myself into the GloryVale Hospital for a medical evaluation. After I go to Switzerland."

"Wait!" Texas yanked his head toward Victoria. "You can't go back to Europe. The International Police will arrest you."

"I'm sorry, honey," she squeezed his hand tightly, "but I have to get my money. Karen's transferred five million dollars into a Zurich bank account. Daniel will meet me there, and together we'll access a bank deposit box." Victoria removed the small gold key from her purse and held it up. "With this!"

"Why now?" Texas wanted her to marry him.

"I don't know. It's what I want. I'm giving most of the money to the Christian Protection Agency." Victoria's eyes moved from face to face. "The rest, I'll use to live on," she said.

"Wow!" Jon exclaimed. "Talk about tithing."

"That's mighty generous of you, Victoria." Texas swallowed. "Do you want me to come with you to Canada?" He knew the answer before he asked. The woman was independently spirited.

"No. This is something I must do alone. When I am a whole woman again, and I have faced up to Sheriff Grimes and the rest

of my accusers, I will be ready to discuss my future with you."
She peered into her suitor's longing eyes. "Please don't be mad."

"I understand," Texas replied, hurting to the core. "But—"

"If you're thinking I'll change my mind about you, Texas,
you're mistaken." Victoria interrupted. "You're my rock, my
hero. I want a life with you, but . . ." words trailed off to tears.

"But . . . there are a few wrinkles in your life you have to iron
out first," he completed her sentence. "I understand. But when
you need me, just whistle. Lucas and I will be at the ranch."

How could he let this lovely creature walk out of his life
again? The idea was inconceivable. Worse, how would he handle
God's calling her into a ministry like he and Jon had discussed?

No, he wanted to be by her side all the way.

Somehow, Texas would convince Victoria to let him help.
He was the stand-by-your-woman kind now, not the spiritually
weak wimp who had abandoned his first wife in her time of need.

14

Bobby's Trailer Park

It was after sunset on Saturday when Sarah Boswell pulled into the driveway of the office that rented spaces for RVs. Down the hill, a couple hundred feet in front of her, she caught a glimpse of a rising pumpkin moon between the trees, hanging like a Halloween lantern over the shimmering Tennessee River.

Bullfrogs cried loudly from their perches. Katydids scraped their hind feet in a clattering fashion, seemingly keeping time in unison. A coyote howled. A couple of large owls screeched.

When Sarah was a kid, she had come to the river with her Pop, making memories that would never be erased until old age caught up with her. Those were carefree days when every second counted, when playing hard was a reason for getting out of bed, a time when she felt no threat of harm under the protection of a loving mother and father, and a reliable job was selling lemonade.

Adulthood was a rude awakening. Nothing came free in life and performing as expected was a curse. She was no longer naïve about sex, or the fickleness of friends. Gray was a better color for society than black or white. And fitting in was all that counted.

Still, young Sarah Ann Boswell had graduated high school with good grades and entered the police academy. And for a while, she was deliriously happy—though she never married.

After the environmental ruckus with Hearty Meats in 1989, and the town gossip had died down, most people believed the evil that had touched Attorney Jeffrey Tempest had left town with the people involved. While Victoria Tempest lay for months in a coma, the town resumed its normal activities. Sarah had breathed a sigh of relief, thinking the tragedy was not her problem.

True, Sarah's first cousin was dead because of environmental poisoning. She was sad about that, but it had no bearing on her immediate circumstances. After the family put James Hornsby in the ground, her daddy had decided to take a vacation to grieve his nephew's death. So he had rented a trailer, attached it to the back of his old truck, and drove west. There was something about the cowboy mentality in him that pulled him to the open prairies.

Sarah missed her daddy, but she understood his need to be alone for a spell. Pop was gone for a long time. At first, she didn't worry, knowing he could take care of himself. He was stout and worked out at the gym. But as time passed, no word came.

Sarah called the police in Albuquerque and reported him missing. Gave a description of his red Ford truck and the tag number, but no evidence ever turned up to suggest if he were alive or dead. No wrecked or abandoned vehicle by that description, or a body, was ever found. Folks out West claimed that people got lost in the mountains when they didn't stay on the paved roads.

The news media reported a series of avalanches brought on by the late spring snows in 1990. God only knew what territory Alvin Boswell had chosen to explore on his own. It was Pop's first real vacation and he was ambitious to climb a mountain.

Sarah couldn't fault Pop for that. Refusing to take a cellphone—which he claimed wouldn't work in the mountains and open spaces anyhow—he was bent on roughing it. May 1, 1990, was the last time Sarah had spoken to or seen her father. Pop just disappeared from the planet. Gone, without a trace.

And now here Sarah was—a mature woman with no illusions of what 2014 might bring into her life—finally facing up to the harm done to many innocent people because an enterprising company had failed to provide an environmentally safe workplace.

It would be nice to forget about Jeffrey Tempest, Hearty Meats, and the chaos that had resulted following the homicide. And for years, Officer Sarah Boswell had shoved the Tempest travesty to the back of her mind, ignoring how she felt about it.

But now, with Victoria Tempest in the picture again and searching for correct answers about her husband's death, it was impossible for Sarah to ignore her feelings anymore. In some strange way, she even blamed Dick Branson for her daddy's death.

Above all, it wasn't fair for Victoria Tempest to take the blame for a murder she didn't commit. Sarah the cop could not imagine sitting back and doing nothing while a corrupt company ran over a citizen of Fernwood again. No, she demanded justice for everyone who had suffered because someone failed to stand up for what was right. The lies must end for justice to prevail.

Shutting down the engine, Sarah climbed out of the car, locked up, and followed the stone pathway up the steep hill to Bobby's trailer. She tapped on the metal door and waited for a response. It had been years since she'd seen her daddy's friend.

"Sarah Boswell!" The old railroad man reacted by grabbing and hugging her. "You didn't come all this way alone, did'ja?" His black eyes canvassed the yard.

"Actually, I have a friend on her way here from Alabama," Sarah replied. "Any chance you got a vacant trailer I can rent for tonight?" She hadn't called ahead for a reservation.

"You want a view of the river? Gonna do a little night fishin'?" Bobby's eyes grew large with interest.

Sarah laughed. "Yeah, I'm doing some night fishing." She wasn't talking about the kind caught on a pole. She was sorting out the fishy facts tucked away in the copies of Jeffrey Tempest's stolen file. "Just be sure the mattress is soft. Tanya is picky."

"Tanya Mason? Lordy mercy! I ain't seen that kid for years!" Bobby was in a chatty mood. "Why don't you come on in and I'll put on a pot of coffee. The wife's dead—don't know if you knew or not—so it's just me and Colonel, my hound dog."

"I'd love to," said Sarah, counting the years since she had last seen Bobby. "Is this the dog you had when——?"

"Heaven's no!" Bobby exclaimed. "Colonel is the grandson of ol' Colonel. Just couldn't bring myself to give the puppy a new name. Guess I'll always own a Colonel until the day I die."

Sarah stepped inside the two-bedroom trailer, roomy and comfortably furnished, but far from being new.

"I could use a bite to eat, too." She felt hungry.

"Sure," said Bobby. "I make a mean Cajun omelet, if that'll do. Promise not to burn it while you talk to me."

"Perfect," said Sarah, collapsing at the table in the corner nook. She was more tired now that she had reached her destination. Running hard on nerves, her legs were beginning to give out. "You still get a lot of folks out of Fernwood?"

"Git 'em frum all over, child. Recreation's something tha's always popular." Bobby banged some pans around.

"You don't get lonely up here, away from civilization?"

"No way—me and Colonel does jus' fine. Don't 'spect we ever met a stranger. You kind'a get used to life the way it comes."

"No, I don't expect you have met a stranger." Sarah glanced at her wristwatch, inhaling the odor of coffee grounds as Bobby uncapped a new can of Folgers. "Tanya should be here soon."

"Good. I need to hear what's goin' on with that girl."

"She's married now, has a fine husband and two kids. Tanya's happy, has let bygones be bygones." Sarah let her voice trail off. *No use getting into everything.*

"You mean she's forgiven that sorry meatpacking company for the damage they done to her family," Bobby spurted, stirring the eggs with a whisk and dumping in a bag of precut vegetables with added spices. "Don't blame her for leaving Fernwood."

"Yeah," said Sarah, wondering if she wasn't doing the same thing right now. When she knew what information the files contained, would she feel safe in going back to her house? Should Cheryl Grimes tell the sheriff she'd borrowed the files, well . . .

About the time the omelet was coming up, Sarah heard a honk out front. "That's gotta be Tanya." She scrambled out the door and began waving her hand at the SUV.

"Hi, girlfriend!" Tanya called out as she stepped out of the Chevy Blazer. "I smell food cookin'. Hope I'm not too late to eat." She grabbed an overnight bag from the back of the vehicle.

"You're not," said Sarah. "Bobby's made one of his Cajun omelets—plenty for the three of us. Com' on in and get comfortable." She wrapped an arm about Tanya.

"Hi, Bobby," Tanya said as the screen door snapped behind them. "What's up? I see you can still cook good."

"You tell me." Bobby slid the omelet on a plate and set it on the table. "Have at it, girls, then tell me what's goin' on. It ain't like either of you to come so far just to chat with an old man unless some'un big is up. 'Course it ain't none of my business anyhow." His gaze skittered between the girls. "What?"

"You don't have to worry, we'll gladly tell you why we're here," Sarah replied. "Three knowin' the truth might be our best defense in avoiding harm's way." She cast a chilly glance at Tanya.

"Uh oh, sounds like monkey business to me!" Bobby chuckled. "I'll get your coffees. Omelet's hot. You girls dig in. Cream? Sugar?" His dark eyes gleamed in the kitchen light.

"Yeah," said Sarah and Tanya in unison, their mouths full as they chewed their food fast like they hadn't eaten in days. "If you don't mind, Bobby, make us another. Me and Tanya are starving." Sarah grabbed a biscuit and smothered it in homemade grape jelly.

15

Kenya, Africa

The sun dwindled on the western horizon as Daniel Tempest and his four peacekeeping cohorts landed at the Nairobi Airport in the Republic of Kenya, a popular stop for tourists.

The area was famous for its exotic animal safaris. Once occupied by the Arabs, Kenya was later seized by the Portuguese and eventually leased to the British East Africa Company.

Encompassing some 218,907 square miles of land, Kenya's population approached thirty-two million, its people speaking a mix of languages, the most official being English and Swahili. In 1963, Kenya had gained its independence from Great Britain.

Daniel wasn't here to hunt lions or sightsee, but there were plenty of roaring beasts roaming about who would like to take his life for a piece of Allah's heaven. His job was to stop them.

"I tried Christean's cell number but Mother's not answering," Daniel informed Daria Langstead, standing outside a jewelry store and peering through its glass window. They had left Switzerland unsure of his mother's final destiny. "I hope your mother bought another cellphone. Christean probably won't get hers back."

"Look at us. Meet the parents, and worrying about our moms like we can control what they do." Daria huffed.

"I feel responsible for my mother's well being," Daniel said.

"I'm sure Victoria's fine. Otherwise, you would have heard from her. She's probably shut off the cell and gone to bed."

Daria resented Daniel's continual doting over his mother's safety. It was inevitable she would reap havoc from her poor choices.

"You don't seem to get it, sweetheart!"

"Oh yeah, I get it," Daria replied rather sarcastically. "Your mother's not thinking straight these days."

"Yeah, and if Karen and I don't do something to help her, she could end up in jail for a crime she didn't commit."

"And you know this because . . .?" Daria tired of the ongoing drama, her lovely transparent blue eyes shifting on Daniel.

"Look, Daria. I know you've got your plate full in dealing with your father's surgery and your mother's hysteria, but . . ."

"I'm sorry," she immediately apologized. "I'm just tired and insensitive tonight. Forgive me? All I want to do is take a steamy hot bath and cuddle up in a soft bed with you lying next to me." She grasped Daniel's arm and laid her head on his shoulder.

"Forgiven." He smiled and patted her hand.

"Isn't there anyone you trust to see after Victoria?"

"Karen, but she's pregnant and just married."

"Hire someone. I know it's not a matter of money." Daria wanted to think of her future with Daniel, not his mother's welfare. "Or call in a favor." Getting Victoria exonerated from the criminal charge might be as simple as making one phone call to someone with international clout. "End this confusion."

"She doesn't seem to want anyone's help," he replied.

"Then respect her wishes." Daria stared into the troubled eyes of the man she deeply loved. "It's out of your hands."

"Perhaps. I keep hoping some piece of physical evidence will turn up to convince Sheriff Andrew Grimes that he's barking up the wrong tree. Then Mother could go home and pick up the pieces of her life." Daniel wondered how she would feel about ending her engagement to Mark when her memories returned.

"You don't have the time to solve the crime, or plan a new life for your mother. You're a peacekeeper, for heaven's sake."

"Yeah, you're right." Daniel's breath went out of him like a deflating balloon. "All I can do is keep track of Mother and hope she doesn't do something crazy, like claiming her money alone."

"What money?" Daria reacted. "You gave a fugitive from the law money! My word, Daniel, you know better than that!"

"It's Mother's money, and she has a right to it."

"But will the authorities see it that way?" Daria's forehead furrowed. "You could be accused of aiding and abetting a criminal and ultimately dragged into a long court trial."

"I know." He sighed.

Regardless of the outcome, Daniel shouldn't let his mother's problems interfere with their wedding plans in September. The bond between a man and a woman should take precedence over any boyish attachment to a parent. "What are you doing?"

"Trying Christean's cell number again." Daniel glanced down the street. People disappeared into buildings as the darkness closed in on the city. "Like you said, maybe she's gone to bed." He slapped shut the cell and placed it in the holder on his belt.

"Right after we deplaned, I overheard you talking to someone at headquarters," Daria said. "What was that call about?"

"The boss says Dr. Ramnes wants to speak to me."

"Privately, or on the phone?"

"Privately," Daniel replied.

"About your sudden departure from Rome," she concluded. "And will you tell him you left to spare your mother from being arrested? If you lie he'll know. What are you going to say?"

"That is one more question than I care to answer," Daniel replied. "I'll take the fifth and think about a good response."

"Wise decision." Daria had an eager eye on a particular piece of hand-made African jewelry in the window display—a gold broach inlaid with diamonds and probably very expensive.

"We should get to the hotel and check in," said Daniel. "I'm worn out." He didn't list the many reasons draining him.

The three other peacekeepers had gone straight from the airport to the hotel to confirm their reservations. The American Embassy was across the street, within walking distance in case their presence in the country became a problem and they needed support. In an unstable environment, one couldn't be too careful.

Tomorrow, the young negotiators were meeting with representatives of an international terrorist group who had its roots in the philosophy of Hekmatyar, a *mujahadeer* Sunni-fundamentalist who supported Taliban leader Mullah Muhammad Omar in an effort to carry out *jihad* in Afghanistan during the early part of the century. NATO's goal was to reach an agreement with the radical Muslims and prevent a movement to oust the president of a democratic American-supported South African regime, privately funded by a group of wealthy American businessmen.

Ironically, Hekmatyar, received millions of dollars in U.S. aid following the 1990 Gulf War because his war methods were viewed by the American CIA and Pakistan Inter-Services Intelligence as most effective in ridding Afghanistan of Soviet troops. Placing restraints on Soviet occupation had served to fuel the zeal of religious underground movements in Russia, and Christianity flourished as Communism waned in the early 1990's.

Until Alexander Luceres Ramnes came on the scene in 2011, the world was a religious battleground and fear prevailed.

But could anyone make peace last? Daniel wondered. *The world was a powder keg with many attached strings already lit.*

Shoving aside political issues out of his control, Daniel considered calling Karen to see how the wedding event came off. By now, she may have heard from their naughty mother.

"Daria, why don't you go on ahead and check us into the hotel? I need to see Baker Byers at the Embassy about a matter."

"What matter?" she curiously asked. There were no secrets between peacekeepers. "Is this personal?" She pulled out her VISA card. "I think I'll buy that beautiful broach in the window."

"Suit yourself. See you at the hotel." Daniel pecked Daria on the cheek with a quick kiss and walked down the street toward the embassy, a cellphone held by his chin as it rang and rang. Karen was suddenly there. "Hey, Ka! I was afraid I'd missed you."

"You almost did, Bro. Mark and I are at the Memphis International Airport about to board a Delta flight to Miami. What's up?" She had to keep the conversation brief.

"You ask me that?" It was 7 p.m. in West Tennessee, six hours later in Kenya. Daniel was emotionally spent from the trip to Iraq—which had ended in a stalemate because the Muslims made all kinds of promises and kept none of them. Hate between the Palestinians and Jews was greater than ever, the twenty-five-hundred-year-old conflict seemingly everlasting and unsolvable.

"Yeah, I ask that," Karen fired. "Aren't you busy keeping the peace so the rest of us can pretend that terror doesn't exist?"

"Supposedly." Daniel chuckled, the issue not a bit funny.

Family relationships were every bit as complicated and time-consuming as peacekeeping efforts. He recalled his swift return to Switzerland to get up with his mother. Believing she was safe in Zurich on a shopping spree, he had flown Daria to London to comfort her mother while her father had four heart bypasses.

Meanwhile, his infamous socialite mother had flown the coop and returned to America. Daniel had no idea where she was, or if she were safe. He was sure hoping Karen had heard from her.

"Daniel? Are you there?" Karen thought she'd lost him in cyberspace. "Speak up, I can't hear you clearly."

"I'm still here," Daniel said in a louder voice. "I tried Mother on Christean Langstead's cellphone—which I might add she's confiscated without permission. I didn't get an answer."

Karen chuckled. "You won't. She's on the run again."

"Again? Has something happened I should know about?"

"Mother showed up at my wedding," Karen informed her little brother. "Walked right in and found herself a pew."

"What? Has she lost all reasoning? Did the police arrest her?" Scenarios flashed through Daniel's mind like a whiplash.

"Nope, not this time," said Karen. "Mark and I helped her escape. You should have been here for the show."

"How did you pull it off?" He had the American Embassy in his sight as he crossed the street and walked briskly.

"I traded clothes with Mother and she took off in the limousine following the wedding. The sheriff didn't have a clue. Mark stalled everyone for a good forty-five minutes before Andy demanded I remove my veil. His expression was priceless."

"It's a wonder he didn't arrest you."

"Oh, he wanted to, but Dick actually stopped him."

"Dick? That's a surprise." Daniel shook his head as he envisioned the scene. "And how is Mark dealing with all this?"

"He's been amazing. I actually believe Mark and mother came to a mutual understanding," Karen professed, thinking that happiness was actually attainable. "They parted as friends."

"Wow, that was some undertaking." What his mother would do next was unimaginable. "So where is Mother now?"

"I have no idea. Mark spied that handsome Texan fellow of Mother's sitting in the driver's seat when the limousine rolled away. I know the guy cares about her, so I'm trusting he'll keep her safe," Karen said. "No doubt, she's not thinking clearly."

"What about the money?" Daniel asked. "Did you tell Mother what we did?" He should be prepared for her return.

"Oh, yeah! She liked the idea of having five million dollars in her bank account. I expect she'll be calling you in the next few days for instructions as to how to get her hands on the lump sum squirreled away in Zurich's Union Bank of Switzerland."

"I'm not so sure it's safe for Mother to return to Europe. Interpol has an all-points bulletin out for her arrest. When she showed up in Rome, the higher-ups began to wonder if she had an assassination in mind." He stood outside the American Embassy.

"What? They think Mother wanted to kill somebody?"

"Yeah, Alexander Luceres Ramnes. She's made no secret of her distaste for the important leader." Daniel paused at hearing Karen whisper something to Mark. "Do you need to go, Sis?"

"No. What were you saying?" Karen asked.

"Just that Mother's being spotted in Rome has gotten her mug posted in every federal outpost in the world. I'm worried she'll be arrested if she returns to Europe," he explained.

"I wish she wouldn't be so outspoken."

"Me, too. And how to help her is beyond my expertise."

"I'm sorry, Daniel, but I have to go now. They're about to close the doors to the plane. We'll talk later, won't we?"

"Tomorrow. Call me tomorrow. I'm in Nairobi."

"Why? On holiday, or work related?"

"Peacekeeping business," Daniel answered. "In a few days Daria and I should be winding up things here and returning to London to check on the medical status of her father. Although the doctors believe Joshua will recuperate with no major setbacks, Daria still worries." *Just like I do about Mother.*

"We all worry about something, don't we?" Karen sighed. "Gotta go now, Bro. Take care." Mark tugged at her sleeve.

"You, too, Sis."

"Call soon?"

"Count on it."

16

D aniel Tempest shut down his cellphone after speaking to Karen and peered up at the brand-new American Embassy, reconstructed after a terrorist bombing had grounded the old one.

Jihad experts had learned how to turn planes into bombs in 2001 when they leveled the New York Twin Towers. In the radical Muslim movement, death was a welcome party into Allah's heavenly home. Beliefs were more difficult to change than laws.

Presenting the proper credentials, Daniel entered embassy foyer, a vaulted concrete room decorated in pastel-green stucco.

Although the hour grew late, Daniel was certain that Baker Byers would not be sleeping. The man was a think-machine during crises, sleeping only when exhausted, sometimes operating on nervous energy and caffeine for days.

In tough times, the tough stay going.

Daniel had heard a disturbing rumor in Baghdad he wanted to run by Baker. The CIA would better receive the news floating about cyberspace if it came from the American ambassador, especially since it involved the President of the United States.

After phoning Baker in his suite, Daniel waited at the embassy hotel bar. Two empty glasses rimmed in white foam sat on the counter in front of him by the time Baker greeted him.

"Hi, Daniel. You're out and about mighty late. What can I do for you?" Baker hiked a leg and claimed a barstool.

"Hello, sir." Daniel glanced over at Baker and grasped his taut hand. "Thanks for receiving me at so late an hour. I've come to give you a head's up on a situation that could prove explosive."

"I'll have a glass of milk," Baker told the barmaid. "What's this all about?" He gave Daniel his undivided attention.

"Decaf coffee for me," Daniel directed his gaze at Baker. "I guess you know why I'm here." Weariness weighted him down.

"To settle some jihad matters, I assume."

Baker's eyes were dark and foreboding. Formerly on staff at CIA headquarters in Langley, Virginia, he was bumped up to an American ambassador while Daniel was still receiving training for covert operations. Later, Daniel was assigned to fieldwork.

"Let's take our drinks over to the corner table," Daniel suggested. The nature of his news was highly confidential, mere conjecture based on Internet chatter.

"I received a brief memo about the peacekeeping team coming to Kenya," Baker reported. "What's *this* meeting about?"

"A matter of importance to the President," Daniel replied as they crossed the room, heading toward a vacant booth.

"Oh. Well, it's no secret that President John Bacon has good reason to worry about winning the next election. His unpopular stance supporting Christianity hasn't earned points with the ACLU or liberal democrats. But I get the feeling you're not here to discuss politics." Baker craned his neck to alleviate muscle spasms in his neck. "You know I'm a busy man."

"I know," Daniel replied. "But this is important."

"Okay." Baker collapsed in the leather seat of the booth, removed the wrapper from a stick of gum and popped it into his mouth. Chewing helped relieve the tension. "What is it?"

Daniel knew rumors could be as deadly to a career as facts. Taking a seat across from Baker, he evaluated his testimony.

"Speak freely, son." The diplomat leaned forward with anticipation. "What we say here is safe inside these walls."

"Have you spoken to George Cross in the last few days?"

George was Baker's friend, an American in his mid-forties who had been working for the French Embassy in Nairobi for the past two years as a language specialist. A graduate from Emory in Atlanta, the diplomat fluently spoke five African language dialects.

More importantly, George had spies in Washington who kept him informed regarding governmental affairs as they developed, the kind that didn't ordinarily make the morning news.

In conjunction with the American CIA and the African-British intelligence, George had effectively coordinated the meeting about to take place between the five NATO peacekeepers and the three ragged Saudis who represented the nasty-fighting Hekmatyar-Islamic sect that promoted *jihad* around the world.

Foremost, Baker Byers implicitly trusted George.

"Well, no. I've been out of touch with George for about a week now," Baker said, not explaining. "Why?"

"Just asking." Daniel had to wonder if there had been a rift between the two men. They were like brothers, united in thought to the point it was almost scary. While most people in the world believed the threat of terrorism had ended with PEACE FIRST, men like George Cross and Baker Byers knew better and acted on their hunches. Daniel only hoped one day to be as perceptive.

A gal in a short black skirt and white apron sashayed over to their booth and delivered their orders, a cup of black coffee and a tall glass of milk. Baker waved her away signifying the order was complete and he needed nothing else to satisfy him.

"So what is it you've come to say, Daniel?" Baker downed half of the two-percent white liquid. "My mother taught me to drink healthy." He smiled. "I never touch the hard stuff."

"Mine taught me to distrust life," Daniel stoically replied. "As for alcohol, I use it discriminately."

"Smart Mama," said Baker and belched. "Excuse me."

"I'll get right to the point." Daniel paused to sip the black coffee set before him. "I had the privilege of meeting with representatives of *Quadaffi's Boys* in Baghdad this past week." He leaned back and collected his thoughts. "We convinced them to talk and not act. I won't go into detail, but they had plans to punish an Israeli organization more popularly known as *Jews for Christ*. We convinced them to let us talk to the group first."

"Wow!" Baker exclaimed. "Will a successful peace ever be negotiated between the Christians and Palestinians in the Middle East? I thought we had that problem nailed down in 2005."

"So did everyone else," Daniel acknowledged. The rivalry existing between the Arabic tribes was legendary.

"While in Baghdad, I heard a rumor concerning President Bacon that was disturbing—some Internet chatter picked up by an ex-CIA agent. I didn't think I should be the one to warn—"

"Wait! Are you telling me there's a contract out on the President's life?" Baker's expression expressed alarm.

"No, that's not what this is about," Daniel quickly answered.

Baker was a small man with a hooked nose like a hawk and eyes as beady as black marbles. His thick raven-black hair was a mark of his Egyptian heritage, a genetic gift from his mother.

Baker's father, a native-born Latino, had worked for the Democratic Party during the nineties to plot America's defense against terrorism. 9/11 of 2001 was indelibly printed on his American heart, and that was why he was so good at his job.

"Then, what is this about?" asked Baker.

"Word is out that the President's son is going to be abducted," Daniel stated. "I thought you should know."

"For what purpose? The lad has been nothing but trouble for his parents. Kicked out of private elementary school for his malicious pranks, accused of witchcraft by televangelists before he was seven. His grandparents won't even come to visit him."

"So true," Daniel agreed.

Baker's face was ablaze with emotion. "I'd say whoever takes that boy off John's hands will be doing him a big favor," he quipped. "Might even get him elected for a second term."

"I had no idea the general population knew about the lad's exotic nature," Daniel replied, coming short of labeling the boy as "evil," taking a moment to let the sarcasm melt from the air.

"The general population doesn't know yet, but they will." Baker's smile was faint, hands folded together on the tabletop.

"Although Lazarus Bacon has emotional problems, his family still loves him dearly," Daniel revealed. "He's John's son."

"What could possibly be accomplished by the lad's abduction?" Baker asked, puzzled over the development.

"I have no idea," Daniel admitted. "I'm only passing on what I've heard. Handle this matter as you will." He glanced at his watch. It was after midnight. "I should get some rest."

"Thank you for telling me." Baker slid from the booth.

Daniel placed enough Euros on the table to pay their tab and leave a healthy tip. "Let me know what comes of this."

"I will," said Baker, his murky gaze stirring in thought. "You take care, son." He made eye contact with Daniel. "The world is depending on your bright young pack to keep the world at peace. Nobody wants to go back to the way it was. Nobody."

"Peace?" Daniel tossed a sideward glance. "It's only a clever illusion." He wasn't smiling. "Rest well, Baker."

17

Dickson County, Tennessee

Electricity sparked the night skies as Jon Branson rolled the wafer-brown van into a makeshift parking space between two large trees. Dozens of vehicles were perched between the trees like sleeping beasts. A whale of a storm was brewing.

Sliding open the metal door to the van, Texas assisted Victoria and Lucas in getting out. Ten seconds later his eyes adjusted to the dark. "We didn't invite the snakes," he teased.

"That doesn't mean they won't decide to come," Victoria replied. Peering up into the heavens, she felt a slight chill as thunder rolled over the landscape. "Is it supposed to storm?"

She knew that summertime storms had the potential to be violent, producing high winds and hail, threatening human safety.

"Doesn't matter," said Jon, placing a firm hand on Victoria's shoulder. "The cave is wide and deep and we shall all be quite safe there until Mother Nature has her say. Let's go."

"Want to hold my hand?" Texas asked Victoria.

Slipping her small hand into the hand of the man she adored sent a thrill down Victoria's spine. She only hoped Texas was right about nature. It sure had its say the night of her fourteenth wedding anniversary. "Marilyn? Can you make the walk?"

"I can, child." The older woman touched Victoria's arm. "Just look at that glorious path, all lit up with fireflies to show the way." There was a lilt of excitement threading Marilyn's voice.

Victoria focused in the darkness. "It sure is."

And God smiled on them as a faint moon emerged from the clouds. Light had always been a guide for mankind—Jesus, a hope for the disoriented. Tonight, Victoria was among friends.

"Shall we go? We've got about a twenty minute walk." Jon grasped his mother's arm to steady her. Ahead of them the moonlit path appeared rough and hilly, and it would soon rain.

"Hey, Jon!" Texas exclaimed. "Let's make a seat with our hands and carry Marilyn down the hill. It'll be fun, just like some of us kids used to do in grade school."

"Oh, no you won't!" Marilyn defensively put up a hand. "I'd rather walk than have my bones groaning and crackin' from being tossed around like a sack of potatoes. Thanks, but no thanks."

Victoria laughed. "There you go, guys! Marilyn's going on her own steam." She snickered at tripping over a rock.

"Well, Mama, if you get tired, you just holler." Jon switched on a large flashlight and pointed it in the direction of a wide pathway cut out by a tractor blade. "Just be careful."

"I will, son." Marilyn clasped Jon's arm for support.

Texas took Victoria's hand as they began the hilly descent.

Sounds of animals—the yelping of coyote pups, owls hooting in the trees, katydids chirruping, the flapping of birds' wings in a sudden rush, and cattle bellowing in a distant pasture—all joined the faint thunderous chorus of clouds gathering steam overhead.

Though invisible to the naked eye, Victoria sensed the presence of fearful animals scurrying for shelter as their entourage brushed past bushes and brambles. The evening walk reminded her of the time she and Texas had taken a walk behind Western State Hospital and visited the secluded prayer retreat—absent of the unsettling storm. And here they were again, on an adventure.

"You're shaking, Victoria. Are you cold?" Texas held tightly to her hand, gently guiding her down the crooked pathway.

"In eighty-degree June weather, how could I be?"

"Don't be afraid of the storm, honey. Nothing bad is going to happen tonight. If anything, God is planning some fireworks to celebrate His presence at the meeting. Just stay focused."

"Focused?" Victoria's gaze fell on Texas.

"Like when the tongues of fire baptized Jesus' disciples when God sent down His Holy Spirit," Lucas remarked, skipping alongside the entourage. "I read about that prayer meeting in the Bible, Papa." The lad peered up at Texas, glossy black eyes huge with interest. "Is God gonna do some miracles tonight?"

"He might." Texas smiled. "Who knows the mind of Jesus?"

"Some of the people spoke in tongues when the Holy Spirit showed up in power," Jon said. "It brought people closer."

"Correct," said Texas. "The gathering of disciples following Jesus' resurrection was a unique setting. Many people of different cultures and languages gathered in one place to hear the message of salvation presented. So that they could understand, they all spoke one language," he explained the spiritual phenomenon.

"Some people said they were drunk because they couldn't stand up and spoke funny," Lucas recalled what he learned from a recent Internet Bible lesson. "Everybody who got the Holy Spirit understood what the other person was saying."

"That's right, Lucas. But not everyone's heart was right with God, so some failed to comprehend the miracle." Texas glanced over at Victoria. "God is an all-consuming fire when it comes to judgment on sin and the disbursement of spiritual gifts."

"Even when it storms?" Lucas raised an eyebrow.

"Yep. God is a spectacular Creator who enjoys a good show sometimes." Texas hoped his words would quell Victoria's concern over the storm. "Our Savior is always in control."

"I know you're right." Victoria sighed. "But I've always been a fearful person." Still, God had delivered her from harm's way.

"But you don't have to be afraid," said Lucas, wisely. "God will take care of us. Papa says so!" And that was the gospel.

"Preach on, Lucas." Marilyn began singing: "Amazing Grace, how sweet the sound, that saved a wretch like me. I once was lost, but now am found, was blind but now I see . . ."

The faithful words of the old hymn resounded in the surrounding hills as a chorus of voices in the distance joined in on the second verse. Soon, the hillside was alive with singing, echoing through the forest like a majestic choir of angels.

"When we've been there ten thousand years, bright shining as the sun, we've no less days to sing God's praise than when we first begun." When the song ended, there was a reverent silence, the forest sounds magnified in an epilogue of nature's praise to God.

"I think I might need a little help, son." Marilyn, ghostly pale, caught Jon's eye as she paused, leaned over, and gasped for breath. "The walk is a little more tiring than I anticipated."

"No problem," said Texas, eyeing Jon as he picked Marilyn up in his arms like she was weightless. "We've no less days to sing God's praise than when we first begun," he continued singing, his bass voice fading out as the skies blackened and rain peppered in his face. "Let's get to shelter!" he hollered to the others.

"Better hurry, it's fixing to rain like we haven't seen in some time." Jon joined Texas in carrying his mother to dry shelter.

Lucas squealed as he rushed ahead of the others. Marilyn giggled as huge raindrops were squeezed from the grumbling clouds and began to fall in giant sheets, the large flat green leaves of trees sheltering them as they ran from the deluge. Soon, they safely reached the dry cave and greeted friends they recognized.

Wrapping a sweater about her wet shirt, Victoria praised God as she gazed at the magnificent cave, tall like an amphitheater and alight with dozens of flaming gas torches. Many had already claimed their spots by placing colorful blankets on the dirt floor.

A lot of hugging and greeting was going on, too. Whispers of praise echoed in the air like angelic praises before God's throne. It was the gathering of the future church where color and race and language barriers meant nothing in the holy presence of God.

"There's Jacob Cooley from Nashville!" Victoria pointed out the elderly man. "Come on and I'll introduce you." She rushed off to greet him, dragging Texas like a mother would a child.

"Jacob, it's me!" Victoria tapped him on the shoulder.

"Whoa?" Jacob Cooley spun around, the fire of recognition burning in his gaze. "Victoria Tempest!" He grabbed her in a ferocious hug. "Been keepin' my eye out for you."

"Me, too." She hugged him back.

"Pretty as ever! But, honey, you shore ar' wet." Jacob ran his rough hands down Victoria's dripping-wet arms. "Hope this awful weather don't make you sick." His eyes drifted to Texas.

"I'm too happy to get sick," Victoria exclaimed. "This is my friend, Texas. You can't imagine what we've been through today to get here. This meeting feels like the dawning of a new day."

"Hopefully, we'll all git our cups filled," Jacob replied. "Good to meet you, young fella." He squeezed Texas' hand.

Trying not to shiver, Victoria briskly rubbed her cold arms. The temperature in the cave was twenty degrees lower than outdoors. When Jon made a quick stop in Dickson, she'd changed into a pair of jeans, a short-sleeve shirt, and a pair of comfortable tennis shoes. Bottom line, she was soaked to the skin

"Where's Angela?" Victoria glanced around for the girl.

"Cold, baby?" Texas was sensitive to Victoria's discomfort and wrapped a dry shawl about her shoulders. "Compliments of Cynthia." He pointed to a smiling woman over in the corner.

"Thank you," Victoria mouthed, lending Texas her spicy-brown eyes for a millisecond. "Jacob?"

"Angela's about somewhere." The old man held Victoria at arms' length to view her better before cutting his eyes over on Texas. "So Texas, why are you hanging out with Victoria?"

"Texas Holmes is my—" Victoria leaped in to answer, suddenly not knowing how to describe her relationship with this handsome, whimsical man who showed up at hopeless times.

"Victoria and I are friends." Texas chuckled, amused at Victoria's loss for words—a new thing under the sun. "Working on being more." He caught Jacob's eye. "A whole lot more."

"I guessed that," Angela interrupted as she arrived. "I'm Jacob's granddaughter." She extended a warm hand of friendship to Texas. "Pop and I had the privilege of meeting Victoria while she was in Nashville. On the run," she teasingly added, making eye contact with Victoria. "We all ran, didn't we?" Angela laughed, the incident at Opryland seeming somewhat humorous.

"I'm still on the run." Victoria pulled Angela to one side and briefly described what had happened at Karen's wedding, how they had traded places so she could escape arrest.

"Thank God, you didn't come home with us. No telling where you'd be today if Donald Wetherfield had nabbed you."

"Right," said Victoria. Who knew why the creep was so intrigued with her. Her thoughts skittered to the Antichrist.

Surely, Luceres wasn't behind the unbelievable chase.

"Agent Wetherfield demanded that we tell him where you were," Angela told Texas. "Of course, we didn't know anything. He finally gave up and left the house in a huff. When we had settled our nerves a bit, Jacob and I went to bed. End of story."

"I wish I knew why Donald wants to get his hands on me so badly? I can't be *that* important," Victoria assessed her situation. "Surely, the international leader has a more important agenda."

Wait! Was Alexander Luceres Ramnes mad enough at her refusal to sip tea with him that he'd sent his goon to fetch her?

"We may never know," said Angela. "It's over now."

Is it? Victoria wondered, noticing how well Texas and Jacob were hitting it off. Jon had another agenda as he escorted his mother down to the front to meet the pastor holding the revival.

Pastor Joe received Marilyn warmly. Seeing it was a private, tender moment for his mother, Jon stepped away while she made her requests—whatever those needs might be.

"Pleased to meet you, Brother Joe." Marilyn held to the pastor's hand like she would drown if he let go. "I've been praying for a long time that I would get a chance to attend a healing revival like this one. Thank you so much for coming so far to share God's Word with us." Her frail body was a cruel reminder that her time on earth was fast running out.

"My pleasure, Sister Branson." Joseph Glower glimpsed death in the woman's clouded vision. "I've been praying God would send the folks He has prepared to receive His blessings."

Marilyn had a few comments about the weather while Joe held tightly to her bony hand. Then she shared the trauma of living with cancer for years. "I've tried to be brave."

"If you've come believing, dear one, you won't go away disappointed." Joe shared a few critical testimonies.

A kindness emanated in the minister's face seasoned by years of obedience to Christ's gospel. Yet, Joe knew full well that not everyone would receive the kind of healing they wanted.

"I have come believing," Marilyn said with certainty. "I sure have. I'm ready for whatever God offers. He knows best."

"Then, tell me your needs and we'll pray together."

18

Back in Fernwood

Marjorie Branson drew her obese husband a Jacuzzi tub of bubbly water and placed a glass tumbler of bourbon on the marble edge as he slowly undressed. Dick's sigh was profound.

"Here. Drink this, Poopsi. You badly need to relax." Pale violet eyes brushed over her husband's enormous torso before making eye contact. "You look like you lost your best friend. What did Andy Grimes have to say that upset you so?"

Why ask? Dick's answer would likely be a twisted version of truth. Marjorie had heard the phone ring in Dick's office not fifteen minutes before. With the door shut, only muffled tones of his conversation had sifted through the walls. But from the look on Dick's face, it wasn't a congenial conversation. Regardless of what was going on, she was prepared to stand by her man.

"Thanks, sweetie." Dick labored to bend over and remove his black socks. Grunting, he crawled into the hot water and cursed. "She got away!" He angrily grabbed the glass and downed the liquor in a few gulps. "Blame woman is as slippery as an eel with more lives than a cat." He would have the devil of a time sleeping off his anger. Life was not going smoothly. The Tempest situation was spinning way out of control again.

"Ah . . . yes! Victoria Tempest." The woman had become a thorn in Dick's side. Marjorie sat down on the edge of the tub clasping an oversized cottony-white towel in her arms. "It's not your fault, Dick. You phoned Andy and told him she was in town. He didn't do his job. There were more than a dozen police about and they all failed to apprehend the fugitive."

"Yeah, I know all that, but . . ." Dick sank in the massive tub, his buoyant blubber afloat in the water. Spewing hot water from jets rolled like waves over his belly and splashed in his wide face.

Gasping for air, he professed, "I let Mark James talk me into giving his precious *Little Vicki* a little more time before the arrest. I should've known somethin' was amiss. My gut told me to grab her while I could." What was he waiting for? A miracle?

"And do what? Strangle the woman to shut her up?" Marjorie was so tired of the ongoing murder drama. "Dick, listen to me," she urged. "I was present and witnessed the entire affair. Nothing seemed out of order. If you have to blame someone, blame Karen Tempest. She's a very clever woman. I just hope Mark James is up to her games." Few people could be trusted.

Games, huh? Dick cranked his head to one side and studied his wife, beautiful and witty, always keeping his best interest at heart, the only person in the world to whom he was submissive.

"I never understood why you disliked Karen so much. What in the world did the girl ever do to you?" Dick said, sinking like a leaking ship to the bottom of the tub. Bubbles engulfed his head.

Marjorie waited for him to resurface. "You really don't have a clue, do you?" Her eyes narrowed, lips clamped together sealing her dour expression. Dick blinked, waiting for her to expound.

"The experienced Karen Tempest murdered her first husband, then aborted her baby. Escaping judgment, she walked away with lily-white hands. No doubt she manipulated Mark's feelings in the wake of her mother's dilemma at the wedding."

"What's your point, Marjorie?"

"Just this. Who knows what the wench is capable of doing? I'd keep my eye on the daughter if you want to find the mother."

"Oh, I know all that." Dick waved his hand. "Theodore Lawrence Carter was a scam artist. Mark asked me to make the unsavory incident go away and I did. Karen was a victim of brutality and not a murderer." He swabbed soap on a bath rag. "As far as having an abortion, it's a non-issue in today's society."

"Why are you so protective of Mark?" Marjorie huffed. "What's to say that Karen won't step outside the law again? Wealth and family position have liberated the girl until she has no boundaries of decency. Who seduces her own mother's lover?"

"Okay, I get it, Marjorie. You dislike Karen. However, Teddy's death was an accident," Dick retorted. "Mark explained all that years ago!" He lathered his body in creamy soap. "The pumped-up athlete was a philanderer, a womanizer. All Karen did was fight back. If I treated you like that, wouldn't you?"

"So you really believe Karen's story, that Teddy drank too much and accidentally overdosed on sleeping pills?"

"If Mark said it, I believe it."

"Doesn't matter what I think because I know you'll take Mark's side." Marjorie adjusted the Jacuzzi jets and watched the exploding bubbles of water calm. "So where did Victoria go after she left the wedding chapel? Surely, someone has a theory."

"The Jackson police found the white limousine parked outside the Shackelford Funeral Parlor—amongst a dozen other vehicles just like it. Took 'em over an hour to locate the right vehicle since somebody was smart enough to switch the license tags. I fear we're dealing with pros, here."

"So Victoria has *smart* people on her side."

"No doubt about it." Dick swiped water droplets from his forehead with a soft oversized towel. "Of course, the limousine was vacant and nobody around saw anything. Ain't it just like people not to get involved?" Dick disparagingly shook his head.

"But you are involved, Dick," Marjorie pointed out.

He studied his wife a second. "Fix me another drink?"

Marjorie reached over and took Dick's empty glass. "When I come back, I want you to explain to me in detail why nailing Victoria for her husband's murder is so important to you." She paused at the door. "If you did something horrible, Dick, I need to know now. I'm on your side, always, right or wrong."

Tormented over his circumstances, Dick ducked under the rolling water thinking all he'd done was hire some men to steal three files. So he made a mistake. He wasn't a murderer. It was all a horrible set of circumstances that ended badly.

Hadn't he paid for it dearly through the years?

Could he help it if everything that could go wrong went wrong that stormy evening of April 13, 1989? Wouldn't the past ever let him alone? Would the nightmarish murder haunt him until he took his last breath? Somebody had to pay for murdering Jeffrey Tempest, and it wasn't going to be him. *Nosiree!*

The hired looters were just kids, untrained to handle a crisis. One of them was carrying a gun and used it before thinking. Jeffrey's death was a fluke of fate. Why should he take a murder wrap when he could prove someone else was responsible?

No, Dick decided, *I will not tell my wife what I did that resulted in Jeffrey Tempest's death. Let the past go to hell and stay there!*

Mark James was just as guilty. They had both profited from that night. Andy Grimes, too. Mark in receiving megabucks to pay off his gambling debts while Hearty Meats avoided immediate prosecution for environmental negligence. And young Andy Grimes in gaining special privileges afforded a rising politician.

Ten young men had died from environmental poisoning. Yes, *ten!* Attorney Jeffrey Tempest had been aware of only three. And Dick wasn't telling how his Mafia buddies took care of the problem. Victoria had been allowed to live because she was a vegetable with no memory. But now, everything had changed.

As hard as it was, those involved should keep their mouths shut and wait for the final drama to unfold. All the evidence was in place to convict Victoria. The big insurance policy taken out on her husband two weeks before he died was motive enough.

How could she possibly wiggle out of a conviction?

19

The Tennessee River Campsite

When Sarah Boswell and Tanya Mason had finished eating the delicious Cajun omelet prepared by Bobby Graves in his beat-up old trailer located at the top of a hill overlooking the Tennessee River, Sarah retrieved the materials from her car she had illegally stolen and copied. It was time to examine the facts.

The screen on the trailer door popped as Sarah returned. "It's gonna storm tonight." Waves of lightning flickered on the western horizon. "You got your car windows rolled up, Tanya?" Brown eyes the size of poker chips shined in the dull lighting. "We'd best make our nest here and wait out the storm."

"Locked up and battened down for the night," Tanya replied. "Do we need to speak in private?" She glanced over at Bobby.

"No problem, use my bedroom." Bobby nodded to the door on Tanya's right. "Only kind of bugs I got is the crawly ones."

"Thanks, Bobby," Sarah said and headed down the hall.

After Tanya had been briefed on the scary scenario contained in the Jeffrey Tempest file, she agreed with Sarah that it would be wise to include Bobby in their little powwow, seeing how Sheriff Andrew Grimes might come after Sarah for stealing the file.

Tanya was in danger because she was Sarah's friend, not to forget a sister to the deceased Terry Wilson who had died from exposure to environmental poisoning on Hearty Meats' property.

Would Andy guess that a third party had seen the file's contents? Probably not, they decided. And should Sarah get caught, Tanya could run while Bobby contacted a higher authority for help. It was a failsafe plan—as safe as you could illegally get.

Tanya had suffered about all she could stomach from Dick Branson's malarkey over the years. It was time for her to take a moral stand and put the criminal in his place. It was the least she could do for Terry. Whatever it took, she would do it.

"You sure you wanna do this?" Tanya asked Bobby after Sarah explained the situation. "Being privy to this information is extremely risky. We won't think hard of you if you ask us to leave right now. In fact, it might be good for your health."

Bobby shook his head and grinned. "If you two girls need my help, you better believe I'm in. Ain't got too many more years left on earth, so if 'n I can be of help to somebody, I wanna be."

"Okay." Sarah nervously laid out the first group of papers on the table, her eyes warily tracing the material.

Tanya was trembling, in too deep to leave.

"I thought the file I took from Sheriff Grimes' place was the original one compiled for the circuit court judge to review in 1989," Sarah revealed. "It appears we've gotten lucky."

"How so?" Bobby asked.

"Because there's a lot more here than I thought."

Huh? Tanya leaned over the table to study the hand-written notations. "Jeffrey Tempest made these notes?"

"Yep." Sarah made eye contact with Bobby.

"Read 'em aloud to us," Bobby said. "My eyes ain't so good anymore. Besides, I like hearing your sweet voice."

Sarah held the page in her hand and began:

January 8, 1989

I arrived at my office located on the second floor of the Union Planters Bank building around 8:25 a.m. this morning. I know the exact time because a black lady with a sassy attitude blocked the way to the elevator.

"Mr. Tempest," she said.

"Pardon me," I replied as we stepped on the elevator and the doors closed. We stood there like dunces for a couple of seconds while the elevator jerked and ascended. "Do I know you?" I noticed her harried, ghostly-pale expression. It was evident the woman was troubled.

"No, you don't know me," she answered. "And after I get through telling you what I know, you ain't seen or heard of me. You got that?"

Gaining my interest in her plight, I stepped off the elevator and invited the woman into my office, shutting the door and locking it for privacy. I had a part-time secretary and she was off that morning.

"What's this about?" I asked Elizabeth Wilson.

"He's talking about my mother!" Tanya cried, interrupting Sarah's dialog. "Apparently, she called on Jeffrey Tempest at his office three months before he was murdered."

"Go on, child," Bobby told Sarah. "Read us the facts."

The cop cast her eyes upon the page and read:

"I didn't call for an appointment because I didn't want anybody to know I was here. Thank you for seeing me," Mrs. Wilson said, laying a pair of despondent eyes on me. "After you hear what I have to say, you will understand why this matter must be kept secret, so bear with me."

"No problem," I replied, realizing that whatever it was on the woman's mind must be of utmost importance.

"You don't know me from Adam, Mr. Tempest—" Mrs. Wilson's sentence shattered as tears filled her dark eyes. "But my son, Terry—bless his sweet heart—is dead now because of that no-good, low-down bunch of criminals runnin' that new meatpacking company."

"Are you referring to Hearty Meats, Inc?" I clarified which company she was lambasting. "What did the company do to your son, Mrs. Wilson?"

"Terry was a good boy. He graduated high school with honors in 1983. He was going to college when he saved a couple thousand dollars."

Mrs. Wilson pulled a tissue from her purse and blew her nose then continued. "I worked hard all my life to give my son a better life than I had." She was nervous and shaky, eyes skittering to the locked door.

"*Relax, Mrs. Wilson. We're quite alone and you are safe,*" *I said, hoping to put her mind at ease.* "*So tell me what happened to Terry? Did he suffer a work-related injury? Is this what your visit is about? Do you want to sue the company?*" *My mind leaped ahead, speculating in many directions.*

"*Oh, yeah, I want to sue the company! I know of at least two other boys who died of weird illnesses. They worked on Terry's crew clearing the land the summer of 1984, before the packing company put up their buildings.*"

"*Weird illnesses? Do you mind explaining?*" *I switched on my tape recorder, took a pen from the drawer, and began making notes.*

Mrs. Wilson talked freely. I was astounded at the story she told. Her son Terry had unearthed thirty rusty metal canisters leaking black oil while clearing debris on the twenty-five acres of land formerly leased by the tannery. Mrs. Wilson learned about the incident when Terry came home after work one day with black oil all over him, telling her what had happened.

According to Terry, Abel Manspeaker, the crew foreman, immediately reported the incident to Burt Clayborne, who was the assistant manager of Hearty Meats at the time. Work temporarily ceased until Abel returned and told the boys that the contents of the barrels contained harmless oil substances.

Of course, that was a lie. Abel ordered the crew to remove the canisters and bury them at the back of the property, twenty feet beneath the surface so that leaking would not be a problem. The unsuspecting crew obeyed, with no idea of the extreme danger involved in handling the toxic material.

"*When did you first notice Terry had a health problem?*" *I asked Mrs. Wilson, growing more concerned over the troubling matter.*

"*Well . . .*" *she thought a second.* "*Terry went off to college in spring of 1985 and made if fine through one semester. The following fall, he developed headaches that aspirin wouldn't cure,*" *Mrs. Wilson explained.* "*His hands started shaking so hard he couldn't write. He missed a lot of classes before deciding to quit and come home.*" *Mrs. Wilson's lips twitched as grief took new hold.* "*A doctor in Memphis said Terry had nerve damage to the brain.*"

I cringed as Mrs. Wilson let out a wail.

"*It was the beginning of the end.*" *Her grief was so profound it touched me deeply, until I wanted to weep with her.*

"*Terry died?*" *I uttered then let my brain reign over my emotions.*

She nodded. "February 15, 1988."

"I'm sorry," I said, "but it's possible that the canisters of oil had nothing to do with your son's illness. People get sick and die, young and old alike. Trust me, there is no way of knowing when death will descend."

"I know that's right," Tanya muttered.

Sarah eyed her friend a fragment of a second then continued with reading Jeffrey's critically revealing notations.

"Terry had a stoke at age twenty-two, Mr. Tempest. Twenty-two!" Anger in Mrs. Wilson's eyes replaced tears. "The coroner did an autopsy and reported that my son's organs were plum full of PCBs. Do you know what that is, Mr. Tempest? That's the chemical stuff that causes nerve damage and cancer in humans. I know because I went to the library and looked it up." Elizabeth Wilson's pasty-red lips were hard twisted.

I didn't know what else to say.

"That's why I'm here today. To get you to help me set things right."

"You want me to prosecute Hearty Meats for operating on environmentally unsafe soil," I said—more a statement than a question. "Can you give me names of the other young men involved?" I needed to show a pattern of illnesses in those who had worked alongside Terry.

"I sure can." Mrs. Wilson retrieved a list of sick children from her purse—three of them deceased, seven still sick and possibly dying.

I was incensed something so heinous could happen in my own hometown and vowed that I would speak out against the injustice.

"Do you know these boys personally? Do you think their families will agree to participate in a class-action suit?" I asked, knowing that coming against so large a company with powerful lawyers would not prove easy.

No one could know about my involvement until I had finished gathering the evidence, evaluated the facts, taken depositions, and was prepared to prosecute the people responsible for this gross environmental negligence.

"Those who have buried sons will," Mrs. Wilson replied. "The others, I'm not sure. Most of 'em were financially compensated and moved away."

"Financially compensated? The management of Hearty Meats knew that they had done wrong and paid off the parents of the injured parties?" I had to be sure I understood exactly what Mrs. Wilson was inferring.

She nodded. "They knew."

"Do you know what kind of oil was in those barrels?"

"Yes, sir. The kind used in electric transformers and greasing roads."

I cringed. *Since 1979, the federal government had passed laws making it illegal to produce and distribute the highly toxic transformer oil. The Environmental Protection Agency had identified similar super-clean-up sites and lawsuits against the negligent companies were spreading across America. The issue was so hot it seared my mind. No doubt, Mrs. Wilson had a case.*

"Can you come back tomorrow morning and give your deposition, Mrs. Wilson?" I needed my secretary present to take dictation, and as a witness. *"I'll also need the phone numbers of the other two plaintiffs you mentioned."*

"No problem," she answered. *"The three of us will come tomorrow and tell our story. I've got fifty-thousand dollars saved—if that's not enough."*

"That's plenty, Elizabeth." I found myself on a first-name basis with my newest client. *If the meatpacking company is found guilty of ignoring an environmental problem, and lying to the work crew, I promise you they will pay plenty for their negligence."* I had my first big class-action law case.

"That's all that Jeffrey Tempest wrote." Sarah yawned and gathered the pages strewn across the metal table.

Tanya stared into space, reliving a clip of the past.

"I don't see copies of any legal depositions pertaining to the environmental case against Hearty Meats in the file," Sarah noted.

"Whoever hired the thugs that broke into Jeffrey's office either has 'em or they're toast," Bobby said. "What else is inside that folder?" He retrieved a legal-sized paper. "What's this?"

"Let me see." Sarah grabbed the document. "It's the investigative summary of the detective assigned to the case. Apparently Greg Diamond reviewed the file when Victoria went missing and new information regarding the case surfaced."

"As in *planted* information?" Bobby raised a bushy eyebrow.

"From what I understand, a copy of Jeffrey Tempest's insurance policy was anonymously mailed to Sheriff Grimes. Victoria's signature was at the bottom." Sarah's eyes rolled.

"Here, let me take a gander." Tanya grabbed the material from Sarah's hand and flipped through the copies. "So this proves that Victoria took out the insurance policy on Jeffrey?"

"That's what Sheriff Grimes would like us to believe."

"It doesn't make any sense that Jeffrey's hand-written notes are in the file," Tanya continued. "Especially if someone is trying to blame Victoria for her husband's death. Jeffrey's notes leave no doubt that the meatpacking company was negligent."

"Does seem plum strange," Bobby interjected.

"Why remove the depositions of the three plaintiffs and leave the attorney's notes?" Sarah posed the critical question.

"You're right, it doesn't add up," said Tanya.

"An oversight," Bobby suggested, thinking not likely.

"Or . . ." Sarah speculated. "Maybe the notes were recently reinserted into the file. No one anticipated that the folder would be stolen underneath the sheriff's nose and copied."

"You mean, whoever stole the notes the night Jeffrey died might have put them back thinking nobody would see them?"

"Yeah," said Bobby. "Like us. Who would do that?"

"The file was at the sheriff's house. Who do you think?"

"In that case, Andrew Grimes is definitely involved in a deliberate cover up. We're in a heap of trouble," Tanya said.

"Not yet," said Sarah. "It's possible that Cheryl Grimes might not tell her husband I picked up the file folder."

"Dream on, honey!" Tanya exclaimed, thinking her life was about to get crazier than usual. "What you did is illegal."

"And if Andy Grimes finds out?" Bobby interjected.

"He won't ignore the theft." Sarah nudged Tanya out of the way and plucked through a few more sheets of paper. "Bingo!"

"What did you find?" Tanya and Bobby squealed.

Sarah slapped the file with a hand. "Rookie Grimes was the first police officer on the crime scene the night of the robbery."

Tanya grabbed the report, an insightful gaze skittering to Bobby. "Well, I'll be." She handed Bobby the police report.

"See." Sarah's pointed finger landed on the page. "The sheriff's name is signed at the bottom of this page—which means that he had plenty of opportunity to remove the hand-written notes from Jeffrey's desk drawer before EMS arrived."

"Goodness!" Bobby let out a long sigh and collapsed in a kitchen chair. "You girls got a grenade in yo'r hands. How you gonna keep this matter from explodin' in your face?"

"I don't know." Sarah hated she had involved Bobby and Tanya in her scheme. Now their lives were in danger, too.

"Do you think Andy knew the robbery was gonna happen?" asked Tanya. "How did he get to Jeffrey's office so fast?"

"'Course, he knew," said Bobby, not stupid. "The company's had the man in their dirty pocket from day one."

"If Dick tells on Andy, Andy will tell on Dick."

"Exactly," said Sarah. If Bobby's right, the three of us are in real danger now that we've read Jeffrey's notes."

"We can't trust the crooks or the cops." Tanya cursed. She should have listened to her first impulse to let well enough alone.

"I don't know," said Sarah. "I need to think about my choices. Do I go to Greg with this information?"

"And if he's in cahoots with Andy?" Tanya raised an eyebrow. "I think we should keep our mouths shut."

20

North Dickson County

A hush came over the congregation as Joseph Glower raised his hand. Only the brisk winds of the fleeing storm interrupted the profound silence that followed. Camaraderie and prayers had gone on for over an hour, and now it was time to do business.

Brother Joe began singing "What a Friend We Have in Jesus." Guitars in the hands of masterful musicians plucked out the beautiful melodies of the familiar hymn passed down through generations. Mumbles of praise rose above the singing.

As Joe wound down the first hymn, other praise-and-worship tunes came to mind like "Bringing in the Sheaves," and "When the Roll is called up Yonder." As he sang, the host of male and female voices joined in, blending harmonies in regal praise.

Thirty minutes later, as if on cue, the music and singing ceased. In respect, the wind outdoors grew silent.

"Thank you for comin', brothers and sisters in Christ," Joseph said in a hushed tone that reverberated through the cave. "I believe it would be proper to pronounce a benediction right now and go home. Surely, we would all leave blessed."

A few amens erupted, Brother Joe smiling in response. "But you know I won't miss an opportunity to preach, don't you?" He whipped open his well-used Bible and read from a choice passage:

"Great is the Lord and most worthy of praise; his greatness no one can fathom. One generation will commend your works to another; they will tell of

your mighty acts. They will speak of the glorious splendor of your majesty, and I will meditate on your wonderful works. They will tell of the power of your awesome works, and I will proclaim your great deeds . . ."

Brother Joe clutched the Bible at his side and said, "You recognize the passage I just read. It's from Psalm 145. David spoke those words, a man after God's own heart."

"Tell it like it is, preacher!" a man at the back exclaimed.

"Tonight I want to speak about the awesome works of the Lord and remind you that He reigns on a heavenly throne, still mightily in control of human events. I should emphasize that nothing is impossible with Jehovah God, Creator of all things."

A few nods were exchanged.

"And me," Joe added. "God loves you and me. Not a hair falls from your head or mine that He does not see. Do you believe that? Really take it to heart?" His penetrating gaze reached the soul level, convicting sin and inciting sweet release.

If there was a chill in the cave, Victoria didn't notice because she was so focused on the words Brother Joe was saying. *God is in control.* Hadn't that one belief carried her though many fiery trials?

I want God to know I'm willing for Him to use me.

"Some of you are asking yourself: how can God use me? What qualifies me to proclaim the gospel to a world of unbelievers?" Brother Joe was so in tune with Victoria's thoughts.

"Well, I can't answer that question for you," he continued. "I wish I could tell you exactly what God expects from each of you, but I can't. God has placed within you His Holy Spirit to help you discern your individual spiritual gifts. You have an idea what those talents are. The question is: will you use them for God?"

Whispers echoed through the cave as thoughts were quietly shared. Victoria profoundly pondered Joe's sermon.

"You were not born by chance," Joe declared. "God planned your life and has important work for you to do. No life is an accident. He knew you before you were formed in your mother's womb." Joe paused, raising his hands in praise fashion.

The silent crowd waited for revelation.

"There are folks here who are confused over their mission in life. I tell you, God knows your doubts and sympathizes."

A unified sigh rose from the audience.

"How will you meet the challenge of evangelism?" Joe boldly asked. "Will you purpose in your hearts tonight to serve and glorify God with your talents? Will you give Jesus the reins?"

"Preach on," a man near the front exclaimed.

"Don't let fear cripple you, folks," Brother Joe continued. "I don't know about you, but I want Jesus to be proud of me when I meet Him in Glory." His smile was radiant, his countenance glowing in the flaming lantern lights. "Hallelujah!"

Shouts of praises to God went up all over the cave.

Victoria pondered over her talent for interpreting languages. She had no idea how she came to understand and speak Spanish, much less Italian. Was she gifted with the interpretation of tongues? Or was it a malfunction of her screwed-up brain?

God, help me, she silently prayed. *I need to be sure.*

21

Late Saturday in Fernwood

Sheriff Andrew Grimes privately cursed the grueling day, psychologically defamed from failing to capture Victoria Tempest at the wedding chapel. The woman had more lives than a cat! How else could she escape harm's way so many times?

Given the chance, Andy would gladly choke the life out of her, no charge. Victoria was a menace, a do-gooder who didn't fit in society. Just when his political career looked promising, she had to go and remember what happened to her husband in 1989.

Andy swiped his white handkerchief across his perspiring forehead. Stress was not good; it drove up his blood pressure.

Sure, Dick Branson said not to worry about the situation, that he had the problem under control. For all the good that would do Andy now that he was the laughing stock of Fernwood.

Imagine that! After all these years of success, one woman's meddling could pull him down. Andy felt his pulse, purposely breathing more slowly. A stroke was not a good idea.

No, he should get on home and thumb through the crime report he had checked out of the police archives. It had been years since he'd worried over the unsolved murder case. *Years!*

Andy grimaced. And now that was all he thought about.

First on the crime scene, Rookie Andy stumbled on Jeffrey Tempest's personal notes regarding the proposed lawsuit against Hearty Meats. He'd read through the file while Jeffrey was still lying on the floor bleeding to death, failing to call an ambulance.

Did that make him a murderer?

Without forethought, Andy had impulsively stuffed the notes inside his shirt, fully intending to turn them over to the detective put in charge of the case. Then he evaluated what he knew.

Privy to the file's damaging contents, young Andy had other plans for the notes. For the first time in his life, God had smiled on him. Information like that could earn a rookie respect.

Later that evening, Andy paid a visit to Richard Branson the Third, the newest big Whig in town. The Hearty Meats' manager hadn't known that Officer Andrew Grimes existed until that fated evening. Who could forget such a classic conversation?

"So what've you got to say to me, Officer, that can't wait until tomorrow?" Dick had received him poorly, obviously busy with other matters. "You need to hear me out," he'd replied.

Shy of ten o'clock, it had been a stormy Wednesday evening when Victoria Tempest underwent surgery. Involved in a terrible automobile accident, she was not expected to live. Her husband Jeffrey had already been pronounced dead on arrival at the same ER and taken over to the morgue for autopsy and embalmment.

So there young Andy had stood in Dick's living room, shaking like a leaf in front of the manager of Hearty Meats, Inc.

"I found something of interest at the young attorney's office tonight," Andy had informed *Mister* Branson.

"Jeffrey Tempest's office?" Dick sat up in his chair like he'd had an electric jolt. "What have you there, son?" His gaze shot to the papers clutched in Andy's right hand. "Speak up, Officer!"

"Some personal notes of a sensitive matter." Andy had come with the idea of using the information as a bargaining chip.

Nobody climbed up the ladder of success unless backed by money and powerful people. The justice system in America was as corrupt as any other business. Young Andy wanted to be more than a meter reader or a traffic cop. He desired respect, to wield a powerful influence in Fernwood. And now he could.

"Are you gonna let me see what you have, or play games, fella?" Dick had reached over and jerked the loose note pages from Andy's hand. Then he read the attorney's notations.

Andy sat still, waiting a good ten minutes while the business guru digested the content of the notes.

"Who did you say you were?" Mr. Branson inquired.

"Andrew Grimes. My friends call me Andy."

"So, what exactly do you plan to do with this information?" Dick was suddenly on friendly terms, his brow beaded with sweat.

"Well, that depends," Andy had wisely responded.

"Seems to me we have a sensitive situation here."

"I'm aware of that, sir," Andy had answered respectfully.

When all this came about, he had just graduated from the Police Academy and was in excellent physical condition. While in his teens, Andy had acted foolishly and stolen a few store items to purchase some drugs. Fortunately, he had not been caught.

Later, when he chose to go into law-enforcement work, he'd turned his delinquent tendencies into a plus since his experience with crime enabled him to more fully understand the criminal mind. With no illusions, he would outsmart most perpetrators.

Andy never expected to confront his dishonest nature ever again. Until the moment he found Jeffrey Tempest's notes.

So there young Andy had stood in front of Dick Branson on April 13, 1989, ready to cut a pact of a criminal nature. With no hesitancy, only the anticipation of getting on with his law-enforcement career, he'd told Dick: "I think we should keep this information under lock and key, somewhere safe, out of the eyesight of folks that might do Hearty Meats serious harm."

"I agree," Dick had said. "What's the catch?"

"In exchange, I want your loyalty. That's all."

That night Andy had presented a clear picture of the deal.

In response, Dick had burst out laughing. "That's all. You'll keep quiet if I stroke your back. And exactly how do you want me to do that, Andy?" His dark eyes sparkled like polished onyx.

"My career is important to me," Andy had replied.

The fat man dug a cigar out of his shirt pocket and lit it with a long match. After taking two puffs, he handed it over to Andy.

"Is this a peace offering—like the Injuns did in their powwows?" Andy had nervously quipped before sucking on the pungent smoke that made him cough. "Are we partners?"

Dick chuckled. "I don't see how helping you build your career can hurt me at all, Andy. Do you? But I gotta let you know I don't take lightly to folks who cross me."

"We're clear, then." A handshake was in order.

Andy understood then as he did now: Jeffrey Tempest was dead because he took the wrong peoples' side and tried to expose Hearty Meats' environmental negligence. The young attorney had no idea what he was up against in opposing Richard Branson. He should have come to terms with Dick and kept on breathing air.

Andy had concluded his business that night and gone home. The notes had been safely locked away in a bank deposit box for twenty-five years. No longer feeling safe, he had removed them fearing that a court order would result in a search and seizure.

And now, he was going home to destroy the evidence that would make him party to the unsolved crime.

22

Bobby's Trailer Park

"What will you do with this incriminating information?" Tanya asked Sarah, eyes illuminated with conflict.

The Fernwood cop took a moment to debate her choices.

"To be perfectly honest, Sarah, I'd rather you didn't mention my name in conjunction with the notes. I can't afford to put my family in danger again." Eyes widened as Tanya internalized the dangerous consequences of more involvement with the case.

"Chicken!" Bobby squawked and flapped his elbows.

Tanya cleared her throat, embarrassed.

"First of all," Sarah said, "I'm going home and think about who I can trust with this newest piece to the murder puzzle."

"And do whut?" Tanya scowled.

"No wonder this crime never got solved," Sarah went on to say. "With Rookie Grimes withholding incriminating evidence, the cause of justice was doomed to failure from the beginning."

"I don't know about takin' that business home with you, Sweetcakes," Bobby put in his two cents. "Maybe you oughta jus' leave the copies here with me, for safekeeping."

"Not a bad idea," Tanya agreed. "What about Victoria's daughter? Should we call her and tell her what we found?"

"Karen Tempest James?" Sarah smirked. "Might as well give the notes to the devil. Don't forget who she's married to?" The woman was loyal to number one, likely to protect her own turf should it come down to choosing between hubby and mama.

"You think?" Bobby reacted. "I don't know. Seems to me that family bonds are stronger than most things in this life. Maybe you should go see Karen. Feel her out. It can't hurt."

"Maybe," Sarah paused to yawn, "but not until tomorrow."

"That may be too late." Tanya pointed out. "Likely Karen is on her honeymoon by now, off to Timbuktu, or other farther parts of the world. You should track her down tonight."

"Of course, you're right." Sarah stretched and yawned. "Now that we've talked and you both know . . ." she directed her gaze at Tanya, then Bobby, "I'm headin' home. I don't think this storm is gonna do much damage, and I gotta git some rest."

"But not before you talk to Karen," Tanya insisted.

"I'll phone her when I get home," Sarah replied.

Tanya picked her gargantuan purple purse off the vinyl floor. "I don't want the kids to wake up in the morning and wonder where Mama is." She had another four-hour drive ahead of her.

"You gotta bed here if you like," Bobby offered.

"Thanks Bobby," Tanya said, "but we both need to git on home." She fondly patted the old man on his shoulder.

"Thanks." Sarah gave Bobby a ferocious hug. "You guard this envelope like it was solid gold. I'll be back for it if I can."

"What do you mean, *if* you can?" Tanya spun around, eyes wide with speculation. "You *do* think you're in danger."

"Maybe, maybe not." Sarah collected her things to leave.

"You don't think Andy will tell Dick Branson, do you?" He'd protected killers before. "He and Andy are pretty tight."

"Don't start worrying prematurely," Sarah warned, jingling her car keys in one hand. "I'm a cop, remember."

"And cops die every day in the line of duty," Bobby said.

"I'll be fine. Be able to think a whole lot straighter after a few hours of sleep. Maybe Cheryl Grimes will forget I stopped by."

"Not a chance," Bobby proclaimed.

"Oh dear . . ." Tanya began to tremble.

The Anointing

***

Back in Fernwood

"I'm home, honey!" Andy Grimes called out loudly, shutting the front door and bolting it. One couldn't be too careful with crooks lurking about. He noticed that Cheryl's car keys were lying on the table beside the door—which meant she'd been out of the house for a while. The hour grew late, and likely she was sleeping soundly. Andy trudged up the steps toward their bedroom.

Like he thought, Cheryl was nestled under the covers of their king-sized bed, a faint snore escaping her plump pink lips, perfectly pursed, like they needed kissing.

Hard as Andy tried, tiptoeing around the bedroom to put his things away, he couldn't keep from waking her.

"Andy? Is that you?" Cheryl's long eyelashes fluttered. "Why are you so late? What have you been doing? I was starting to really worry about you." She blinked at the bedside clock.

"I'm fine, honey. Go back to sleep." He peeled off his shirt and threw it on the back of a chair. "Been a long day, hon."

"Were you working all this time?" Cheryl asked, squinting in the dim lighting of the bedroom. "I'm worried about you."

"Well, don't. There was a lot of winding up at the office to do." He dropped his pants to the floor and stepped out of them.

"Oh, the Tempest case, I suppose," Cheryl mumbled.

"What?" Andy's eyes were suddenly wide open.

"You left the file on your desk," Cheryl clarified. "Why did you send for it?" She rolled over in the bed, her back to Andy.

"Come again?" Her question struck Andy like a lightning bolt. "What are you talkin' about, Cheryl?"

He reached over and shook her. His pulse was chasing heartbeats like a fox after a jackrabbit. *The Tempest file?*

Cheryl sat up in bed. "Okay, Andy, I'm fully awake now. Obviously you're upset at something I said. You did send that officer over to the house earlier to get the file, didn't you?"

"Huh?" Andy's gaze zoomed in on Cheryl's face.

"The Tempest file, honey. Sarah somebody—that black gal who works in Traffic Violations—she said you needed it."

"You didn't give Sarah the file, did you?"

"The officer had a signed form. It was your signature, Andy. Did I do something wrong?" Cheryl tossed back the covers. "You left on the bathroom light. Shall I turn it off?"

Andy was stunned for a moment, having grossly underestimated Sarah's commitment to justice.

"You're as white as a sheet, Andy. Are you ill?"

"Just tired," Andy lied, his heart jumping like Mexican beans. "I'm going downstairs to get a snack. Want something?"

"No." Cheryl yawned. "The file's back. It's lying on your office desk. Sarah returned it hours ago. As far as she could discern, there was no earthshaking problem. "Go have some warm milk and come to bed. You look like a train ran over you."

Andy grunted, losing interest in food as he tramped down the hall to his office. Sure enough the file was there, with the notes.

Tiptoeing down the stairs to the kitchen, Andy's blood pressure probably shot up twenty points as he approached the kitchen phone. Grabbing the receiver, he dialed Dick Branson's cell, dreading to divulge the latest mishap. A royal screw-up!

The dratted day just kept on getting worse.

First Victoria slips through his fingers, and now this screw up with the file! With his cholesterol running high, he was prime for a heart attack. The phone rang twice before Dick answered.

"What is it, Andy?"

"You got caller ID on your cell?"

"I've upgraded all my electronics," Dick replied. "So what's this call about? Do I need to remind you it's almost midnight?"

The day had seemed like a year, like he'd been eating crow for months. "We've got a big problem," Andy hurriedly said.

SUNDAY, JUNE 29

23

Josh Tenny had telephoned Sarah Boswell's house five times and gotten her voice mail every time. Sure it was after midnight, but Sarah was usually a night owl. It wasn't like her to ignore his call.

Like him, she was probably dog-tired from the day. No cause to worry, she'd evidently shut off the ringer and gone to bed.

Still, he'd be in big trouble if he didn't inform Sarah that she had to report at work at 6 a.m. Sunday morning. Gosh, it was already Sunday. He might as well go over to her house and rouse her. Josh picked up his truck keys and rushed from his apartment.

A storm had passed through the town not long before, tossing broken tree limbs and scattering debris in the streets. Overhead streetlights flickered like the electricity was going to crash. Not in a big hurry, Josh drove his 2008 green Chevrolet truck east of town and located Sarah's quaint 20th-century neighborhood. All Josh could afford right now was a flat.

Born in the early eighties, Josh had missed the "good ol' days" according to his mama, who had died when he was twenty. Devastated by Janie Tenny's early death, his daddy had taken off to somewhere in Florida to blow off some steam and rethink life.

Josh guessed Clayton Tenny was dead by now since nobody had heard from him in over five years. The only family he had left was his aging grandma, cynical and sick with rheumatism, threatening to call the doctor in for a dose of voluntary cessation.

Like his Nana always says, "Folks in the New World Order don't have the guts to face hardships no more." Disgustingly true.

Always a cowboy at heart, Josh had taken life as it had come, one day at a time. He had never done anything huge to earn him recognition, always erring on the side of justice. He already had the only job he ever wanted, right smack in the middle of town.

Yes sir, answering the phones for the Fernwood Police Department was something Josh could do well, although it paid pennies in comparison to other high-powered occupations.

But he was content. And that counted for something.

Chivalry came in many forms, Josh believed. Making sure the precinct ran without a hitch, he took personal. Sarah was his closest friend, so he didn't want her to get into trouble because he failed to deliver a message. So here he was, after midnight, driving across the sleepy town, once again doing his duty to assist a fellow cop. Surely, there were some rewards in Heaven for his efforts.

Josh parked his truck in the driveway of the vacant house across the street from Sarah's house and walked over.

"Sarah?" Josh called out from the portals of her front porch.

Above him, a moon attempted to escape a dark cloud and miserably failed. There was even a cool breeze astir.

"Sarah! Open up. It's me, Josh." He banged on the door, glancing around the dark yard, deep in green grass and needing a fresh mowing. Just when you got things done around a house, it was time to do them again. Call it laziness, but Josh didn't want to own any personal property. A house could become a mistress.

And with ownership of property came yards and all the junk that went with it. A house had to be occasionally repainted and a new roof put on. That wouldn't come cheap. No, Josh's messy apartment worked just fine for him. One bedroom, a den, a kitchen and a bath, were all that one lonely body needed.

But, should he find the perfect woman in the future, somebody like Sarah, he might change his mind and marry.

Josh smiled. A man ought to keep his options open to include love and a family. And kids. He really liked Sarah.

He jumped off the porch. Maybe he'd come over on his day off and mow the yard for Sarah. Maybe, if he wasn't playing poker with the guys down at the local pub. It'd be the nice thing to do for a friend, and Josh had fewer friends than he did toes on one foot. Oh, well . . . he backed up and stared at Sarah's house.

The lights inside the white clapboard structure were out. In fact, the whole street was cloaked in shadows because of a busted-out streetlight. He should report that outage to the city.

A black cat scraped against Josh's leg, mewing for attention.

Leaning over, he picked up the feline and massaged the plush fur around her neck with his hand. "Hey, baby, who do you belong to?" he asked as if the cat could answer, feeling a little jolt inside at the idea of a black cat's showing up.

Wasn't that a sign of bad luck?

Josh mounted the front porch again and tapped lightly on the front door. He got no response. Maybe he'd leave her a note. He peeked through the glass in the door. It was pitch dark inside.

Not a mouse stirring, Josh recalled that Sarah kept an emergency key over her back door. What a place to hide a key, he chuckled. Why, everybody and his grandma knew that people hid keys on the ledges of doors or under pots, so what was the use locking up?

Josh crept around the right side of house, his feet sinking into the mushy grass, a firm reminder that he should make an effort to do Sarah's yard in return for one of her scrumptious home-cooked meals. He was tired of eating out of cardboard boxes and cans, tired of being alone. She enjoyed his company, too.

But Josh was shy and didn't usually fair well with women. How old was Sarah anyhow? *Forty? Forty-five?* He was thirty-three and never had a steady gal since high school, but what did age matter when it came to relationships? And Sarah was wonderful.

Once in a while Josh allowed himself to daydream about romance, the kind squirreled away in those risqué novels. But those were unreal people doing stupid things, not at all like him.

Retrieving Sarah's house key from the ledge, Josh unlocked the back door and opened it. Hesitating a second, he sniffed.

What was that odor? Gas?

Probably his imagination, Josh decided, having recently worked on his Chevrolet truck and spilled gasoline on his pants.

"Sarah?" he called out, barely able to see through the murky darkness. If he remembered correctly, the kitchen light switch was on the left wall beside the door. He hoped to high heaven that the electricity hadn't crashed because of the wretched storm.

In the distance, thunder angrily rumbled, signaling the approach of another storm front. Like his mother said, when it rains it pours. Josh heard the first drops pinging on the roof.

Yep. It was going to be an awful night. Josh's right hand groped along the smooth wall in search of the light switch.

Dadgummit! He left his umbrella in the truck.

Unfortunately, Josh was the kind of person who limped through life unprepared. He tried to decide whether to proceed with his search or brave the rain and get the umbrella before a deluge set in. *Oh well*, he'd just borrow Sarah's and return it later.

That is, if Sarah hadn't taken her umbrella with her.

There. Josh's finger lingered on the light switch a nanosecond before he flipped it up. Light filled the room like Josh had never seen before, followed by a roaring heat that consumed everything in the room. There was no time to think or react as a green haze swallowed him. There was no pain, only a strange floating feeling.

The explosion rocked the neighborhood and turned on every light in every house lining the serene street. Within minutes, Sarah Boswell's house was obliterated, going up in dirty plume of black smoke, the consuming fire squealing like a band of demons.

Sarah rounded the street corner just in time to see her house disintegrating in flames. *What the devil happened?*

Then she reached a chilling conclusion. Obviously, Andy Grimes found out about her visit to his house, knew she had borrowed the Tempest file. Then he told Dick Branson.

This was how they thanked her. *Duh*.

24

Flight to Baghdad

When Lazarus Bacon woke up, he was on an airplane. Where was he going? Was this Airforce One, his daddy's plane?

Suddenly becoming aware of the seatbelt restraints, the lad scrubbed sleepy bugs from his eyes with the back of his fists, blinked, and glanced around. Grasping his pounding head, he felt dizzy and disoriented. Beside him sat his so-called new friend, Gordo, who had promised to show him a giant chocolate bunny.

"Mr. Gordo?" Lazarus poked the lean man with a finger. "There really isn't a big chocolate bunny, is there?" He already knew the answer. His daddy had warned him time and time again to never trust strangers. But Gordo had seemed so sincere.

"You awake, bud?" Gordon erected himself in his seat and yawned. "What time is it?" He glanced down at his watch, which registered 2 a.m., Central Standard Time. "Are you hungry? You've been asleep a long time." He patted the lad's hand.

"Yes." Lazarus chose his words carefully. He wasn't going to resist and be put to sleep again. No sir, he'd play it smart. Wait for the right moment to steal Gordo's cellphone and call Natalie. His nanny would know what to do. He'd been in a crisis before from not minding her. She would make him feel safe again.

"About the big bunny—no, there isn't one, but we're taking a far more interesting trip," Gordon informed Lazarus.

"I see." Lazarus spied only one other person on the leer jet, a lady wearing a blue uniform carrying a tray with food.

"Hey Miss!" Gordon called out to a young, plump flight attendant. "Would you get this young man something to eat?"

Lazarus approved, he was starving and very thirsty.

"How many more hours to Baghdad?" Gordon whispered to the flight attendant, but Lazarus had keen ears and overheard.

"We've been in flight for about four hours. Give us another few and we'll put you safely on the ground," she replied. "What would you like to drink, young man?" she addressed Lazarus.

"Water. A big bottle of water."

The lady in blue rushed off to comply, disappearing behind a curtain at the back of the plane. "This is not a commercial plane, is it?" Lazarus asked Gordo, already knowing the answer.

"No, it isn't. It's a charter."

"You rented a plane just for us?"

"Yep. Don't you like the ride?"

Lazarus nodded, wondering if Natalie had told his parents he was missing when they called to ask how he was doing. They usually phoned around 10:30 p.m. when they were traveling. They trusted Natalie to do the right thing. What a huge mistake!

"Yeah, I thought it would give us more privacy," Gordon said, creating a story behind the trip he hoped was believable.

Lazarus listened and evaluated his predicament.

It wasn't long before the flight attendant returned with food. He was surprised to see a juicy cheeseburger underneath the hot paper wrapping. Loaded down with onions, lettuce, pickles and ketchup, he could hardly wrap his mouth around the sandwich.

But first Lazarus drank all the water. Then he lit into the sandwich like he hadn't eaten for days. Tina had brought a Coke, too. He knew her name because it was printed on a button she had pinned to her blue vest. The flight attendant was pretty and seemed nice. Maybe the trip would be fun, after all.

Lazarus asked for another Coke. His mama never let him have regular Coca-Cola because it contained caffeine. But Natalie sometimes broke the rules and gave the beverage to him anyhow.

Gordo told Tina goodnight in Spanish. Lazarus knew because he had studied the language. He spoke Italian and German, too. Learning came easy for him. He was smart.

"I'm not sleepy, Mr. Gordo. Can we play a game?"

"Sure," said his captor. "Name the game and we'll play it."

Lazarus chose checkers, so Gordon pulled out his laptop and called up a game for two. They played for hours before Lazarus got sleepy and said he was finished. Maybe he'd nap again.

Perhaps taking a vacation from his parents wasn't all that bad, Lazarus thought. Besides, Gordo was a barrel of fun and would do just about anything to please him. At home, Lazarus didn't always get his way, but here . . . he was the main attraction.

Lazarus wiped his face with the hot, wet cloth and turned to his assailant. "Gordo? Why are we going to Baghdad?"

Gordon smiled. "I was wondering when you were going to ask me that question. Your brother wants to talk to you."

"My brother?" Lazarus blinked. "I don't have any sisters or brothers." At least none that he knew about.

"Yes, you do," Gordon replied, fearing if Lazarus decided not to cooperate, everyone on the plane would be in trouble. The lad possessed phenomenal psychic gifts including mind reading. Labeled cruel and insensitive, he had left a trail of dead animals.

"For real?" Lazarus said.

"Son, I wouldn't trick you on this fact."

"Okay, is my brother younger or older?" Lazarus grew curious. Maybe he'd wait a little longer before putting Gordo to sleep and calling Natalie. Didn't he want to see his brother?

What is Baghdad like?

"Your brother is eighteen years older than you are." Gordon saw no reason to lie. "You share the exact genetic makeup." Weird as it seemed, that was the story he had been told.

Lazarus' smile faded. "But if we share the exact genetic makeup, that would make my brother my twin. How is that possible?" Twins were born at the same time by the same mother.

134

"Good question!" Gordon exclaimed. "Don't ask me to explain how it happened, but I'm told it's true. Scout's honor." He made the sign and chuckled. The boy was fun to have around.

Humph. "I bet you never were a scout, Gordo."

"You're correct, son. But nevertheless, I'm telling you the truth about your brother. Few people know of your situation."

"You mean, *him* being eighteen years older than me?"

"No, I mean they don't even know you have a brother."

"I can ask my daddy, if you like. He knows everything. Let me borrow your cellphone." Lazarus reached for Gordo's belt.

"I don't think so." Gordon chuckled, restraining his young captive's hand. "You're a mighty clever little man, Lazarus Bacon. I can see why your brother wants to meet you. I would."

"Will I like him?" asked Lazarus, considering whether to put Gordo to sleep anyhow and call Natalie. But if he did that, the security police would immediately come for him.

"If your brother is exactly like you, only older, do you think you'll like him, Lazarus?" It was a unique question to ponder.

"I think I'll love him," Lazarus replied, now anxious to get to Baghdad. "I know I will, and he's bound to like me."

25

Switzerland

Georgie Hendricks had slept through most of the flight to Zurich. Right after her last Coke, she'd passed out like a light. Apparently her captor had slipped a sedative in her drink.

Leave it to Donald to get the job done. Regardless of how PI Georgie felt about betraying Victoria, she was going to Switzerland to meet the famous Alexander Luceres Ramnes.

Beside her sat Donald Wetherfield, fully awake and looking suave. As usual, he appeared in full control of his faculties. Did the man never sleep? Always scheming and planning his next move, could she possibly be clever enough to escape his tight clutches? *Probably not*, Georgie decided with a rude yawn.

No, the wise thing to do was play along. Be cool and learn what the Antichrist had in mind. Now why did she think that?

Antichrist was the name Victoria applied to Luceres—not that she was buying into that religious crap. But her client sure believed in Biblical prophecy. She eyed Donald with distaste.

"What? You hate me?" He chuckled.

"Worse."

"I've ordered you some food. You're as thin as a rail. A breeze could easily disassemble your gangly bones."

"Thanks, Donald," Georgie quipped. "You look nice, too."

"You'd be almost attractive, girl, if you didn't have such a foul mouth on you." Donald wanted to slap the detective and throw her to the wolves. "Maybe my boss will have the patience to teach you some manners." He doubted that was possible.

"What you think of me doesn't matter," Georgie replied. "And I could care less what your boss thinks. I just want to get this trip over with so the rest of my life can begin."

Donald smiled. "So you claim."

The food was better than Georgie expected, and she ate like there would be no other meal. After wolfing down two turkey sandwiches and three bottles of spring water, she dusted the crumbs from her hands and said, "What is Luceres like?"

Donald slowly rotated his head toward the captive. "He is like no other man you will ever meet." The bright subject was one he was well qualified to discuss. "The diplomat is smart, clever, rich, and he knows exactly where he is going in this life."

"Is he married?" Georgie inquired.

"As far as I know he has never even dated," Donald answered. "But Luceres doesn't tell me everything."

"Is he gay?" Georgie asked before thinking.

"No." Donald chuckled. "He would have made a move on me if he were. Luceres is single by choice. The man has class and ambition. He obviously doesn't want a woman interfering." Like Beverly James would do should Donald let his heart wander there.

"I thought most men liked women," Georgie said, getting more into the strange conversation, not that she put too much stock in male friendship. "Exactly what does Luceres *like*?"

"He prefers to orchestrate grandiose systems designed to help mankind deal with seemingly unsolvable problems, such as saving the environment or arriving at a peaceful solution to war."

Donald paused to evaluate Georgie's level of interest.

"I see."

"You should ask him yourself?"

"And for all that *grandiose* planning, he gets what?" Georgie's turquoise eyes sparkled with interest, having never personally met an unselfish person. "A little attention, an award?"

"You misunderstand, Georgie. Luceres' receives satisfaction in executing his plans. He delights in implementing programs that will make life better for everyone on planet Earth."

"Sounds to me like he's playing God," Georgie quipped.

"As a human being, Luceres is one of a kind. You should take notes while he speaks to you. That is, if you want to improve your life. Don't sell him short until you have met him."

"Wow!" Georgie remarked. "Sounds to me like Luceres aspires to be the next savior of the world." The idea of a false Christ arising in the end times came to mind. Was she getting a touch of religion? Was Victoria's faith rubbing off on her?

"*Savior?* You might say that," Donald replied. "Luceres is a philanthropist of the highest order, a Mother Theresa and Lottie Moon all rolled into one. I can't imagine where the world would be today without him, he seems so in tune with world events."

Georgie didn't know who Lottie Moon was, but she must have been somebody important. "When we get to Zurich, what are we gonna do first?" she asked, moving to a new subject.

"We'll check into a hotel, get cleaned up, and rest for the night. In the morning after we've had breakfast, we'll go over to my boss's chalet for a visit. He is expecting us."

"Why me?" Georgie's eyes widened. "Why does Luceres want to see me? I'm absolutely nobody in his personal directory."

"You're wrong, Georgie. Luceres is interested in everyone he meets. He places great value on humanity. In particular, he wants to question you about your client, Victoria Tempest."

"Why?" Georgie was big into motives.

"Luceres respects the woman. Don't ask me why, Victoria seems to be nothing but tricky trouble." She had managed to escape the authorities at every turn of the corner. "But she explicitly trusts you, Georgie." Women had strange bonds.

"He expects me to betray a client?"

"No. He wants you to talk some sense into Victoria."

"So he can . . ." Georgie motioned with her left hand for Donald to supply more data.

"So he can help Victoria get back her life. I assure you, Luceres has your client's best interest at heart."

"And he wants to do this service because . . ."

"Because he is a nice person and likes to do the right thing," Donald replied. "Hear him out, and if you decide not to help, he won't force you. He wants your loyalty, freely given."

"All right," Georgie agreed, knowing that nobody could force her to betray Victoria. But if Luceres could actually help clarify the situation, accelerate justice in Jeffrey's murder case, she should listen to his ideas before running off with no sane plan in mind.

***

Dickson County in Tennessee

The cave meeting had been in progress for three hours. Victoria was too excited and involved to be tired or sleepy. She had never heard so powerful a sermon as preached by the visiting evangelist from California. Brother Joseph Glower made Bible prophecy come alive. An altar call had brought scores of people to the front. People anticipated Brother Joe's prayerful touch. Even Lucas had gone down for prayer. But Victoria hadn't.

When people began to faint under the influence of the Holy Spirit, Victoria became frightened, failing to comprehend the omnipotent power of God, having never experienced so great a move of His Holy Presence. About to excuse herself from the service, Texas reminded her of an incident that occurred in Acts.

The Bible Scripture described manifestation of tongues of fire as first-century believers of different nationalities assembled to worship. During the miraculous gathering believers spoke in unfamiliar languages and shared their amazing testimonies.

Skeptics accused the participants of being drunk. Accepting the fact that it was impossible to understand how God worked, Victoria prayerfully listened and watched all that was taking place.

"Victoria?" Texas leaned over and whispered. "Don't you want to go down to the altar? Maybe you should tell Brother Joe about your language gift. I'm sure he has some ideas."

Shaky inside, Victoria shook her head no.

"Baby, listen to me," Texas made a second appeal. "If God has granted you the intelligence to interpret languages, don't you think you should explore the idea? Don't be afraid, please."

"I am afraid," Victoria admitted, tears scalding her cheeks. "What if I pass out like the others?" All she could think about was the coma she'd experienced years before, going in and out of reality. She didn't want to be in that state of mind ever again.

"Why are you so afraid, dear?" he asked.

Victoria shrugged her shoulders. "I'm a coward."

"No, you're not. We'll prove it."

Victoria allowed Texas to take her by the hand and lead her down the aisle. For some reason, she did not resist. Maybe her desire to confirm God's will for her life was greater than her fear. Perhaps Brother Joe could explain why God had entrusted her with so powerful a gift. One question loomed in Victoria's mind.

Was she God's anointed?

26

Fernwood, Tennessee

The explosion was loud, bright and sizzling. Sarah Boswell's dark eyes widened in disbelief as she whipped her car around so fast in the middle of the street it made her dizzy.

Wow! Witnessing the incineration of her house suddenly reduced her to a whimpering child as fear stabbed her in the gut.

"*That* was meant for me."

After Sarah quit shaking, she realized what had to be done next. "I have to call Tanya." She grappled for her cellphone inside her purse, her right hand shaking so hard she dropped the cell on the floorboard. "Calm down, Sarah," she warned herself, her heart thumping out of her chest. "It's all right, you're alive."

Instinctively, Sarah knew life had forever changed. Five minutes later and she would have been inside the exploding house.

"What were you thinkin', girl?" she babbled to herself. "Getting mixed up with someone like Victoria Martin Tempest."

Sarah held one hand to the steering wheel while she felt for the phone on the floorboard with the other. Grasping it, she laid the cell on its back and hurriedly punched in Tanya's number.

"Com'on, Tan. Answer before I lose it here!"

The line rang five times before the message center clicked on.

"No, Tanya! I'm not leaving a message," Sarah rasped, driving the car down the middle of the street like a maniac, cutting corners and screeching the tires. "I'm driving to Birmingham tonight to see you, Tan. And you'd better be there or else."

The path leading away from clear and present danger was laid out in Sarah's mind like a roadmap. God help her to succeed.

***

Barbados Island in the Caribbean

"I can't sleep, Mark." Karen nudged him in the back with a hand. "Get up and let's take a moonlight walk along the beach." The insomnia that went with pregnancy was getting on her nerves.

Huh? Mark rolled over, opened one eye and winced. "Are you serious? Is this what married life is going to be like?" he insensitively quipped, lying back down and closing his eyes.

"Mark!" Karen reacted. "Wake up!"

"Sorry, dear." He yawned.

Like a fuzzy old bear aroused, Mark slowly pulled himself to a sitting position, rolled his legs off the bed, and glared at the blinking clock. "What time is it?"

"I don't know. I think the electricity went off."

"Oh." Mark came to his feet, slipped on his khaki shorts and peered down at Karen. "If this is a baby thing, and you're hungry for something outrageous to eat, I will forgive you for waking me this time." He was too routine-oriented for a late-night stroll.

"Actually, I'm craving a juicy dill pickle," Karen admitted. "I think I'm getting past my nausea and into the eating stage. I'll probably get as big as a hog before I deliver this bambino."

"Let's hope not." Mark put on his tee shirt, a grin tugging at his lips. "I kind of like that cute little figure you walk around in." He grasped Karen's cold hand and kissed her knuckles, feeling cold air blowing through the overhead vent. "Do I need to turn up the AC?" He thought women overheated while pregnant.

"No, we'll warm up outdoors." Karen ran her long manicured fingers through her frosted-blond hair. "After that amazing display of affection you showed me a few hours ago, I don't want to get away from this bed for very long."

"Me, either." Mark pulled Karen to her feet and sweetly kissed her on the forehead. "Come on, honey. Let's go feed that little fella in your tummy." He could humor her this once.

The sand on the beach glistened. It was a balmy evening, the half moon overcast in a thin silvery haze. Wet sand clung to their sandals like glue as Mark and Karen joined hands and walked alongside the receding ocean. The night was very peaceful.

"Look!" Karen pointed to large crabs scurrying about the beach in search of smaller critters.

"In a big hurry for something," Mark commented. Jellyfish lay beached all around them, now dead and abandoned by the waves. A distinct odor of decaying fish clung to the humid air.

"Food, Mark. Everything living needs food."

They found a small restaurant open a quarter of a mile down the beach from the hotel where they were staying. Mark ordered breakfast, but Karen kept to her first craving and had a huge, juicy half-pound hamburger with all the vegetable trimmings.

"Thank you for coming out with me." Karen wanted a second glass of milk. "It was sweet of you to humor me."

"Anything for you and the little one," Mark replied, thoughts returning to the wedding that was certain to make the morning papers describing the role of mother-in-law versus the bride.

As if reading his mind, Karen said, "Don't worry about Mother. She'll be fine." Tears were poised to flow. *Would she?*

"I'm not," Mark answered. "But I sure hope Dick saves us a copy of the Sunday morning *Fernwood Gazette*. I bet we got more coverage than any other wedding held at the country club chapel."

He chuckled, envisioning Victoria as she walked past Dick Branson and climbed into the bride's white limousine.

"For now, I just want to enjoy us," Karen remarked. "Ready to go back to the hotel?" She was a bit sleepy after having food.

"Yeah, if you are," said Mark.

When he'd paid their tab, they left the diner and took their time in walking back to the hotel, enjoying the sounds of the roaring waves white capping and rolling onto the beach with each breath of the ocean. Here, they were far away from confusion.

"I wonder what Mother is doing now," Karen wouldn't let the subject alone. "Was it sad saying goodbye to her?" She lent Mark her large hazel eyes, truly confident in his love. "I mean— you were very close to her for almost a year." *Intimate.*

Mark stopped in his tracks and turned to Karen. "If you're asking me do I still love Vicki, the answer is yes. I will always have a place in my heart for your mother. She was my best friend and first love. You can't forget a feeling like that."

Karen glanced down. She hadn't been asking for that much honesty. Mark's statement of undying love for her mother rattled her ego a bit. There was still a place of unrest in her heart.

"Should I be jealous, Mark?" Karen explored the touchy topic, needing all of Mark's affection and hoping that she would eventually become the most important person in his life.

A baby would make all the difference.

"Jealous? No. I love you, too. In a slightly different way, but much more settled than my former relationship with your mother. I was always on edge with Vicki."

"How so?"

"Vicki kept me guessing about her feelings, and deep down, I always knew her heart belonged to Jeffrey."

"What a shame!" Karen kicked off her sandals, bare feet sinking into the spongy sand. "Mother missed a great chance at a second happiness. Daddy has been dead so long, you'd think she would move ahead." It was futile to think she'd solve his murder.

"Well, I'm not so sure about that. It appears Vicki has another man in her life now." Mark envisioned the tall, handsome Texan with sea-green eyes—the man with her in Rome.

"Mother always did like an adventure," Karen sarcastically noted. "Well, she certainly has her saga now! A fugitive running from the law, homeless and living on the streets, befriending strangers like family—" the truth left a foul taste in her mouth.

"Hey, baby." Mark put an arm around his new bride and hugged her. "I sense a bit of sarcasm in your words. Forgive your mother. I have. Life goes on. This is *our* honeymoon, not hers."

"Really?" Karen's eyes misted. "You truly mean that with all your heart? We can put our past grievances behind us and start anew? Build a life together and become a real family?"

"That's what I'm talking about, honey." Mark hugged Karen. "Now let's go back to the hotel and get some rest. We have plenty of time later today to play."

Karen yawned. "You're right. Now that my stomach is full, I'm really sleepy." The hotel was within sight now.

"Good girl." Mark fondly patted his wife on the rump, his mind turning to pleasant memories. But the face in his mind was Vicki's, not Karen's. He could not yet give Karen his whole heart.

27

Fernwood, Tennessee

One of Dick's goons phoned him on his cell after the explosion on 106 Kenneth Street occurred. The police were on the site investigating the catastrophe. The deed was done.

"The house is gone," the informer told Dick. "You don't have to worry about anything, Mr. Branson."

Dick smiled. "Thank you for the good report. I'll be in touch." Money purchased a lot of gratification in life.

Poor Sarah Boswell had forgotten to turn off a gas eye and look what damage one little mistake had done. A charred body would be found in the rubble—at least, part of the bone structure.

"Anything else I can do for you, Mr. Branson?"

"Not tonight." Dick hung up the phone.

"Well, well," he mumbled as he entered the master bedroom.

"Who was on the phone?" Marjorie roused from a deep sleep. "I can't imagine anyone being so rude. What time is it?"

"Late," Dick said. "Go back to sleep. It's nothing for you to worry over." He peeled off his robe and crawled into bed.

"1:15 a.m." Marjorie read the clock dial and rolled over.

No longer sleepy, Dick began to worry over what he didn't know. According to Andy Grimes, the Tempest file was missing from his house for over an hour. His wife Cheryl had stupidly believed Officer Sarah Boswell's lie that Andy had requested the file and let her have it. Maybe the pesky woman only viewed its contents, but Dick couldn't discount the possibility the cop had made copies and placed them somewhere or with somebody for safekeeping. There were a lot of unknowns hanging out there.

No, Dick thought he shouldn't just assume that the Hearty Meats' environmental indiscretion was still a secret. He had to know exactly what Sarah Boswell had done from the second her greedy-little hands had touched the file until the second she handed it back over to Cheryl Grimes. To do that, he would need an investigator. Dick dialed Jake Kyle's number and woke him.

"Get up Jake. I need a favor and it pays well." Dick explained in detail how he wanted the matter handled.

***

The revival meeting at the Dickson County cave ended shortly after midnight. Surprisingly, Victoria wasn't a bit tired. She'd had a wonderful moment of rededication at the altar, and Brother Joseph Glower was a great listener. She'd told him about her husband's death, her amnesia for twenty-five years and recent recovery, the situation with flip-flopped memories, and her determination to solve the crime that had stolen much of her life.

The issue of Victoria's ability to speak and interpret foreign tongues was not something that could be boxed and its parts examined, Brother Joe had said. But at least Victoria had been reassured that God was the gift-giver and in control. Joe suggested that she pray about the gift and wait on the Holy Spirit for direction. Meanwhile, she should live every day for Jesus.

The five of them were in Jon's SUV headed home. Jon was driving and Lucas had long drifted off to sleep in Marilyn's lap. Texas was in the back seat with Victoria, quieter than usual. There was much Victoria wanted to say to him, but not now.

Marilyn informed Jon that she felt physically better after Pastor Glower had prayed with her. Victoria was afraid that hope was not enough to produce healing from cancer. In Victoria's experience, miracles were rare. But then she'd forgotten much.

If Marilyn Branson was immediately healed, it was not evident. The woman still looked sickly around the eyes, thin as a rail, bearing a ghostly countenance. Definitely, time would tell.

"Where are we going now?" Victoria peered at Texas.

"Back to Jon's apartment in Selmer. I left my helicopter parked nearby, at a private airport. Lucas and I are flying home tonight. Do you want to come with us?"

Victoria seriously considered the proposal before answering.

"No, I'm going directly to Canada, to see my mother. It's been way too long. She'll think I've abandoned her."

I'll think you've abandoned me, Texas thought but didn't say.

"I would offer to take you to GloryVale if I didn't have to deliver microchips to Seattle the first of the week. Also, Lucas is due at camp bright and early Monday morning. Alice will hate not seeing you." He reached over and grasped Victoria's cold hand.

"Tell Alice I'll be over to sample her great cooking before long." She squeezed Texas's hand. "I know you want me to go with you and Lucas, but I have a couple of matters I need to take care of first." The money in Zurich's bank came to mind.

"Mmm, should I ask?" Texas raised an eyebrow. "You're not thinking of going over to Zurich to try out your shiny key?"

Victoria blushed, Texas knew her so well. "Oh, that thing!" She nervously wound a strand of hair around her finger. Why should she be embarrassed over recovering her own funds? Did Texas think it was wrong to have money?

"The key that holds potential," he said with a sigh.

"It's not the money," Victoria protested. "There are a lot of other things that are more important to me." She was not shallow like most people believed, or was she? Did she just forget?

"Like what?" Texas toyed with Victoria, a smile clawing at his lips. "I have the time to listen. Lay it on me, baby."

"Well," Victoria swallowed hard. "Like going to visit my mother." Taking care of the elderly was important. "Oh, did you know that Tom Hopkins wife, Mimosa, recently died?" She was suddenly struck by the fact she had not told Texas.

"No." Texas' expression turned raw. "What happened to Mim?" He was ashamed he had neglected to stay in contact with Tom. "Is there anything I can do to help?"

"I'm not sure. Mother said it was sudden. A heart attack, I believe. Everyone was totally surprised," Victoria added.

"That's too bad. Tom must be devastated." He had been there and done that. "Soon as I'm able, I'm going to spend some time with Tom. He was a lot of comfort when my—" he stopped.

"When your wife died," Victoria finished his statement. "You don't have to tiptoe around the subject, Texas. I know you loved Joann and miss her. A person never forgets a lifetime partner, no matter how short or long the marriage lasts."

"You're talking about Jeffrey now, aren't you?" Texas asked. "His death is still fresh in your mind because of your amnesia. I'm so sorry, honey. Sometimes I'm an insensitive boar."

"No, please don't think that!" Victoria reacted. "We've gotten pretty close in the past two months. Friends, I mean." She didn't know how to describe her feelings or what to say next.

"Yes, we have. And our friendship is growing." He cleared his throat. "You'll be at GloryVale when I get there, won't you?"

"Sure." Victoria licked her dry lips. *Would she?*

"I'll miss you, Victoria. Will you find some time for me?" Texas smiled. "We need to talk about our future." She had avoided his affections long enough. It was time to take the lead.

"Of course, I always have time for you."

"You don't sound very convincing," Texas noted.

Victoria smoothed out a wrinkle in her linen pants with a hand, mulling over the idea of a deeper relationship with Texas. Jeffrey's murder was unsolved and she was a fugitive running from the law. Shouldn't she get her life in order before tying Texas to her problems? Would that be fair to him?

149

"What are you thinking?" Texas could see Victoria's mind working by the troubled expression on her face. "You're not having second thoughts about us, are you?"

"*Us?* No," Victoria replied. "It's just that—"

"Good." An explanation was not required. He settled back in his seat and peered out the window. The sky had partially cleared, but there were rumblings of new storms on the horizon.

Victoria wanted a little space. She had shared quite a lot of herself with many people during the past few hours. There were private matters she preferred handling alone—like consulting a CPA surgeon about removing the lesions on her brain.

Surgery would not be a pleasant experience.

But afterwards, she might be able to recall her former life— which might be tricky since she had once loved Dr. Mark James and was prepared to marry him until April 14th when her memories suddenly flip-flopped. Was she ready to deal with that?

However, Victoria argued with herself, recall would give her a clearer picture of who she had been before her memories flip-flopped, and the kind of life she had formerly chosen. Then she could better deal with her past sins and seek God's forgiveness.

What about my ability to interpret languages?

As far as Victoria knew, her linguistic abilities were limited to a few languages, like Spanish and Italian. If the phenomenon were a quirk of her brain, she might lose the gift when the scar tissue came out. But if the gift were Spirit-driven, it would persist.

Regardless of the consequences of surgery, Victoria had to know for sure whether her unusual ability stemmed from a physical condition or the spiritual realm. She wanted to look Old Fear in the face and shoot her little stone at it, like David had Goliath. Her future hung in the balance.

What was it that the evangelist said to her? "God will soon reveal His plan to you. The voice will be clear, the path made plain. There will be no way you can mistake His divine purpose for your life. Pay attention, Victoria. God is on His throne."

Texas scooted closer to Victoria and wrapped an arm around her shoulder. "Don't you know I love you, Victoria?" he softly whispered. "I thought we were a team. I thought we formed a bond in Italy. But I feel you pulling away from me. Why?"

"I'm sorry." Victoria made eye contact. "I didn't mean to give you the impression we were permanently parting ways."

But she had mentally distanced herself from him. There were some issues she must face alone, her reasons difficult to explain.

"Don't ever leave me or forsake me," Texas pleaded.

"I won't, I promise." Victoria had not yet fully defined her commitment to Texas. Were they simply comrades in Christ? Good friends who had met by chance? Or were they to become lovers in God's time, wearing golden rings on their fingers to signify a permanent belonging? "You've blessed my life, Texas."

"Thank you for saying that, Victoria."

"Okay guys, I hear the whispering," Jon called out over the back seat. "What are you two planning? If it's a wedding, the minister shouldn't be last to know," he teased.

"Jon has hit on a great idea, honey. Why don't we get married at the safehouse?" Texas formulated a plan. "Jon can perform the ceremony and I'll take care of the legality through the CPA when I get home." His eyes were wide with speculation.

"What about the honeymoon?" Victoria was reminded of Karen and Mark's trip to Barbados. "Remember I'm going to Canada." She eyed the guys. "You're teasing, aren't you?"

Jon chuckled, eyes on Texas through the mirror.

"I'm not. We can have a belated honeymoon, after you've had surgery," Texas proposed. "We can spend a whole week in, uh," he stopped short of saying *bed*, cheeks blushing orange.

Victoria squeaked a giggle. "Sounds intriguing."

"So am I going to try out my new credentials?" Jon hollered back. "Is there going to be a wedding later today or not?"

"Not," answered Victoria. "I think we need more time to plan." She was flushed with embarrassment over the subject.

28

Detective Jake Kyle had been a private eye for the past ten years. A newcomer to Fernwood, he preferred working independently of the police, so he'd rented a cubbyhole in the basement of the courthouse to see clients.

However, when it came time to solving a major crime, Jake was very much a team partner with the law. He loved the ruse.

Most residents didn't know of his discreet connection with a crime family in Miami, Florida. His attorney ex-brother-in-law took care of the family's business enterprises. As hard as Jake tried to abide by the law, his genes ran on the side of wrongdoing.

When Richard Branson first requested Jake's professional services, he realized from the conversation that the businessman had already explored his references. One call to his brother-in-law confirmed his suspicion. Dick was satisfied with his credentials.

So Jake had agreed to work for Richard Branson and trace the footsteps of Officer Sarah Boswell after she illegally obtained the Jeffrey Tempest file. He began at the most obvious place.

The Speedy Print Copy Shop was a popular place in town. Besides making photocopies, one could also mail UPS packages. Eleanor Mayo was the exclusive owner, and since Jake knew her home address, he decided to get her out of bed and find out if Sarah Boswell had made any copies at her shop the day before.

Jake pulled into Elli's driveway and climbed out of his yellow-and-white, two-tone vintage Buick and rapped on her front door.

"Sorry to wake you up, Elli," Jake said as soon as she cracked the front door. "But . . ." he flashed his credentials, "it's police business and criminals don't keep business hours. Hope you don't mind the imposition." He shoved open her door and secured it with his big foot. They were going to talk, like it or not.

"For heavens sake, Jake, it's 3 a.m.!" Elli exclaimed. "Can't this matter wait until morning?" She glanced around the yard like she expected to see squad cars parked there.

"Sorry, it can't." He pushed past the lanky woman and entered her lamp-lit den. Closing the door, she followed him.

"What is this about?" Elli clung to her flimsy robe to keep it from falling open. "Did the neighbors see you come in?" she asked like they would think something hanky-panky was going on.

Jake shook his head "no" to put her at ease.

A clanging grandfather clock belatedly registered the hour.

"It's important, Elli," he said. "May I sit down?"

"Sure. What kind of emergency brings you to my door at this hour?" she asked. In her early forties, already graying, Elli had crow's feet ensconced around her widely set pale-green eyes.

"Officer Sarah Boswell died tonight—in a gas explosion at her house. I'm investigating the steps she took yesterday before the trail grows cold. I was hoping you could lend some insight."

"You think she was murdered?" Alarm spread over Elli's angular face. Almost pretty, her hard eyes gave her a used look.

"I don't know, Elli. I'm simply after the facts."

"Why, come to think of it," Elli placed a polished fingernail at her temple, "Sarah was at my shop late yesterday afternoon. Around five o'clock, I believe. She was making a lot of copies. Pretty secretive, if you ask me," she whispered. "Is that helpful?"

"Very," Jake replied, a smile curling his lips. "Do you have any idea where Sarah was headed when she left your shop?" He jotted down Eleanor's statement on a notepad. "Did she say anything to suggest what materials she was copying?"

"No. Every time I came close, Sarah covered her papers like they were top-secret," Elli recalled with clarity. "Did her death have something to do with what she was copying?"

"Let me ask the questions," Jake suggested, "then I'll answer yours." He hoped he hadn't responded too harshly. "I appreciate your help, Elli. There will be a small check in the mail to you."

"Who's paying?" she asked. "I don't want any trouble."

"My client, but he wishes to remain anonymous. He really liked the Boswell gal and wants to know more about what happened to her." Whether Dick Branson was involved in the cop's death was none of Jake's business. "Do you want to add anything to your statement?" He waited for a response.

"No, I think that's all." Elli yawned. "Want some coffee?"

"No, I need to go."

"You might call first the next time you want to visit."

"Sure," said Jake with a smile. "Sorry for the trouble. See you at the copy machine." He got up to leave.

"Sure. Do you ever take time off for lunch?" Elli hinted at a date with Jake. Single and a known swinger, she was an easy conquest. Her husband had been dead for over a year and Jake guessed she was extending her horizons.

"Sometimes." Jake smiled. "But right now I'm pretty busy."

Elli's countenance took a dive. "Can't blame a girl for tryin'." She squeezed Jake's arm. "Hope you find out what happened to Officer Boswell. Dying in a fire must be a terrible fate."

"I will," Jake said. "And thank you for your time."

"Just so you know, I do entertain male guests on occasions." Elli winked at Jake. "Just so you know."

"You're all right, Elli. No pretense."

"I can be a lot of fun if you let me." She laughed.

"I bet you could." Jake opened the front door and left the house. Sometimes when he was lonesome, he might just give her a call, get together for a little R and R to suit them both.

Jake returned to his Buick and put in a call to Dick, relaying what he had learned from Eleanor Mayo. That Sarah Boswell had made copies at the Speedy Print Shop didn't make Dick happy.

"What do you want me to do next?" Jake asked.

"Find out where Sarah went after she left the copy shop. I want to know the names of everybody she talked to and what she said to them. She's bound to have left a trail you can follow."

"Let's hope," Jake replied. "I'll get back to you."

"You do that, son. And don't let no grass grow under your feet," Dick said. "I don't like leaving loose ends."

"No, sir. I understand." He would start with a list of names of people who frequented the Speedy Print Shop. Then he'd start asking a lot of questions, if anybody had seen Sarah late yesterday.

Questions like, what kind of vehicle she was driving. Was she driving east or west of town? Was anybody with her?

Then Jake would check all the local gas stations to see if Sarah had gassed up her car. After that, he would examine a Tennessee map to determine where she might have gone.

Did Sarah use her cellphone after 5 p.m.? Her phone service would have a record on file. Somehow, some way, Jake would turn up a lead. Investigating a homicide was his job.

***

Baghdad, Iraq

Ahmed Ramallah kept his promise to Alexander Luceres Ramnes, a man he had met at Harvard University a decade before. Trust was very important in any friendship, and theirs had resulted in a mutual respect canonized with an occasional exchange of favors—which in this case involved a personal matter.

At this moment, Luceres' bad half-seed was aboard a charted jet en route to Baghdad. Ahmed trusted that Luceres would later return the favor when he achieved more political power by sanctioning a Muslim jihad movement designed to create a holy utopia united under the one true God, Allah.

Ending the domination of false religions was the dream of all true Islamic peoples. Mohammed was the last prophet in a holy succession of Allah's chosen beginning with Ishmael, Father

Abraham's firstborn. Why should Isaac's descendants through the line of Judah be allowed to acclaim Jesus Christ as the one true savior of the world, when the rightful heir was Mohammed?

No, truth was worth fighting for, even if bloodshed was required. Ahmed joined millions of other devout Muslims prepared to die for their beliefs. He had Luceres "tagged" from the beginning as a brother because of their common goal: to unite the world. Although the politician did not embrace the Muslim faith, or any other religion, he was a man of ingenuity and reason.

However, Christians had quickly labeled Luceres as "the" Antichrist predicted by the Bible because he had sponsored PEACE FIRST, a decree denying Christians the right to proselyte.

When Luceres arrived in Baghdad tomorrow, Ahmed would remind his good friend of their future plans to unite the world under a Muslim government. Only then would true peace occur.

As far as the half brother, Lazarus Roger Bacon, he was already dead if Luceres gave the word. Death was not the end of life. It was only the beginning. *Praise Allah!*

29

When the private jet landed in Baghdad, Lazarus Bacon deplaned with Gordon. The boy had slept most of the way and seemed excited about seeing Iraq. Just keep him happy.

Holding tightly to Gordon's hand, Lazarus passed through the umbilical tube and entered the bright lights of the terminal.

Gordon paused to get his bearings, then headed toward a sign marked BAGGAGE. He was extremely pleased that the captive had followed him like a sheep being led to slaughter.

Whimsically caught up in his private musings of Baghdad, Gordon realized he had not been in the Baghdad Airport since he was fourteen. The facility had been enlarged and modernized by the Americans during the rebuilding of Iraq following George Bush's "War for Iraqi Freedom." American occupation in the country had continued for years after the fighting ended, to ensure that a democratic puppet government was firmly established.

Regardless how hard Americans tried, they never changed the political view of the Iraqi people when it came to religion and government. Allah was supreme and ruled over all matters.

The Muslim faith prospered under the surface of a calm, so-called democratic Iraq. Young people who had lost family in the Iraqi War had grown up with grudges against the Americans for interfering in old-world customs and religious practices.

Gordon knew the time would eventually come when millions of devout Muslims would rise up and forcefully reclaim their right to practice their faith. To accomplish so magnificent a task would require an exceptional leader with diplomatic and social skills like those of Alexander Luceres Ramnes. To many, the man was the savior of the world because of his revolutionary ideas in creating a one-world government under the auspices of brotherly love and peace. Not that Gordon believed in all that, or trusted in any god.

"Gordo? When can I meet my brother?" Lazarus asked.

"Soon." Gordon made eye contact. "Someone will meet us outside the terminal and transport us to our final destination."

"I hope Natalie doesn't get into trouble because of me." It was unusual for Lazarus to be concerned for another person's welfare, but he actually liked Natalie. And he knew she loved him.

"Good thing we phoned her then, to put her mind at rest," Gordon lied. "Natalie will understand that visiting Baghdad is a great learning experience. You'll be back home in no time."

"I don't think my daddy will approve," the lad said.

"Then don't tell him."

"I've always wanted to visit the Middle East," said Lazarus. "I like the way people think over here."

"Oh?" said Gordon. "And how is that?"

"Fight for what you want," he answered.

"Well, I suppose that is what gets a person ahead in life," said Gordon. "Don't worry about Natalie. She can take care of herself. By late Tuesday, we'll be on the plane and headed back to Washington. You can jump into your soft bed as if nothing ever happened." Gordon had no idea if what he said were true.

"Can I take my brother home with me?" Lazarus asked.

"You can ask him that question yourself."

"When?"

"Soon," said Gordon.

Lazarus was impatient. He wanted to meet his brother *now*. When he didn't get his way, it made him cranky. He felt the anger rising in him like smoldering smoke from a fiery pit. When the rage surfaced, he had to send it somewhere. *Where?*

He spied an old man hobbling down the terminal. *There!* Lazarus released the building energy as he blew out his breath in the direction of the sick man. A nanosecond later, the man grasped his tightening chest and keeled over. *Rest, now.*

"Help! Help!" a woman standing nearby cried out as the man collapsed in the middle of the terminal. A Delta attendant rushed over and knelt beside the man, feeling his pulse. "This man is dead," said the attendant. "Call security at once!"

Lazarus felt a whole lot better now. He hated the way the angry energy felt inside him. He had to let it go or it would only grow worse inside him. And since there were no animals around, well . . . in fact, Lazarus was beginning to feel hungry again.

30

Zurich, Switzerland

It was 11:00 a.m. Sunday when Donald Wetherfield arrived at the private residence of Alexander Luceres Ramnes. At his side was Georgie Hendricks, appearing unhealthy from weeks of illness, lack of nourishing food, and drinking tainted water.

The female detective, though crude, was an invaluable asset when it came to luring Victoria Martin Tempest. Only a friend might convince the international fugitive to come forward and cooperate with Luceres. Donald's job was to make that happen.

"You're sure your boss wants to see me?" Georgie asked as Donald formerly rang the doorbell to the lacquered chalet glistening in the bright morning sunlight. "You don't have to do this, you know." She jerked her arm from his grasp.

"Do what?" Donald chuckled. "Introduce you to one of the most famous individuals on earth? I should think you'd be jumping up and down for the privilege."

"*Yippi-i-kiya!*" Georgie made a half-hearted leap into the air and landed with a thud on her weak ankles, nearly spraining them as she recalled a Bruce Willis' victory cry from an old flick thriller.

"I saw that movie. Pretty good, wasn't it? If I remember correctly, Bruce got banged up pretty bad for resisting the bad guys. Don't follow suit." He penetrated her armor with his gaze.

Georgie caught the gist of his warning. "No sir, I won't." She saluted. "I'm in the army now." She whistled "Dixie," using her hands to mimic playing a flute. He didn't seem amused.

The door swung open and Georgie sobered. This was not a trip to the mall, she realized. These two men had the power to take away her last breath. She'd better shape up and hear them out or suffer the consequences. She had tried getting cute with the men who kidnapped her in front of Devin Baldwin's house, and just look where she'd ended up. *Nope.* Just play it cool, girl.

"Hello, Luceres." Donald was on a first-name basis with his boss when he wasn't working out in the public.

Mouth clamped and irritated to the core, Georgie wasn't in a social mood, especially since she was the bacon Donald was bringing home to feed the political leader's insatiable curiosity.

"And who is this beautiful lady?" Luceres' strange olive eyes eclipsed in the sunlight and fell solidly upon Georgie.

"Detective Georgie Hendricks," she announced, sweeping a lock of sun-streaked hair off her forehead. "At your service."

"Don't pay any attention to Georgie, she's just feeling her morning oats." Donald pinched the detective's arm hard.

"*Oats?* I'm afraid I don't understand." Luceres scrutinized his guest. "Is she taking drugs?" His gaze swallowed Donald.

Half smiling, Georgie wrenched her arm from Donald and peered at Luceres. "My friend Donald said you had a few questions you wanted to ask. So what'd ya wanna know?"

The world leader burst out in laughter, eyes cutting over on Donald. "I thought you said the woman was difficult. She's absolutely delightful." Luceres crossed his muscular arms over his chest, feet spread to support his impressive frame. Wearing a white turtleneck sweater, dark pleated slacks, and Italian leather loafers, the leader might have stepped off a fashion magazine.

Delightful? What's this? No eye for an eye?

"Come inside." Luceres pulled back the door.

Nudged through the doorway, Georgie cast her eyes upon the chalet's opulent contents, anxious to be offered a seat and a foreign beer. Didn't happen. So she waited for instructions.

"I've prepared some hot decaffeinated tea." Luceres smiled. "I don't drink beer, or allow strong beverages in my house."

Humph. Somehow, Georgie felt slighted. "Decaf tea sounds like a winner," she cooperated. "With lots of lemon, please."

Donald chuckled. "I told you he's nice."

La-de-da! Georgie couldn't resist elbowing Donald. Being around him seemed to bring out the mischievous child in her.

"I'll do the talking from here on out," she leaned over and whispered in Donald's ear. "Go play captor somewhere else!"

"Not a chance," he returned. "I'm watching you like a hawk. Make one wrong move—well, don't test me, all right?"

If Luceres overheard Georgie's outrageous conversation with Donald, he didn't act like it, playing nice like he really meant it.

"Won't you have a seat, Miss Hendricks?" Luceres pointed to the leather sofa. "After tea, we'll speak briefly then nap."

Nap? That's all Georgie had done for the last eight hours.

"You've had a long ordeal, Miss Hendricks. You must be exhausted," Luceres insisted. "You'll use the bedroom at the end of the hall to your right. If you need a sedative to sleep more soundly, there's packaged Benadryl on the bathroom counter."

Not enough for an overdose, Georgie figured.

A whimsical smile materialized on her host's face.

"No, I'm good," she said in response, "and I'm not a bit sleepy." Was he trying to sedate her so she'd talk more freely?

The teapot began singing so the three musketeers adjourned to the kitchen. While Luceres filled three dainty china cups with teabags and boiling water, Donald commented on their long trip.

From the way the men conversed, Georgie could tell they were good friends. And in spite of her dislike for being brought to Switzerland against her will, she found her captors entertaining. The world leader was all that the news media had promised. His manners were impeccable—not to mention his kindness and sensitivity to her physical needs after a long international flight.

Was she so easily duped? Caution captured Georgie's thoughts.

"How is your tea?" Luceres asked Georgie after she had sampled the delicious peach blend and consumed a half dozen frosted cookies to boot. "Do you need more sugar?"

"Please," she answered, scooping more granules in her cup.

The three of them sat down at the round, polished cherry table with a vase of fresh fall flowers placed in the center. Luceres talked about the unusual weather in Switzerland, then Donald detailed a few amusing events he had experienced during his adventure to America. After a bit, Georgie rudely yawned.

Noting his guest's boredom, Luceres inquired of Georgie, "How does a relaxing dip in my hot Jacuzzi tub sound? It's just what we all need before a delicious lunch."

Not enchanted with the idea, Donald walked over to the box on the wall that controlled the Jacuzzi and pulled the switch. "The water needs to warm up before we get in," he said.

"Dip, Miss Hendricks?" Luceres restated his invitation.

She was a *dip wad*, all right, but a soak with Donald in the tub was out of the question. Besides, she didn't bring a bathing suit.

"Go on, Donald." Luceres shooed him away. "You're tough. Get on your bathing suit and hop in. The heater will soon have the cool water at a perfect temperature."

When Donald didn't budge a muscle, a subtle rage washed over Luceres' face. No one crossed the leader, Georgie suspected.

"Actually, a float in your hot tub sounds nice," she said to bring the moment into harmony. "What about it, Donald?"

"I'll get Georgie a swimsuit and put it in her bedroom." Donald tromped out of the kitchen appearing distressed.

"There's a chenille robe hanging in the closet in your room, Miss Hendricks. We'll see you in the Jacuzzi in a few minutes."

"Sure," said Georgie as Luceres walked into the den and disappeared behind a door she assumed was the master bedroom.

Fifteen minutes later, they were all cozy in the Jacuzzi.

The "dip" was not unpleasant, the water warm and bubbly. Georgie relaxed, thinking spending a few days in Switzerland free gratis wasn't so bad. Nobody had tried to push her buttons. *Yet.*

Luceres had an opinion regarding everything going on in the world from politics and religion to the unreliable stock markets and banking practices. Georgie had been so poor most of her life that the leader's assessments had no real significance, other than to draw attention away from her—which was just fine.

Georgie yawned and stretched in the Jacuzzi.

"See, Donald." Luceres grinned. "Like I said, the lady needs to relax. Everyone out! It's time we had our lunch."

The leader stepped from the hot tub and grasped a towel from the wooden rack, briskly drying water droplets from his bronzed skin. A perfect human specimen, his complexion was flawless, his sculptured features as perfect as a Roman god's.

Lunch was prepared and waiting in the refrigerator. Luceres removed a tray of cold cuts, tasty cheeses, sliced tomatoes, and crisp lettuce. From the oven he pulled a tray of warm sliced homemade bread. Georgie's sandwich melted in her mouth.

Everyone ate ferociously. At the end of the meal, a slice of cheesecake floating in orange sauce was placed before Georgie, perfectly satisfying her craving for sweets. She widely yawned.

"Why don't you turn down our guest's bed?" Luceres said to Donald. "I let the housekeeper leave early today."

Georgie's gaze swung between the two.

"No problem," said Donald. "You said she was to take the back bedroom?" His eyes skittered to Georgie.

"That's correct, Donald. After you have done that, get some rest, will you? You seem slightly out of sorts today."

Georgie suppressed a giggle, amused at the interaction. "Out of sorts" aptly described Donald, she thought, attempting to absorb the idea that she had actually landed in the lap of luxury.

Then, as Donald left the kitchen, Luceres had to go and ruin everything. "Tell me, *Georgie*, how did you and Victoria Tempest first meet?" He moved to a first-name basis, smile widening.

Grrrr! Georgie stiffened. *So, it was time to talk.* When she answered Luceres' questions didn't matter. She would never betray Victoria's trust. The host patiently waited for a response.

"Shoot! I might as well get this over with," she said.

"You won't be sorry," Luceres responded.

A reassuring pat on Georgie's hand came next.

"Okay, my first contact with Victoria was in Memphis, Tennessee, by phone when she called my apartment in April and asked to meet with me at O'Charley's to discuss a legal matter."

"Why contact you?" Luceres inquired.

"It was a referral, from a local Memphis attorney." Georgie saw no reason to give Devin Baldwin's name. "Victoria was lookin' for a private eye to assist in finding her husband's killers."

"I assume you know Victoria pretty well by now. Do you think your client is capable of cold-blooded murder?"

"Wow! You don't waste time, do you?" Georgie intended to give Luceres enough information to satisfy his need to know.

"Answer the question, please."

"No, I don't believe Victoria has a malicious bone in her."

Luceres smiled. "More tea?"

Tea? "Yes, please," Georgie replied, the room temperature feeling chilly after being in the hot Jacuzzi water.

Luceres poured boiling water into their cups and added fresh teabags. Georgie said thanks and followed the host into the den. The large cushy recliner near the fireplace looked inviting.

"Take the recliner, if you like," Luceres said, as if to read Georgie's mind. "You want to tell me the truth, don't you? But you feel it's unethical," he said to disarm her. "Client privilege."

"So you read minds, too." Georgie sighed. "Unlucky for me." The recliner suddenly felt more like a ball and chain.

"I'm clairvoyant," Luceres admitted. "However, some minds are more difficult to decipher than others." Victoria Tempest was an unusual human specimen, her thoughts virtually unreadable.

"Then I'd better be careful what I think, hadn't I?" Georgie felt like an open book waiting to be psychologically scanned.

"All I want is an opinion, Georgie. If your client has been falsely accused of murder, consider it my privilege to assist her in solving the crime. Let's keep it simple, shall we?"

K.I.S.S. She smiled. *Keep it simple, stupid.*

"Why do you want to speak to Victoria so badly?"

"First-hand testimony is far more revealing than second-hand knowledge. Isn't there something you want very badly in life, Georgie? What will it take for me to earn your cooperation?"

Luceres dangled the bait for a nanosecond.

"As you can see, buster, I am very needy." Georgie came out of her seat, indignant. Her apartment had been bombed, she had no cash, and little hope of resuming a normal life under the circumstances. "I'm not the kind of person you can buy."

"I know that," Luceres replied, waving his hand for Georgie to be seated again. "Convince your client to speak to me, and I'll see that at least a part of your carnal dreams come true. I am willing to meet Victoria anywhere she chooses on neutral ground. You can be present to see that my tactics don't get out of hand."

Tactics? At that, Georgie guffawed. "What about your thug, Donald? Anthony Vorices is even worse. If that's how you get things done, forgive me if I want no part of it. Can I leave now?"

"You drive a hard bargain, Georgie."

"I drive no bargain at all!"

"Even if I give you my word that I will treat your client with the utmost respect? Victoria needs my help and you know it. Why not expedite our meeting and become the hero?"

"Why are you so interested in her plight?" Georgie tilted her head to one side. "She's nobody important in society."

"I'll decide that, Georgie. Beside, it's in my nature to help. Ask anyone who knows me well. That's why I was named the International Man of the Year. I am a philanthropist at heart."

"So, say I believe you," Georgie said. "What's in it for me?"

"Freedom," Luceres replied.

"Does that include protection from Richard Branson?"

"You have my word."

"Victoria has a daughter who lives in Fernwood." Georgie's tongue came unglued. "I could give Karen a call and ask if she knows how to contact her mother. That's the best I can do."

"The phone is over there." Luceres pointed. "Make your call." He walked out of the room to give her privacy.

Georgie had Karen's cellular number memorized. She used the phone Luceres had placed on the coffee table before leaving the room. Karen's message center clicked on: "This is Karen Tempest James. Leave a message and I will get back to you."

After *click click*, and many beeps, the recording played out and Georgie hung up. "At least I tried." She profoundly sighed.

***

Around 3:00 in the afternoon, Luceres asked Donald to drive their guest into Zurich and show her a good time. The poor girl had never had an opportunity to travel abroad and experience the culture. A wad of cash exchanged hands. "Have fun."

The idea of sightseeing appealed to Georgie, lifting her drab spirits. For a little while, she could act like a normal tourist.

Donald had just driven away from the chalet when Luceres' cellphone rang. It was Ahmed Ramallah calling from Baghdad.

"I hope you have good news," Luceres remarked.

"Your brother has arrived. When are you coming?"

"I'll be there sometime after my dinner speech scheduled for Monday evening—a fundraiser for the newly elected president of the Independent Democratic States of the Middle East."

It had taken awhile to rid the Middle East of United States occupation and convince the countries of Iraq, Iran, Turkey, Syria, and Saudi Arabia to form a united government under a central body patterned after a democracy. However, there was still a strong Muslim presence in Iraq driving the public elections.

"We're fine here," said Ahmed. "The lad seems interested in learning all he can about the history of Baghdad. He's smart and absorbs information like a sponge," he used perfect English.

"Don't be fooled by the lad's whimsical moods, friend. I've heard my brother has a nasty side when he feels threatened."

"Trust me, I'm keeping him happy." Ahmed laughed.

"Good." Luceres had confronted his own demons and periodically wrestled with setbacks. But Lazarus—like the man Jesus raised from the dead—still had much to learn about himself.

"I will personally attend your brother every step of the way," Ahmed assured Luceres. "Today, we are going into Baghdad to visit a war museum featuring relics collected during the American War for Iraqi Freedom. Don't worry, I have a stun gun with me."

"Don't let Lazarus near an American Embassy," Luceres warned. "His cooperation and interest in foreign affairs may be a ruse. Let's not forget he is the American president's son."

"He wants to phone his nanny. Lazarus doesn't believe Natalie will report him missing if he reassures her he is safe."

"Good. Give the boy a phone," Luceres ordered. "Make sure Lazarus understands the consequences of betrayal. He must not mention his location, or whom he is with."

If the press got wind of the kidnapping . . .

"I think this is smart," Ahmed agreed. "We should satisfy Natalie her charge is unharmed. You can visit with Lazarus, and I'll see that he's home before his parents return to the White House on Thursday. Why create an international crisis?"

"I knew I could count on your ingenuity." Luceres applauded his friend. "I will see you soon."

31

Birmingham, Alabama

After returning home early Sunday, Tanya Mason shut off her cellphone. Unable to sleep, she got out of bed and turned on the tube. A CNN news clip reported the explosion in Fernwood.

Tanya fought panic. The house unmistakably belonged to Sarah Boswell, her dearest friend in the world. No, it couldn't be.

Shoving aside worry over Sarah, reality soon kicked in. Was someone coming after her, too? Should she pack a suitcase for her family immediately and get them out of town?

Tanya's thoughts shattered and raced in several directions.

Her husband Billy was still sleeping, but when he woke up he would question what was going on. Bobby's Trailer Park was no Baptist Women's retreat. She had been party to a criminal act.

Dick Branson found out! That scumbag sheriff, Andy Grimes, told him. And now the meatpacker was making sure Sarah never showed anyone what was in Jeffrey Tempest's notes. As certain as the sun would come up in Birmingham, the "big bad wolf" of Fernwood was coming. Branson never left loose ends untied.

Fifteen minutes later, Billy stumbled out of the bedroom and heard Tanya banging pans in the kitchen. "I thought you went on a retreat with Sarah," he hollered. "Bring me some coffee?"

Billy switched the TV channel to FOX and caught the headlines. Tanya whistled as she made him a big breakfast of biscuits, ham and eggs. Later, when they had chatted about family matters, and his stomach was full, she launched into her drama.

Billy took it pretty well, said it would be okay, that they would pack up and leave the house immediately. What about his work? Tanya wondered. Didn't he need to notify his boss that he was taking some vacation days? She had a ton of "ifs" to consider.

The Postal Service could do without him until he was certain the danger had passed, Billy said. As if on cue, the phone rang.

"It's for you, Tan." Billy handed over the receiver.

Tanya's eyes grew the size of walnuts. "Is that really you, Sarah? I thought you were dead. The reports say a body was found in the rubble of your house—burnt to a crisp except for a few skeletal parts." She was exhilarated over Sarah's resurrection.

"Yeah, it's me. Five minutes later and it would've been me inside the house going up in smoke." Sarah had no idea who had broken into her house. "Somebody died in my place."

"Why didn't you turn off your stove?" Tanya had heard the theory of a gas explosion exploited by the news media.

"I did. I didn't even cook yesterday—had a double-decker at McDonald's for lunch. I always turn off everything before leaving the house." Sarah reviewed her departure from Fernwood.

"Well, something caused the explosion," Tanya said.

"I know. Does Billy know about your involvement?"

"Yeah, he's on his cell right now talking to his boss about taking vacation time. I think we're going to Florida to visit his brother for a couple of weeks. Let this thing blow over."

"That's a good idea," Sarah supported Tanya's decision. "Things aren't exactly normal these days."

"Where are you now?" asked Tanya, eyes skittering to Billy, who had shut down his cellphone and was walking down the hall.

"Not far from you," Sarah replied. "I'm in my car, about five miles from your house. May I come see you?"

"No!" Tanya emphatically replied. "Somebody might be watching the house. Are you familiar with the Utopia Mall off the interstate? Beside it there's a brand new Ramada Inn."

"I can find it," said Sarah.

"Rent a room under the name of . . ." she let her mind grab an identity out of the hat, "under the name of Lucy Boyd."

Billy called out for Tanya to come pack up the kids' things.

"Lucy Boyd. All right. Are you coming alone?"

"Yes," Tanya replied. "Billy is going to pack up the kids and meet me somewhere—we haven't worked out the details."

Tanya sucked in a quick breath, beginning to hyperventilate.

"I hate I involved you," Sarah said.

"I have to admit I'm terrified. Are *they* going to kill us?"

"*They* will have to catch us first. As long as Sheriff Grimes and Dick Branson believe I'm dead, we're got some time to plan."

"You're dead, but what about me?" Tanya rasped. "There could be a sniper lurking outside my house right now. How can I protect my family? Did you call Bobby and warn him?"

"No, but I will." A squad car passed Sarah on the interstate. "I don't think anybody will connect him with us, do you?"

"I hope not," said Tanya. Bobby was their safety net. When he heard about the explosion and Sarah's death, he was sure to contact the FBI "You shouldn't spook him, he's elderly."

"The old die, too." Sarah sighed.

"I'm worried that when forensics gets hold of the charred body come Monday morning they'll know the DNA doesn't match yours. Then what?" Tanya asked.

"I don't know, Tan. I can't think that far ahead."

"Whatever happens, we have about forty-eight hours to get our ducks in a row," Tanya remarked. "See you shortly."

***

Fernwood, Tennessee

Detective Greg Diamond was working in his home office set up in the second bedroom of his compact apartment. Unable to sleep, he had crawled from the tangled sheets to check his messages. A call came in reporting a possible homicide caused by an explosion. The charred remains of a body had been found in the rubble that had once been Officer Sarah Boswell's house.

Likely Sarah's body, Greg deducted. *Too bad*, he thought. *Did someone have a grievance against her? Or was it only an accident?*

There would be an inquiry into the cause of the explosion and verification of the victim's identify. The conclusions of the CSI team would determine the nature of Greg's involvement.

The detective made his way into the kitchen and emptied the decanter of day-old coffee into the stainless-steel sink. Placing a clean filter in the coffeemaker, his thoughts shifted to a more important unsolved case, the murder of Attorney Jeffrey Tempest.

Unlike Sheriff Andrew Grimes, Greg was unconvinced that Jeffrey's wife, Victoria Martin Tempest, was guilty of murder one. However, the evidence certainly implicated her involvement.

The D.A. had the actual life insurance policy signed by Victoria, plus an affidavit from an employee of Caldwell Insurance Company stating she had witnessed Victoria's signature. The fugitive's name and mug was on every major crime network in the world. Why Victoria hadn't been caught was anybody's guess.

"Slippery and conniving," Andy had said of the woman.

Greg had never personally associated with Victoria, but he knew of her benevolent work with the Fernwood Chamber of Commerce and support for other community organizations. She'd given money to schools and helped sponsor sport events.

George Clydesdale was pressing Greg hard to get the case ready for court. "Bad press for the town," Dick Branson had complained, and Sheriff Andy Grimes heartily agreed.

The content of the Tempest file was sketchy at best. All Greg really knew was that the young attorney's office had been ransacked twenty-five years before, his file cabinets cleaned out, a new computer stolen, and petty cash removed from his wall safe.

News of the young attorney's death and his wife's comatose condition drew public sympathy. Newspaper and magazine reporters from all the major U.S. cities responded by printing heart-wrenching stories about the unfortunate incident.

However, lack of criminal evidence to support a murder trial had resulted in the case getting shoved to the side. By the time Victoria regained consciousness, people had lost interest in the case, and it was filed under "unsolved." Suffering from amnesia, she did not press the police to continue the investigation.

A lot of time passed. No one ever expected that Victoria's memories would resurrect. When she began snooping around town and asking a lot of unsettling questions about Jeffrey's death, it was not well received by townsfolk. People wanted to forget.

Victoria's daughter and Dr. Mark James objected to reopening the case, thinking it was irrational to believe the widow could solve the crime when the police had miserably failed.

Dick Branson had reported one instance when Victoria burst into his office without an appointment and accused him of having a hand in the heist. *Unbelievable!* He'd shouted obscenities.

Greg had dug into Fernwood's history and learned Richard Branson was the manager of Hearty Meats at the time of Jeffrey's death and had later raised money to pay Victoria's hospital bills. One would expect the recovered amnesiac to be grateful rather than hostile toward her benefactor. Dick even had a hand in setting up a Gift Trust Fund for Victoria and her children.

So why did Victoria blame Dick for her husband's death?

More recently, in April, Victoria had collapsed at her daughter's condo and was hospitalized in critical condition. Hours later, she mysteriously disappeared from the Hardeman County General Hospital during a power outage caused by a storm. The following morning, incriminating evidence surfaced pointing to her guilt. Greg did not believe in coincidences.

Thumping his pencil eraser on his desk, he let it thrum to a stop. The Tempest case was shrouded in mystery. No one knew exactly what information was inside Jeffrey's stolen files—which made Greg wonder how important the files were to the thieves.

Dr. Mark James said he knew nothing about what was in those files. Was he lying? If so, what was he hiding?

Karen Tempest was too young to remember much about what happened, and her brother Paul was deceased.

In fact, Greg had no eyewitnesses to the theft. The official police report revealed that no windows had been broken from the outside, and that the door locks weren't jimmied. So did someone have a key to Jeffrey's office and use it that night to get in?

Then there was the strange friendship that existed between Dick Branson and Mark James. Greg was huge on motives. Andy Grimes was the third spoke in the wheel, also in tight with Dick.

What am I missing? Greg belabored the case.

Emotions had run high over the murder incident. Jeffrey Tempest came from a long bloodline of attorneys and was well respected. Some people wanted to forget the incident, sold their homes, and moved away without an explanation to neighbors.

From experience, Greg had learned that ten, twenty, thirty years could go by before some piece of evidence in a case showed up. DNA often entered into the equation. Solving a crime was the divine providence of justice. The truth usually came out.

Why no one had mentioned years ago that Victoria had taken out a large life insurance policy on her husband two weeks before he died didn't compute for Greg. Someone must have known.

Why hadn't a representative of Caldwell Insurance Company reported Victoria to the police? Was everyone in Fernwood brain dead at the time? Or was fear a factor in the equation?

Those were critical questions Greg had to ask to solve the cold case. Who were the players in Jeffrey's saga? Who stood to gain from his death? Does the insurance policy still exist?

Or did someone collect the money on Victoria's behalf? Why did Hearty Meats set up a gift trust fund for Jeffrey's widow? Did Dr. Mark James' attentiveness toward Victoria suggest *guilt*?

Greg thumped his pencil on his desk, letting the ratty-tat-tat die out. Much had changed over the decades to alter the landscape in Fernwood since Jeffrey's death. Greg was doing the best he could to get at the truth. He would soon have to give an evaluation to the District Attorney regarding whether the case was ready to go to court. George Clydesdale didn't like losing.

Unbeknownst to others, Greg had placed an ad in the *National Inquirer* offering a healthy reward for any information leading to the name or names of persons who had formerly worked for the Caldwell Insurance Company in Fernwood, Tennessee, in 1989. All Greg needed to exonerate Victoria was one witness willing to testify in court that Jeffrey Tempest initiated his life insurance policy and had asked his wife to sign for him.

But if Victoria isn't responsible for her husband's death, who is? Greg still had a lot of hard investigative work ahead of him.

32

Baghdad, Iraq

After Gordon Smyth delivered Lazarus Bacon, the American President's son, into the hands of Ahmed Ramallah in Baghdad, he was instructed to take a hike while they talked. Gordon left the premises, anticipating he would be paid well.

"Go ahead and call your nanny," Ahmed told Lazarus to downplay the kidnapping. "But remember what I said. You are not to tell Natalie where you are or who brought you here, only that you are fine." He hoped the lad would be cooperative.

"Yes, sir," Lazarus replied, using good manners when it mattered. Traveling overseas and seeing Baghdad was fun, an opportunity of a lifetime. All he'd ever seen of the Middle East were the images on the television or pictures in magazines.

Lazarus dialed Natalie's cell number. It rang and rang and rang. "I don't think she's answering," he told Ahmed.

"Hello. This is Natalie Brooster."

"Hi Natalie," Lazarus said. "You didn't tell my parents I was missing, did you?" His serpentine gaze drifted to his captor.

A minute passed as the nanny fussed.

"I'm fine, Natalie. Really! You don't have to worry. I'm having a good time, just wanted you to know." He made light of his situation. "I'm with friends. Good friends."

Ahmed shook his head, warning Lazarus not to give names.

"With friends!" Natalie reacted. "I'm going to kill you myself, Lazarus! How dare you pull a stunt like this and go off with a stranger. Where are you? I demand that you come home immediately!" She had looked all over Washington for the boy.

Lazarus cupped his hand over the receiver and made eye contact with Ahmed. "Natalie's pretty mad. She had to lie to the CIA guys about where I was and says for me to come home *now*. What do you want me to tell her?" He wanted to please his host.

"Let me speak to Natalie." Ahmed took the phone from Lazarus' small hand. "This is the police chief in Washington D.C. I found Lazarus wondering around in the park, skinned up and needing some medical attention. He needs to have bed rest for a couple of days. I will personally guarantee his safe return to the White House by late Tuesday. Is that satisfactory?"

"Yes sir, I suppose. And you're sure Lazarus is fine? Maybe I should tell President Bacon so he can check on his son."

"I've already talked to the president," Ahmed lied. "Just stay close to the phone in case I need to ask you a question."

Ahmed winked at Lazarus.

"That's not a problem," Natalie agreed. "I don't want to lose my job over losing Lazarus at the mall." Her voice was shaky.

"You won't. The matter is settled then. Lazarus is in my safekeeping until he goes home," Ahmed said.

"I guess," Natalie replied. "Let me speak to Lazarus."

"It's me," said the boy. "I promise to be good."

"Are you sure you're safe?"

"Positive." Lazarus looked up at his new friend. "I can take care of myself." He knew that he could. Let somebody cross him and he'd give 'im a dose of death. He could do anything he wanted, anytime he wanted. The trick was to keep his talent a secret until he needed to act. Then pretend nothing happened.

***

Back in Fernwood

Dick Branson was worried. Donald Wetherfield should have called by now to report he had found Georgie Hendricks. How could he predict what the future held when the fugitive was on the loose, still pointing an accusing finger at him? No, he had to do something besides sit around and hope life would turn out fine.

Dick picked up the phone and punched in a two-digit code for the governor's private cell number. It rang five times before Charles Dunn answered. "Hey, Charles. It's Dick Branson," he said in a jovial voice. "Am I catchin' you at a bad time?"

"No problem. Actually I'm taking the day off and playing a few holes of golf." The governor knew Dick wanted something. The man only called when he needed a favor. Such was politics.

"Where at?" Dick had given up golf when he couldn't swing his golf club past his widening stomach. "You can call me back if you're in the middle of a game. I don't wanna be a nuisance."

"You're not, now's fine. I'm in Memphis playing with the mayor, doing a little politicking while I'm here. What can I do for you?" Charles took a few steps away from his caddy.

"I need to find someone—a man named Donald Wetherfield who works for Alexander Luceres Ramnes," Dick made his request. "He came to Fernwood not long ago to see me."

"Why?" the governor asked.

"Wetherfield was low key in his visit, but he asked a lot of unsettling questions about Victoria Tempest."

"And you'd like to know his angle?"

"Yeah. He said he was tracking down Victoria because his boss wanted to speak to her. Wetherfield promised to call me when he found Victoria, but I haven't heard a word."

"Have you discussed this development with Andy Grimes?"

"No, not yet. I want to get my facts straight first."

"I see," said Charles, puzzled over why a world leader like Dr. Ramnes was interested in a fugitive fleeing from the law.

"Can you help me locate Wetherfied?" Dick pressed.

"I get it." A light went on in Charles' mind. "You think Wetherfield is after the reward money you're offering."

"It's possible," Dick answered. "If by chance Wetherfield finds Victoria, I don't want him to bungle it and let her get away."

"I still think Andy should be involved," Charles said.

"He will be, when I know more," answered Dick. "I actually met Luceres when I was in Rome at the end of June. He's quite impressive. I can't imagine why the most recent *International Man of the Year* would give Victoria Tempest the time of day."

"I had the same thought, but didn't say so."

"There's always more than meets the eye, isn't there?"

"Underlying motives drive the day," the governor spurted.

"Back to locating Wetherfield?"

"I guess I could call in a favor from the CIA and find this guy for you. Exactly what are your intentions?"

"Look, Charles, if Victoria Tempest murdered her husband, she doesn't deserve an international pardon, if that's what Wetherfield and his boss have in mind. The D.A. has all the evidence needed to convict Victoria in a court of law."

"I get it," said Charles. "You want the crime solved."

"Exactly. Doesn't the United States have first claim on a fugitive?" Dick asked. "I want Victoria returned to Fernwood to face trial. No interferences. She should pay for her crime."

"Let me see what I can do to expedite your goals," Charles said. "I'll call you when I know something definite."

"Thanks, friend. I'll owe you." Dick smiled.

Passing the buck is so easy, Dick thought as he hung up the phone. Victoria's meddling had brought to light Branson's environmental soil problem, but due to quick thinking, he had avoided prosecution. She would not bring down his drug dynasty if he had to wrap his fingers around her throat to shut her up.

Dick wanted the crime solved so he could resume living his life without a threat hanging over his head. He wanted to find

Victoria first and bring her home. She would be arrested, arraigned, and go to trial. Case opened and shut.

Mark James was married to Victoria's daughter and had bettered his position should a murder trial materialize. Dick was certain Mark wouldn't testify to self-incriminating information—especially now that a baby was on the way.

Karen James was another matter. She wanted her mother absolved from the murder charge, but would never do anything to hurt Mark, the father of her baby. It could be a win-win situation.

But if Donald Wetherfield found Georgie Hendricks and somehow convinced her to coax Victoria into a compromising position . . .

Dick did not want to think about the outcome.

33

West Tennessee

Jon Branson switched on the radio as the van rolled past the Selmer city-limits sign. A local DJ was graphically reporting the gas explosion that had rocked a Fernwood neighborhood. When Officer Sarah Boswell's name was mentioned as the possible victim found inside the house, Jon turned up the volume.

"Hey, you two lovebirds back there. Listen up!"

"Why is he talking about my friend, Sarah?" Victoria leaned arms on the back of the front seat to bring herself closer to the radio. "When I saw her the other day, she was doing just fine."

"Maybe it wasn't her in the house," Texas pointed out.

"Texas is right," Jon agreed. "Until the DNA tests have been done, no one can be for certain if the body found in the house was Sarah's." He wanted to give Victoria hope.

"But Sarah lives alone. And it was after midnight."

"I know, dear. Just don't jump to any conclusions, all right?"

It had to be Sarah, who else? Dick Branson, the snake!

"I see the anger rising in your face, honey . . ."

"Yes, I'm mad! If Sarah's dead, you and I both know who killed her—" Dick Branson would pay plenty if he did this.

"Wait a minute, Victoria," Jon interrupted her tirade. "It's entirely possible the gas leak that caused the explosion was accidental. Don't go placing blame without knowing the facts."

Of course, Jon was right, Victoria seethed in the back seat. People believed she was guilty of having her husband murdered even though all the facts weren't in. And now she was passing judgment on Dick like she was God Almighty. Still, she was mad.

"Lucas and I have our bags with us, Jon. You can drop us off at the Selma airport and we'll be on our way back to the ranch." He glanced over at Victoria, who was in a silent world of confusion. No use asking if she wanted to come along, she didn't.

Victoria stood at the base of the helicopter, her hair whipping in the wind created by the rotor blades. Texas hadn't kissed her goodbye—which meant he was disgusted with her attitude. She wanted to rush over and leap inside the open cockpit, but didn't.

Texas should go about his business and let her be about hers. Later, they could work on a relationship—or would it be too late?

After Jon had dropped his mother off at her house, Victoria climbed into the front seat of the van. Neither of them said anything until they were in the underground tunnel en route to the safehouse located on the premises of Western State Hospital.

Privately, Victoria could kick herself for letting Texas leave without telling him how much she needed and loved him.

"Your old room is still available," Jon said, glancing over at Victoria. "Why don't you get a good night's rest and we'll work on your new identity later today." Church was in a few hours and Jon was preaching. "We have to talk about your future, Victoria."

She blinked. "You think I have made some bad decisions."

"Yes," Jon said. "So *we*, you and me, are going to decide what identity best suits you and map out your next few weeks. If you dare divert from the plan, I will have to oust you from safehouses across the world. You put everyone you know at risk by your rash actions. I am responsible for peoples' lives."

Jon hated being so strict, but with Victoria it was necessary.

Victoria was too stunned to respond. Was she such a rebel that even Jon distrusted her? How would God ever use her in a ministry position? She needed deliverance from hating Dick Branson, forgiven for her selfishness, cleansed by the Holy Spirit.

Selfish ambition is the sin of witchcraft.

182

God, I am so sorry. Victoria closed the door of her bedroom and let out a loud wail that sounded like a wounded animal.

***

Birmingham, Alabama

It was nearly sunrise when Lucy Boyd, a.k.a. Sarah Boswell, checked into the Ramada Inn, anticipating Tanya Mason's arrival.

When a knock came at the door, Sarah squeaked like a mouse. With one ear glued to the door, she quietly listened.

"Tan? Is that you?" Sarah whispered.

"It's me, Sarah. Open up."

Sarah removed the security bar, turned the lock, and flung open the door. "Git in here, girl!" She grabbed Tanya by the shirt collar and pulled her inside the dark room, glancing down the hallway to see if anyone watched. "You're sure you weren't followed?" She slammed the door and double locked it.

"No, I'm not sure." Tanya jerked away from Sarah. "Don't tear my clothes off!" She tossed her large purse and a set of car keys on the bed. "So what's your big plan to get Dick off our backs?" She sassily planted hands on her hips.

"I'm not the enemy." Sarah deflated from fatigue. "I made some coffee. It's on the sink in the bathroom, so help yo'rself."

Tanya walked into the bathroom and used the john before filling a Styrofoam cup with the dark steamy liquid. Peering at her image in the mirror, she didn't like what she saw. A middle-aged woman with graying hair, puffiness under her eyes from fatigue, and a wiped-out expression that showed exactly how she felt.

When Tanya returned to the bedroom, she noticed that Sarah had switched on the TV and tuned into Fox and Friends. A clip came on showing the gas explosion in Fernwood, Tennessee.

According to the report, authorities had not ruled out a homicide, but Sheriff Andrew Grimes did not believe the incident was a malicious act, rather accidental due to a faulty gas stove.

"I guess Andy is glad to be in the spotlight again. Not acting too upset that I'm dead, is he?" Sarah quipped to Tanya. "I'd sure like to know if his wife Cheryl told him I borrowed the Tempest file yesterday. Never mind, I already know she did."

"And we can't just call and ask Cheryl, now can we?" Tanya's dander was up and fluffing out like an alley cat's.

"I can't let anyone know I'm alive. Not yet. I talked to Bobby a few minutes ago and told him what happened. He's going to let a friend run the trailer court while he takes a trip. He's a good man, Tan. No wonder my father liked him."

"A trip to where?" Tanya reacted. "I hope you didn't send Bobby on a dangerous mission. He's an old man."

"Bobby said he always wanted to see the Rocky Mountains," Sarah replied. "I didn't twist his arm, Tan. He wanted to do it."

"Do what? You're scarin' me." Tanya shivered, fear gripping her like a pair of strong hands. "It's too cold in here."

Sarah walked over to the AC unit beside the window and adjusted the temperature then faced Tanya. "Bobby's on his way to see Beverly James in Denver as we speak."

"Driving alone?"

"That's the way he wants it."

Alarm shrouded Tanya's expression.

"Look, I know Bobby's old but he's not stupid," Sarah defended her actions. "Won't nobody be able to trace his steps if he uses cash to buy gas along the way. When he gives Beverly the copy of Jeffrey's notes, and she comprehends the significance, we'll have two people on our side. I'd bet my life on it."

"Just don't bet Bobby's!" The enlarged pupils of Tanya's eyes reflected the light from the only bulb glowing in a lamp. In the bathroom, the lights over the sink blinked on their way out. "And you're certain that Beverly will help and not hurt us?"

"No, I'm not certain!" Sarah exclaimed. "But if Victoria trusts Beverly, the woman must have some integrity."

Humph. Tanya wrung her hands. "What if after seeing the notes Beverly decides to contact Karen Tempest. Who, I remind you, happens to be married to Dr. Mark James."

"Who," Sarah added, "is definitely in cahoots with Dick Branson. Like I said, nothing is for certain. But we have to try."

"I hate all the ifs!" Tanya plopped down on the edge of the bed, placing her empty coffee cup on the bedside stand. "I hope Bobby made an extra copy and left it in his safe deposit box."

"I don't think that was the plan," Sarah said, propped against the wall. "Tan! We gotta trust our instincts and pray that Jeffrey's notes get into the right hands. We've helped all we can."

"You really believe that Dick Branson will go down for Jeffrey's murder," Tanya said. "What about Hearty Meats? Won't they pay, too, for environmental negligence? What about Terry?"

"I think the environmental issue is no longer a factor, Tan. Dick came out smelling like a rose when he called the governor and reported a toxic spill on his property. The *Fernwood Gazette* reported that a private firm was cleaning up the mess under the guidance of the Environmental Protection Agency."

"Well, la de da! And people call this justice?"

"Goodness, Tan, don't be so negative!" Sarah moved to a chair and collapsed in it. "We're not finished here, not yet!"

"So what's to celebrate?" Tanya huffed. "Your house has been obliterated and you're as good as dead."

"I know." Sarah removed a tissue from her purse on the table and blew her nose as Tanya stretched out her lean body on the bed, hands supporting her head. "I have a plan."

"Yeah? Details, please, seeing I'm the one you called."

"We need to locate Georgie Hendricks since she was eyewitness to Branson employees dealing drugs," Sarah said.

"What gravestone are you gonna look under?" Tanya came to her feet, crumpled the empty Styrofoam cup in her hand, and threw it in the garbage can. "I hope this story gets better."

"It does." A smile curled Sarah's lips. "If we can show Detective Greg Diamond that Georgie is alive and her testimony verifies that the criminal evidence the Memphis Police Department is holding is valid, Dick will go down for drug dealing. Without him in the picture, I think Victoria will go free."

"So much of your theory hinges on Georgie," Tanya said.

"I'm afraid so." Sarah's eyes closed in fatigue.

"Okay, assuming you are right," said Tanya, "where do we go from here? Are we gonna keep runnin' until Georgie shows up? My kids will soon be in school, my husband has a job, and I want my boring life back. I hate all this detective stuff!"

"I understand your concern, Tan. But until Branson is arrested for his crimes and taken off the streets, there isn't much more we can do to protect ourselves but lie low."

"Maybe Georgie Hendricks will show her mug in public," Tanya said. "Isn't it time our luck turned?"

"Tan, keep to your plan and stay out of sight. When Bobby calls me on my cell, I'll decide what needs to be done."

"You gave Bobby a cell?"

"Yep," said Sarah.

"Registered in your name? Isn't that traceable?" Tanya grabbed her purse off the bed. "I don't like it."

"Yeah, me either, but I don't think anybody will start looking for me until Monday at the earliest." The long night dragged on Sarah like an anchor. "By then, I'll have a better plan."

"Well, I'll be at my brother-in-law's house in Florida." Tanya used a Ramada Inn notepad to jot down the address and phone number for Sarah. "Don't call me unless you have good news."

"Chicken," Sarah teased.

"Whatever you do, Sarah, please don't contact Gloria Gordon. We can't take any chances with friends. I love my family, and Dick Branson will stop at nothing to cover his sins."

"Okay, if you say so," the cop mumbled.

"Meanwhile, what are you going to do?"

"I'm not sure, but I'll play it safe."

"Good." Tanya was satisfied there was no more to say on the subject. "I don't think I could survive knowing you weren't by my side. We've been together too long as friends."

"Or . . ." Sarah speculated, "I might contact Jon Branson."

"What? Dick's son! That's crazy, Sarah."

"Victoria didn't tell me a whole lot about her life underground, but she did mention that Jon was a good person and reliable friend. He just might know how to contact Victoria."

"And he sure knows how to find Dick Branson."

"Jon's not at all like his father."

"How do you know this?"

"Victoria told me."

"Oh."

Silence filled the motel room.

Sarah walked over and gave Tanya a hug. "Thanks for coming. I'll keep you and your family in my prayers."

"You do that, honey. I need to leave now."

Sarah opened the door and watched Tanya walk to the elevator. One brief glance back and she was gone.

34

Safehouse #36

Victoria was in and out of a restless sleep, unconsciously praying for God's intervention and guidance. Shadows of old events danced on her subconscious like horror flicks, including the regrettable night when Jeffrey met death and she ended up in a coma after carelessly crashing her Mazda.

Cold, then hot, Victoria kicked off the covers only to retrieve them for comfort. When she finally awakened, there was a sober reality gripping her psyche: except for God, she was alone, having alienated most people. But she had family. Maybe she should phone Daniel and get his opinion before going a new direction.

Time was running out. Texas was gone.

And after the morning worship hour, Jon would expect to hear and approve her immediate plans—which were far from clear. If she decided on first going to Zurich to collect her five million dollars, he was sure to disapprove because she knew far too much about the work of the Christian Protection Agency and the safehouses they sponsored around the world.

Did Jon believe she would betray safehouse secrets?

The conclusion was disturbing. Would he think any better of her if she immediately returned to GloryVale for brain surgery?

Confusion over what to do next was mounting.

When a surgeon removed the scar tissue from her brain, it was sure to alter her pattern of thinking with all those neurons and synapses running about in new circuits. Sure, she might have back the missing twenty-five years of memories. Did that mean her old feelings would return? How would she view Mark then? Would she love him and hate that she had ended their engagement?

What about Karen? Would she be mad at her daughter for marrying Mark when he was on the rebound?

What about Texas?

All of these unknowns were scary. Worse, would she revert to her old ways of thinking and let selfishness rule? Or would the Holy Spirit convict her more completely for her years of sinning?

Certainly, Victoria Martin Tempest would not be the same person who had innocently awakened on April 14, 2014, with an intense determination to solve her husband's twenty-five-year-old murder. Suppose she resumed her old selfish characteristics, wanting her way no matter what, caring nothing for God's ways.

So what was a girl to do?

Victoria was deliberating her difficult situation when someone knocked on the door. "Yes?" She cracked it open and spied Jon standing there with stress multiplied on his face.

"You missed breakfast. Are you coming to church?"

"I'm sorry about last night."

"Forgiven." He almost smiled. "I think we're adults enough to discuss your future without explosive emotions, don't you?"

Are we? Victoria questioned.

Jon leaned against the door jam and crossed his arms. "I like you, Victoria. I only want what's best for you."

"I know," she sighed. "Did Texas call?"

"No. He was pretty put off by your attitude last night."

"I know . . ." Victoria knew she had hurt his feelings. He wanted to marry her and carry her away on his big white Texas horse, but life was not a fairytale. "I'm sorry. Really."

"Get dressed and I'll see you in church in twenty minutes."

"Sure." Victoria closed the door and rushed off to take a shower, having made a decision about her future.

There were new faces gathered in the mess hall that Victoria didn't recognize. Before the service began, she'd overheard some of the residents talking about a new safehouse about to open in Whiteville, Tennessee. One elderly couple was considering transferring, reminding Victoria of how Southern Baptists moved their church membership from one local fellowship to another.

Jon seemed very much at home at the pulpit. He said an opening prayer then opened his Bible to 1 Corinthians 3, written by a first-century Christian, Paul of Tarsus. In Victoria's Bible, the topic was **WATERING, WORKING, WARNING**

Jon explained the scripture eloquently. It was obvious he lived life as nearly as possible to God's dictates. The gist of the passage indicated that it didn't matter who sowed the seeds of Christianity, or who did the harvesting, God always gave the increase, changing human lives through His Holy Spirit.

"There is no other acceptable foundation in God's sight other than faith built on Jesus Christ," Jon was saying. "Men's works will be tested by fire at Christ's Judgment Seat. Will your works endure?" Jon perused the audience. "Dear ones, God deals in motives and awards accordingly. Be firm in your faith!"

Victoria needed to think about the quality of her works. When she was asked to operate the safehouse computers in the elevator shaft, what had she done? Put on a blond wig, a fake nose, and taken a job as a maid—to accomplish her own agenda.

Was that being responsible? *Duh.* Didn't God's principles still apply today, and disobedience bear eternal consequences?

Won't I answer for my mistakes when I face Jesus?

Victoria realized what she was contemplating doing in the next few days was both selfish and dangerous. Yet, she was bent on having her own way. Not everything a person did had spiritual ramifications. But if she were doing the right thing, why did she feel so confused? The answer was obvious. It was time to evaluate her true motives in bringing Jeffrey's killers to justice.

Was she doing it for Jeffrey, to vindicate the loss of a life? Or was she appeasing her own conscience because she had failed him?

More pertinent, was solving the crime about punishing the despicable Dick Branson? Victoria deeply sighed.

Why can't I move on, God? What is driving me?

Solving Jeffrey's murder would definitely make her feel better, she decided. It would seem like penance for failing as Jeffrey's wife, for not being more involved in his life at the time, and recognizing the impending danger. The truth hurt a lot.

What am I going to do?

She should decide soon.

Deep in retrospection, Victoria had barely heard the sermon. The service was over and people moved about. Time to act.

Leaving the mess hall, Victoria hurried back to her room, deciding on a course of action, whether right or wrong.

Grabbing her duffle bag from under the bed, she filled it with a few worldly possessions—a far cry from the way she'd once lived. No time to assume a new identity, she was leaving.

"I'm sorry, Jon, but I have to go," she muttered.

35

Luceres' chalet in Switzerland

Zurich sweltered with abnormal heat. Georgie was dog tired when she returned from her afternoon of sightseeing and went straight to her room to shower, change clothes and rest.

"Well, how did you like your tour of the city?"

"Oh, hi," Georgie answered NATO's perfect specimen standing in the open doorway like they were going to be friends.

"I trust Donald showed you a good time."

"Uh huh." Georgie was lounging on the bed, a tourist magazine on her lap as she perused the pages.

Luceres chuckled. "If you're trying to be rude, you're succeeding. I trust you have what you need to be comfortable."

"Sure, what's for supper?" Georgie couldn't get enough food in her stomach to satisfy her hunger." Her stomach rumbled like a troubled train. "Sorry," she apologized for the noise.

"Supper isn't until later, but there's a bowl of fresh fruit in the kitchen," Luceres offered a remedy. "Help yourself." He lingered in the doorway. "What are you reading?"

"How the rich and famous come to Zurich on holidays," she replied. "I think I'll mosey into the kitchen and grab a bite."

The detective threw her long legs off the bed. Wearing a pair of shorts and a tee, she came to her feet, stretched and yawned.

"By the way," she said, "what time is supper?"

Georgie walked over to the dresser and ran a guest comb through her tangled bleached hair, badly needing a color and trim.

"Seven thirty, usually," Luceres answered.

"Oh." Georgie guessed a banana would have to do.

A smile tugged at Luceres' mouth. "We'll fatten you up, Georgie, give us a little time. Did I tell you my grandmother is joining us for dinner?" He knew Georgie had no close family.

"Really?" Luceres had the door blocked so she couldn't exit.

"A chef from a nearby village is coming over to make a wonderful mutton with potatoes." The leader popped his knuckles, reminding Georgie of her own nervous habit.

"Mutton? As in the fatted lamb?" Georgie hoped she wasn't being prepared for the sacrifice. Was Luceres Jewish?

"I promise you'll love the preparation and ask for more," he said with a chuckle. "You are a strange woman, Georgie. You dress like a man and have the emotions of a child." He swayed in the doorway, hairy arms crossed over his chest. "But delightful."

Georgie peered at her abductor. *Delightful?* That wasn't a compliment. It was a camouflaged dig if she'd ever heard one.

"To pass the time before dinner you can take a walk up the trail behind the chalet. There's a lovely view of Zurich from the top of the rise. Our sunsets are spectacular in the area."

Georgie considered accepting the challenge and taking the hike. Maybe there was an escape route on the other side of the mountain. At least it would earn her some quality breathing time.

"Regardless of how you spend the rest of your day, we'll see you in the dining room at half past seven. Don't be late, Georgie. My grandmother is punctual and expects no less from others."

Mmm . . . Georgie could only imagine what Grandma Ramnes was like. This family gathering . . . was it designed to break down her defenses? It would take more than a hug to soften her up.

"A walk up the trail sounds like a winner," Georgie decided.

"Good. Donald will accompany you."

"Shoot! Don't you trust me?" Georgie spouted. "Why don't you get rid of your watchdog and lets you, me, and Grandma have a nice quiet dinner alone." She laid her cards on the table.

"Does Donald really make you that uncomfortable?"

"Yes," Georgie replied. "We're not buddies."

"I see . . ." Luceres thumped his forefinger on his chin in speculation. "Then I shall send Donald on an errand. At your request, it will just be the three of us for dinner. I'm looking forward to knowing you better." He left Georgie to her devices.

Quickly changing into a lightweight exercise suit, Georgie grabbed an apple from the fruit bowl on her way out the back door of the chalet. Hoping to beat the jujitsu expert up to the top of the rise, she scurried up a well-beaten trail through the woods.

Let Donald chase after her. He was good at that.

As promised, the sun hovered on the horizon, firing lavender and reds over the countryside. Overhead, the stars began to bleed through the deepening-blue skies. One could almost believe in a Heaven and the goodness of a God at such glorious moments.

Georgie reached the top of the trail and inhaled the mountain air. Alone, she felt perfectly safe, far removed from Victoria's melodrama. For a few seconds, she forgot she was a prisoner.

Then Donald Wetherfield rounded the corner, fuming and huffing to catch his breath. The man was an unrelenting pest.

"Well, look who the cats' dragged up," she quipped.

Halting in front of Georgie, Donald leaned over and grasped both knees with his hands, gasping for a breath. "You're in better shape than I thought," he said. "How's the view?"

"You missed it," Georgie mouthed. "The sun's already set. Don't you have an errand to run or something better to do?"

"You are my errand," he said, finally catching his breath.

"Gee, ain't you heard? A gal needs her space."

"So that's why Luceres is sending me into town with a long grocery list." Donald realized what the pressing errand was all about. "It was your idea to get rid of me."

Georgie considered a response. The man was too smart for his britches. "I don't run this show, or have you forgotten?"

The bruiser erected his body and breathed deeply. "I've got to get back to the gym. I'm losing some of my edge."

"Well . . . gotta go now or I'll be late for supper." Georgie brushed past Donald in a half run and headed back down the mountain trail. "Take your time," she called back. "Count the stars." She picked up speed, gratified at outrunning him.

Going down the mountain was much easier than the climb up. Sort of like looking back on a difficult case after it was solved.

It was dusk in the woods by the time Georgie reached the chalet and passed through the kitchen. The visiting chef was busy at preparing the evening meal and the food smelled scrumptious.

After showering, Georgie gazed at the only dress hanging in the bedroom closet. A size twelve, it was far more feminine—not to mention expensive—than any garment she'd ever worn on her athletic body. Not even Anthony Vorices could top this outfit.

Wearing only a sports bra and bikini briefs, Georgie slid into the shimmering silk dress the color of mango. Scooped and rounded in the neckline, it left plenty of skin to tease.

Ridiculous! Georgie wasn't into impressing anyone.

Assuming the string of authentic-looking pearls and matching earrings lying idly on the fancy antique dresser were designed to fill in the space between her chin and the dress, she put them on.

"Oh, well," Georgie murmured, "might as well please the host." She admired her image in the mirror. *Not bad.*

Continuing to dress, Georgie slid her size ten feet into a pair of pumps made solely of leather straps then sprayed perfume on her wrists and neck until she coughed from lack of oxygen. *Done.*

Voices came from the formal dining room as Georgie stepped into the hallway. Smoothing down her short wet hair, slicked back like the pelt of a seal, she glanced through the French doors and saw the oval table eloquently set. Martha Stewart couldn't have done a better job, and Donald was nowhere in sight.

Good.

On a pale yellow linen tablecloth were three floral china plates with settings of sparkling silverware that glimmered in the chandelier's brilliant lighting. Thinking no one was watching, Georgie lifted the lid of a large silver platter and inhaled the delicious odor of simmering roasted lamb. Man, was she hungry!

"And look who's come for a visit!" A woman resembling Moses' grandmother stepped into the dining room.

"Good evening," Luceres said to Georgie with a smile.

"Oh, hi," she responded, embarrassed at being caught with investigating the contents of the silver platter.

"The mutton smells wonderful!" Grandma Ramnes said, eyes bright for her age with a smile that dismantled one's defenses.

"This is my maternal grandmother, Tabitha Anne Ramnes," Luceres said. "Grandma, greet my guest, Georgie Hendricks."

What was a girl to do after that introduction? Georgie stuck out her hand and shook the woman's frail paw. "Pleased, I'm sure."

"Grandma brought cookies and cream with her," Luceres said. "I noticed you have a sweet tooth, Georgie."

"That was thoughtful." Georgie produced a genuine smile. *Had she missed something significant, like her birthday?* The whole scene was surreal, like the unfolding of a Walt Disney fairytale.

"Don't let my grandson fool you, Georgie, he loves my desserts, too." Grandma walked around the table and stood behind a chair. "The cookies are from a famous bakery in Bern, Germany, the ice cream so rich it is usually served for royalty."

Is she pulling my chain? Georgie wondered.

"The table looks exquisite. Did Madeline arrange the fresh flowers?" Grandma asked Luceres. "Madeline is the maid who comes three times a week to clean," she explained to Georgie.

Luceres seated Georgie at the table opposite his grandmother and chose the chair at the end. Wearing a green silk shirt under his tooled jacket, with no tie, he looked beautiful, if a guy could be so described. Grandma looked nice, too. They were a regal pair.

"Agnes is the best chef around these parts," Grandma said. "Let the male chefs think they can cook better." She chuckled.

Placing her beige linen napkin across her lap, Georgie waited for someone to say grace. Instead, Luceres rang the dinner bell and the soup de jour arrived, a blend of sweet cold cream and cucumber, a preparation Georgie had not expected to like. Still, after tasting it, she ate every drop in her beautiful china bowl.

Agnes lit a large scented candle on the sideboard and dimmed the chandelier lights. A warm glow filled the room. Outdoors, it grew rapidly dark. Katydids chorused in the nearby woods, the rushing rapids of a creek in competition with their song.

Luceres served the lamb, slicing each piece carefully. Georgie could not help but notice the fine details of his slender fingers and manicured nails. It was as if every hair on his head had been counted and properly documented. Was his mind as organized?

Is that why he usually got his way?

"I don't always get my way." Luceres made eye contact with Georgie, a faint smile pulsing his lips. "How's your food?"

"You read my mind?" Georgie rudely placed both hands on the table, thinking she'd like to turn it over like the cowpoke did when he'd lost at cards. *How dare you invade my privacy!*

Luceres heartily laughed. "And you're right, I usually get my way. But please don't tip over this beautiful setting."

"Don't pay any attention to Luceres. He's a big tease," Grandma Ramnes said. "Be sweet, or I'll get out my paddle."

Dumbfounded at the conversation, Georgie searched the vault of her brain for a response and came up with nothing.

"My grandson is clairvoyant," Grandma went on to explain. "He's been able to discern thoughts since he was old enough to talk. Don't let him get your goat, he means well."

So sweetly said, Georgie felt more at ease.

"It's a gift, Georgie," Luceres interjected. "My grandmother has it, too. However, she is more discreet about her talent."

Grandmother smiled at Luceres. "Sometimes a curse, isn't it, dear? Knowing what others are really thinking. But, of course, we don't always let on we know." Her dark round eyes came to rest on Georgie. "Don't let us spook you, dear."

"I won't." Georgie's stony gaze slowly shifted to Luceres. "So whatever I'm thinking, you—shoot! That's no fun."

Grandma chuckled as Luceres grinned like the Cheshire cat in *Alice in Wonderland*. "Georgie thinks we should say grace."

"Then, by all means, let's please our guest," said Grandma.

Embarrassed, Georgie lowered her head for the blessing.

Luceres closed his eyes. "Great God of the Universe, ruler of all things, we ask your blessing upon this meal. Keep us safe through the night. Give us divine guidance. Amen."

Georgie had been watching, rather mesmerized by her captor.

"It's not like I don't appreciate the meal, I do . . ." Georgie groped for the right words, "but after we've finished eating, uh, I'd like to know why you have brought me here. This is not a social visit." She held her fork so tightly her hand was hurting.

Grandma smiled. "Of course, it is, dear. Everything we do in life is social. Men and women are a special creation of our universe, designed to interact. Like family, we all need each other. I would hate to think you were our guest and felt uncomfortable."

Georgie frowned, getting nowhere with being nice.

"Exactly what is it you want to say?" Luceres asked.

"The problem is, I am enjoying your company too much, and it frightens me." Might was well come clean. Luceres already knew how she felt. "Like Dorothy, I want to go home."

"Dorothy?" Grandma peered at her son.

"From the *Wizard of Oz*, Grandma."

"Oh," Grandma said as Agnes brought in a potato soufflé.

36

Safehouse #36

With Sunday services over and people moving about, no one paid any attention to Victoria as she was leaving. Residents flooded the hallways, returning to their rooms to make preparation for the many afternoon activities Jon had scheduled.

I'd better hurry. Victoria sliced her card through the security lock to open the exit door and hopped into the electric trolley.

She was traveling through the underground tunnel when she noticed that the ground was trembling. Was it an earthquake?

The New Madrid Fault ran through Reel Foot Lake and spiraled southward down the Mississippi River delta through West Tennessee. No major earthquake had occurred in the region since 1812. Thinking she was paranoid, Victoria dismissed the idea.

When the trolley rolled to a stop, she hurriedly climbed out and entered the old cold-storage building, quickly passing through the musky old relic. Once outdoors, she retrieved Jon's car keys from her pants pocket and unlocked the door to his sports-utility vehicle. With haste, she climbed in and switched on the engine.

Jon is going to be so disappointed in me when he finds out . . .

A few minutes later, shaky with heart racing, Victoria raced down the paved road toward the state mental hospital's main exit.

What? She jammed the break with her right foot as she spied flames shooting out the windows of the four-story brick building that housed Safehouse #36. *How did the fire happen so fast?*

Victoria considered returning to the safehouse and helping the others get out safely. But with dark smoke billowing into the sky, the fire was sure to be noticed by hospital personnel working in the other buildings. Before long, fire trucks and police personnel would arrive. No, she could not risk getting caught.

Obviously, there had been an explosion—which would explain why the ground was shaking inside the tunnel. Victoria whipped the car on the highway and raced west.

Breathing a little easier now, she took the ramp to the interstate, realizing that God had removed her from safehouse premises in the nick of time. *Thank You, Lord?*

Then a sinking feeling settled into the pit of her stomach. By now, Jon would be searching for her and conclude that she had left the premises without telling him. What would he think of her when he later discovered his truck was missing? Would he realize that she only borrowed the vehicle and was going to return it?

Oh dear, she should have left Jon a note explaining.

No, he would not understand, or like her taking off by herself without anyone knowing about her plans. She couldn't go back.

Victoria picked up speed, glancing in the truck's rearview mirror to see if anyone had followed. It was imperative she escape the authorities. Air trapped in her lungs wouldn't let go.

Breathe, sister. She furiously drove toward Jackson, Tennessee.

***

Switzerland

Dinner was exquisite and Georgie felt quite gratified. The mutton was deliciously prepared just as Luceres had promised, and she had eaten enough potatoes to sprout plants out her skin.

Grandma's almond cookies served with vanilla ice cream were delicious. Georgie found herself on a first name basis with the elderly woman. Tabitha Anne outshined her grandson when it came to friendliness to the point she almost trusted her.

Grandma and Luceres led the way into the den.

A fire was glowing in the hearth. Evenings were always cool in the Alps. Offered a shawl, Georgie graciously accepted. With her stomach pleasantly full, she sank into her favorite leather recliner near the fireplace hearth and soaked in the warmth.

Beautiful! Her turquoise eyes were aglow with firelight as she felt for her missing silver medallion usually worn around her neck. She'd lost it in South America while a fever ravished her body.

No, some Columbian thug had stolen it.

"We'll get your medallion back, Georgie," Luceres said.

"Thank you." She didn't question his ability to do so.

The serene setting was perfect for an evening of fellowship—which was sure to follow. Georgie's thoughts flipped to the "Brady Bunch," a television flick that had entertained family audiences for decades. But she wasn't one of the gang, was she?

So why had she been included in the family setting?

Agnes, the exquisite chef, soon brought in their coffees—a rich blend of chicory beans reminiscent of the strong coffee Georgie had been served during captivity. Even though her hands weren't bound, she was beginning to feel that the chalet was a very upscale prison. No longer could she sit quietly by and pretend to be content. It was time to negotiate her freedom.

"How do you like Switzerland thus far?" Luceres lent Georgie his balmy gaze, like he was her "best" friend.

"This is unbelievable!" Georgie came to her feet, suddenly tired of the politeness and pretense. "C'mon! What's the use of asking me questions when you already read my mind?"

Luceres chuckled and glanced over at Tabitha Anne. "Aren't American women charming, Grandma? They never hesitate to say what's on their minds. It's called free speech."

Georgie seethed inside as she sat back down.

"I'm sorry we make you feel uncomfortable, dear," Tabitha remarked, her smile so sweet it could be canned and sold at the supermarket. "Luceres is a big tease. Don't let him taunt you."

"Do I have a say whether I stay here or not?" Georgie was spent from the civility. "Given a choice, I'd rather leave Switzerland tonight. Going home seems mighty appealing."

"You hurt my feelings, Georgie. Haven't I made you feel at home here? Given you your basic needs—food and shelter? Donald rescued you from Colombia, and you probably haven't even thanked him. Haven't *we* bettered your life?"

Georgie blinked. *That's a lot of bull to take in*, she was thinking as Tabitha leaned forward and patted her hand. *But so true.*

"Don't be frightened, dear. You are our guest, and nothing bad will happen to you, I promise. Luceres is only trying to get to know you better. He doesn't mean any harm."

"So you say." Georgie was unconvinced.

"My grandson asked me to come here tonight—to lend support in case you feel uncomfortable answering his questions. Luceres has a heart of gold and would never do anything to hurt you or your friend, Victoria. He saves lives, not takes them."

"Do you know about Victoria—about her predicament, I mean?" Georgie couldn't believe either of them would care.

"Donald Wetherfield has filled us in on the details."

"Oh." Georgie's gaze swooped on Luceres.

"I have one requirement, Georgie," the world leader stated. "I want to speak directly with your client and hear her side of the story. If I deem her innocent, I will offer my assistance."

"What kind of assistance?"

"As you know . . ." Tabitha interjected, "Luceres knows a number of influential people. If Victoria is innocent as you must believe, she will only be vindicated if facts are brought to light."

"Right." Georgie couldn't have agreed more. "You would do that for a stranger?" Georgie glared at Luceres in disbelief.

"Sure, why not?"

"You'd help Victoria Tempest prove she is innocent of murdering her husband when most people believe she is guilty?"

"I said I would, and my word is good."

Georgie was bowled over. "Why?"

Luceres shifted in his seat and made eye contact with his grandmother. "I am a person who has respect for the truth. And I can tell if a person is lying. Call it discernment."

"Some call it witchcraft," Georgie pointed out, wishing she hadn't. Her life rested in the hands of these powerful people.

Luceres smiled, cupping his hands between his knees.

"Interesting slant on my comment, but be assured that I use my gift to explore ways of helping others achieve a better life."

"Who can fault that, dear?" Grandma chimed in.

"Not me." Georgie didn't think the idea was worth arguing over. "So . . . let's just say I buy into the theory that you are a genuine do-gooder and only interested in helping my client. You can't, because I don't know where she is—and that's the truth."

"I believe you, Georgie," Luceres professed.

Tabitha's dark eyes were wide with interest as she sipped on her coffee, but she kept her opinions to herself.

"It's the truth."

"In that case, I will have to rely on what you know, won't I?" Luceres set his china cup aside and took out a notepad. "Start from the moment you met Victoria. Don't leave anything out."

37

All pandemonium broke loose at Safehouse #36 when an explosion occurred in the kitchen. Five minutes earlier, residents would have been at the morning service and many would have died from the initial blast. But the service had ended earlier than usual, so the majority of residents had already left. A few were still fraternizing in the hallway when the incident occurred.

Frightened by the loud noise, leaping flames, and rolling waves of thick dark smoke, people scattered to their rooms to grab a few essential items before crowding at the exit door.

Unfortunately, the area was impassable, blocked by debris.

Jon Branson's mind raced in many directions. He heard the children's screams and their sobbing parents, recognizing it was his responsibility to control the confusion sweeping through the safehouse. But first, he would have to clear a way for escape.

People were unkind in a situation such as this, pushing and shoving each other to get out of harm's way. Finally, Jon made his way to the exit door and spied the wooden beam that had collapsed through the ceiling tiles. "Watch out!" he screamed.

Convincing people to move away from the door, Jon and another strong arm removed the beam and opened the heavy fire door. One of the electric cars was missing. Who had taken it?

"Both cars were here before the service, weren't they?" Jon asked Guy. "Who was the last to leave—?" the question died on his tongue in the midst of the shoving and screaming.

"Hold up," Jon tried to control the panic. "Be calm."

Everyone wanted out of the building all at once to escape the leaping flames and suffocating smoke. Jon asked around and learned that no one had seen anyone leave the safehouse.

In his way of thinking, the person who took the trolley might be the person responsible for the blast in the kitchen.

A bomber?

Rumors flew around the complex like confetti, perpetuating more panic and speculation. Jon did the best he could to coordinate the mass exit, gaining an appreciation for Moses' organizational skills in getting a million Israelites safely out of Egypt. As he prayed for divine deliverance, one of the larger men took charge and told everyone to line up in an orderly fashion.

Seeing Carl's calm leadership had controlled the crowd, Jon placed a hand on his shoulder and thanked him. Once at the other end of the tunnel, the big man promised to see that both cars were returned so that more people could safely ride out.

As a long line formed at the exit door, Jon noticed that Victoria was missing. He hurried back into the dense smoke to see if she had been injured in the blast and left behind.

He checked the kitchen area first, but the flames were too hot to enter. Maybe she was still in her bedroom packing.

"Victoria!" Jon screamed her name as he ran through the hallway and entered her bedroom. *Where is she?*

The closet door was left open and Victoria's clothes were missing. Assuming she was in the first trolley car en route through the tunnel, Jon hurried to his room to grab his truck keys.

Fire crackled overhead like a demon crying out in the old ceiling. The interior of the building would soon ignite and go up in flames like a matchbox. Who would do such a terrible thing?

Jon's truck keys weren't on the dresser where he left them.

No matter, he had to get back to the exit and see that everybody got out safely. Joining the flow of hall traffic, he realized the situation was deteriorating. People might die.

"Walk, don't run," Jon reminded folks.

There was no way to extinguish the panic as people pushed and shoved to get out. Jon plowed though the hysterical crowd screaming for them to step away from the plugged doorway.

Lord, help! I don't know what to do.

Jon prayed for God's direction and deliverance. He was dirty, hot, thirsty and discouraged. Ignoring his basic needs, it was his responsibility to restore order. Which seemed an impossible feat.

"Excuse me, ladies and gentleman, but I need to get outside and see what's going on," Jon said, as kindly as possible.

Miraculously, the sea of people parted and Jon stepped into the dark tunnel, spying two men up ahead on foot racing away from the burning building through the dark passageway.

"How are we gonna get out of here?" a kid cried out.

"Be patient." Jon sucked in the acrid air, feeling the heat fuming at his back. "Carl and Guy will be back with both electric cars and we'll load them first with those who have trouble walking." He tried to appear calm, fearing the toxic fumes.

People would likely die if the mass exit took much longer. Time was now moving in slow motion, like in a movie. It seemed to take forever before one of the electric cars came jolting down the tracks. "Okay, let's get some people loaded in the cars."

Two elderly couples climbed aboard a trolley while others impatiently ran past them on foot in pursuit of fresh air at the end of the tunnel. Some carried weeping children in their arms.

It isn't just a fire, thought Jon. The explosion was a disaster that would end the CPA's occupation of the building. Police and fire departments would soon arrive on the site, firemen showering the building with water, soaking walls and destroying the interior.

And when the flames were all snuffed out, the insurance inspectors would go through the rubble to estimate the damage.

Then everyone would know that the lower floor of the building had been occupied. They would find the elevator shaft and the sophisticated communications equipment at the top.

It was time to notify the Christian Protection Agency and ask for help. No, he'd call Texas and have him do it.

Jon tried to use his cellphone—which didn't work.

Last to leave the building, coughing to get his breath, he raced through the tunnel, gasping for breath as he entered the cold storage building. Coming into the sunlight, he noticed scores of residents hightailing it into the woods. His truck was missing.

Missing? Who took it?

Somebody had stolen Jon's car keys and taken off minutes before the explosion. *The bomber?*

Jon took a moment to be still and prayed: *Dear God, I don't know what to do, please tell me? Amen.*

In the midst of the confusion, Jon felt quietness settle over his being. *God is still in control.* This storm shall pass.

Instead of running toward the woods, Jon cut down a narrow paved road and entered an occupied state-hospital building.

"Hey! Did somebody hear the explosion?" he asked an attendant, acting like he was as surprised as they must be.

"Yeah," said the blond at the desk checking people into the facility. "I dialed 911 and the authorities are on their way. I told the manager just the other day that they oughta tear down that piece of junk before it went up in flames. It'll cost more to clean up than it's worth. The building was condemned, you know."

"No, I didn't know." Jon entered a long hallway, swiping sweat from his brow and trying not to cough—a tale-tell sign he'd been in the building. "Hey! Did you sign in?" Blondie called out.

"Earlier." Jon kept walking until he reached the entrance of the cafeteria. In time for lunch, he got in line and waited for his turn to order. Being a beautiful Sunday, friends and relatives of inmates would assume he was a visitor. Good. Perfect.

Seated alone at a table, Jon purposely slowed down his breathing and took a few bites of his food before ringing Texas on his cell. An answer came after the second ring. "Yeah?"

"It's me, Jon."

"What's up, pal? Miss me already?"

"You have no idea. Not forty-five minutes ago, there was a huge explosion at our complex. Whether an accident or arson, we will probably never know." Jon sighed over the incident.

"What? Did anybody get hurt?"

"No, just cuts and scratches as far as I can discern."

"Where are you?" Texas asked.

"I'm fine, in the cafeteria of another building. If the explosion had occurred during the church service, I hate to think of how many casualties we would have had."

"What about Victoria?"

"I'm not sure. She wasn't in her room when I checked, and somebody borrowed my truck keys," Jon reported. "I hate to say it, but I think Victoria took off in my vehicle."

"Before the explosion?"

"It appears so," Jon answered.

"You don't think she had anything to do with the mishap, do you?" Victoria had been acting strangely. "She's not a RUA, is she?" Hadn't she pumped him for personal information?

"If Victoria's is a spy, she's fooled us all." A RUA was a religious undercover agent working for the federal government to investigate the activities of subversive religious groups.

"But you think it's a possibility?" Texas asked.

"I don't know—maybe," Jon replied. "If Victoria borrowed my truck and took off somewhere, her timing stinks."

"And you're in no position to report a missing vehicle," Texas concluded. "I assume you are on foot."

"Yes."

"Uninjured?" Texas was about to leave for San Francisco.

"Actually, I'm fine, eating lunch though I'm not a bit hungry. When all the hoop-de-la passes and the fire's put out, I plan to hitch a ride into town and pick up my motorcycle at the shop.

"Then where to?"

"My Selmer apartment, probably." Jon still had a lot of loose ends to tie up. "I think the safehouse is gone."

"Have you called the CPA to report the incident?"

"No. I want you to do that for me," Jon said. "And let's give Victoria an opportunity to do the right thing about returning my truck. She's confused over a lot of issues."

"Not about me," said Texas. "She flat turned down my marriage proposal. I don't intend to ask her again anytime soon."

"Don't be bitter, friend. Give it some time. Victoria might wake up and realize what a great guy you really are." Jon saw two badges entering the cafeteria. "Gotta go, the police are here."

"Keep me posted," Texas said and hung up.

Standing beside Texas, Lucas longingly peering up. "Who was that?" he asked. "Is Miss Victoria in trouble again?"

"I'm not sure," Texas never lied to the boy. "There was an explosion at the safehouse. We need to get on our knees and pray that all the residents escaped." He was worried about Victoria

"Is *she* okay?" Lucas asked.

"You are referring to Ms. Victoria?"

"Yep." Lucas had a big grin on his face.

"I don't know, son. Jon says she's missing."

"Then we have to go and find her," the lad proclaimed.

"Not this time, Lucas."

"But, Papa—"

"My decision is final, son. Victoria is on her own."

38

Victoria entered the city limits of Nashville, Tennessee, on Sunday around 1 p.m. Jon's truck drove like a dream. Fearing the police might stop her she obeyed all the traffic signs while maneuvering through the city, no easy feat in traffic.

By now, Jacob Cooley and his granddaughter Angela should be home from church services. They were Victoria's only hope of escaping the authorities now that Safehouse #36 was gone.

Taking I-65 North out of the city, Victoria drove with intent, watching like a hawk for the right exit, counting on recalling something familiar to indicate that she was on the correct road.

Forging ahead, trusting her gut impulses, Victoria took rights and lefts into neighborhoods, praying that she would end up at the correct house. With great relief, she knew that she was on target when she spied Angela's yellow Cadillac parked in the driveway of a white-clapboard house. *Thank you, Jesus.* She killed the engine.

Jacob was standing like a wooden Indian on the front porch, a Sunday paper in his hands as he gazed at the headlines, acting as if he hadn't heard the SUV drive up. Victoria honked the horn.

Looking up from whatever news item held his undivided attention, Jacob strained aged eyes to see through the tinted window glass of Jon's truck. To end his curiosity, Victoria opened the door and climbed out of the vehicle. "It's me, Jacob," she called out, walking fast toward him. "Thank God, you're home!"

"Victoria!" A smile curled Jacob's dry lips as he opened his arms and warmly received her. "When you left the meetin' last night, I thought it would be a spell before we laid eyes on you a'gin. What happened?" Sincerity graced his expression.

The hug was all Victoria needed to loosen her lips.

"Quite a lot." Her thoughts skittered to the fire raging at Safehouse #36. "Could we go inside and talk?" Wary eyes scanned the neighborhood for police cars.

"Sure." Jacob opened the screen door and waved Victoria inside. "Got a guest, Angela!" he hollered.

The odor of food cooking permeated the house, reminding Victoria of how very much she missed her own home.

"Angela!" Victoria exclaimed as Jacob's granddaughter appeared in the open arch between the living room and kitchen.

"Heavens to Betsy, Victoria! What are you doin' here?" The pretty young woman appeared astonished. "Are you in trouble again?" Her eyes skittered to her grandfather for an answer.

"I don't know—she just arrived."

"Sort of," she admitted, beginning to think that most people identified her with problems. "Trust me, I'm just as surprised as you are to be here." Her throat burned with dryness. "May I have a drink of water? I drove all the way here without stopping."

"Here from where?" Angela sauntered over to the kitchen cabinet where she removed a plastic tumbler and filled it with filtered water from a big plastic jug marked SPRING WATER.

Jacob could no longer restrain his curiosity. "Why are you here? Why aren't you with that handsome Texas fella of yours?"

"Jacob!" Angela cautioned her grandfather.

"Way you two was lookin' at each other I thought you'd be married by now." Jacob took off his hat and clutched it tightly in his hands. "Is that Donald fella buggin' you again?"

"No, nothing like that." Victoria guzzled down the water in big thirsty gulps. "Something happened at the safehouse."

"What?" Angela asked, forehead furrowing.

"It was a fire, happened just as I was leaving."

211

"It's good you got out in time," said Jacob. "You better sit, honey, you look kind of pale." He pulled out a kitchen chair.

Victoria accepted and collapsed at the kitchen table, eyes alight between her two friends. "I did something bad."

Angela and Jacob looked at one another.

"I borrowed a friend's truck without asking. I was afraid he might report it missing before I had an opportunity to return it."

"Could be worse," Jacob surmised.

"Did you call the owner and tell him you *borrowed* it?" Angela asked concerned over where the admission was going.

"No, I didn't," Victoria replied, body heat rising around her neck. *Why not admit I am a thief, among other things?*

"Why not?" Angela's eyes latched onto Jacob's as she tried to discern the reason for Victoria's confession of theft. "Wouldn't your friend have lent it to you if you had asked?"

"Maybe—I don't know." Victoria visibly wilted from hunger as she inhaled the blended odors of cabbage and onions cooking on the stove. "It's a long story." And she was weary to the bone.

"We've got time," Jacob remarked. "I think you better tell us everything. Maybe you should start with last night."

"Wash up and we'll have a bite to eat first," Angela suggested. "I don't want you going and fainting on us. You look like you had your last meal yesterday." She accurately sized up the situation.

"I am hungry." Victoria hadn't eaten any breakfast.

"Does Texas know where you are?" Jacob asked as Angela took up the hot dishes with potholders and placed them on the oblong kitchen table covered with a blue linen cloth.

"May I use your bathroom?" Victoria asked, avoiding the tough question. Texas was the least of her worries.

Would Jon ever forgive her for stealing his truck?

"You know where it is," Jacob said. "Clean towels are under the sink. He'p yourself. But don't be long, I'm hungry."

Angela removed the metal lid of a large boiling pot of field peas, dipped in a spoon and sampled her creation. "Mmm."

"What a trick!" Jacob said of Victoria as he pulled the salad bowl from the refrigerator and set it on the table. "Too bad trouble follows that girl like fleas after a mangy hound."

"Yeah." Angela sighed. "She hasn't had it easy in life."

The hosts were seated at the table when Victoria joined them for lunch. "Thank you for having me." She bowed her head.

"Will you say grace?" Angela peered at Jacob.

"Sure." He reached across the table and clasped Victoria's hand, pronouncing the most beautiful prayer she'd heard in a while. Tears crowded her eyes, regret sweeping over her.

"Let's eat!" Angela declared and passed the bowl of salad to Victoria. "Then Jacob and I want you to tell us *everything*. By coming here, you've involved us in your problems—not that we won't go out on a limb to help. We just need to know."

"Thank you, Angela. I understand, and if it's all right, I'll tell you about my situation when we've had lunch."

Jacob nodded at Angela.

Victoria picked up her fork and began eating. Cabbage had never tasted so wonderful, and the tea was perfectly sweetened.

Angela talked about life in Nashville, bringing Victoria up to snuff on the latest news about singing stars and their families.

Jacob discussed the weather and his plans to put out a flower garden in the fall. He was so looking forward to the changing color of the leaves and might take a trip to the Smoky Mountains.

Victoria enjoyed the good, heart-warming fellowship.

Later, after the three of them had each polished off a slice of chocolate cake, they retired to the den for more talk, a full glass of tea in their hands. Victoria saw the expectation in the faces of her newest friends and gathered her thoughts for an explanation.

Regardless of how embarrassing, or how difficult, she was determined to reveal everything that had taken place since she'd last seen them at the Dickson County cave—even her rejection of Texas when he had proposed marriage. Life was on a spin again.

"Jon Branson—" Victoria began. "You met him at the cave revival last night. He wanted me to map out a plan for my life, but I couldn't." She sucked in a sob.

"I don't understand," Jacob professed.

"Wow!" Angela let out a sigh. "How does one map out life?" She made eye contact with Jacob.

"Exactly," Victoria replied, feeling a little more comfortable in sharing why she had come to them first for help.

"So, how can we help this time?" Angela asked.

39

The Island of Barbados

The day couldn't be more perfect. Karen and Mark James had slept until 11:00 a.m. Sunday and ordered brunch sent up to their suite. A bellhop served the meal on the veranda overlooking the teal-blue Atlantic Ocean rambunctious with white-capped waves slapping in perfect rhythm on the sandy shoreline.

Karen was never happier, having everything she ever wanted out of life: a husband she dearly loved and a baby on the way. That Mark seemed just as content was comforting.

Besides, if Mark's *Little Vicki* wanted to discard a precious relationship with him, it was her prerogative. It wasn't as if Karen had stolen Mark from her mother, rather filled a void left when their engagement ended. Ultimately, Karen had found a way to ensure that Mark would never forsake or leave her.

The baby was their eternal link.

After brunch, while Karen took a nap, Mark ventured down to the office to grab a free Sunday paper.

"You from Fernwood, Tennessee?" asked the youthful guy manning the front desk. "Your town is in the news." He punched the paper with a stout finger. "Printed right here."

"Oh, yeah?" Mark answered, puzzled over why it mattered. "Is there something in the paper you want to show me?"

"I guess you ain't heard about the big explosion last night." The kid turned to the second page. "Says so right here—a big gas explosion in Fernwood, Tennessee. Kilt some female cop."

"Really? Give me that paper!" Mark snapped it out of the clerk's hands. "I can read the article for myself."

He hurried upstairs to their suite and found Karen asleep on the divan, looking like a China doll in her gauzy, pink gown.

No use disturbing his bride over a matter that had little significance in their lives, Mark thought. If Karen had known the victim well, he might wake her. An uneasy feeling crept over him

Carrying with him a glass of ice water out on the veranda, Mark sat down and began reading the newsworthy article.

The charred remains of a body thought to be Officer Sarah Boswell were found in her demolished house.

Wait! Wasn't that Victoria's friend at the precinct?

Mark continued reading. A fire inspector believed that the explosion had occurred because of a leaky gas stove. The blinking lights from the electrical storm had set off a spark and ignited the gas fumes accumulating in the kitchen area. The rest was history.

Mark read the entire news article. There would be an investigation into the incident to be sure there was no foul play.

If Sarah Boswell was murdered . . .

Mark slowly folded the newspaper, walked back inside the condo, and shoved it in the nearest garbage can. Why tell Karen about Sarah's unfortunate accident when it would destroy her serenity? They were having such a great honeymoon—except for an occasional thought about what life might have been like with Victoria. But he couldn't go there now. Life had marched on.

"Why did you throw away the newspaper?" Karen sat up on the divan and asked. "You know I love reading the Sunday issue."

Mark flipped on the television, ignoring the question.

"Mark!" Karen set her feet on the floor and walked over to the trashcan, retrieving the paper. "Is there something in there you don't want me to read?" She challenged him.

"No, there's nothing that would interest you," Mark gazed at Karen. "Why don't we take a walk on the beach?"

Karen didn't budge a muscle.

"Honey?" Mark approached Karen, removed the paper from her hands, and placed it on the coffee table. "Let's just shut out the world today. Okay?" He cut off the TV and heaved a sigh.

"Sounds like a plan," Karen replied with a smile. "Are you sure it's all that's going on? I have a funny feeling—"

"I'm sure. I love you, Karen." He embraced his bride.

"I love you, too, Mark." Karen pushed him away and picked up the paper, sensing something forbidden was there. "Why don't you let me decide if what you *don't* want me to see is important?"

She opened the pages and scanned the front page. "There's a hurricane coming." She glanced up. "Shouldn't we make plans to leave the island?" Her hazel eyes sparkled with mischief.

"Where?" Mark grabbed the paper.

"Right here." She pointed to the weather page. "The eye is going right through our hotel."

"No, there isn't. Mark scanned the paper. There was a hurricane in the Atlantic but it was farther south than the islands.

Karen crossed her arms and grinned.

"You were teasing me, you sly little wench." Mark grabbed Karen by the arms, pulled her to him, and kissed her on the lips.

"You see how half truths get you in trouble." She wasn't just talking about weather predictions. There was his hidden past.

"Forget about the weather. If you don't want to walk on the beach, what'd ya say we practice our honeymoon some more?"

"Maybe . . ." Karen kissed Mark again, delving a little more deeply into her feelings. "Beat you to the bed!" She screamed and ran for the door, with Mark at her heels laughing all the way.

When Mark fell asleep after making love, Karen carried the Sunday paper out on the veranda and sat down to read its contents. "So now, Mark, what is it you don't want me to see?" She scanned the topics recorded in the pages. "Nothing here."

Turning to the second page, the photo of a burning house leaped off the pages and gripped Karen's heart. The headlines read: BODY FOUND IN FIRE'S RUBBLE.

"Sarah Boswell—my mother's friend!" Karen felt her heart sink a notch. "What's going on?" She needed to find out.

***

Zurich, Switzerland

Georgie told Luceres everything she knew about the mystery shrouding Attorney Jeffrey Tempest's death, including her own consequences for becoming involved with his widow, Victoria.

Grandma Ramnes politely listened, occasionally commenting about how truly sorry she was over Victoria's sad predicament, the woman's expression so earnest it was obvious she cared.

"That is an amazing story," Luceres remarked.

"It isn't *just* an amazing story. Everything I've told you is true," Georgie insisted. "There's nothing more to tell. I know it sounds bizarre—the environmental cover-up with Hearty Meats, the drug issue, and Richard Branson's role in it. If someone doesn't help Victoria, she'll pay for a crime she didn't commit."

"I believe you." Luceres glanced over at his grandmother, who nodded. "I'll have Donald check out your facts and judge for myself what is evidence. Thank you for your candidness."

"I have another problem," Georgie hesitantly admitted.

"What is it?" Luceres' strange eyes targeted her.

"Are you certain you can trust Donald?" Georgie asked in a hushed voice. "He seems like a man with his own agenda," she daringly pointed out. "Greg Diamond is the detective assigned to the case. Why not give him a call and get the facts yourself?"

Luceres sat in quiet repose for a good thirty seconds.

"Maybe I will call Detective Diamond and hear what he has to say about the case. I'd also like to assess the town temper concerning Victoria." The trial would likely be held in Fernwood.

Georgie guffawed. "Oh, I can tell you that the town's temper is maddening. In most people's minds, Victoria's already been tried and convicted. Just the matter of her arrest left to do."

Luceres response to her outburst was a somber glare.

"Thank you for your input, Georgie." He cleared his throat. "Meanwhile, enjoy your visit in Switzerland, my friend. And remember that all good things eventually come to an end."

Georgie sobered and zipped her lips.

"Are we done for tonight?" Tabitha yawned, tightly hugging her knitted shawl about her shoulders for warmth. All that was left of the fire in the hearth were a pile of glowing embers.

"You are weary, Grandma." Luceres turned his attention to his other guest, helping Tabitha to her feet. "Donald can sleep on the sofa when he returns. You'll have his room tonight."

"Speak of the devil," Georgie quipped as Luceres' bodyguard came through the front door with two bundles of groceries nestled in his muscular arms. "Are we having a bedtime snack?"

"No." Donald ground his teeth. "I like to never have found fresh smoked salmon." He kicked the door shut with a foot.

"Are we eating?" Georgie repeated her question.

"No," Luceres said. "It's time for sleep."

"Did I miss something?" The jujitsu expert peered at his boss, suspecting PI Georgie had tried a few of her sly tactics.

"Just a little conversation, that's all. And thank you for going for groceries. Grandma loves smoked salmon and she's staying another night. She'll be sleeping in your bedroom."

Donald's jaw tightened.

"Oh, by the way, I'm flying out in the morning, Donald. I have an appointment." *Some things he must do alone.*

"Shall I come with you?" Donald inquired.

"No need. Stay here with the girls so they won't get lonely. Take them to Zurich. Arrange for a tour through Saint Peter's Church and a leisurely sail on Lake Zurichsee. They'll love it."

"For real?" Georgie's eyebrows lifted.

Luceres laughed. "For real."

The detective tilted her head to one side, enjoying the idea of sailing. "A big boat and fishing gear, all my own."

"No, nothing so elaborate," Luceres replied.

"Don't worry about us, Boss, we'll be just fine," Donald said. "Won't we, Georgie?" Donald caught her eye.

"Fine, if you say so." Georgie made a face, still needing to negotiate a favor for supplying Luceres with information about her client. Meanwhile, Switzerland wasn't so bad a vacation spot. *Staying a few more days couldn't hurt.*

When Luceres returned from his short trip, Georgie planned on asking him to buy her a ticket to Memphis. But first, he should set Dick Branson straight so his thugs wouldn't come after her again and make her staged death permanent. Luck was on a roll.

40

Western State Hospital

"Are you Jonathan Branson?" a woman in uniform inquired as Jon mopped up the last of the roast-beef gravy in his plate with cornbread. Her staring was unsettling, like she *knew*.

"Yes, Officer. What can I do for you?" Jon casually replied, sliding his plastic orange tray to the side, eyes meeting hers.

"I need to see your credentials," said Officer Janice Kelly.

"Sure." Jon stood and dusted breadcrumbs from his hands. "Is something the matter?" Glancing past the young woman, he spied two policemen standing at the cafeteria's only exit door.

Trouble had arrived. Jon removed his fake I.D. credentials from his billfold and handed them over to Officer Kelly.

Barely looking at them, she said, "Sir, you are under arrest."

"What?" Jon came to his feet, acting indignant.

"You have the right to an attorney. Anything you say can and will be used against you in a court of law . . ."

Something told Jon the arrest was prearranged. He knew the routine and didn't resist, just allowed the officer do her job, snap on the handcuffs, and walk him outdoors to a squad car.

"Am I allowed to ask why?" He already knew the answer. Whoever had set the kitchen bomb had fingered him.

"All I know is I'm supposed to pick you up."

"And you've done that," Jon said with a sigh.

Obviously, a religious mole had slipped into Safehouse #36 under false pretenses and done a bang-up undercover job. The fire was meant to draw attention from the outside world, and it certainly had. Jon was going to need the smartest available CPA attorney to defend him. There was no doubt in his mind that the evidence had already been gathered to try and convict him for religious crimes against the mandates of PEACE FIRST.

The squad car slowly rolled forward and picked up speed as it neared the front entrance of Western State Hospital. Jon glanced over at the burning building. Tall ladders scaled the sides of the building and firemen were entering through fourth-story windows.

It was only a matter of time before the contents of Jon's office and the radio tower would become police property. He was busted, and Safehouse #36 wasn't the only complex shutting down, either. Would Victoria's rash actions bring them all down?

***

Goodlettsville, Tennessee

Middle of the afternoon, after Victoria had taken a long nap and a hot bath, she dressed in the clean clothes Angela Cooley had provided for her. To support a new identity, she would need believable credentials to move about the planet safely.

Angela knew a CPA undercover agent living in Nashville who would help Victoria. "Adam is trustworthy, I promise," she said, aware of how skittish her guest was over yet another change.

"Thank you, Angela. For everything." Victoria tried to hide her mounting fear. Without God on her side, she would collapse.

"This nightmare will soon end," Angela promised. "Trust, me, I've learned that God's will prevails in all circumstances."

Taking a jerky breath, Victoria nodded in agreement. It was an eternal truth that uplifted the human spirit. *Why not end now?*

"When?" Victoria rasped, hating how she felt. "When will this nightmare be over? When I'm caught by the police and locked up in prison?" Bitterness rose unbelievably fast.

"Don't be so negative, honey," Jacob interjected. "You know us Christians can't expect everything to always go smoothly. Persecutions come alongside blessings. Tha's just the way it is according to the Apostle Paul. It's how we git stronger."

"Well, I'm already busting out of my persecutions," Victoria announced to Jacob. "When trouble outweighs blessings, it's not an easy pill to swallow." She would can this pickle herself.

"You do what you have to do in life," Angela philosophized. "For now, Victoria, you must concentrate on changing your image so the police won't recognize you. We'll help."

"I hate to involve you and Jacob again," Victoria said to Angela, "but I have no where else to turn."

"We know." Angela led Victoria to the bathroom and pulled out a bottle of bleach from beneath the cabinet. "Use this."

Victoria had been here before. "I'm sick and tired of running, changing hair colors, and trying to vindicate my actions."

"I know." Angela covered Victoria's shoulders with a towel.

Jacob stood at the door as Angela sectioned the back of Victoria's hair and applied bleaching lotion. "About mapping out your future, Victoria—what do you have in mind?"

"Two possibilities," she vaguely replied.

"Well, are you going to tell us?" Angela paused from her task.

"No, I'd rather keep my activities private—to protect those innocently involved with me. If the police come looking for me here, you don't know anything—the absolute truth."

If you see me, I'll be there for a reason, Victoria recalled Georgie's cryptic words regarding her investigation into the shenanigans of Dick Branson. So much had happened since then.

"Is that wise, Victoria?" Jacob offered an opinion. "If we don't hear from you, an' you get into a heap of trouble, how 're we gonna find you? Do you really want to act alone?"

"Yes." Victoria's eyes skittered to her caretakers.

MONDAY, JUNE 30

41
Baghdad, Iraq

The private jet landed at the Baghdad Airport. Three men who worked for Ahmed met Luceres at the gate and walked him out of the terminal. Tossing his duffel bag into the back of a jeep, he prepared for a bumpy ride across the untamed desert terrain.

Few words were exchanged during the drive from Baghdad to the campsite. Luceres was quite content to sit back and enjoy the beautiful scenery, his thoughts centered on the country's history.

Using the latest technology, Baghdad had been reconstructed by Westerners following the Iraqi invasion led by the American President, George Bush. Thought to be the seat of civilization and possible location for the biblical "Garden of Eden," the city was once called Babel—the site where disobedient humans supposedly attempted to build a tower to reach Heaven.

According to Old Testament Scripture, God was displeased and confused the languages of the people, causing a division among them. As a result, they disbursed and populated the world.

Later, during the reign of King Nebuchadezzar, the city was called Babylon, its brave warriors famed in Iraqi history for enslaving the Jewish nation. As late as 2002, the ruthless Iraqi leader, Saddam Hussein, envisioned himself as the "knight" who would once again conquer and enslave the Jewish nation, and declare Islam as the supreme religion of the entire Middle East.

After Saddam failed to achieve his goal, and was tried for war crimes, much of his terrorist kingdom crumbled. However, religious zealots of the Muslim faith refused to give up and let the Christian West establish a pure democracy in their country. Resistance to American mandates persisted as the jihad movement grew around the world. Threats of violence existed on all fronts.

PEACE FIRST halted the religious conflict in 2012, but it had not ended warring Muslims' desire to force the Christian infidel to worship the one true god, Allah. Emotions boiled.

The continuing conflict between the Jews and Palestinians was nothing new, rooted in centuries of disagreement. Since the day Israel became a nation in 1948, many Americans supported the Jewish effort to fend off the Arab world, primarily because they embraced Christianity, a religion rooted in Judaism.

Following the bombing of the New York Twin Towers in 2001, world opinion changed in regard to which nations deserved UN support. The face of America had been altered by the influx of immigrants representing all nationalities and religions. No longer did the white European Christian dictate American politics.

Presently, a strong NATO, weakly backed by the United Nations, was the backbone of world civility. An undefeated U.S. military force continued to maintain world peace, but harmony would not prove lasting as anger burned deep in Jihad organizations waiting for the right leader and a divine signal to act.

That is where I come in, Luceres thought. Whereas the French Napoleon Bonaparte, and German Adolph Hitler had failed, he would succeed in rallying the world under his leadership. Weapons of mass destruction made it possible to eliminate large populations. While many world citizens thought WMDs had been eradicated, Luceres knew differently. In private moments, he envisioned commanding an invincible army composed of millions of *jihad* soldiers who served him, their king, in the name of Allah!

Let Jesus Christ top that one! Luceres let out a maniacal laughter that pierced the deep darkness and resounded into the spiritual realm where fallen angels were poised to defy the true God of the Universe in support of the Antichrist as they prepared for a spiritual battle that would shake the very foundations of the physical world. *Jihad!* It was to be the culmination of all wars.

"What pleasant thoughts bring a smile to your face?" Ahmed Ramallah inquired as his Harvard friend stepped from the jeep.

"Where is the boy?" Luceres was anxious to see his brother.

"I sense this will not be a social visit." Ahmed smiled. "Your sibling is inside the tent entertaining my men. Lazarus has rather strange gifts. Come, see for yourself."

"How so?" Luceres lifted the flap of the tent.

"He moves objects with his mind."

Ahmed entered the tent first. Startled at seeing a portrait of his younger self, Luceres stared into the face of his twin brother.

"Hello, Lazarus. I am your brother, Luceres."

A pair of strange green eyes clung to Luceres, the thin blanket dancing in the air suddenly falling to the ground with a thud.

Lazarus mentally communicated his greeting. In response, Luceres laughed and hugged the boy. Ahmed motioned with his hand for his soldiers to evacuate the tent. No words exchanged, the brothers communicated silently, responding emotionally.

Alone with his older brother, Lazarus collapsed on the blanket he had levitated and folded his arms into his lap. "I am glad to have a brother. I am not well liked. Are you?"

"Pretty well," Luceres replied. "So we'll just have to polish your social skills at bit." He could not resist touching the child's thick, dark locks of hair. "What it is you want in life?"

"I am happy when I have control," Lazarus fervently replied.

"You mean—as in manipulating your nanny, or your parents?" Luceres delved deeper into his brother's psyche.

"If you are worried I will hurt you, I won't."

"No, I don't think that." Luceres chuckled.

"I'm not afraid of you, either. We are the same."

"Pretty much," said Luceres. "What about your gifts?"

"I find them entertaining. I get bored sometimes. You ever will a living creature to die?" Lazarus candidly asked.

"So you are fascinated with death. Is that what excites you?"

"I don't want to die, if that's what you mean."

"Neither do I," replied Luceres. "Are you aware that a man named Lazarus is in the Bible? He was brought back to life by the prophet named Jesus Christ." He noted the similarities.

"My father is a Christian, you know. I read the Bible."

"But you are not, I assume?"

"I'm not sure. Are we going to be friends or enemies?" There was a strange discernment in the lad's eyes.

"Yes, I believe we are," Luceres replied.

"You came to kill me, didn't you?"

"I considered it briefly. But, Lazarus, you are my twin."

"How is that possible? I am younger," the lad reasoned.

"We came from the same egg, but at different times. Our father is a Catholic priest who donated a sperm to a New York facility before he entered a monastery. I was hatched first—so to speak." Luceres smiled. "You were frozen and introduced into the womb of your mother twenty years later."

"We are a strange phenomenon, are we not?"

"Yes, we are," said Luceres. "But destined to greatness."

"So you believe that I am identical to you, only a younger version." The idea was enchanting, a medical wonder.

"It feels as if that is so . . ." Luceres considered if their souls might intertwine. Were their destinies already sealed? What has been, was, and is to come. It was a divine approach to living.

"I am no threat to you, my brother. I love you." Lazarus crawled to his feet and embraced his older twin. "Take me with you. Train me. Together, we can do anything we desire."

"You know of my plans?" Luceres reacted, stunned.

"I know everything you think—all at once. I am more intellectually evolved than you are. Does that bother you?"

"I don't know," Luceres answered honestly, the idea of their priestly father's joining forces with his prodigies immensely appealing. With the backing of a Catholic Pope, much could be achieved in the world arena. They were an unstoppable trinity.

Lazarus grinned. "I agree."

42

A Trailer Court South of Orlando

A seemingly pregnant Victoria Martin Tempest stood outside the third-hand trailer staring at the closed mini-blinds. It was after 10:00 a.m. Monday, and anyone alive should be awake.

Should she knock? More importantly, would she be welcome?

The name on Victoria's driver's license was Tobias K. Juniper, but a Christian-Protection-Agency undercover agent in Nashville said the recently deceased woman went by Tobbie.

Fine by me, Victoria thought, as long as Tobbie's credentials got her safely through the bus and airport terminal checkpoints.

She laid her fist to the door and let 'er rip.

Thirty seconds later, the misplaced soda jerk from Fernwood cracked the door, her expression crunched like Cornflakes in a cereal bowl. "Whut is it?" Gloria Gordon acted like the plague had shown up. Victoria smiled at passing the litmus test.

She was neither pregnant, nor Tobbie, nor the plague. Gloria had not recognized her. *Good.* The moment was too precious to ruin with words. So Victoria stood there enjoying the ruse.

"Well . . ." dark eyes impatiently flashed, "ain't you gonna say something? If you're lookin' for a handout, lady, you've knocked on the wrong door." Gloria wasn't shy about the way she felt.

"Wait! Don't close the door!" Victoria anticipated Gloria's next move. "That isn't why I'm here!" she replied, her voice pitched high with hope. "It's me, Gloria."

"Huh?" Gloria backed up like she'd seen a ghost.

"Yeah. It's your ol' soda buddy." Victoria couldn't help but grin. Gloria's shocked expression was priceless.

"Wait a cotton pickin' minute! I know that voice!" Gloria pointed a finger at Victoria. "And it don't belong to no Tobbie thing-u-ma-jig." She took a step backwards and tripped over a magazine rack in the den, landing hard her buttocks.

"Careful," Victoria said too late, reaching out to catch her.

"Ouch! I knew I should've stayed in bed."

"You'll live." Victoria entered the trailer and closed the door, sidestepping Gloria on the floor. "Are you alone?"

Gloria made no attempt to answer or stand up.

It took a few seconds for Victoria's eyes to adjust in the dark room. "Why are you still in bed?" Victoria peeked out the trailer window, drew the blinds, and flipped on the light switch.

"Do I need permission to sleep?" Gloria, still wearing pajamas, reached over and set the magazine rack upright.

"How are you, girlfriend?"

"How am I?" Gloria repeated, crawling to her feet "Don't you believe in calling first. How in the world did you find me?"

"I have my ways," Victoria replied. "If you had known it was me knocking, would you have answered the door?"

"Not a chance." Gloria glared at Victoria.

"I thought not. If I've interrupted something important, I apologize, but I don't have time for formalities."

"So I see."

Victoria pulled the walloping maternity blouse over her head and haphazardly tossed it on the rocking chair. "You can't imagine how distressed I was to learn you'd left town."

"Sorry about that," Gloria said, "but when Jon Branson showed up at the soda shop, it scared the willies out of me. Somebody had to be watchin' us talk. Bottom line, I got paid to leave town. I ain't claimin' going was the right thing to do."

"Who knows . . ." Victoria adjusted the foam pillow strapped to her waist. "You know how to use a phone, don't you?"

"Telling you would make matters worse. I don't think so."

"What's goin' on?" A sleepy-eyed Sarah Boswell stepped from the bedroom. "What time is it—who's that?" She pointed a half-painted, green fingernail at the big-nosed blond wearing glasses, glaring through curls stringing down her forehead.

"Which question you want answered first?" Gloria sacked a hand on her waist and frowned at Sarah.

"*About-to-deliver* over there?" Sarah nodded toward Victoria.

"My name is Tobbie Juniper—not really." Victoria giggled, feeling the rubbery texture of her fake nose. "I'd like to remove this prosthetic, but it appears to be rather permanent."

"Did we just let in a serial killer?" Sarah remarked to Gloria, shaking her head. "I know *that* voice?" She looked closer.

"Don't worry, I'm not a serial killer." Victoria's eyes skittered between the two women. "Don't you recognize me, Sarah?"

"Well, I'll be, if it ain't the fugitive from Fernwood!" Sarah quipped, truly astonished. "Decide to vacation in Florida?"

"Life should be so simple." Victoria glanced past the women through the open door leading into the kitchen. "I thought you were dead, Sarah. Any other surprises I should know about?" She inhaled the addictive aroma of brewed coffee.

"Well, I ain't dead—no thanks to Dick Branson!"

"Git Vicki some coffee 'fore she faints!" Gloria bossily ordered Sarah. "Take a load off yo'r feet, honey." She eyed Victoria. "Since you've come all this way, we should talk."

Spontaneously obedient, Sarah hustled off into the kitchen and returned with a plastic tray loaded with three filled-to-the-brim coffee mugs and individually packaged creams and sugars.

"Help yo'rself, girls." Sarah grabbed a mug from the tray.

Gloria chose the red cup and drank down the hot black liquid like a thirsty sailor, hoping the caffeine would clear her head for the courage she needed. "You were about to say, Victoria?"

Off with the lily-white gloves! Victoria removed the foam pillow and settled into the soft folds of Gloria's well-used sofa, probably purchased at a Goodwill Store. Lifting the last mug from the tray, she added powdered creams and two packs of sugar to her coffee.

Sarah chose the rocking chair as Gloria claimed the sofa.

"Thank you, Gloria. The coffee's delicious." Victoria's gaze fell on the hostess. "You always had a knack for fellowship."

"You all comfy now?" Gloria raised an eyebrow, her gaze transferred to Sarah. "Ready to talk about why you came?"

Victoria peered at the two people she believed were her friends. "Why do I feel like a bombshell is about to be dropped in my lap?" She savored the odor of the coffee.

"If knowledge ain't a bombshell, it's close to it." Gloria plopped her empty mug on the coffee table with attitude.

"I'm not here to cause trouble for either of you," said Victoria. "I just feel we needed to share information."

"What kind of information?" Sarah asked.

"Are you certain you weren't followed?" Gloria ventured over to the window and peeked through slits in the vinyl blinds.

"Nobody followed me," Victoria said with certainty. "So why are you here, Sarah? This isn't exactly your regular beat."

"Like you, I find I have no place to lay my head."

"It was *all* on the news," Gloria said.

"About the explosion at Sarah's house."

"Yeah, not to mention I'm presumed dead!" Sarah interjected, coffee spewing out of her mouth on the carpet.

"Look whut you've gone and done!"

"Sorry." Sarah peered at Victoria. "Like the reports said, my house went up in smoke early Sunday morning."

"Details, please. They don't exactly air CNN and FOX on a Greyhound Bus," Victoria came back. "How did it happen?"

"CSI claims lightning set off sparks in my kitchen and ignited gas fumes from the stove. Looks like somebody broke into my house and got what was planned for me. Five minutes later, and I would've been toast. I was driving down the street toward my house when the powerful explosion occurred," Sarah explained.

"Thank God, you weren't hurt!" Victoria began to worry about Jon Branson and the others at the safehouse.

Had the same person set off both fires?

"I did something illegal," Sarah shyly admitted.

"This sounds like a bacon-and-egg conversation if I've ever heard one," Gloria interjected, feeling hungry. "Let's git in the kitchen and make some breakfast. Then we'll share stories"

"Does this *something* illegal have to do with Jeffrey?"

"Breakfast first, then talk." Gloria shook a testy finger at her two guests. "'Fore morning's over, the three of us is gonna make some sense out of whut's been happening in Fernwood for decades. Doggone, if we ain't gonna end this confusion."

"I'm all for that," Victoria agreed.

"Me, too." Sarah trailed Gloria into the kitchen.

"You microwave the bacon, while I'll git the canned biscuits in the oven," Gloria said to Sarah, eyes gliding to Victoria.

"Okay, I'll take care of the scrambled eggs." Victoria opened the refrigerator and grabbed a full carton, privately ruminating that Dick Branson was somehow at the root of all the confusion the three of them were experiencing. His kingdom would not prevail.

While breakfast was in progress, Gloria talked about her new job at the fruit-packing company as they lit into the bacon, eggs and biscuits like they were starving. By the time they had finished breakfast, they were swimming in coffee refills and orange juice.

With renewed anticipation, the three musketeers returned to the living room and took their seats, all feeling as if a powerful powwow had been called. "Okay, Vicki, you first," Gloria said.

43

The Fernwood City Jail

"You have a visitor," an officer addressed Jon Branson. Unlocking the jail cell, he motioned for Jon to come out.

"Who is it?" Jon wasn't expecting his attorney. Feeling dirty and sweaty from poor ventilation in the cell, he guessed that criminals weren't supposed to have all the comforts of home.

"Name's Marilyn Branson," Ted sourly mouthed, a ring of keys in one hand, a cup of coffee in the other. "You can use the interrogation room." He nodded to his left.

Jon followed Ted down a hall and entered the visitation room to his right. His mother stood there, looking unbelievably well.

"Hi, Mom." He embraced her, childhood memories rushing in with the need to know she viewed him as an honest citizen.

"Hi, son. How are they treating you in here?"

"Fine, and you should not have come."

"How'd this happen, Jon? You getting arrested?"

Marilyn's pale lime-colored eyes were so like Jon's it raced over every emotion reflected in his evolving expressions.

"Have you spoken with your father?" she inquired

"Now there's a thought!" he scoffed. "You think Dad would stoop so low as to come down to the city jail?" God, forgive him for being bitter over the situation, more for his poor judgment in trusting Victoria Tempest. Because of her, people would suffer.

"I'm so sorry, son. I know this is hard on you. I wish your father had more compassion, but he fails to comprehend what being a good parent means. Jesus could change him into the man he needs to become if only he would listen to reason."

"If wishes came true, I'd be free," Jon said. "I don't want to talk about me or dad—how are you feeling?"

"See for yourself, dear. I'm better." A smile trickled over Marilyn's kind face. "Of course, I'm very worried about you and the precarious situation you're in. What will happen next?"

"Sit down, Mother." Jon pulled out a straight chair for her.

Marilyn sat down and watched her son pace the room.

"You know about the safehouse," he said. "We take a lot of fugitives into our complex, and apparently one of them was a religious mole. Whoever it was must have reported me."

"I never thought I'd live to see Christianity viewed as a subversive organization," Marilyn sadly remarked. "The principles of PEACE FIRST have stolen my religious heritage and deemed practicing faith according to grace a crime. Too bad somebody can't get to Alexander Luceres Ramnes and tell him off for good!"

Jon smiled. "I love you, Mother. Thank you for standing by me now and sharing Christ with me at an early age."

"That's what mothers do." A tear swelled and poised to fall.

"I know . . ." Jon hugged his mother.

"God promised me that if I raised you up according to biblical principles, you would not depart from them as an adult—that's a paraphrase." She smiled. "God's principles are eternal."

"I had a divine appointment with Jesus," Jon admitted.

"You bet!" Marilyn reached out and pulled her son to her, hugging him ferociously. "I'm so proud of you."

"I'm proud of you, too, Mom." Jon knelt beside Marilyn and held her hands tightly. "All you can do *now* is pray for me."

"No, I can do more. We can't sit idly by and expect justice to be correctly served," she said. "If you won't call Dick, let me."

"I'm not sure if he wants to help." Jon stood and stretched.

"Trust me, he does. Besides, Dick has a strong advocate. He and Andy Grimes go way back. Accept your father's help."

Jon sighed, considering the offer. "I've broken international law, Mother," he admitted. "I've harbored religious fugitives. I can't see a court of law letting me off in light of my actions."

"It's not an American law yet," Marilyn pointed out.

"No, but it soon will be. People want peace without conflict. Christians are viewed as narrow-minded, trouble-causing bigots who profess Jesus Christ is the *only* way to enter God's Heaven."

"Which—need I remind you—is the absolute truth!"

"Even so, the law rules." Jon was resigned to facing the legal charges filed against him. He'd known the risks involved when he agreed to oversee Safehouse #36. By receiving God's forgiveness, and accepting Christ as his savior through grace, he expected there would be persecutions alongside abundant blessings.

"Before, Jon, you asked me how I was feeling?" Marilyn's smile was beaming. "I just came from the doctor's office and my hemoglobin count is up. I have twice as many platelets as I had a week ago. Dr. Baker says my immune systems is kicking in and fighting the cancer. I believe I am slowly healing from leukemia."

Jon blinked in disbelief. *A miracle wrought in the midst of trials?*

"Mother! That's wonderful news!" He hugged her again.

"There's more, son." Marilyn's grew serious.

"What?" Jon stared into his mother's aging face.

"Brother Joe Glower phoned me last night and invited me to visit him in California. He suggested I see the doctor to verify my improved health. He wants me to travel with him to revivals and give my testimony." Marilyn studied her son for a response.

"What can I say? You've always believed that God had a divine purpose for your life. You've lived a sheltered life in Fernwood for sixty-five years. I suppose Moses wouldn't be surprised at all, since he was eighty years old when he led the Israelites out of Egypt into the Sinai dessert." Jon gave a thumbs-up. "I'm proud for you, Mom. Go and preach the gospel!"

"Oh, son! I knew you would approve. It's just that I hate to leave you, in jail like this." Tears poured from Marilyn's eyes.

"God is in control, Mother. I'll be fine."

"My plane leaves from Memphis later tonight. I don't know when I'll be back, or if I'll be able to contact you while I'm gone. Best I can do is get a message through to your friend in Selmer."

"Latisha Mangosa?" Jon realized he should have warned her that the police would be coming around. "If you don't mind, Mom, call my apartment and leave a message for her to leave town immediately. I don't want her involved in my troubles."

"Where will she go?" Marilyn asked.

"She's engaged. Her fiancé will see that she gets out of the country or safely moved to a new location. Whoever bombed the safehouse probably has my personal files and knows everything about me. A lot of people will be hurt because of the fire."

"I'll do it," she said, "and I'll stay in Fernwood, if you want."

"No, go to California, I'll be fine," Jon reiterated. *Would he?*

"I have only one other thing left to do before leaving."

"What? Talk to Dad about helping me?" Jon was no fool. "He won't like you interfering. If it's not his idea, he won't care."

"I think you're wrong, Jon," said Marilyn. "Your father loves you in his own way. I'm going over to his office right now and have a little chat with him. I'll make sure he gets off his fat rump and does the right thing. Count on it!" Determination set in.

44

South Florida

Gloria Gordon had known Vicki Martin since the eighth grade. She was as honest as they came, no pretense. There was no reason to believe she had lost her integrity just because Dick Branson said so. No, Victoria Martin Tempest was no liar.

"Just start at the beginning." Gloria fondly patted Victoria's hand. "Ain't nobody in this room pointin' an accusing finger." Inquisitive dark eyes rolled on Sarah. "Are we?"

"Not me," Sarah said. "Talk to us."

Victoria mustered her courage. "First, I must apologize for involving you in my personal problems." She reached back into her memories to the morning of April 14, 2014, when her world "flip-flopped" and wiped out twenty-five years in a nanosecond.

"That was pretty traumatic, if you ask me," Sarah said.

"Yeah, you have no idea." Victoria launched into describing what Switzerland was like and her encounter with the Antichrist.

Having worked the Sunday evening eleven to seven shift, Gloria often yawned, though not a bit bored. Work at the fruit-processing plant was hard and she wasn't getting any younger.

Victoria's saga lasted an hour and fifteen minutes according to the wall clock hanging over the kitchen door. "So what do you think, girls?" she concluded, praying for a bit of friendly advice.

"Wow, that's quite a tale!" Gloria said. "When you came into the drugstore that Saturday . . ." Victoria would know which day she meant, "and ordered a chocolate soda, I had no idea you were so confused—not that I didn't add to your trauma by opening my big mouth and criticizing Mark James. I hope you'll forgive me."

"I do forgive you." Victoria grasped her friend's hand. "What you said about Mark and Dick Branson was true—their crazy friendship. To be honest, I wasn't sure I could trust you, given Karen and Mark were also treating me with kid gloves."

"I understand, believe me. You sure asked a lot of unsettling questions," Gloria recalled. "I'm so sorry I ran out on you."

"Really, it's not a problem. When I came to see you at the drugstore, I was desperate to evaluate Mark's' involvement with Jeffrey's death. I should have told you about my memory switch. Had you known, I'm sure you would have been more help."

"Don't count on it, honey!" Gloria whistled. "I knew far too much to want to be involved with your situation."

"I understand now why you were so afraid."

"I hope so. When Dick Branson's son popped through the door of the drugstore, I lost it. I'd already said far too much, and I had to get out of there fast. I was a coward, I confess."

"I've done the same thing since. Twice," Victoria admitted.

"Wait! Both of you had good reason to fear Dick Branson," Sarah chimed in for the first time. "He probably gave the order to burn my house to the ground." Bitterness stuck in her craw. "And don't think because you ran away you're safe. Dick won't rest until *everyone* who opposes him is out of his perfect picture!"

Head slowly rotating on its axis, Victoria focused on the savvy Fernwood cop. "And that brings me to another thought."

Only the ticking of the clock measured the moment.

"Whut?" the girls queried.

"I've been entertaining the idea that Dick Branson may have hired someone to tamper with my brakes the night Jeffrey died."

"What?" Sarah and Gloria said in one voice.

"The problem is . . ." Victoria sighed, "I can't prove Dick had anything to do with my accident or Jeffrey's death. It's so frustrating. I'd give my right arm to put that crook behind bars!"

Sarah sarcastically laughed, realization unwinding like a coil as it struck home that no prey Dick chose was untouchable.

"Don't expect the man to let you go on breathing if you go after him," Gloria warned. "He has friends all over the globe."

"Yeah, I know. I recently met Donald Wetherfield."

"Who's he?" Sarah asked.

"A European thug you don't want to meet," replied Victoria

"See, I told you," said Gloria. "*All* over the globe."

"I can't worry about what Dick will do next. I have to concentrate on what I'm going to do about my situation," Victoria stated. "God is faithful and has the power to protect me."

"So what do you want us to do?" Gloria asked.

"About now I could use your support. I'm in so deep into Dick's illegal drama I could drown just thinkin' about it."

"Or crash and burn." The flames that had engulfed Sarah's house flashed like lightning through her mind.

"Go ahead and tell her," Gloria urged Sarah.

"Tell me what?" Victoria's eyes shot to the cop.

Sarah's dark eyes focused on Victoria.

"What did you do, Sarah?"

"I did some nosing around in the police archives not long ago and ran into Henry Carter while I was in the cellar of the courthouse. He's an old buddy of my Pop's—a retired cop."

Sarah's gaze shifted to Gloria as she took in a breath.

"Henry's niece works as a clerk in the police archives," Sarah continued. " I didn't move on my plan 'til I heard the sheriff had his team at the country club trying to apprehend you, Victoria."

"What plan? Sarah, get to the point!" Victoria exclaimed.

"Well . . ." Sarah thought back, "Elizabeth Carter—that's Henry's niece—told me that Andy Grimes had checked out Jeffrey's case file. That started me to speculating."

"Speculating how?" Victoria blinked. "Isn't reviewing the case Detective Greg Diamond's job?"

"Andy checked out the file on a Thursday, a week before you showed up at Karen's wedding and upset everybody's applecart."

"I don't understand. Is there some new development with the cold case I don't know about?" Dare she hope that the truth would surface and free her of the false murder charge?

"You might say that." Sarah made eye contact with Gloria. "Learned quite a lot from the file I borrowed," Sarah bragged with a wink of the eye. "*Stole* is a better verb. Just look where the good deed got me? Homeless, with folks thinkin' I'm dead."

"I'm so sorry." Victoria walked over and hugged Sarah. "I never should have involved either of you in my fiasco. It's all my fault." Her eyes slid to Gloria. "Both of you would still be living in Fernwood had I not poked my big nose into your lives."

"Wait a cotton-pickin' second!" Sarah took exception. "This mess ain't ours! It belongs to Dick Branson—dumped in our laps because we happen to know what he did. I say we dump it back!"

"Okay, ladies!" Gloria interrupted the heated conversation. "Threats are fine and noble, but until we settle on a plan of action to catch the crooks, we ain't got a leg to stand on."

"Agreed," Victoria and Sarah unanimously replied.

"Sarah, tell Victoria exactly what you did after you stole the file," Gloria coaxed her friend. "And don't leave nothin' out!"

"Well," Sarah leaned back in the wooden rocker. "Backing up a bit, I went to see Cheryl Grimes with a signed release to pick up Jeffrey's case file—a release I forged, which is a crime in itself."

"And?" Victoria urged Sarah to continue.

"*And so* . . . I made a beeline down to the Quick Print Shop and copied every scrap of paper in Jeffrey's file."

Like a spark of electricity, anticipation charged the moment.

"An hour later, I returned the file to Cheryl Grimes, praying she wouldn't mention my borrowing it to her husband."

"But he found out anyhow," Victoria deducted.

"My guess is Cheryl spilled the beans when Andy came home Saturday night, giving him plenty of time to notify Dick so he could set a trap for me at my house. I wish I knew who died in my stead." Sarah groaned. "I guess we'll all know when the coroner completes his report on the charred corpse."

"You're certain Dick torched your house?" Victoria thought of the victim who died in the fire, reminded of how Jesus died on the cross for all people, and that eternal life was far more precious.

"I could be wrong," Sarah admitted. "And like the police report said, there was an electrical storm that doused the lights. Just maybe my stove really had a gas leak. Accidents happen."

"Git real!" Gloria guffawed. "The gas explosion has the mark of Dick Branson's doing written all over it."

"Birds of a feather stick together," Sarah remarked.

"Which makes me question *why*?" said Victoria.

"Because Dick and Andy are involved in something shady as sure as two peas grow in a pod," Sarah deducted. "How else can you explain Jeffrey's case gettin' shoved under the rug?"

"Of course, you're right," Victoria remarked. "For twenty-five years, I was no problem. With no memory of Jeffrey's death, it was easy for Dick to convince the public there wasn't enough evidence to keep the case active. And Andy Grimes helped."

"Exactly," Sarah responded. "And anyone who rises to the occasion to support you in bringing Jeffrey's killers to justice gets a dose of Branson's lethal, attitude-adjustment tactics."

"Apparently Dick Branson is quick to react to anything that threatens his security," Victoria pointed out. "When I awakened from amnesia and began asking questions about Jeffrey's death, he tried to shut me up with a pack of lethal cigars, then he went after the only person on my side, Georgie Hendricks, my private eye."

"Ol' Dick seems to like fire. Neat and clean, with little evidence left." Sarah sighed, weighted down by the gravity of losing everything she owned—her family photos and fine antiques—the loss becoming more real to her by the second.

45

Back at Gloria's Trailer

Exhausted from expounding theories to explain why Sheriff Andrew Grimes would protect a criminal like Dick Branson, the three women were frantic to decipher the truth.

"So what do you think?" Sarah rolled her eyes.

"I'll go first," Gloria volunteered, eyes on Victoria. "Before Sarah's house was burned to the ground, she called Tanya Mason and they met up at the river—did I already tell you that?"

"Tell me again," Victoria replied, gazing at Gloria.

"Let me tell it," Sarah said. "I met Tanya at Bobby Graves' trailer park. Bobby's old—worked in traffic violations back in the eighties and loved kids," she recalled. "A real friend of Pop's."

"You probably remember ol' Bobby?" asked Gloria.

The fugitive had no visual of Bobby's face materializing in her brain. "I don't think so. Sorry, I'm sure he's nice."

"No matter," said Sarah, "Bobby's off doing us a favor."

"Do you believe the contents of the file is enough to convict Dick?" Victoria thought of Mrs. Wilson's intervention on behalf of her son, Terrance. "By chance, was the third plaintiff involved in the lawsuit against Hearty Meats named in the file?"

"Yeah, Donothan Craswell's name was mentioned in Jeffrey's notes as one of the victims who died from lung complications."

Silence told its own sad tale.

"As I recall," Sarah continued, "Donny was best buddies with James Hornsby and Terry Wilson. They graduated from high school together. What one did, they all did. Good or bad."

"Yeah," said Gloria. "All the boys wanted was a summer job that would earn them extra bucks. Look where good intentions got them. Working for Hearty Meats in 1984 was a bad choice. "

"If James and Terry hadn't moved the unidentified toxic oil barrels, they would probably still be alive," Victoria concluded.

"I hate all this!" Gloria fussed. "Talk doesn't change the past or git those boys back. We gotta git our heads in the future."

"You're right, Gloria!" A light bulb switched on in Sarah's mind, redirecting her thoughts as she turned toward Victoria. "Did I mention contacting Timothy Cates in Memphis?"

"*My* Timothy Cates?" Victoria jumped in her seat. "The one who prepared Jeffrey's life-insurance policy for me to sign?"

"*Junior*," Sarah clarified. "Senior died a few years back."

"You went to see Timothy—does he know anything about Jeffrey's death? Did his father ever say anything about why Caldwell Insurance folded at the end of 1989?" Victoria bombarded Sarah with questions, her mind in a quandary.

"Which question you want answered first?"

"Sorry," said Victoria. "You tell me."

"No, I didn't see Timothy in person, but I phoned SunTrust Bank and left my name and phone number for him to call."

"A number which is no good anymore," Gloria reminded Sarah. "Your address is disconnected, too—what's left of it."

"I should give him another call," Sarah said.

"And let him know you're living," Gloria remarked.

"Let's just hope young Timothy stays healthy," Victoria mumbled, knowing how fast Dick's grapevine worked.

"Look at us, down in the mouth like we're losers!" Gloria fussed. "This *thang* ain't over 'til we say it's over."

"You're right," said Victoria. "Back to what you were saying before, Sarah, about your clandestine meeting with Tanya Mason."

"Well, Tan was as shocked as I was to learn there were seven other boys who had suffered harmful physical effects from carting off the toxic barrels of oil," Sarah recalled. "The problem is, we don't know any of their names. Dead end, again."

"Maybe not. Jeffrey's notes prove that the environmental travesty committed by Hearty Meats touched many lives," Victoria pointed out. "Maybe some of the boys' relatives are still living."

"And how are we gonna get hold of that information without names to start with?" Sarah mewed. "Who's gonna risk their lives at this late date and admit they knew bout this crime?"

"Jeffrey would, if he were alive." Victoria believed her husband was a straight shooter when it came to justice. "He would never ignore anyone who needed his help. Bottom line."

"Jeffrey's not most people," Gloria remarked.

"No, he's not." Victoria agreed. "He was better."

"So all that we have to show the court is a copy of Jeffrey's handwritten notes—which are sketchy at best." Sarah noted the sadness in Victoria's face as a tear slipped down her cheek.

"I'd like to read those notes. Where are they?" Victoria hoped she could read between the lines as the widow of the victim. She and Jeffrey often operated on the same brainwave.

"I'm sorry," Sarah said, "but I don't have the copy of his notes with me." She was sensitive to Victoria's turmoil.

"Why not?"

"Bobby Graves has them."

"What? None of this is fair!" Victoria blurted out. "All my husband ever wanted to do was help the families of the victims and save Fernwood from future pollution mishaps. It didn't have to end with his death!" Her words were loaded with emotion.

"We know," the women empathized.

"The courts could have settled the dispute between the grieving families and Hearty Meatpacking Company with financial compensation," Victoria said. "Justice would have been served."

"What can we say, honey?" Gloria was out of ideas.

"It's Dick Branson's fault. He was too busy making money to stop production and comply with federal regulations," Sarah fussed. "He should pay for his crimes."

"I agree," said Gloria. "We both agree."

"Are you sure there's no way we can trace the whereabouts of the other victims?" Victoria grasped for a thread of hope.

Sarah and Gloria shook their heads.

"Let's face it," Sarah said, "nobility is not fashionable."

Victoria sighed. "I wish I could turn back the hands of time. If I hadn't been so upset at hearing the gunshots and wrecked my car, I would have been there to defend my husband's cause."

"And become one more body to bury," Gloria mumbled.

"It ain't your fault, Victoria!" Sarah exclaimed.

"Sarah's right, honey. Don't beat up on yourself."

"Can't at least one person stand up against Dick?"

"No. I tried to help, Vicki, and look where it got me. Scared and homeless," Sarah answered, confused and heartbroken.

"Okay, okay!" Victoria raised her hands. "Our complaining isn't getting us anywhere. Let's examine what evidence we have."

"Jeffrey's notes is about it," Sarah replied with a sigh.

"Did his notes indicate Dick was personally involved?"

"No," Sarah replied. "But you and I know that he was. The man probably had his finger in everybody's pocket in town."

"So that makes him party to the cover-up," Gloria stated.

"Square one: we can't prove it," Victoria concluded.

"But at least we still have the copy of Jeffrey's notes," Sarah pointed out. "No question Hearty Meats was illegally operating on contaminated soil. It isn't a big leap to blame the manager."

"Can Bobby Graves be trusted?" Victoria asked.

"Absolutely," Sarah replied.

"But neither does Dick's knowing about the environmental cover-up prove that he planned the break-in at Jeffrey's office."

"Oh brother, I need another cup of coffee." Gloria rushed off to the kitchen. "Or somethin' a little stronger," she grumbled.

"I'm so sorry, Victoria," Sarah said. "I thought we had the evidence to prove Dick Branson had a motive for killing Jeffrey."

"Thanks for caring." Victoria peered at Sarah. "What we have is partial evidence to convict Dick Branson for interfering with solving a murder. Before long, more pieces of the puzzle will surface. Soon, we'll know what happened the night Jeffrey died."

"We have to believe that," said Sarah.

"When we do, the opposition had better watch out." Victoria stood up and strapped the foam pillow to her stomach.

"What are you going to do *now*?" Gloria returned from the kitchen. "You ain't leavin', are you? Where will you go?"

"I can't tell you," Victoria answered. "If Dick's people catch up with either of you, they'll force you tell them how to find me."

"You're right. *Some things are best left unsaid,*" Gloria quoted Beverly James' insightful statement.

"Right." The fugitive slipped on her maternity top and picked up her K-Mart purse. "I'll be going now. Take care."

"Wait! How did you get here?" Sarah asked.

"Taxi. I phoned the driver not long ago and he's coming back to get me." Victoria peered out the window. "He's here."

"Oh, do be careful, Vicki." Gloria hugged her high school friend. "I'd hate for something bad to happen."

"It already has," Victoria stoically replied. "Really, I'll be fine, girls. I've got God on my side. Who can ask for better?"

46

Fernwood, Tennessee

Dick Branson was on the horn with Andy Grimes, fuming. "So, forensics said the body found in Sarah Boswell's house wasn't her." His fists were doubled in readiness to hit something.

"Correct," Andy replied. "I have even worse news."

"No more bad news, please!" Dick huffed. "Got any idee whose body was found in the charred remains?" he asked, backing into his swivel rocker and letting his weight pull him down.

"Josh Tenny hasn't shown up for work. He was supposed to tell Sarah she was on schedule to work the early shift on Sunday. It's Greg Diamond's guess that Josh met with the accident when he went over to her house. Too bad, I liked the young fella."

Dick moaned, not about to tell Andy he'd paid someone to set the stage for the accident, a little welcome-home party for Sarah Boswell to repay her for being so nosy. The officer should not have illegally borrowed the Tempest file. Didn't Sarah know that poking her nose where it didn't belong would reap trouble?

"Does Josh have family?"

"Only a grandmother," said Andy.

"Too bad for her."

Basically, Dick applauded Andy for performing his job well as county sheriff. But as a young rookie policeman, he'd committed a criminal act when he stole Attorney Jeffrey Tempest's personal notes from his desk, notes that related to an environmental case against Hearty Meats. Notes he later used for personal gain.

That was the one secret Dick had shared with Andy during the past twenty-five years, making the Tempest murder case personal, and solving the crime more dangerous.

No, Andy was not entirely innocent when it came to Jeffrey Tempest's death. Dick had been taking care of obstacles for years. Officer Sarah Boswell was just another clog in the engine.

Following the break-in at Jeffrey's office, the three hired thugs skipped town and never came back to collect their pay. Dick never even knew which one of them had pulled the trigger that left Jeffrey in a pool of blood. The storm had caused greater havoc than most people in Fernwood would ever realize.

How could forgetting one umbrella create such a mess?

"Just a minute, Andy." Dick's phone buzzed.

"Yeah?" he hurriedly answered Jeannie. "Send her in."   It was his first wife, Marilyn, waiting at the front desk to see him.

What did she want? Money?

"Gotta go now, Andy." Dick punched the button to break the connection. "Oh, hi, Marilyn."   He looked up and saw that she was already through the door. "I'm sorry the check was la—"

"This isn't about alimony, Dick. I've saved most of what you've sent me over the past ten years and I'm not living in poverty." Marilyn plopped her purse on his desk, eyes drawn to a man she once adored and trusted. "I have news about Jon."

"Oh, no! I knew he'd get in a motorcycle wreck before it was over! What was the boy thinkin'? Driving over the speed limit and riskin' his life!" Dick's horoscope chart indicated tragedy for the week. He should have called his personal psychic in Dallas.

"Mind if I sit down?" Marilyn had no patience for Dick's theatrics. She had gotten her fill of him while they were married. Both angry and sad at Dick's misplaced values, she had realized long ago that only Almighty God had the power to change him.

"Can I get you a cup of coffee?" Dick nervously fidgeted in his seat, convinced Marilyn's visit meant he was about to suffer. At a closer look, he noticed she appeared in better health.

"Decaf coffee would be nice," Marilyn replied, needing to calm her rapid heartbeat and prepare how to tell him that Jon was in jail sited for a religious crime against the government.

"Jeannie? Two decafs," Dick told his secretary. "Now." He crossed his thick arms over his chest. "Why are you here?"

Marilyn removed a tissue from her purse and blew her nose.

"This isn't a social visit, is it?" Dick already knew the answer. "Just tell me the bad news and get it over with." He puttered around the desk and straightened folders, brushing donut crumbs into the wastebasket, doing anything to avoid eye contact with his ex-wife whose very presence made him feel insecure.

"About *our* son," Marilyn said, clearing her throat.

If anyone had the clout to help Jon, it was Dick. Marilyn was packed and ready to go, her suitcase stored in the trunk of her Toyota. When she had finished her business with Dick she was leaving for the Memphis International Airport. This was goodbye.

"All right, Marilyn . . ." Dick ran his pudgy fingers over his mustache, the corners of his mouth twitching. "What is it about Jon that's so important you couldn't tell me over the phone?"

"Have you recently spoken to Andy?"

Huh? Jeannie came into the office and delivered two mugs of coffee and a handful of miniature creams and sugar packets.

"Thanks, Jeannie. Please close the door on your way out." Dick walked over and handed Marilyn her coffee. "What's Andy Grimes got to do with your visit?" He found his seat again.

"Your son has been arrested and needs your help. Will you go see him and talk to Andy about dropping the charges?"

"My son is in jail? What's he done now?" Why hadn't Andy mentioned Jon's arrest while they were talking a few minutes ago?

"I don't know all the details." Marilyn measured how much Jon would want her to share with his father about the safehouse. "Why don't you ask Jon yourself? Go and see him."

"I will." Dick stood and jacked up his pants, loose from eating too many Weight-Watcher meals.

"Thank you, Dick." Marilyn stood in preparation to leave.

"Shall I call you after I've talked to Andy?" Making Jon's bail shouldn't be a huge problem. Money always talked.

"No, you can handle it," Marilyn replied, aware that her home phone would be disconnected by tomorrow. No one would know where she had gone except Jon, who would never divulge her whereabouts. Secrecy was mandated in the Lord's service.

"Suit yourself," Dick replied, in a hurry to get over to the station to confront Andy, not caring a whit about what his ex-wife did with her time. "Is that all? I should get going."

"By all means." Marilyn gathered her things from Dick's desk. "Just go easy on the boy. He's a wonderful person."

"Have a nice day, Marilyn." Dick didn't want to hear about how nice Jon was, or what his mother thought about him.

"I will." Marilyn turned to leave Dick's office, probably forever. She looked back one last time, her thoughts private.

Goodbye, husband. Too bad you never cherished my love. May God convict you of wrongdoing and bring you into a right fellowship with Jesus.

47

Zurich, Switzerland

Victoria had Christean Langstead's cellphone reprogrammed, using the deceased Tobbie Juniper's number. How she came by that number was both heart warming and heart wrenching.

In her late forties, never expecting to have children, Tobbie had been delighted to learn that she was pregnant with twins. While vacationing in the Appalachians with her rugged mountain-climbing husband, James, Tobbie went into premature labor and miscarried. The delivery happened so fast she bled to death from complications before help arrived. James was devastated.

As a Christian, James was aware of the substitution program the Christian Protection Agency utilized to give Christian fugitives new identities. Since it was Tobbie's desire to be cremated, he had her burial ceremony in the mountains, scattered her ashes over the beautiful cliffs, and donated her identity to the CPA.

The CPA representative in Nashville had a master list of available identities and thought Tobbie's profile would fit Victoria. She had agreed, convinced that Tina Banks and Ruth Matthews were no longer safe identities. Still, wearing another woman's face and using her credentials felt weird. But it was the best option.

"Oh, hi, Daniel," Victoria said when he answered his cell.

"Mother? Where are you?" He turned to Daria and mouthed that it was his runaway mother. "Karen called and said you came to her wedding. Why did you attempt something so foolish?"

"It was a beautiful wedding, honey. I hate you missed it." Victoria thought back to Saturday and the foolish game she had played with her life by attending. "The picture looked pretty grim for me at first, but it all worked out, thanks to Mark and Karen."

"One day I want to hear all about it, but not now." Daniel was on a tight schedule. "Did you phone for a reason?"

"Yes," said Victoria. "Will it be possible for you meet me at UBS in Zurich tomorrow morning? I want my funds."

"Are you here, in Switzerland?" Daniel inquired. "Mother, the cellphone you are using is traceable."

"Don't be concerned. Can you meet me?"

"Maybe." He considered how to rearrange his schedule to do what his mother had asked. "Can I get back to you on this?"

"Sure. My plane just landed. I'm going to get a room in Zurich for the night and lie low." She didn't think a pregnant woman would be shopping late at night. "I'll call you, all right?"

"Call me in the morning," Daniel said. "Daria and I are en route to Schaffhausen as we speak. We both desperately need a few days of downtime after our ordeal in Africa. You want to come over to the chalet? I'd really like to see you in person and talk to you about your future plans." He hoped she would agree.

"I don't think that's possible, Daniel. I need to get my money out of the bank and move on with my plans."

"What plans?" Daniel waited for an explanation.

"Is this line secure?"

"Yes, mother. I'm a peacekeeper for NATO and all my conversations are private. If that were not so, the people I deal with wouldn't call me," he explained. "So continue please."

"Oh," said Victoria, not really comprehending the depth of Daniel's job. "I don't have anything to tell, son. Sorry."

"Look. I know that getting your hands on some money is important. Don't take this wrong, because I don't want you living off other people, but I also have a request."

"What is it?" Victoria thought she wouldn't like it.

"Promise me that after we go to the bank you'll come back to the chalet with me for a couple of days. I miss you, Mom, and I am very worried over your private agenda."

"You don't have to worry, I have things under control."

"What *things*? I may be your son, but I don't know a single *thing* about you anymore." Daniel eyed Daria. "You know Daria and I are planning a September wedding. I was hoping you could help us with that." It was the last ploy Daniel knew to try.

"Won't the police expect me to show up at the chalet? Do you want me to get arrested, Daniel?"

"Of course not! I'm on your side, Mom. I hope we can get this murder charge against you dropped. I need to hear your side of the story. Let me help you hire a lawyer, so you can go home and straighten out this mess," Daniel said. "Please, Mom."

"I can't do that yet, son. I might as well tell you that I am going to have brain surgery as soon as I have the funds."

"What? Where?"

"I can't tell you where and you can't come with me." Victoria answered. "I have faith God will see me through this."

Daniel sighed. "You believe a full memory will permit you to put Dad's death in perspective. I understand, and I agree."

"Thank you for your vote of confidence," Victoria replied. "I need to evaluate my existence based on a full set of memories. You can't imagine how difficult these months have been for me."

"No, I can't, Mom. No one can walk in another's shoes. I'm sorry." He let a couple seconds slip by. "So what time do you want me at the bank?" No use arguing with a signpost.

"Eleven o'clock. I'll find you."

"Are you coming incognito?"

"Never in a million years will you recognize me," Victoria said. "I like it that way, so I can move around without worrying about getting arrested. But, if I don't show up, leave. All right?"

"That goes two ways."

"Agreed."

"Then I'll see you tomorrow."

"Bye, son." Victoria slapped shut the cellphone and slid it inside her purse. *Now, to safely exit the terminal!*

While standing outside the Zurich International Airport, cabbies rushed over to offer Victoria a ride. Looking eight months pregnant definitely had it advantages, she decided.

Crawling into the back seat of a taxi, as Tobbie Juniper, Victoria instructed the driver to take her to the nearest economy hotel. The Euros left over from her last trip were dwindling, but first thing tomorrow morning, she would rectify that problem.

After modestly tipping a bellhop for carrying her suitcase to her hotel room, Victoria latched the door and let out a whoop of praise to Jesus. Never would she have made it this far without God's blessings, so many people had helped her along the way.

48

Denver, Colorado

Privacy didn't seem to be a problem for Beverly James. Bobby Graves had obtained her personal information via the Internet. Sarah Boswell said to look for NEWBRIGHT COSMETICS, INC. on the web, so he had. He might be old, but he wasn't inept.

The site listed home-based sales representatives and how to contact them. After cross-referencing Beverly's phone number, he learned her Denver address. She had a flat on the first floor.

To be on the safe side, Bobby parked his car down the street under a tree and walked to the upscale apartment complex.

While standing on her porch, he questioned the wisdom of becoming involved in so intricate a murder case. However, after coming thousands of miles, it seemed too late to turn tail and run since he'd promised Sarah he would personally deliver the illegal copy of Jeffrey Tempest's personal notes to Victoria's friend, the ex Mrs. Mark James. And like the good boy his mama always believed he was, Bobby usually kept his promises.

He knocked on Beverly's front door.

It had been a long trip in his old Ford truck and Bobby was tired. He wasn't energetic like he once was, couldn't push his old body like he used to. All he could do was his best.

He knocked again. If Beverly decided to help Victoria, that was her business. Once Jeffrey Tempest's notes were out of his hands, he was finished with his business in Denver, deed done.

In response, Beverly peeked through the donut hole in the door and spied a black man standing on her porch. Not having any idea who he was, she did the safe thing and punched the intercom button. "Is this a delivery?" she asked, not expecting a cosmetic shipment. "Please state your name and business here."

"It's a delivery, you might say that," Bobby answered, his image distorted through the beveled glass insert. "My name is Bobby Graves, Mrs. James. Your friend, Victoria Tempest, sent me." He was certain she would be curious. "Can I come in?"

"You're not a cop, are you?" Beverly inquired.

"Retired railroad. No guns." Bobby reached inside his pants pockets, removed the loose change, and pulled out the linings, grinning like the fox that caught the hen. "You wan' me to strip?"

"No, that won't be necessary." Beverly removed the chain on the door and opened it. "What do you want, Mr. Graves?"

"Don't know if you know Officer Sarah Boswell or not." Bobby peeked inside the murky condo, the only light coming from a small lamp. "She works for the Fernwood Police, and—"

"Come inside." Beverly glanced down the street then jerked the old man inside the condo. "Sarah Boswell's dead. Ain't you heard? I don't know anything, and if I did, I wouldn't say."

"Sarah's dead?" Bobby's sooty eyes rounded like silver dollars. "When did this happen?" He'd been traveling for the past two days. "How? Did she have an accident?"

"It happened early Sunday morning. It's all over the news—about the explosion and all. Where have you been, man?" Beverly asked, nervous as a blind bat flying in a hurricane.

"Been on the road since late Saturday. Ain't stopped to read no paper and my radio died 'fore I left. No use me taking up anymore of your time. Here." He handed Beverly his brown-wrapped package. "Sarah Boswell said to give it to you."

"What's this—a bomb?" Beverly listened for ticks. "Anthrax? Why are you doing this?" Fear tore at her face. "I don't know anything more about Jeffrey Tempest's murder. I told Victoria and her handsome boyfriend everything I knew."

"Oh?" said Bobby, learning a thing or two. "When was Victoria here? And who is her boyfriend?"

"You might as well take a seat," Beverly mumbled as she tore into the package. Inside was a manila envelope that contained several pages of hand-written notes. "What's this?"

"Read fer yourself." Bobby collapsed in a chair.

"I certainly will."

Beverly rushed off to the kitchen and laid the papers out on the breakfast bar. With a flick of a switch, bright florescent lights flooded the kitchen area. Bobby got up and followed, taking his time in getting to the kitchen. The woman was in a dither.

"Well, if this don't take the cake!" Beverly's eyes scanned the pages until realization knocked the breath out of her. "These are Jeffrey Tempest's personal notes—before he was murdered. It tells everything about Hearty Meats' environmental negligence."

"Exactly," said Bobby. "The problem is, nobody I know has the guts to take this information to the police. Will you?"

The woman's baby blues turned stagnant.

"Are you crazy? If Dick Branson finds out I've seen *this*, he'll kill me. But not before he takes care of you first! Who are you?"

"Nobody important—used to work for the L & N Railroad out of Jackson, Tennessee. Sarah's father was my friend. After I leave here tonight, Ms. James, I'm gonna disappear for a while. If anything bad happens to you, I promise to contact the FBI."

"That's real comforting, Bobby," Beverly huffed. "You wait until I'm dead, then you take over. Why don't I disappear and you take Jeffrey's notes to the Fernwood Police instead? Here."

Bobby smiled, pushing away Beverly's hand.

"I could do that," he said, "but I think being the ex-wife of Dr. Mark James might get you through more doors. Tha's whut Sarah thinks, too. Do the right thing and help Victoria."

Bev stared into space, deliberating the consequences.

"Well," she said. "I actually know one person who might be willing to help us." Donald Wetherfield came to mind.

"I don't care how you handle the matter, just do it," Bobby said. "And as far as Sarah being dead, I don't believe it. The cop is too smart to get herself kilt. She'll show up one day, mark my word." Bobby turned to leave. "Pleased to meet'cha, Beverly."

"Wait! Will you be all right? For a minute there I forgot my manners?" Beverly saw that the old man was weary.

"Doin' just fine." Bobby grinned. "Thanks anyhow."

"I hope you are right, Bobby—about Sarah's being safe. There's already been too many deaths in Fernwood, and far too much heartache." Beverly was familiar with grief.

"I agree," Bobby said. "I'll be goin' now."

"Sure I can't offer you a cup of hot chocolate or coffee?"

"No, but tha's mighty kind of you to care."

Beverly walked Bobby to the door. "Don't say anything about my having the notes," she warned him.

"No ma'am, I won't. Don't talk much to anybody."

"Good night, Bobby."

"Night, Ma'am."

Bobby Graves went out into the night and disappeared into the shadows of the trees lining the street. As the wind blew across the yard, Beverly began to wonder if she'd encountered a ghost.

With a chill running down her spine, she closed the door and latched it. Call it paranoid, but she put on the security system and closed the drapes tighter. Hot chocolate sounded like just the thing to chase away the cold fear invading her spirit.

After rereading Jeffrey's personal notes, Beverly thought about what she'd said to Bobby, about knowing someone who might help Victoria. She hadn't heard from Donald Wetherfield since the night they connected—literally. But she still had his cellphone number in case of an emergency.

Wasn't this an emergency?

The jujitsu expert, slash ex-marine undercover agent, had said to phone if any information about Victoria came to light.

And this news shines like a beacon!

"So, Donald, where are you?"

TUESDAY, JULY 1

49

Zurich was small in comparison to other towns, but it had all the world-class advantages of a big city. Situated on the northern shore of Lake Zurich, one could easily find fantastic views of the surrounding wooded slopes and distant Swiss Alps.

One of the key financial seats of Europe, Zurich boasted at having an enormous gold-bullion market. Headquarters for many major financial institutions, banks lined the *Bahnhofstrasse*, an elegant tree-lined avenue that ran through the heart of the city.

Alexander Luceres Ramnes lived fifteen miles from Zurich on hilly terrain. Though he enjoyed the countryside, for all practical purposes, he needed access to an international airport

Zurich was alive with sounds and odors today, the essence of life in perpetual motion. It was Tuesday, and Luceres had an appointment with the UBS bank manager at 9:45 a.m. to move some funds. He was also transferring two million euros into an account in Baghdad under the name of Aristotle Haddad.

Luceres had his driver pull the limousine up to the curb. "Wait here and keep the engine running," he instructed Robert. "I won't be long. Watch out for Donald," he added. "He's arriving in a taxi shortly with my guest from America."

After transacting his business, Luceres had promised to treat Georgie Hendricks to breakfast in *Alstad,* or Old Town. The woman needed a dining experience other than McDonald's. He pushed though revolving glass doors and entered the UBS facility.

Guards wearing blue uniforms stood near the front entrance of the bank to question anyone entering who appeared suspicious.

Considering how to infuse culture into Georgie's bland life, after breakfast Luceres would instruct Donald to escort her to the *Landesmuseum* and view a world-class collection of artwork. The woman needed to awaken her taste buds for more than hotdogs and Coke. Zurich Opera House also had decent offerings.

***

"So . . ." Georgie eyed Donald as the taxi turned the corner, "are we here in Zurich so you can send me back to the states?" It was a winning idea, but not likely on his agenda.

Not responding, Donald's eyes were on the outdoor scenery.

"Luceres said something about breakfast—" Georgie tapped her captor on the shoulder to gain attention. "Am I being treated to a last meal before your boss throws me to the sharks?"

"Cute, Georgie." Donald made eye contact and brushed away her hand. "Sit tight. I'll let you know what comes next."

"I was afraid of that." Georgie groaned and slid down in her seat. "You never said where we were going?"

"Not far. I can see the limousine from here."

"Are we taking a drive through the city in style?" She straightened up in her seat, peered out the front window, and spied the white limousine parked in front of a bank.

"You ask too many questions, Georgie."

"It's the curse of an investigator."

Robert Laurence was watching for Donald's taxi. He always did as his boss instructed, deemed trustworthy because he had driven over five years for Dr. Ramnes. There they were.

"Stop!" Donald instructed the cab driver. "We're getting out here. Come on." He grabbed Georgie by the arm.

"Off with the hands, I can get myself out of the cab!" the PI fussed as she pushed open the door and felt Zurich's heat slap her in the face. It was going to be a hot one, in more ways than one.

"Get in," Donald ordered Georgie as he opened the door to the sleek white limousine. "Back seat, please."

"Please?" She grinned and climbed aboard.

Air conditioning blew through the vents in competition with operatic music. The inside smelled like expensive leather and the glasses on the sidebar sparkled. "Are we having cocktails?"

"Bottled water. Want one?" Donald replied.

Georgie shook her head no.

"How are you doing today?" the driver asked Donald.

"We're fine." He ran his fingers through his hair.

"No, *we're* not. I need to pee," Georgie said. "Can I get out and go over there?" She pointed to a McDonald's restaurant.

"Can't you wait fifteen minutes?"

"No," said Georgie. "When you gotta go, you gotta go."

"Then I'll go with you," Donald said with disgust and opened the door. "No funny business, you hear?" He climbed out first and took Georgie by the arm. "Let's go. I'll be watching you."

Robert smiled over the incident, perusing a magazine while he waited for his boss to reappear from the bank.

Arm in arm, Donald and Georgie crossed the busy street and approached the front entrance of McDonald's. Kids played on the equipment in the caged yard reminding Georgie of America.

"I'll go in alone." Georgie jerked loose from Donald. "You can watch me through the window. I know how to find the restroom, and frankly, some things you have to do by yourself."

"Whatever." Donald lingered outside the door, observing a trail of kids leaving the restaurant with greasy sacks of food.

There were only two exit doors to the restaurant, and from where Donald stood he could see both. Georgie wasn't going anywhere far. If she tried, he would make her tremendously sorry.

Georgie angrily shoved open the door to the restroom and entered a stall. Her business didn't take long. While washing her hands, she noticed a woman entering—at least eight months pregnant. An American, she guessed, by the way she was dressed.

A pair of dark eyes, startled and wide, fell on Georgie, sending chills up her spine. "Do I know you, lady?"

The pregnant woman shook her head no and hurried into a stall. Curious as to why the woman reacted as she had, Georgie waited for her to come out. "Can I talk to you a minute?"

Obviously, the woman didn't speak English.

"Look, I'm only making conversation here." Georgie made the mistake of placing her hand on the woman's shoulder.

"Get your hands off me!" Eight Months took a few rickety steps backwards. "What are you doing here? Following me?"

"Victoria? Is that you?" The probability of Georgie running into her client in a foreign country by accident was about a billion to one. "I don't believe this! Pinch me so I can wake up!"

"What are you doing here, Georgie? Did you follow me from the states?" Victoria adjusted her maternity top.

"No," Georgie replied. "Life is not all about you."

"Why did you run off like you did? I was so worried."

"I was kidnapped!" Georgie half expected Donald to barge in the restroom any second and grab her. "I have to go now."

"Me, too, I'm leaving Zurich this afternoon."

"You should know I'm with Donald Wetherfield."

"What? That creep!" Anger raced over Victoria.

"You know him?"

"Yeah, he chased me in Nashville, but I outsmarted him. Please don't let him know I'm here." Fear crept in.

"My feelings are hurt that you think so little of me. I wouldn't turn you in, you're my client," Georgie professed.

"Really? I don't recall paying you."

"You haven't. But you will. You've really gotten into this undercover thing, haven't you? I understand you spy, too."

"I don't want to talk about me, Georgie. I was worried sick something bad had happened to you, but it appears you're doing just fine, hobnobbing with European nobility."

"You have it all wrong, Victoria, but now isn't a good time to hash out our differences. I really need to go."

"Yeah, me too. I have pressing business that needs my attention." It was time to meet Daniel at UBS across the street.

"Monkey business." Georgie poked the foam pillow underneath Victoria's tent blouse. "So why are you here?"

"It's a personal matter." Victoria's eyes were on the door like she expected the police to charge in and arrest them both.

"Isn't everything? Your friend Dick Branson did a number on me and Donald Wetherfield rescued me," Georgie revealed.

"How sweet of him. You're not taking his side, are you?"

"Never. But I am in a good position to negotiate my future."

"Yeah? Tattling on me? Sounds like a case of bribery."

"I hate it when you do that," Georgie fussed. "Makes me feel like a traitor." The wind sailed out of her lungs.

"Are you?" Victoria evaluated Georgie's sincerity.

"That hurts, you know. Donald Wetherfield is outside the restaurant waiting on me. Don't go bumping into him. He'd love to turn you over to his boss like a trophy on a silver platter."

"Yeah, I get that. I better not tarry, lest Attila the Hun drag me away by the hair on my head." Victoria searched Georgie's troubled face. "Come with me. We'll leave Zurich together."

"Believe me, I'd like nothing better."

"Good. We'll exit through the back—you can hide—"

"I can't," Georgie put a halt to Victoria's inventive escape plan. "As my client, I have to advise you to linger awhile at McDonald's. Have a juicy hamburger and lie low until the white limousine parked across the street is gone."

"What is it you're *not* saying, Georgie?" Victoria knew there was more to the situation. "You're scaring me."

"Your good buddy, Luceres, is at the bank across the street as we speak," Georgie revealed "Don't cross his path."

Victoria wilted as she leaned against the bathroom sink.

"I'm meeting my son Daniel at the bank." She glanced down at her Mickey-Mouse wristwatch. "And I'm already late."

"Let him wait thirty minutes," said Georgie.

"If I don't show up as planned, Daniel will leave."

"That's his problem. Don't you like your freedom? Going into the bank right now is a very risky idea."

"So it seems." Victoria contemplated her choices.

"And don't forget that Luceres knows Daniel."

"It doesn't matter, Luceres won't recognize me in my disguise." Victoria prayed God was up to something miraculous.

"I did," Georgie pointed out.

"When will I see you again?" Victoria asked.

"I don't know. Memphis, maybe?"

"That might be a while." Victoria became realistic. "We should talk soon. I have a lot to share with you about Jeffrey's murder case. Sarah Boswell and Gloria Gordon are on *our* side."

"Our side?" Georgie said. "Does that mean you trust me?"

"Yeah, I guess we have a bond."

"How can I contact you? Where will you be staying?"

"You can't. I'm going to see my mother when I leave here and have brain surgery. I'll contact you through Devin Baldwin."

"Not a fun idea," said Georgie. "He failed the friend test."

"Oh?" Victoria suddenly gave Georgie a tight hug. "You've been a wonderful addition to my life," she said. "It feels more like you are my daughter than my private eye. Please be careful."

"Aw now, don't go getting' all mushy on me!" Georgie was privately touched. "If you're bent on meeting Daniel at the bank, let him take the lead. Whatever he tells Luceres will be believable. He's a negotiator, after all. Keep your mouth shut."

"I will." The next thirty minutes were critical. "Wait," said Victoria as Georgie cracked the bathroom door. "Do you have any idea why Luceres wants to see me so badly?"

"Claims he wants to hear your side of the murder drama." Georgie turned around to face Victoria. "He says he'll help you out of your legal mess if you can convince him you're innocent."

"That's mighty nice of him. Does he read minds?"

"As a matter of fact, he does."

"Give me a break!" Clairvoyance was a gimmick of Satan, fortune-telling strictly forbidden by the Bible. "I don't want to hear *anything* that man has to say!" Victoria exclaimed.

"It couldn't hurt to talk to him."

"Forget it! What about *us*, Georgie? I thought we were a team. I don't need or want that man's help. I'm about to wrap up Jeffrey' murder myself." Victoria hoped it was true.

"Oh?" Georgie's eyebrows lifted. "How?"

Victoria glared at her friend a nanosecond. "Don't trust Luceres, Georgie. His goal is to bring about world government, a system that limits individual rights and religious freedom."

"I don't want to hear this, Victoria."

"The man opposes the principles of Christianity. He will lie, cheat, and manipulate people to accomplish his agenda," Victoria plead her cause. "Peace may sound wonderful and safe, but in the end it will turn society into the worst kind of dictatorship."

Victoria knew people would be required to have a mark on their foreheads or their hands to buy and sell. Eventually, they would be forced to submit to the Antichrist, a puppet of Satan.

"Come away with me, Georgie. Now!"

"Not a bad sermon, but I'm not into that sort of stuff."

"It's real, Georgie!" Victoria was passionate about her beliefs. "I wish we had more time to talk about this." Every life was a story waiting to be told, and she would sure like to hear Georgie's.

"Do what you have to do, Victoria. As for me, I'm going to cooperate with Luceres so I can go home and get back my old life. I'd better go now before Donald comes in here after me."

Tears filled Victoria's eyes. "I'm sorry you feel that way, but we'll meet again soon." She felt it was true. "I'm not through talking to you about God's plan for your life."

"Whatever . . ."

"Is this it for now?"

"It seems so." Georgie hated leaving Victoria to fend off the wolves. "Are you going home to face the music? It would indeed be a pleasure to watch Dick Branson pay for his crimes."

"You can take it to the bank. Justice is on my side."

50

Donald Wetherfield paid close attention to those entering and leaving McDonald's, not trusting Georgie any farther than he could throw her. She'd been in the bathroom a long time.

What is going on? He stepped to the side as a pregnant woman passed him and headed across the street. His cellphone rang.

"What?" Donald peered through the plate-glass window of McDonald's, scanning the busy restaurant for Georgie.

"Is that you, Donald?"

"Yeah. Who is this?" He was in no mood for distractions.

"Beverly James," a warm, sexy female voice came back.

"Oh, hi. I've been meaning to call you—" Donald's anger at Georgie melted like cheese at hearing Beverly's voice. He had a soft spot in his heart for the lady. "Can you hold a minute?"

Donald cupped his hand over the phone and peeked inside the restaurant. Where the devil was Georgie? Uh oh, there she was, in a long line of customers waiting to purchase food.

"Sorry, I'm back," said Donald, cursing under his breath.

"Did you hurt your fingers?" Beverly sarcastically remarked. "So bad you couldn't call me?" Silence filled the void.

"Uh, I—" Donald stumbled around with his words, having no reasonable explanation why he hadn't phoned. "Sorry."

"Admit it! You like one-night stands. I suppose having a real woman in your life would cramp your style. I get it, believe me."

Donald grinned. "I gotta say I've missed that wit of yours. Maybe I'll make my way back to Denver before long." He was uncertain what he wanted from the feisty female. In times past, he'd yearned to find the right person and settle down. But then, he had never met a woman who challenged him. *Until now* . . .

"If you plan on breezing through Denver like a ship passing in the night, you can forget calling me! I'll be busy," she said.

"Then why did you call me?"

"Because I have new information regarding Victoria and her deceased husband," Beverly answered. "Right here, in my hot little hands, is a valid copy of some old hand-written notes penned by Attorney Jeffrey Tempest a few months before he was murdered. I thought you'd be interested."

"Yeah, I did say call, didn't I? I'd like to read what you have. Could you fax the notes?" Donald gave Beverly the number.

She took a moment to jot it down.

"I assume Jeffrey's remarks in some way supports Victoria's innocence." His boss would want to evaluate the information.

"In my way of thinking, it does."

"I guess this is not good news for Richard Branson."

"No, it isn't. Possessing this information makes me a bit nervous. I don't wanna end up on a cold slab in some morgue."

"Right." Donald respected the woman's stark reality.

"But if it helps Victoria get her life back . . ."

"Your involvement is worth it," he finished her sentence.

"Correct. So what do you think I should do *now*?"

"Sit tight. Fax me the notes," Donald said. "Can't talk any longer, I'm in the middle of something. I'll be in touch."

"You know how to find me," she said.

"Yeah, I do." He closed his cell, noticing Georgie coming out of the restaurant carrying a big white sack of smelly food.

"Who was that?" Luceres startled Donald.

"A friend." Donald turned around and faced his boss.

"Sorry to disturb you, but I need an item from the limousine. Apparently, Robert has locked up and stepped away for a few minutes. Do you happen to have an extra set of keys?"

Donald dug into his pants pockets. "Here."

"What's this?" Luceres asked as Georgie arrived with her snack sack. "You're going to ruin the breakfast I have planned."

"Too bad." She munched on a salty French fry. "I got hungry." She sipped Coke from a plastic straw. "Want one?"

"You can take the girl out of the country, but . . ." Luceres chuckled. "Do me a favor, Donald. Take this woman to the limousine and don't let her out again until I'm done in the bank."

"Sure." Donald grabbed the detective by the arm, watching his boss cross the street ahead of them and retrieve what he needed from the vehicle. "Move it, Georgie!"

"All right, already!" Georgie balked as Donald pulled her along. "I'll get salt all over your pretty limousine."

"Eat faster," Donald ordered.

***

"Fine, so far," Victoria mumbled as she entered the UBS and gingerly glanced around for Luceres, nowhere in sight.

Good! Apparently, he'd completed his business and departed.

Victoria spied Daniel chatting with a suited bank executive seated behind an impressive desk. Hobbling over, one hand on her stomach like it hurt, she lightly tapped him on the shoulder.

Daniel turned around and smiled. "Can I help you?"

"You might," Victoria said. "I have this little gold key." On a chain, it spun around in the air. "I was told it would unlock my safe deposit box. Ain't sure what I'm s'posed to do next."

"Excuse me, James," Daniel said to the bank executive. "I'll assist this lady in completing her transaction."

"No problem," James replied. "Be the Good Samaritan."

"Are you ready?" Daniel's eyes mischievously flashed.

"You bet." Victoria held her stomach to secure the foam pillow about to slip from under her maternity blouse. If only Karen and Mark could see her now. "Could we hurry a little?"

271

"About to deliver?" Daniel teased, grasping his mother by the elbow and ushering her over to an unoccupied corner. "Don't look now, but your buddy Luceres just walked into the bank."

"What?" Despite Daniel's warning, she glanced at him.

"Uh oh, looks like he's on his way over to speak to me."

Victoria considered running, but it would only draw more attention. The confrontation was unavoidable.

"Keep your mouth shut, Mother, I'll handle this."

Worry creased Victoria's brow. *Relax*, she told herself.

"On second thought, why don't you go up to the counter and ask for help. Lockbox # 1313 is your number?" Daniel whispered in Victoria's ear. "Use the name Brenda Jane Lane. When I see the clerk come out to assist you, I'll step over with my key."

Victoria spied Luceres closing in and froze.

"Go, Mother!" Daniel nudged her elbow.

"Nice day." Luceres arrived. "Who was that?"

"Good morning, Dr. Ramnes." Daniel extended his right hand in a gesture of friendship. "No one important."

"I'm glad I ran into you, Daniel." Luceres glanced at the pregnant woman, thinking he'd passed her on the street.

"What's up?" Daniel crossed his arms over his chest.

"I've been intending to phone and ask why you failed to remain in Rome to receive your peacekeeping award?"

"Sorry about that," Daniel casually remarked. "I had a family emergency. I heard you delivered a great speech."

"The emergency didn't happen to involve your lovely mother, did it?" Luceres sought details, evaluating Daniel's mannerisms.

"Mother? No. Why?" Daniel kept a stoic face.

"That woman talking to you . . . she looks out of place."

"Oh, *her*," said Daniel. "She's not from here, had a couple of questions concerning how to access her lockbox. I might need to step over and lend a hand if she doesn't get help."

"That's very kind of you. Seems odd that she banks here."

"I thought that, too, at first," said Daniel. "My guess is she inherited some money. It really isn't any of my business."

Hmm . . . "So, how was your visit to Africa?" Luceres cleared his throat, curbed his curiosity and moved on to a new subject.

"Fine. My team negotiated a treaty and avoided an uprising in Uganda. Routine stuff, you know."

"You young peacekeepers do a bang-up job." Luceres placed a hand on Daniel's shoulder. "Do me a favor, son. If you hear from your mother, call me? I'd like to help her, if I can."

"Mother is pretty stubborn. I'm not sure she wants anybody's help, including mine," Daniel stated a fact.

"Anyhow . . ." Luceres glanced over at the pregnant woman, "if Victoria needs legal advice, I know a competent attorney."

"I'll mention that to her," Daniel said. "Next time we speak."

***

Daniel's lengthy discussion with the world leader worried Victoria as she assumed a position in the long line of customers waiting for assistance. What were they talking about so intensely?

Not me, she prayed.

After fifteen minutes, there was only one person left in the line in front of her. "Excuse me," a voice from behind said.

Victoria turned around and gazed into a pair of disturbing serpentine eyes. *"Keep your mouth shut,"* came to mind.

"Do you have the correct time?" Luceres asked. "My watch quit on me," he explained, psychically probing the lady's mind.

Liar. Victoria held out her Mickey-Mouse wristwatch for him to see the time. *Read for yourself, bud!*

"Thank you." Luceres set his watch. "Do you need help?"

Victoria shook her head no.

"When is your baby due?" he inquired.

He isn't giving up, is he? Life revolved around words. *How do the deaf and dumb communicate?* In response, she held up one finger.

273

"In a month. You can't speak at all?"

Victoria shook her head again. *What do I do now, Lord?* The silly smile on her face was genuine.

"Excuse me, lady, but it's your turn," an elderly gentleman in a bright blue suit addressed Victoria. "Step forward, please."

Becoming disinterested in the pregnant woman, Luceres stepped over to a vice-president's desk to complete his business.

"Thank you." Victoria quickly retrieved the gold key from her purse, handed it over to the bank clerk, and followed the tall man into a small room located through a door behind the counter.

"Sign here," he said, holding her key in his hand.

Victoria signed Brenda Jane Lane alongside her password number, anxious to get the transaction over with.

"We will need the third party, Ma'am," the clerk said.

"Oh, my associate. He'll be along shortly."

Victoria turned around and looked for Daniel. *Oh dear*, she sighed. *What now?* All she saw was a crowd of people.

51

"Why did you eat so much?" Donald fussed as Georgie polished off two sausage-and-cheese biscuits. The heat was rising outdoors. "Keep this up and you'll get fat."

"I doubt it—not in my genes." She licked her fingers.

"You're purposely irritating me," he complained. "I don't have the patience of Job. For your own good, remember that."

"Oh, you're a Bible scholar now. How interesting."

"Don't provoke me, Detective, I have my limits."

"So you say." Georgie brushed breadcrumbs from her hands. "Ain't nothin' like a McDonald's breakfast to jumpstart the day."

"Get in." Donald opened the limousine door and gave her a nudge. The engine was running and cool air circled the vehicle.

"No roughhousing!" Georgie fussed, thoughts centered on Victoria and what was taking place inside the bank.

Donald took a seat facing Georgie and picked up a magazine to read. Any second, she half expected Victoria to come barreling out of the bank, stomach bucking like a horse and foam stuffing flying. Such was life on the run, interesting and dangerous.

"What?" Donald glanced up from his reading. "When you get quiet, I start to worry." The woman had a tongue on her the size of Godzilla's. "Did something happen inside the restaurant?"

"Uh—no. I was just thinking," said Georgie.

"What about?"

"None of your beeswax," Georgie wisecracked.

"Is that a southern word for business?"

"Take it any way you like," Georgie cockily replied. "Look, Donald, I think it's time you leveled with me. Am I going home? In my way of thinking, I have fulfilled all your expectations."

Donald blinked. "It's not my call."

"Okay, so that we don't misunderstand one another, what I want from you and your boss is a guarantee that Dick Branson and his buddies won't track me down and try to kill me again. I go home, I keep my mouth shut, and you find Victoria."

"Want a piece of gum?" Donald opened a pack of Dentine. "It will clean your teeth and freshen your breath."

"*Gum?* Is that all you have to say?"

"For now." His lips pursed with amusement.

Like life, the tides had shifted.

"Doesn't make any difference whether you need my help, or not . . ." Georgie reminded Donald, "you did promise to let me go home if I came to Zurich with you. Well, *duh*, I'm here. And haven't I spilled my guts about Victoria to your boss? In my book, that means I've fulfilled my contract. Now, fulfill yours."

"I'll think about what you said."

Oh, great! She had better get another plan, and fast.

***

Denver, Colorado

It was well after midnight on Monday when Bobby Graves left the motel. He liked driving at night, when the traffic was at a minimum. And Bobby hoped he'd done the right thing in giving Beverly James the *only* copy of Jeffrey Tempest's notes regarding his work with the plaintiffs suing Hearty Meats, Incorporated.

Like Sarah, Bobby believed Beverly James was in a better position to help Victoria, having been once married to Mark James. It would take a bigger fish than him or Sarah to stir Fernwood's murky waters. Say for instance, he took the notes to the Sheriff Grimes. Likely, the evidence would be buried under a pile of paperwork and not taken seriously. His past grievances with the Fernwood Police Department definitely would not help.

No, going to Beverly with the criminal information was the best way to assure that someone would eventually pay attention to what Jeffrey's notes meant. Beverly would not easily let Sheriff Grimes blow her off, her dislike for Dick Branson most helpful.

Bobby got in his old Ford truck and drove deeper into Utah. Deciding it was time to see the remote part of the Wild West, or what was left of it, he was fulfilling a lifetime dream to view the magnificent desert valleys from the top of mountain peaks.

Certainly, Bobby's new vantage point would prove starkly different from his favorite reclined positioned in front of the television set. Anyhow, he wasn't needed at the fishing camp. His nephew, Spud, was there with Louis, taking care of business.

Yep, no time like the present for some R and R. Bobby enjoyed the dark. The stars above were huge, hanging by invisible threads in the black velvety sky. He felt amazingly good. Having taken his high blood-pressure medication on schedule, he expected no health problems in making the solo trip. *No sir.*

Cruising down the highway, singing an old country tune to the top of his lungs, Bobby periodically munched on a pack of salty, cheese-flavored chips. He'd been on the road for a spell when he felt a pain ripple through his chest. Probably indigestion, he guessed. Nothing major. So he kept on driving.

Feeling uncomfortable a ways down the road, Bobby pulled over to the side of the road and killed his truck engine. *What a bummer!* The pain just kept getting worse. He began to worry.

Bobby's cellphone was useless in the desert.

Dadgummit! He should have purchased a fancy satellite version for the trip. Was he going to have a heart attack and never get to see how the Tempest trauma turned out? *Shoot!*

In excruciating pain, Bobby slumped down behind the wheel of the truck. Two minutes later, his heart stopped beating. All was silent in the desert except for the lone cry of a coyote.

52

Washington, D.C.

Lazarus Bacon tapped on his nanny's door. He was back at the White House earlier than anticipated. It had been a long flight from Baghdad and he was tired. All he wanted was food, a hot shower, and a soft bed. He knocked again, but Natalie didn't respond. Deciding she was probably out of the house on an errand, he opened the bedroom door and walked in without asking. Natalie was wrapped up in sheets with a new boyfriend.

"Did Mama call?" he asked, not about to bolt.

"Lazarus! You bad boy!" Natalie shooed her guest out of the bed. Horrified, her boyfriend raced to the bathroom with a towel around his waist. "I wasn't expecting you until later."

"John let me in." John was CIA and used to Lazarus playing pranks on his nanny. "I'm hungry. Got anything to eat?"

"Let's go to the kitchen." She led him from the bedroom. "Do you know how worried I've been? How dare you run away like that! Ending up in a hospital with injuries. What if something really bad had happened to you? I would have lost my job."

"Yeah." Lazarus was grateful Natalie was totally selfish and keeping her job was top priority. She would never tell his parents about what happened. "Sorry. Can I have chocolate milk?"

The kitchen flooded with light as Natalie flipped a switch.

"Your parents called a couple of hours ago and I had to lie to them. I told them you were busy on the computer. They're going to be livid if you don't finish last week's homework."

Natalie opened the refrigerator door and removed a carton of chocolate milk from the top shelf. "Promise me you won't run away again." She poured the dark syrupy liquid into a glass.

"I promise." Lazarus was thirsty and drank all the milk in a few gulps. "I'm tired. Can I go to my room now?" He yawned.

"First, we have to have a little talk."

"About what?"

"Were you really in the hospital?" She was aware of the boy's devilish nature. "Tell me, so we can keep our story straight." She wanted to shake him, but dared not lay a hand on him.

"Does it matter, Natalie? I'm home now, and safe. Isn't that what counts?" the lad wisely answered. "I'd like a big bowl of Fruitloops, dry, so I can take it to my room for a snack."

"Sure," said Natalie, noticing her boyfriend peeking around the doorjamb. "Go get a shower and change clothes while I fix your snack. I'll bring it to you." She gave him a tight hug.

"Thank you, Natalie. You're the best."

"No problem, Lazarus. I'm just grateful you're home safe."

***

Fernwood, Tennessee

Detective Jake Kyle was on the trail Officer Sarah Boswell had taken Saturday afternoon, after she left the Quick Print Shop.

Sarah had stopped to gas up her car and asked the attendant if he knew if the fish were biting on the Tennessee River, which suggested she was headed out in that direction. After studying the state map, Jake chose the most direct route to the river.

A guy selling fresh fish bait at a gas station told Jake about the fishing camp on the river. Thirty minutes later, he found the row of dilapidated trailers on top of a hill overlooking the river.

Jake climbed out of his truck and ventured inside the trailer that had a vacancy sign in the yard. Louis was in charge.

According to Louis, a renter overseeing the camp, Bobby Graves was the owner and was presently out of state on vacation. Jake asked a few leading questions and got the standard "I don't know" answers when Officer Sarah Boswell's name came up.

Bobby's deranged nephew, Spud, seemed fuzzy about why his uncle wasn't there. "And you're certain you have no idea why Bobby took off so suddenly?" Jake asked Louis again.

"All I know is Bobby tol' me to keep an eye out for Spud. He's not the sharpest tack on the bulletin board, you know."

Jake chuckled, wondering about Bobby's agenda.

"As far as renting trailers, we git folks up here every weekend lookin' for cheap rent. Ain't no problem to run this camp."

Jake was uninterested in how business ran on the river. He could not verify that Sarah Boswell had been at the camp, though he wondered why Bobby Graves took off on a vacation at his age.

Perhaps Sarah had shown Bobby Jeffrey Tempest's notes, and he became frightened and ran away. With Bobby not there to answer Jake's questions, he had reached an impasse.

Then maybe he was barking up the wrong tree. It could be Sarah had gone elsewhere with her critical information.

"Thank you, Louis." Jake gave the man a crisp new fifty with a business card and told him to call when Bobby showed up.

Two hours later, rolling past the city limits of Fernwood, Jake called Dick Branson to give a report. "It wasn't much to go on," he said, "but I'm not through with my investigation."

"Keep digging," Dick replied. "There's more, I'm betting."

Dick disconnected the phone, worried over how many people Sarah Boswell had told about Jeffrey's personal notes. Who knew how many were plotting to collapse his financial kingdom?

Somehow, he had to tip the scales in his favor.

Oh, he could claim the notes were forged, and Andy Grimes would back him up. But, if the female cop got the FBI involved, it might take a little more doing to wiggle out of the obvious.

It had been decades since Dick had read those notes. In the notations, Jeffrey Tempest had detailed incriminating information concerning Hearty Meats' environmental cover-up. Worse, he'd given the names of the boys who died from the toxic poisoning. The notes proved that company's leadership had motive for breaking into Jeffrey's office and stealing the pertinent files.

Dick sighed, angry over the escalating situation and at Victoria's meddling in rekindling the cold case. If he could wrap his hands around her neck, he would squeeze the life out of her.

Should the case go to trial it wouldn't be a giant leap for jurors to believe that the manager of Hearty Meats knew about the break-in at Jeffrey Tempest's office. They would assume he had hired the perpetrators to do the job. The jury would never believe that Jeffrey's death was accidental. "Premeditated murder," they'd declare and blame him. It would be just awful.

Dick grabbed an antacid from his desk drawer and popped it in his mouth. No, the wisest thing he could do was make sure Officer Sarah Boswell never made it back to Fernwood with her copy of the notes. Jake had obtained a list of Sarah's friends, and would begin at the top with Tanya Wilson Mason, the sister of the deceased Terrance Wilson. Eventually, Sarah would get her due for meddling in his business. With that thought, Dick felt better.

53

The Union Bank of Switzerland

"Excuse me, Ms. Florhof," Daniel Tempest addressed the bank clerk, flashing his high-security badge, "but I need to get inside Brenda Lane's safe-deposit box." He indicated the pregnant woman seated on a corner bench. "Will you assist us?"

Confused at first, the young female bank clerk approached Daniel. "I probably can. Are you in possession of the third key necessary to open Ms Lane's lockbox?" she asked in German.

"Yes," said Daniel. "We're here to remove some stocks and bonds from Brenda's safe-deposit box and covert them to liquid funds. Here is the bank account for the electronic transfer."

Elise Florhof began to tremble. "To transfer these funds, I will need my manager's approval." This all said in German.

"No, Miss Florhof, that won't be necessary. You will use your gold key, along with ours, and open Lockbox #1313."

Nervously blinking blue eyes, Elise Florhof scoffed, "You must be joking, sir!" She was inches from pressing the alarm button on the wall and getting the international police involved.

"I'd think twice before I did that," Daniel warned.

"I need to see your identification. Right now!"

Daniel opened his leather wallet and flashed his picture I.D. "I'm a UN peacekeeper with governmental clearance to transfer these funds. Now, can we proceed with this transaction?"

Victoria prayed Ms. Florhof would believe Daniel.

A few seconds passed as she thought about the situation. Then with a profound sigh, Elise invited Daniel and Victoria into her office, promptly presenting the proper forms for them to sign.

"Thank you," said Daniel. "I'll be sure you get special commendation for your cooperation in this transaction."

Daniel followed Ms. Florhof into the bank vault, and Victoria entered behind him. When the lockbox opened, Daniel retrieved the stocks and bonds from the metal container and handed them to the bank clerk. "Please don't keep us waiting too long."

Elise's gaze wafted on Victoria, her expression reflecting concern. No doubt, if she had misjudged the situation, she would lose her job, or worse. "The process will take awhile."

Daniel nodded. "Do your best. We'll wait."

When the metal door clicked, Victoria ripped away her fake glasses and exclaimed, "You did it, son!" She ferociously hugged him. "God bless you for caring so much!"

Their eyes connected on a deep level.

"Of course, I care, Mother." Daniel held Victoria at arm's length. "But we're not finished here, yet. Nor are we home free. When Elise returns we will be leaving the bank, safely I hope."

"Is this transaction going to work? Can I really go into the Bank of Canada and withdraw my funds?" Victoria asked.

"As long as you use Brenda Lane's credentials, the money is yours. Karen and I want nothing to do with how you spend your life's saving, although I admit I am most curious."

"I know you don't approve of my belief in Jesus Christ, or my mysterious associates, but I plan to donate some of the money to a Christian organization that supports fugitives like me."

"People like you—religious *rebels*?" Daniel scoffed. "Please! I don't want details, Mother. Just assure me you will be safe."

"I will be safe. I'm going to see your grandmother—"

"Who is living where?" Daniel interrupted.

"At a safe location in Canada. And when I get there, I'm going to see a surgeon about having these lesions on my brain removed. I want my life back. I want to know who I am."

"I doubt recalling the past will get your life back, Mother. Mark is out of the picture, married to Karen. And too much water has run under the bridge for you to return to Fernwood without consequences. Face it, Mother, you have enemies."

"Dick Branson!" *Humph.* "I'm not concerned about him."

"You should be. He has plenty of clout."

"And I have evidence to incriminate him," Victoria declared.

"What kind of evidence?"

"A friend of a friend has a copy of your father's hand-written notes detailing his legal case against Hearty Meats. Jeffrey's notes prove Dick had motive to break into his office and steal his files."

"Cloak and dagger stuff again! I'd like to see those notes."

"I'm sorry, but that's impossible, son. Trust me when I tell you that it's Dick Branson's fault your father died."

"I'm sorry, but this is not a discussion we should have right now. We need to concentrate on our task at hand," Daniel said.

"I know, leaving the bank safely. But there's one more thing you should know . . ." Victoria drew a breath. "If my surgery goes as well as I hope, and my memories return, I'm going home."

"To face the charges filed against you?"

"Yes."

"Trusting a friend of a friend is going to speak up on your behalf." Daniel half smiled. "Fairly risky, isn't it?"

"What else can I do? I have to prove I'm innocent."

"You're too old to play with fire, Mother."

"And you're too impertinent to be my son," she lashed back.

"Truce." Daniel chuckled.

"You and Karen just don't seem to get it," she said.

"Your plan is very dangerous, Mother. We get it."

"Life is dangerous," Victoria defended her decision. "A person can drop dead from a heart attack, or have a stroke. Get run over crossing a busy street. I refuse to live my life in fear!"

"I like this new Victoria." Daniel smiled.

"When this is all over—I mean, when the murder charge against me has been dropped—I promise to be a better mother."

At that, Daniel melted and pulled his mother to his breast. "You are a good mom. Circumstances are weird right now."

"Thank you for understanding."

"To play the devil's advocate, what if your contact fails to deliver Daddy's notes to the proper authorities? Can you prove they exist? The evidence against you is weighty," Daniel said.

Victoria peered at her son. "I have to go home."

Daniel let out a moan. "Wouldn't it be prudent on your part to tell me the name of this friend with the notes?"

"Officer Sarah Boswell," Victoria replied.

"The cop whose house burned down early Sunday morning?"

"Somebody else died in that fire," Victoria declared. "Sarah is alive and well. I saw her two days ago. Daniel, she's doing her best to help me. I'm convinced the truth will win out."

"Don't tell me." Daniel held up a hand. "Sarah made an illegal copy of the notes. And how did she manage that?"

Victoria nodded. "It's a long story."

"I bet," said Daniel, buzzing for the bank clerk.

"I love you, son. Thanks for helping me."

The door lock clicked. "It's Ms Florhof," Daniel said. "Let me do the talking. When we're through here, walk slowly out of the bank. Don't look at anyone, just keep moving."

"What if Luceres tries to stop me?"

"I doubt he will, but if he does, I'll distract him."

"Thank you, Daniel. I love you."

Elise Florhof entered the vault and handed Daniel the receipt to the transaction. "Anything else, sir?"

"No," said Daniel. As expected, his credentials had checked out and Elise could care less who his accomplice was.

"Follow me." Elise led the way out of the vault.

"Thank you," Daniel said, handing the envelope to Victoria.

Heart palpitating, mouth dry, Victoria's eyes met Daniel's. "Until we meet again." She squeezed his arm and exited the vault.

54

Victoria glanced around the lobby of the Union Bank of Switzerland. Luceres was nowhere in sight. *Thank you, Jesus.*

As Daniel instructed, Victoria walked slowly toward the exit door, eyes straight ahead. "If he's watching, don't look," she kept saying to herself over and over again as the door came closer.

Victoria stepped outdoors and squinted in the bright sunlight, warm on her face, a brisk cool breeze stirring in the air. The white limousine was still parked in the same place, its windows too dark to see through. On the horizon, storm clouds were gathering.

Not a good sign, Victoria thought.

Like my son says, she reminded herself, just keep on walking.

At the end of the short block, Victoria spied a cab idling. Inside, the driver she had hired was waiting patiently for her.

Success was but a few dozen steps away. Victoria ripped off her blond wig, prosthetic nose, and glasses, a sign of victory as significant to her as a soldier waving Old Glory at the end of the Revolutionary War. She'd done it. *Hooray!*

***

Donald Wetherfield glanced out the window of the limousine and got the shock of his life. "Well, I'll be, if it isn't—"

"Victoria Tempest!" Georgie quipped. "Shut my mouth."

"Stay put while I go after your buddy!"

Not on your life!

"Keep the motor running, Robert. I won't be long."

As Donald grasped the doorknob, Georgie suddenly knew exactly what to do, having seen it done dozens of times in old movies. Reaching for Luceres' heavy brief in the floorboard, she raised it above her head, and with all her might, slammed it down on the back of Donald's head. Letting out a mumble, he slumped and fell backwards into the limousine.

"Good riddance, Donald." She crawled over the European thug and hopped out of the limousine, the energy of success propelling her forward as she raced down the sidewalk after Victoria. "Wait up!" she called out. "I'm going, too!"

***

Victoria thought she heard someone call her name but dared not glance back. A few more steps and she would be inside the cab. No one could stop her now. *No one.*

Then a heavy hand fell on her shoulder.

"Going somewhere?"

"What?" She spun around confused, sensing an evil presence as she peered into the eyes of Alexander Luceres Ramnes. The political leader's smile was impeccable, his suit a perfect fit, his immortal soul straight from the pit of hell.

"Are you going somewhere?" he asked again.

"You!" Victoria said with disdain. "Get out of my way!"

"No," he firmly said, his grip on her tightening.

"Don't bet on it, Mister!" She struggled to get free.

Luceres held tightly to the fugitive's forearm. "It's in your best interest to cooperate. I only want to help you."

"Get your hands off me, Mister Know-it-all!!" Victoria stumbled and fell hard against the side of the cab.

"I only want to talk," Luceres said. "Don't be frightened."

"Stop it! Help!" Victoria squealed. "Mugger!"

It was useless to struggle. Luceres was stronger. Victoria was caught like a rabbit in a vise. It was the man's laugh that really made her mad. *It can't end here. Not NOW! Dear God, protect me!*

Victoria felt the mounting energy soaring, and heard the rustling air around her as she was engulfed in a brilliant light.

Is this really happening, or am I dreaming?

"What's going on?" the cab driver asked in Italian, horrified over the bright light as he ducked down in the front seat.

Frightened, Victoria's heart began to palpitate.

Stunned over the mystical event, Luceres suddenly let go of Victoria and shrank from the cab, hands shading his eyes.

"Remind me to thank you later," she quipped.

Now free, Victoria leaped into the cab and slammed the door, surprised to see that Georgie was there and already buckled in.

"Way to go, girl!" The detective gave a thumbs-up.

"Step on it, Vincent!" Victoria said to the cab driver.

He nodded, rammed his foot on the pedal and shot out into the passing traffic. Glancing back, Victoria saw Luceres on the ground, hands on his head, trembling like a wounded soldier.

In disbelief, Luceres could not budge a muscle as he spied magnificent masses of light taking winged shapes resembling Roman gladiators. Too frightened to scream, throat constricting, hyperventilating, he fell faint to his knees and prepared to die.

"Drive faster!" Victoria ordered the cabby.

"What's going on?" asked Georgie, not understanding what was happening as the vehicle seemed to lift off the ground and sail forward. "Help!" She lost her stomach with the propulsion.

"Hold on, Georgie!" Victoria screamed. "God has His hand on us! Don't be afraid, we're in for the ride of our lives."

THE END

DON'T MISS BOOK 6
IN THE RESURRECTION DAWN SERIES
In the continuing saga of Victoria Martin Tempest
COUNTDOWN TO JUSTICE

Dr. Mark James receives a mysterious message from an unidentified caller: "Ask your father about Terrance Wilson and the others." Blown away by the idea that his father's heart attack may not have been from natural causes, he investigates.

After quizzing Carlotta Diagostino about his father's business practices, Mark recognizes Richard Branson for who he really is— scary, unpredictable, and very dangerous. Perhaps it's time to get the F.B.I. involved in solving the Jeffrey Tempest equation.

Meanwhile, Officer Sarah Boswell travels to Memphis, Tennessee, to question young Timothy Cates regarding his father's knowledge of the Caldwell life-insurance application filled out by Attorney Jeffrey Tempest in 1989. Sarah believes proving Victoria did not initiate the $ 2 million policy will go a long way in a court trial.

After Victoria Tempest's miraculous escape from Switzerland, she and PI Georgie Hendricks make their way back to New York via boat. With the help of Colt Adams, they narrowly escape arrest.

Meanwhile, Jon Branson remains in jail accused of crimes against PEACE FIRST. Dick Branson hires an attorney to help his son prove he is no threat to society, making sure that no one opposing his drug dynasty has the opportunity to charge him with a crime.

The story leaps to new and challenging heights. Don't miss the next exciting sequel in the life of Victoria Martin Tempest.

ABOUT THE AUTHOR

Four years past ovarian cancer surgery, Sue has finished all seven books in the *Resurrection Dawn* series. The final three sequels will be published in 2006. During the seven years of its creation, this story became even more applicable to American society as laws were passed to take down the Ten Commandments in public places. The end to our age draws nearer with each passing day.

A couple of heart-warming stories have come to light as a result of people embracing this series. One reader who had a form of skin cancer was healed after reading the first book in the series: *Resurrection Dawn 2014*. Lois believed that if she trusted Jesus as much as Victoria Tempest did, God would heal her. And He did.

When Cindy purchased Book 2: *The Christian Fugitive*, she said it was for a friend who was in the hospital undergoing cancer treatments. Charlsie's husband sat by her bed and read the first book in the *Resurrection Dawn* series aloud. Enjoying the adventure of Victoria Tempest very much, they requested the second book.

There is no magic within the printed pages of Christian books. Miracles occur because people have faith in God. Readily identifying with the characters, readers often draw strength from their statements of faith. God bless the writer and the reader.

WHO IS JESUS TO YOU?

It is never too soon to recognize that Jesus Christ is God's only anointed Son and was involved in designing our universe. Setting the standards for admission into Heaven, God's rules for engagement are recorded in the Bible. When the gospel message of salvation by grace through Jesus Christ has been preached to all the earth, the end will come. Are you ready to meet your Maker?

2 Peter 3:10, and 14 states: "But the day of the Lord will come like a thief. The heavens will disappear with roar; the elements will be destroyed by fire, and the earth and everything in it will be laid bare . . . So then, dear friends, since your are looking forward to this, make every effort to be found spotless, blameless, and at peace with him." Have you made your peace with God?

Forgiveness is an act of God's grace. Romans 3: 23 states: "For all have sinned and fallen short of the glory of God." Jesus Christ provided an acceptable sacrifice on the cross to atone for every sin committed—past, present and future. "If you believe in your heart that Jesus is Lord and that God raised Him for the dead, you will be saved," Romans 10: 9. What will you do with Jesus today?